ANDREW TAYLOR

Call the Dying

Copyright © 2004 by Andrew Taylor

First published in Great Britain in 2004 by Hodder and Stoughton
This edition published in paperback in 2005 by Hodder and Stoughton
A division of Hodder Headline

The right of Andrew Taylor to be identified as the Author
of the Work has been asserted by him in accordance
with the Copyright, Designs and Patents Act 1988.

A Hodder paperback

1

A CIP catalogue record for this title
is available from the British Library

ISBN 0 340 82571 5

Typeset in Plantin by Hewer Text UK Ltd, Edinburgh
Printed and bound in Great Britain by
Clays Ltd, St Ives plc

Hodder Headline's policy is to use papers that are natural,
renewable and recyclable products and made from wood grown in
sustainable forests. The logging and manufacturing processes are
expected to conform to the environmental regulations
of the country of origin.

Hodder and Stoughton Ltd
A division of Hodder Headline
338 Euston Road
London NW1 3BH

'Andrew Taylor's latest addition to his "Lydmouth" murder series prefectly evokes that innocent world of the 1950s. The book is wonderfully redolent of that era, except that it has psychological depth instead of Christie-type clichés. Taylor builds a gripping story, as redolent of the period as brown linoleum. His subtle exploration of provincial society, with its gruesome underbelly, makes this a powerful extension to the series.'   *Independent*

'What's rare and admirable in Taylor's fiction (especially in the Lydmouth series) is his painterly and poetic skill in transforming the humdrum into something emblematic and important. His writing is never pretentious. He strikes no attitudes. His crime scenes and procedures are meticulously observed and followed. *Call the Dying* is expert, ingenious and absorbing.'   *Literary Review*

'Full of nostalgic detail, this is old-fashioned crime at its best – perfect for a cold winter night in front of a roaring fire'
The Sunday Times

'This is top of the class. Taylor's re-creation of the 1950s is absolutely convincing.'   *Publishing News*

'Taylor is an excellent writer'   *The Times*

'Andrew Taylor is one of the most interesting, if not THE most interesting novelist writing on crime in England today'
Harriet Waugh, *Spectator*

'The people depicted here are real and believable and the drabness and genteel facade of Fifties England is skilfully brought to life. Taylor is, as always, adept at showing the reality beneath the surface'   *Sunday Telegraph*

'How skilfully he recreates the atmosphere of the time through innuendo, attitude and detail rather than dogged description . . . Taylor is the master of small lives writ large'
Frances Fyfield, *Express*

'The most underrated crime writer in Britain today'
Val McDermid

The Lydmouth Series by Andrew Taylor

An Air That Kills

The Mortal Sickness

The Suffocating Night

The Lover of the Grave

Where Roses Fade

Death's Own Door

About the author

Andrew Taylor has won the John Creasey and twice won
the Ellis Peters Historical Dagger of the Crime Writers'
Association and has also been shortlisted for the Gold Dagger.
As well as the Lydmouth Series, he has written the Dougal
novels, the award-winning Roth Trilogy, thrillers for
teenagers, and the bestselling *The American Boy*, a
literary historical novel featuring the young Edgar Allen Poe,
which was a Richard & Judy Best Read of 2005.

Andrew Taylor and his wife live with their children
in the Forest of Dean.

For Anna, with love

The author thanks the Society of Authors, as the literary representative of the Estate of A. E. Housman, for permission to quote from A. E. Housman's *Last Poems*, xix.

Around the huddling homesteads,
    The leafless timber roars,
And the dead call the dying
    And finger at the doors.

A. E. Housman, *Last Poems*, xix

THE PRINCIPAL CHARACTERS

DR BAYSWATER – of Grove House

DEPUTY CHIEF CONSTABLE VINCENT J. DRAKE

JILL FRANCIS – of the *Lydmouth Gazette*

MR & MRS FREDERICK – of London

GENEVIEVE FUGGLE – of Whistler's Lane

IVOR FUGGLE – editor of the *Evening Post*; husband of Genevieve

MR GRAY – of Gray's Garage

AMY GWYN-THOMAS – of the *Lydmouth Gazette*

BRIAN KIRBY – Detective Sergeant

DR ROGER LEDDON

HOWARD MORK – of the *Lydmouth Gazette*

MR and MISS MYNOTT

PC PETER PORTER

RONALD PROUT – of Prout's Toys and Novelties

DOREEN RODLEY – of Viney Cottage, Whistler's Lane

JOE RODLEY – her husband

EDITH THORNHILL

DETECTIVE CHIEF INSPECTOR RICHARD THORNHILL – her husband; DAVID, ELIZABETH and SUSIE, their children

CHARLOTTE WEMYSS-BROWN – of Troy House; owner of the *Gazette*

PHILIP WEMYSS-BROWN – husband of Charlotte; editor of the *Gazette*

A NOTE ON THE TRANSCRIPTIONS

The twelve diary entries were written on loose sheets of writing paper and placed, apparently at random, in an envelope found at the residence of the accused. Six entries are undated but their probable places in the sequence have been inferred from internal evidence. Square brackets indicate these conjectural dates.

There is also a thirteenth entry, believed to have been written at an earlier period.

No other relevant documentary material was found at the scene.

[Wednesday, 30 November]

I saw a ghost today. It was very foggy, I know, but I'm sure I wasn't mistaken. He was coming through the door of Butter's, and he looked like a ghost because of the fog. But he really was a ghost from a time that's dead and gone.

I couldn't move. He crossed the road and went into the Gardenia Café. Around me, everything trembled, as though the fog had stopped things being solid and made them wispy and shaky and unreal. I think the fog has got into me, too, into my mind.

Was it a sign, seeing him there? Perhaps she's calling me. There's more than one way of calling. Something dreadful is going to happen. I must find out, and there's only one way to do that.

But it's dangerous.

Chapter One

The past is a foreign country, thought Jill Francis: and I want an exit visa.

She drove over New Bridge and slowed for the level-crossing before the station. The car juddered across the railway tracks and began to crawl up the long hill towards the crossroads at the top of the town. The buildings she passed had the unsettling familiarity of the half-remembered, of a dream landscape revisited.

Behind her, a driver hooted his horn. No point in dawdling. She put her foot down hard on the accelerator and the Morris Minor jerked forward. At the crossroads she turned left into the High Street. So here she was, against her better judgement, back in Lydmouth, at least for the time being: so the sooner she became used to it the better.

The town was smaller and drabber than she remembered. It was only mid-afternoon but thanks to the fog the streets were wrapped in a moist grey twilight. The lights were on in the shops. People hurried along the pavements, anxious to be home. A thickset man in overalls and flat cap was standing on the pavement outside the Gardenia Café. He stared blankly at Jill's jaunty green car and spat in the road.

Nothing personal, Jill told herself; he probably wasn't even aware he was staring at me. Still, it seemed an unhappy omen. She turned left at the war memorial and followed a broad avenue lined with leafless trees and sturdy Victorian villas.

The road came to a T-junction where a gap in the trees and the houses gave her a glimpse of the grey river below. She turned left and a moment later was pulling up outside Troy House.

A curtain twitched in the big bay window of the drawing-room. The front door opened and Charlotte came down the steps, a little unsteadily, hand on the balustrade. Like everyone and everything else, she had become less substantial in the fog and smaller than she was in memory. She had lost weight since September.

'Jill, dear. How lovely to see you – and so early, too. I wasn't expecting you for at least another hour.' There was an un-mistakable note of complaint in Charlotte's voice. 'You must be exhausted. Come and sit down.'

Jill followed Charlotte inside.

'Dr Leddon is here,' said Charlotte brightly. 'Have you met him?'

'No, I haven't.'

'He's up with Philip now.' Charlotte lowered her voice. 'Fortunately Philip likes him. It makes things so much easier. He always had his doubts about old Bayswater. But Dr Leddon is thoroughly modern and very nice to deal with, too.'

The hall smelled musty, as though it had not been properly aired for some time. The dark oak chest near the front door was cloudy with lack of polishing. The Wemyss-Browns' housekeeper had retired a couple of years before and Charlotte had not been able to find a replacement for love or money.

She led Jill into the kitchen, which was at the back of the house, overlooking the service yard. The room was much warmer than the hall. A kettle steamed on the hotplate of the Aga. Jill took off her coat – Charlotte had forgotten to take it in the hall – and laid it across one of the chairs. While Charlotte made the tea, Jill sat down and took cigarettes from a handbag.

'You really should cut down,' Charlotte said over her shoulder, though without her usual conviction. 'Everyone says they're frightfully bad for you.'

'They always say that about something pleasant,' Jill said. 'And then six months later it changes, and something that was meant to be good for you has now become bad for you, and vice versa.'

'That's one thing this ghastly business has done for Philip,' Charlotte said, pursuing a line of her own. 'He hasn't had a cigarette since it happened. I was really getting quite worried about him. He's not meant to drink either, but I sometimes allow him a little glass of claret as a treat.'

Jill closed her eyes momentarily, for the idea of Philip not smoking and hardly drinking was akin to the idea of a fish not swimming. 'How is he?'

Charlotte shrugged and turned away, her body hunched over the teapot into which she was spooning tea. 'Getting better, of course, but it's a slow process. His legs are frightfully swollen and he gets breathless very easily. Dr Leddon is very concerned that he shouldn't get worried or excited.' She glanced at Jill. 'Which is why it's such a blessing that you are here.'

There were footsteps in the hall and the kitchen door opened.

'Oh – hello, Doctor,' said Charlotte in a voice that was suddenly uncertain. 'How is he today?'

'Not too bad.' Leddon was at least half a head taller than Jill and perhaps a year or two younger. 'Very sleepy but quite comfortable.'

'They say rest is the best medicine, don't they?'

'They do indeed.' Leddon glanced at Jill. He was dark, with vivid blue eyes and the sort of eyelashes that many women would pay good money for.

Charlotte said, stumbling a little over the words: 'Jill, this is Dr Leddon, who's taken over Dr Bayswater's practice. And this is an old friend of ours – Jill Francis.'

The doctor held out a hand. 'Roger Leddon.' There was a minute hesitation, a practised glance at Jill's left hand. 'How do you do, Miss Francis?'

'Jill's going to look after the *Gazette* while Philip's convalescing,' Charlotte said. 'Now what about some tea?'

'Not for me, thank you. I must get on.' Leddon was still looking at Jill. 'So you're a journalist?'

'Yes – I used to work on the *Gazette* but I moved to London a few years ago.'

'You and Dr Leddon are going to be neighbours,' Charlotte said.

'Really?' Leddon smiled at Jill. 'You've taken that second-floor flat at Raglan Court?'

'For the time being.'

'That's what I told myself when I moved in last year,' Leddon said. He turned to Charlotte. 'I must be off but I'll look in tomorrow. No – don't worry – I know the way. I'll see myself out. Nice to meet you, Miss Francis.'

The two women listened to his footsteps receding down the hallway. Neither of them spoke until the heavy front door had closed behind him.

'Charming, isn't he?' Charlotte said in a voice not much more than a whisper, in case Leddon were gifted with supernatural hearing. 'I know he's young but he's a very good doctor. Poor Bayswater is becoming *so* cranky. He should have retired years ago.' She turned away to pour their tea.

'Is he still in Lydmouth?' Jill asked.

'Dr Bayswater? Yes – still at Grove House, too. That's rather a bone of contention, actually. They say that—' Charlotte broke off and cocked her head. 'Did you hear something?'

'No – what?'

'I . . . I thought I heard Philip calling.' She put Jill's cup down on the table and a few drops of tea slopped into the saucer; she didn't notice. 'Silly of me – he's got a little bell that he uses when he needs me. But sometimes—'

'Old houses are full of noises,' Jill said. 'And they're always louder when one's by oneself in a room.'

'Yes,' Charlotte said. 'Aren't they?'

She joined Jill at the table, absent-mindedly took one of Jill's cigarettes, and then apologised, having realised what she had done. They sat smoking in silence for a moment.

'It's not going to be easy, you know,' Charlotte said. 'The advertising revenue's down for the third successive month.'

'It's a difficult time.'

'We've got the wretched *Post* yapping like a pack of jackals at our heels. And since Cubbitt went, we haven't been able to find a replacement as deputy editor.' Charlotte expelled a great plume of smoke. 'Spineless! There's no other word for it.'

'Who or what?'

'Cubbitt, of course.'

'You can't blame him,' Jill said. 'He had another job to go to, didn't he, and that fight he got into must have left a nasty taste.'

'Pooh, another job? Do you know who owns the *Rosington Observer*?'

'No – but at a guess you're going to tell me it's the same people that own the *Post*.'

'Precisely.' Charlotte was breathing heavily. 'They're quite ruthless. They were always unpleasant to deal with, but things are ten times worse since they promoted Ivor Fuggle.'

'I know,' Jill said gently. 'You told me.'

'I even wondered about that fight: Cubbitt never actually saw his attacker.'

'You're not saying it was Fuggle trying to frighten off the competition?'

'That was the effect it had,' Charlotte said. 'I know it couldn't have been Fuggle himself, he must be nearly sixty, if he's a day, and he's not exactly fighting fit, but I wouldn't put it past him to bribe someone else to do his dirty work for him. Amy Gwyn-Thomas thinks we should have a word with the police.'

'Don't,' Jill said. 'Imagine what Fuggle would do if he caught the merest whisper of it.'

'I suppose so. But Amy does have a point, and I was thinking if I gave Richard Thornhill just a little hint, mentioning no names, of course, and—'

Jill ground out her cigarette in the ashtray. 'I wouldn't, Charlotte, really I wouldn't.'

'Perhaps you're right. Or perhaps you could say something to him. You two used to be quite pally at one time, didn't you?'

'Not pally enough for that,' Jill said, congratulating herself on how cool she felt and how casual she sounded.

'He's doing rather well, by the way.'

'I'm so glad.'

'And have you heard? He and Edith have another child.' Charlotte looked up, and Jill avoided meeting her eyes. 'A little girl – she's called Susie.'

'How nice.' Jill plunged from one uncomfortable subject to another. 'So Amy's still at the *Gazette*?'

'Yes indeed. She's been a tower of strength since Philip was taken poorly. I don't know what I'd have done without her. She'll soon remind you what's what in the office.'

Jill smiled mechanically. At one time Amy had been jealous of the place she assumed that Jill held in Philip's affections. She opened her handbag and put cigarettes and lighter inside.

'I suppose I should go to the flat now. I'd like to unload the car before it gets absolutely dark. Shall I look in on Philip before I leave?'

'Better not, dear. Dr Leddon says it's very important that he should rest in the afternoon. If he's dozing, I wouldn't like to wake him.'

'No, of course not.'

'Now where did I put the letter from the landlord?' Charlotte wondered. 'In my bureau? And you'll need the keys for the office. You collect the keys for the flat at Raglan Court: Mr and Mrs Merton in Flat Three – they're meant to look after things for the landlord.'

She eventually found the letter on the dresser and the keys for the office in Philip's study. On the front doorstep, Jill hesitated and then kissed her on the cheek. For a moment Charlotte clung to her. When she reached the car, Jill looked back at the house and saw Charlotte still standing in the doorway, with her hand resting on her cheek where Jill had kissed her.

Jill had been at Troy House no more than half an hour, but during that time afternoon seemed to have surrendered to evening. The fog was thicker, and the headlights of passing cars made it seem denser still. She drove back down to the war memorial and turned left into Broad Street. The grimy neo-Gothic façade of Grove House reared up on the corner of Whistler's Lane. A moment later, Jill turned left into Albert Road. Raglan Court was at the upper end of the road, a small block of modern flats backing on to Jubilee Park.

She drove round to the car park at the rear of the block. For the next twenty minutes, she lugged her belongings up to the cold little flat on the second floor. The trouble with owning expensive leather suitcases, Jill thought, was that when you had to carry them yourself, they became a liability rather than an asset. It was a pity Dr Leddon wasn't about.

Most of her belongings were now in store in London; two trunks were due to be delivered by carrier in a few days; the rest of her life was here, piled in a mound of suitcases and boxes in the middle of the living-room. Still in her fur coat, still wearing hat and gloves, Jill postponed unpacking and prowled through her new home. The furniture came with the flat. She would need to find a comfortable armchair to sit and read in. She laughed aloud, her breath visible in the chilly air of the living-room.

So this was what she had achieved in life: a cramped, rented flat without even a decent chair in it. She glanced at the box that contained the bottles. But half-past four in the afternoon was not the time for a glass of brandy, however warming it would be. Instead she lit a cigarette and wandered into the bedroom.

Without turning on the light, she stood smoking by the window. The glow from a lamp-post cast a puddle of murky light on the moist tarmac. From here she had a view of the main gates of Jubilee Park, a prospect which had aroused the estate agent's enthusiasm, if not hers. At right angles to the gates was the cemetery.

As she watched, a sturdy little woman ploughed her way through the puddle of light, towing a very small dog. The animal stopped, forcing the woman to stop too, and pointed his head towards the entrance to the cemetery. He barked shrilly, the sound clearly audible even though the windows were shut. The woman dragged the dog, a tiny terrier, under the archway and into the darkness of the park beyond.

Jill remained where she was. Just inside the cemetery, a match flared. For an instant, in the orange glow of flame, she saw a man's face, so briefly and indistinctly that it was devoid of individuality. The flame vanished. The darkness returned.

With a shiver, Jill pulled the curtains across the window. Richard Thornhill, she thought, though the face hadn't been his, and though in the years she had known him he had never smoked a cigarette: Richard, you bastard.

Chapter Two

Detective Chief Inspector Richard Thornhill hit the wall and bounced.

'Sorry, sir,' said PC Porter. 'Oh – sorry – I didn't mean—'

'It's all right,' Thornhill said, straightening his jacket. 'No bones broken.' He looked up at Porter's red, fat face looming several inches above his own. 'How are you getting on at Mynott's? Settled in all right?'

'Yes, sir. It's very nice. Miss Mynott's ever so kind.' Porter hesitated, and the muscles of his face worked convulsively. 'The only trouble is, sir, waking up.'

'Waking up?'

'When I'm on earlies,' Porter explained. 'Mam used to wake me.'

'I see.'

Peter Porter had lived with his mother all his life. Six weeks earlier, her death had turned him adrift in a terrifying world without landmarks. It was Thornhill who had found him a room above Mynott's electrical shop in Broad Street.

'Let's see,' Thornhill said, dimly suspecting that as far as Porter was concerned he now occupied a quasi-parental role. 'You're on the second floor, aren't you, overlooking the road?'

'Yes, sir.'

'You could try the piece-of-string trick.'

'The what?'

'It's something I used to do when I was a probationer,' Thornhill explained. 'I had trouble getting up as well. So when I was on early turn, I tied a piece of string to my toe and put the other end out of the window. Then one of the night men would pull the string at five o'clock.'

'I've got a ball of string,' Porter said with a touch of pride.

'Well, there you are. It's one thing to sleep through an alarm clock but you certainly wake up when someone tries to pull your big toe off.'

'Yes, sir. Thank you, sir.'

Thornhill nodded and opened the door of the CID office. For three years he had run the Central Office for Serious Crimes, and for three years he had lobbied for a separate office for the men under his command. But they were still sharing the long, first-floor room with Lydmouth's Divisional CID. Sergeant Kirby was sitting at his desk by the window, studying the advertisements in the *Gazette*. An instant later, he had transferred his attention to the open file beside the newspaper.

'I'm just going in to see Mr Drake,' Thornhill said. 'Have we got anything more?'

Kirby shook his head, an action which made his increasingly prominent jowls wobble. Three years of marriage had fleshed him out, but had left the inner man somehow sharper and harder than before.

'It's all down to the beat officers, if you ask me, sir,' Kirby said. 'Haven't had a whisper from the snouts, though they know we're interested. We've just got to hope one of our blue woolly suits gets lucky one night.'

'I'd like to think we'd do better than rely on luck, Brian,' Thornhill said.

He was tempted to add that they might have better results if detective sergeants spent less time studying advertisements for televisions in the local newspaper. But there were several constables within earshot and it never paid to bawl out a man in front of his inferiors. He nodded and left the room.

The office of the Deputy Chief Constable was farther down the corridor. Thornhill found Drake sipping china tea and ploughing his way through a week's worth of divisional reports.

'Sit down,' he said. 'I won't be a moment. Have a look at that editorial in the *Post* while you're waiting.'

Thornhill picked up the newspaper and turned to the editorial. Ivor Fuggle was still hammering at the law-and-order theme. *We are unsafe on our own streets, in our own homes. The innocent walk in fear, the guilty go unpunished. What on earth are we paying our police for?* And so on, for five paragraphs of self-righteous and self-serving invective.

On the opposite page there was a picture of Fuggle himself at the Rotary Club's Christmas bazaar: *The* Post's *editor Mr Ivor Fuggle and his wife Genevieve share a joke with Lady Ruispidge*. Fuggle was beaming at the camera, but his wife looked as gloomy as sin and Lady Ruispidge appeared to be talking to someone else, just out of the shot.

'Pernicious nonsense,' Drake said, closing the last file and picking up his teacup. 'Cheap, rabble-rousing gutter journalism. I've put men behind bars for less than that.'

Thornhill could well believe it. Drake had served as a District Superintendent of Police in India before Partition, and he held a number of robustly unfashionable views which he took care not to express in public.

'He's got a point, though, sir. This has been going on for nine or ten weeks now.'

Drake shook his head. 'The press should work with the authorities, not against them. Fuggle's playing a damned dangerous game.'

'In one way it's nothing to do with us.'

'Eh?'

'That's my wife's theory.' Thornhill grinned. 'Which means that it's the official Mothers' Union view: the *Post* wants to gobble up the *Gazette*, and now's its chance. So Fuggle's going all out to improve circulation. Increased circulation means increased advertising, and that means increased revenue. And if the *Gazette* goes to the wall, then the *Post* scoops the pool.'

'Nasty business. I pity that poor woman.'

'Who, sir?'

'The woman who's coming to hold the fort at the *Gazette*. She used to work there before – I met her once or twice. Quite a looker, in her way.'

Thornhill felt ice cold. He said: 'You mean Miss Francis?'

'That's the one. You must have had dealings with her. Is she any good?'

'She seemed very competent, sir,' Thornhill heard himself saying in a prim little voice. He hesitated, aware that this was less than just. 'She's more than capable of giving Ivor Fuggle a run for his money.'

Drake grunted. 'Let's hope you're right. Any new developments I should know about?'

'I'm afraid not, sir.'

'You've got Kirby handling it still?'

'Yes, sir. I had a word with him just now – he's not over-optimistic. He doesn't feel this is a case where CID can do much that's useful.'

'That's not his decision, Thornhill.'

'No, sir.'

Drake narrowed his eyes as though squinting at the sun. 'I'm not sure Sergeant Kirby is giving us his best at present.'

Old loyalties made Thornhill say, 'It's a difficult case, sir. Low-level. Shapeless. We can't even be sure whether it's one case or several. But I'll make quite sure that we do what we can.'

Drake looked at him for a moment and nodded. 'Filthy evening,' he said. 'The fog's getting worse. I think I'll call it a day.'

Fifteen minutes later, Thornhill reached the car park at the back of Police Headquarters just in time to see the tail-lights of Drake's Armstrong Siddeley disappearing. He climbed into his own car, a box-like Standard Ten Companion, recently bought and not yet paid for. He drove home to Victoria Road. Afterwards he remembered nothing of the drive.

In the conscious part of his mind he was either thinking of Jill Francis or trying with increasing desperation to think of someone or something – anything – else. When these tactics failed, he told himself sternly that he wasn't thinking of a real Jill Francis any more. Longing and unhappiness had combined with faulty memory to make her someone completely different, his own creation. Had she in fact ever been real? Had she always been an expression of his needs, for a time conveniently clothed in flesh and bone and living in Lydmouth? This attempt at metaphysics left him feeling even more depressed than he had been before.

He pulled up outside the house. Clutching his briefcase, he walked quickly up the path to the front door. He was aware of a knocking on the window to his left and waved at his younger daughter, whose golden head was just visible above the level of the sill and who was standing, waiting and watching for him, between the curtains and the window of the sitting-room. As he pushed his key into the door, he heard her shrieking, 'It's Daddy! It's Daddy!'

He hung up his hat and coat, left his briefcase in the dining-room and went into the sitting-room. Susie flung herself at his legs with a squeal of triumph and grasped him round the knees with such force that he almost fell over. He disengaged himself gently, bent down and kissed the top of her head. Elizabeth, his elder daughter, who was nine going on nineteen, was cutting out pictures of clothes from a copy of *Woman and Home* for pasting in her scrapbook. She acknowledged his arrival with a wave but did not look up. Edith was knitting by the fire, with a *Radio Times* open on her lap. For an instant Thornhill saw his wife afresh, which perhaps had something to do with his recent bout of metaphysical speculation: and he knew that he should count himself fortunate.

'Oh, good,' she said with a smile. 'We're glad you're home in good time, aren't we? We wanted to discuss something with you.'

Thornhill sat down in the armchair on the other side of the fire and helped Susie clamber on to his lap. Elizabeth looked up from her scrapbook and he recognised the determination on her face because he had often seen the same expression on Edith's.

'The girls and I have been putting our heads together,' Edith went on. 'We think it's time we got a television set. It could be a sort of a family Christmas present.'

'Please, Daddy,' Elizabeth said. 'Please.'

'Please,' echoed Susie, bouncing up and down on his lap. 'Please, please, please, please, *please*.'

Feeling ambushed, Thornhill said, 'I thought we'd talked about that a few months ago, and decided we didn't really need one.'

'That was then,' Edith pointed out. 'But things are changing so fast.'

Elizabeth said, 'The Queen's going to broadcast her Christmas message on television, Daddy. So it's patriotic to buy one.'

'Pleasey, pleasey, teasey, weasey, *please*.'

'Isn't it just as patriotic to listen to it on the radio?' Thornhill said, wincing and writhing as Susie's latest bounce caught him at a sensitive point.

'No, it's much more patriotic if you can see her as well. It shows you really care.'

'That's enough, Elizabeth,' Edith said with casual authority. 'Daddy and I will talk about it later.'

'But everyone's got one now.'

'I said, that's enough.'

Thursday, 1 December

Everything was unreal. It was still very foggy, too, and that made it worse. At one point I started to wonder if HE was unreal as well. In which case either he was a ghost or he was there in my mind, and I projected him outside the Gardenia.

But I knew I wouldn't be able to sleep if I didn't get some fresh air. I told myself that there was no real risk. Even if he was in Lydmouth, even if he was still here, he couldn't be expecting to see me. Why should he? And at night, and with my face concealed with a scarf and hat, I was quite safe.

But it wasn't him that turned out to be the problem. I got as far as the High Street when I heard the sound of breaking glass.

Then I heard someone running. The next thing I knew there were flames flickering on the other side of the road in a building beside the Gazette. You could see the glass was broken in one of the windows because of the flames flickering and roaring behind it. The fire was growing all the time, and the flames danced. It got bigger and bigger and made a noise like the wind.

I couldn't think what to do. Someone could be sleeping in there. Someone could die. That's what I thought. Except it wasn't like thought, it was more of a jumble. More feelings than words. I ran down the road to the phone box. I put a handkerchief over the receiver as they do in films, and dialled 999. I've never dialled 999 before. And when someone answered, I just said, 'Fire at the Gazette,' twice, and slammed the phone down.

I went home as quickly as possible. I heard the bells of the fire engine.

Chapter Three

The ringing of the phone snatched Jill Francis out of a dream she was glad to leave. She pushed aside the covers and rolled out of bed. As she staggered across the floor, she stubbed her toes against the unforgiving leg of the bed. She swore, both at the pain and at the tendrils of the dream, whose content had now evaporated, though she did remember her own unhappiness and the fact that it had featured Richard Thornhill.

The telephone rang on. It was intensely cold, and still dark outside. She flicked on the lights as she went into the living-room. The phone squatted like a black toad on the little sideboard. Next to it was the brandy bottle, the level of the liquid a little lower than it should have been. According to the electric clock on the mantelpiece it was only a quarter to seven. She seized the receiver.

'Jill? This is Charlotte.'

'What's wrong? Is it Philip?'

'No, thank God. Nothing like that. Look, I'm sorry to ring so early but I thought I'd better let you know as soon as possible in case you went into the *Gazette* at the crack of dawn.'

'What's happened?'

Charlotte was not to be deflected from her own way of telling the story. 'The first I knew was when the police phoned at half-past two. There's been a fire at the printing works.'

Jill sat down in the nearest armchair. She extended her leg and managed to turn on the electric fire with her foot. She was wearing only a nightdress and she began to shiver, though not solely from the cold.

'It was in the storeroom next to the road. Luckily the Fire Brigade got there before it had time to spread.' Charlotte's voice wobbled. 'There's a certain amount of smoke damage, I gather, but it could be much worse.'

'The storeroom?' Jill said, trying to visualise the ramshackle sheds and converted stabling that straggled round the yard beside the *Gazette*'s editorial offices. 'That's on the left of the gates, isn't it? It seems an odd place for a fire to start in the middle of the night.'

'Yes – well, that's just it. I gather there's some doubt about how it actually did start.'

'What are you saying? It was arson?'

'The officer I spoke to was very cagey, but I understand at this stage they're keeping an open mind. There's . . . there's something else. The reason the Fire Brigade got there so soon was that they had a 999 call. The caller didn't leave a name. Truly a Good Samaritan.'

'Unless it was the arsonist himself,' Jill said.

Charlotte wished her luck and rang off. Jill washed, dressed and forced herself to drink a cup of tea and nibble some toast. Afterwards she stood by the window, smoking the first cigarette of the day. The sky was beginning to lighten.

An arson attack at the *Gazette*? And not so long after her predecessor, poor Mr Cubbitt, was beaten up? Coming back to Lydmouth had been a decision forced on her by circumstances. She hadn't expected to enjoy it. But she hadn't expected to feel afraid, either.

It was a little after eight by the time Jill parked the car in the *Gazette*'s yard. She spent the first ten minutes looking at the storeroom with the foreman of the printing works. They stood in the doorway because a fire officer and a youthful police constable were inside. Most of the damage was due to smoke and the attentions of the Fire Brigade, rather than to the fire itself – it was fortunate that the Good Samaritan had raised the alarm so promptly.

'Some bugger started it, Miss Francis,' the foreman muttered. 'It weren't an accident.'

'Are you sure?' Jill asked.

The fire officer looked round. 'The window smashed and the fire went like a rocket.' He waved a gloved hand at the floor beside a filing cabinet. 'See that? A broken bottle.'

'That's worrying.'

She assessed what needed to be done: a good deal of paper would need to be replaced; a window would need mending; and the whole room would have to be redecorated. She hoped the insurance was up to date. She would also have to think about increasing the security of the site as a whole.

Jill went next door into the office. She had expected to be the first there, because the staff did not usually arrive until between 8.30 and nine. To her surprise, she found Amy Gwyn-Thomas industriously collating expenses claims at her desk outside the editor's room. Amy was a tall, angular woman with a long, thin nose which looked as though someone had given it a tweak to one side while it was still in the malleable stage of its development. But she was dressed more smartly than Jill remembered, and wore much more make-up.

'Miss Francis!' Amy stood up, a flush spreading like a stain beneath the powder on her cheeks. 'How lovely to see you after all this time.'

It was an unmistakable olive branch. As the two women shook hands, asked after each other's health, discussed the fire and the weather, Jill noticed on Amy's desk a framed photograph of a middle-aged man with large eyes, a thin moustache and a spotted bow tie. She glanced at Amy's hands: no sign of a wedding or engagement ring.

'I was so glad when Mrs Wemyss-Brown said it was you,' Amy confided.

'Better the devil you know?'

Amy appeared not to hear. 'It's not been easy these last few months, Miss Francis, I don't mind telling you. And when Mr Wemyss-Brown was took ill, and Mr Cubbitt took over, it just went from bad to worse. He could do a lovely obituary, I'll say that for him, but he wasn't very good at running things. Funny, isn't it – some men are and some men aren't. I did what I could to keep things straight, but I couldn't make the decisions, could I? It just wasn't my place.'

'I'm sure you did everything you could. Mrs Wemyss-Brown was saying to me only yesterday how marvellous you've been. And Mr Wemyss-Brown, too.' Jill bent the truth a little in the interests of morale. 'He said they couldn't possibly have managed without you.'

Amy grew a little pinker than before. 'One does what one can, of course. But not everyone pulls their weight, do they, and it's no use pretending that they do.' She lowered her voice. 'And it's been such a difficult time, because of the *Post*.'

'We shall have to see what we can do about that.'

'Will you be here long?'

'I'm just here as a stopgap,' Jill said. 'We hope Mr Wemyss-Brown will soon be back in harness.'

'So you'll be going back to London?'

'Yes – probably.'

'We all thought you were settled up there for life on that magazine,' Amy said.

'Nothing lasts for ever. There was a change of ownership, and the new people had someone else lined up for features editor.' Jill did not add that she and the major shareholder had met over a dinner table in Belgravia and found that their opinions on almost every subject you cared to name were diametrically opposed.

The building around them was beginning to come to life. Doors closed, footsteps mounted the stairs, fragments of conversation drifted along the landing.

'They're not a bad lot,' Amy said suddenly. 'They can all do their jobs. I was talking about it with my . . . my friend.' Here her eyes drifted towards the photograph of the man in the bow tie. 'He said they just need a leader. And that is what Mr Wemyss-Brown was so good at doing – leading, I mean.'

'I know.'

A short but not uncomfortable silence followed. Amy was entirely right, Jill thought: despite the fact that Philip Wemyss-Brown liked liquid lunches and long afternoons on the golf course, he had been a good leader. He talked to people; he made them feel wanted; he told them what they had to do, and then he congratulated them when they had done it. All of which would have made him a hard act to follow, even temporarily, even in the best of times. And these were not the best of times, except, possibly, for Amy Gwyn-Thomas. For years, Amy had nursed a hopeless passion for Philip Wemyss-Brown. Now it seemed she had found another object for her affection, and her temperament had improved dramatically because of it.

There was a tap on the half-open door, and a thin youth sidled into the room. His cadaverous cheeks sheltered a complex network of craters and spots. His dark hair, worn rather long, was slicked back with grease into a duck's tail. The shoulders of his jacket showed unmistakable signs of padding and even more obvious signs of dandruff. His trousers clung to his skinny legs and the toes of his shoes tapered sharply to a point.

Good God, thought Jill, the Teddy boys have come to Lydmouth.

'This is Howard,' Amy said. 'Howard Mork. Howard helps in the post room, don't you, Howard?' She spoke loudly and rather slowly. 'And this is Miss Francis. She'll be taking over as editor for the time being, while Mr Wemyss-Brown is convalescing.'

Howard stared at his shoes. Jill asked him whether he'd worked there long and was rewarded with a mumble that could probably be translated as 'four months'. Amy put him out of his misery by sending him off to collect the day's post.

'Very shy,' she mouthed to Jill when he had left the room. 'But such a nice boy. His father is the manager of Butter's. His mother died rather unexpectedly – it was all rather tragic.' Suddenly brisk, she opened her desk diary and raised her voice to its normal level. 'Would you like me to run through your appointments now or later, Miss Francis?'

'Later, I think. Unless there's anything urgent.'

'It's Thursday, so there's the press briefing at Police Head-quarters.'

'That's a regular thing now, is it?'

'Yes, Mr Drake's idea, I understand. Sometimes they're more a matter of form than anything else, but not recently.'

'Oh?'

'There's been a lot of petty crime in the last few weeks. Worse than petty, in some cases – look at poor Mr Cubbitt, he had to have four stitches and he lost a tooth.' She coloured, glancing at the photograph. 'My friend – Mr Prout – has been another victim, though nothing like as bad. I'm afraid the *Post* has been quick to make capital out of it.'

'I'll go,' Jill said. 'It'll be a good opportunity to meet people again.' But there would never be a good opportunity to meet Richard Thornhill. If she had her way she would never see him again. She went on: 'I'll have to talk to the police about last night, in any case.'

'I've put the fire on in your room,' Amy said smugly.

'I think I'll go round the office first. The sooner people know what I look like the better.'

Jill made her way methodically through the building, from the reporters' room with its long central table, where she had worked when she first came to the *Gazette*, to the printing works; from the accountant's lair in the attic to the cellar which contained the only complete back file of the *Lydmouth Gazette* in existence. She talked to advertising clerks and printers, to reporters and cleaning ladies.

She spent a quarter of an hour with Jamie Marr, the advertising manager, going through the figures for the last twelve months. The first quarter held up to expectations. Thereafter a decline began, at first gradual, but, since September, increasingly rapid.

'It's a combination of things, if you ask me,' Marr said. 'The main thing is, since Fuggle took over at the *Post*, he's slashed their rates. He can't have done it off his own bat – it must be part of a wider strategy. They're practically paying people to advertise with them. And there's no denying it, since Mr Wemyss-Brown was took poorly, things have got much worse. A lot of our advertisers felt they had a personal relationship with him – the old established, family businesses, like Butter's and Mynott's. But with him not around, it's much easier for Fuggle to poach them.'

'He must be losing money over this too.'

'Of course he is,' Marr said. 'But he's not worried, not in the short term.'

'Because the *Post* is now part of the Champion Group?'

'Yes – they must have fifty or sixty provincial newspapers, and other interests as well. They can afford to make a loss for a few months in order to turn a profit later. But most people in Lydmouth can't. We're all feeling the pinch. There's even talk of lay-offs at Broadbent's.'

Broadbent and Jones was a large engineering company on the outskirts of town, one of Lydmouth's largest employers. When Jill had last been in Lydmouth it was widely assumed that a job at Broadbent's was a job for life, as secure as a job with the railways or the Post Office or the Council.

'I don't want to talk out of turn about Mr Cubbitt,' Marr continued, 'but he didn't get the same coverage that Mr Wemyss-Brown did. And Fuggle's damned good at his job, there's no denying that. So our circulation's been declining.'

'Which makes us even less attractive to advertisers?'

Marr shrugged. 'It's a downward spiral, and everyone knows it, I'm afraid.'

'What goes down,' Jill said, 'must come up. If you try hard enough. And that's what I'm going to do until Mr Wemyss-Brown is well enough to do it for himself.'

Jill was uneasily aware that rousing words were not going to solve the problem. She arranged to meet Marr again on Friday morning and discuss tactics. In the meantime, she asked Amy for coffee and biscuits to be sent to the reporters' room. She talked to her colleagues as a group and individually. It was not a subtle way of trying to raise morale, but it was better than none at all.

At 11.30, she borrowed Philip's umbrella, the fabric green with age, and walked through the rain up the High Street to Police Headquarters. This occupied what had once been a large Victorian house; car parks and ancillary buildings sprawled through the grounds. A few great trees – a cedar of Lebanon, a copper beech and a pair of limes – reared up among the Nissen huts and tarmac, ungainly reminders of the garden which had once been there.

She did not recognise the man on the desk, but when she introduced herself she was waved into the Conference Room on the ground floor. She opened the door and hesitated. The room was tall and high ceilinged, dominated by an elderly mahogany dining-table and a nicotine-stained portrait of a Victorian Chief Constable. It was full of smoke and the sound of voices. One by one the voices died away and for a moment the only sound was the rumble of traffic in the road outside.

'Well, well,' said Ivor Fuggle. 'Look who it is, gentlemen. It's our famous lady reporter from London.'

'Good morning, gentlemen,' Jill said, welcoming the sustaining spurt of anger. 'No, don't get up. I'm sure you need to conserve your energy.'

Most of the men were strangers to her, but there was a murmur of greeting from the two or three whom she had met before. There were only four vacant chairs – the three at the head of the table, beneath the portrait of the Chief Constable, and one on the corner beside them, the chair next to Ivor Fuggle's. Jill walked round the room to it, sniffing the familiar smell of wet dog and old tobacco that characterised the working journalist in winter. She put her handbag on the table and hesitated a moment – long enough for Ivor Fuggle to look up, pantomime surprise, draw back the empty chair and wave his hand in a courtly gesture.

'Thank you so much,' Jill said, sitting down.

Fuggle grinned at her. He was a portly man in his late fifties whose gleaming white false teeth were the cleanest thing about him. 'According to my English master, Dr Johnson said that he who is tired of London is tired of life.' His voice sounded as dirty engine oil would sound if dirty engine oil could talk. 'I hope that's not true in your case.'

'No, Mr Fuggle, it's not. Would you mind moving your

chair just a few inches away from mine, and then I can get my legs under the table. Thank you so much.'

The door opened, and the moment Jill had been dreading was suddenly upon her. Detective Chief Inspector Richard Thornhill came into the room. For a split second he looked at her. The years had treated him well – better, in all probability, than they had treated her. She knew at once that he had been expecting her.

A uniformed sergeant and a secretary followed him into the room. He walked round the table, choosing the route that enabled him to avoid passing behind Jill's chair. Then he was standing a few feet away from her beneath the portrait of that long-dead Chief Constable.

'Good morning, gentlemen,' he said. 'And good morning to you, Miss Francis.'

You bastard, Jill thought, you bastard. Why did I waste my time on you for so many years?

Chapter Four

The weekly press briefing had been Mr Drake's innovation, his way of keeping his finger on the pulse of what was happening in the town. The DCC knew the power of the press and he wanted to harness it. Often the briefings were near-formalities – on the one hand almost social occasions and, on the other, ritual opportunities for the police and press to grumble to each other. They were usually chaired by an inspector or chief inspector.

Today Thornhill wished he were anywhere else but here. He had often wondered how he would feel if he met Jill again. If you saw someone in your mind every day for more than three years, you grew accustomed to your version of her presence. As time passed, you modified her, you talked to her, you expanded her history – and sometimes, as Thornhill knew, you let her invade your dreams. Now, confronted by a dark unsmiling woman with a notebook in hand and a raincoat draped like a cape over her shoulders, he was forced to face a real person endowed with all the inconveniences of independent existence.

For an instant Jill caught his eye and he saw, or thought he did, a wave of dislike wash across her face. In the same moment he realised that he had miscalculated badly. He had hoped that what he felt for her would be analogous to measles – that once you had had one attack you would no longer be susceptible to infection. But now he discovered that malaria would make a better analogy for his condition: he suffered from a disease that could return at any time, possibly with renewed force, whenever circumstances were favourable to it. A jolt of misery ran through him like dark electricity.

Routine was a blessing. Sergeant Lumb took the seat to his right, and Miss Arkwright, the stenographer, the seat to his left. Thornhill cleared his throat but the words wouldn't come. He tried again, and this time they flowed in a way that seemed normal enough, though he himself had no way of knowing because he wasn't really listening. There had been an outbreak of poaching in the Mitchelbrook area. The Clearland estate had been particularly badly hit. Police had arrested and charged three men that week, two from London, in connection with the offences. On Tuesday afternoon, there had been a burglary in a house in Broadwell Crescent, and the police would be glad to hear from anyone who might have seen or heard anything suspicious in that area on the afternoon in question.

And so on. At last Thornhill paused and asked for questions. Fuggle raised a hand with a smoking cigarette.

'This is all very well, Chief Inspector, but I'm sure you realise that it's not what we really want to hear. What are you doing about the man who beat up poor Johnny Cubbitt? What about the fire at the *Gazette* last night? And what about the Pisser?'

'I beg your pardon?' said Jill.

'Granted, I'm sure,' Fuggle said. 'Well, Chief Inspector?'

'It's true that there have been several outbreaks of rowdy behaviour in the town over the last few weeks, particularly on Friday and Saturday evenings. It's also true that these have been accompanied by isolated bursts of vandalism. However, we—'

'The Pisser,' Fuggle interrupted.

'Yes indeed, Mr Fuggle. The Pisser.' Thornhill could bear it no longer. He turned towards Jill and addressed her directly. 'We have had several cases of somebody urinating through letter boxes, Miss Francis. It doesn't seem to be a random outbreak, in that all the targets are connected with the Baptist Chapel.'

'First there was Mr Prout of Prout's Toys and Novelties. He's the organist,' Fuggle put in. 'Then we had the chapel itself. Great big puddle waiting for the worshippers on Sunday morning. I mean, it's not nice, is it? Next weekend, it was the turn of Mr Smethwick, the minister himself. He's got little kiddies, you know, and Mrs Smethwick isn't in the best of health. Then Mynott's – the old chap acts as Prout's deputy. And then last weekend it was back to Mr Prout himself.'

'Thank you, Mr Fuggle. As Sergeant Lumb explained to you last week, we're increasing the numbers of uniformed constables on the beat, especially at closing time on Fridays and Saturdays. We have every hope of an early arrest.'

Fuggle made a noise that sounded like *pfui!*

'Our investigation into the attack on Mr Cubbitt is continuing. It was a savage and, as far as we know, entirely unprovoked attack. Unfortunately it was dark and he was taken unawares so he was unable to describe his attacker.'

'Have you got a suspect?' Fuggle demanded. 'Have you even got an investigation?'

'We are following several lines of enquiry, sir, and the press will be the first to know when we have any news.'

'Business as usual, in other words.' Fuggle sighed in a way that made his lips vibrate. He made a show of writing in his notebook. 'Police are baffled,' he murmured. Then, looking up, he went on: 'And what about this latest thing, the fire at the *Gazette*?' He leaned towards Jill, and leered at her. 'I'm sure this little lady would like to hear what you think about that.'

'Luckily the Fire Brigade was alerted before the fire had time to take hold,' Thornhill said stiffly.

'Who by?' asked Fuggle.

'The caller rang from a nearby phone box and did not choose to leave their name.'

'And what's this a little bird told me?' Fuggle asked the ceiling, as though the little bird were cruising in circles over the table in case it needed to repeat its information. 'That the fire didn't start by accident? Could it be arson?'

'It's too early to speculate, Mr Fuggle. The investigation is still in its early stages.'

Fuggle lowered his eyes and looked directly at Thornhill. 'I see. But I'm told that someone chucked a Molotov cocktail through the window. If that isn't arson, I don't know what is.'

Chapter Five

At the end of his shift, Peter Porter returned home. Except it was not home, and never could be: it was Mynott's ('Television and Electrical Services For All Your Needs') on Broad Street, between the southern end of the High Street and the junction with Chepstow Road.

As a lodger, he had a key to the side entrance, but he went into the shop because he wanted to ask Miss Mynott about his laundry. Since the death of his mother, PC Porter had found himself in a strange new world where shirts had to be ironed, stains removed from tunics and socks washed and darned.

Old Mr Mynott was in the showroom at the front of the shop, waving his arms about and showing a lady the controls of one of the television sets on display. Porter saw Miss Mynott in the workshop behind the counter talking to a broad-shouldered man he didn't recognise. He walked down the shop, trying to minimise the clumping of his boots on the linoleum. The customer turned as he approached, and he recognised the lady.

'Hello, Porter,' said Mrs Thornhill. 'How are you?'

'Fine, thanks, Mrs Thornhill.' He didn't know Mrs Thornhill well, but he had often met her when he acted as her husband's driver.

'I was very sorry to hear about your mother.'

Porter felt his eyes filling with shameful tears. 'Yes,' he said, because he could think of nothing else to say.

'And Mr Thornhill tells me you're lodging here.'

'Yes,' Porter said, glancing wildly from the remote and bony face of Mr Mynott to the slight figure of his daughter in the workshop. 'It's . . . it's very nice.'

'That's good. Well, I mustn't keep you.'

She smiled at him and turned back to Mr Mynott. Porter walked on, stumbling into a large walnut-veneered cabinet housing a television set. Mr Mynott tutted behind him.

Miss Mynott came out of the workshop. She was in her twenties, a slim girl with close-cropped yellow hair; she was said to be more interested in televisions than men. 'The sheets came back from the laundry, Peter,' she said. 'I've left them in your room. I left a note of what's owing on top of them. Were you late again this morning?'

'Yes – a little. But I won't be tomorrow.'

'New alarm clock?'

'No. I'm going to hang a piece of string out of my window and tie one end to my big toe. And the chap who's on nights is going to give the other end a tug as he's on his way back to the station.'

Miss Mynott burst out laughing. 'I hope he doesn't tug too hard. Is there any news, by the way?'

He blinked. 'About what?'

'You know.' She lowered her voice to a whisper. 'The Pisser.'

He took a step backward as though she had threatened to hit him. It wasn't nice, hearing a lady say that word. 'No, miss. But we're working on it.'

As they were speaking, the strange man had come out of the workshop. His face reminded Porter of an American film star's whose name he could not recall. He wore a brown cotton work coat over his clothes, as did Miss Mynott, and was carrying a valve in one hand.

'You haven't met Mr Frederick, have you, Peter?' Miss Mynott said. 'Not with you being on earlies. He's down from London for a couple of nights, and we've put him in the room next to yours.'

Mr Frederick extended a hand. He was shorter than Porter, with fair hair beginning to recede from the temples. 'A police officer, eh?' he said, running his eyes over Porter's uniform. 'So we'll sleep safe at night?'

'Not entirely,' Miss Mynott said, with a significant glance at the letter slot in the door of the showroom.

Porter blushed.

'Excuse me' – Frederick turned back to Miss Mynott – 'I wouldn't use these Miskin valves, if I were you. We never do. They have a tendency to overheat.'

Porter's cheeks burned in sympathy.

Chapter Six

Outside the window, the black rain fell, kicking up the sheets of water on the road like a hail of bullets. There were footsteps on the stairs and in the hall. The lights snapped on in the room behind her. Jill turned.

'Draw the curtains, would you?' Charlotte said. 'These dark winter afternoons are so depressing.'

Jill pulled the heavy curtains across the bay window of the drawing-room. As she did so, she noted that the paint on the window frame was flaking.

'Philip's ready for you now,' Charlotte said.

'Are you sure I won't tire him out?'

'Dr Leddon said that short visits from old friends would be fine, but do try not to upset him. Any sort of strain could—' She broke off and twisted her engagement ring around her finger. 'I haven't told him about the fire. He didn't hear the phone ringing in the night so he knows nothing about it. Have the police said anything yet?'

'Not officially. But they're obviously treating it as arson.'

'How did Fuggle know so much?'

'He must have heard something. I'm sure he has his sources, just like Philip does.'

'Philip wouldn't use information like that.'

'Fuggle's clever. If we're not careful he's going to come out of all this as the people's friend.'

'Do you think he's responsible?'

Jill picked up her handbag. 'For the arson? It seems unreal, that a man one knows could do something like that. On the other hand I wouldn't put it past him.'

'I wonder if we could have a word with someone,' Charlotte suggested, uncharacteristically hesitant.

'With the police? Without any evidence whatsoever?'

Charlotte sat down suddenly on the sofa. 'Jill, we need to talk. About the *Gazette*, about lots of things. There are decisions to be made . . .'

Jill sat down beside her. If Charlotte had been another woman, she would have taken her hand. 'You need a holiday.'

'That's out of the question,' snapped Charlotte. 'But we can't talk here, not properly. I'm always half listening for the bell, you know, and anyway Philip's expecting you. What about tomorrow? I could come down to the *Gazette* at about midday.'

'Why don't we go out for lunch instead? My treat. No, don't say anything. I'll come and collect you in the car at about twelve o'clock, and we'll go somewhere outside Lydmouth.'

'All right. Thank you.'

The capitulation was so sudden that it took Jill by surprise. She had thought of Charlotte and Philip for years as the epitome of security, permanence and comfort: often dull and obstinate, sometimes small-minded, but always safe. Now they were showing themselves to be as vulnerable and uncertain as anyone else. It gave Jill a queer sensation of panic, as a child feels when he first discovers that his parents are frail and mortal.

Charlotte heaved herself to her feet. 'We mustn't keep Philip waiting. It's funny' – and here her voice took on a querulous note – 'he knows you've been here since yesterday, and he's becoming quite agitated about not seeing you. But please don't excite him. Don't let him talk about work.'

Jill promised to do her best. She and Charlotte went up the wide stairs to the first-floor landing. Troy House had been built for Charlotte's grandparents. Everything was a little taller or wider or larger than was necessary, as if to suggest that the residents themselves were more than life size.

The biggest of the bedrooms was at the front of the house, directly over the drawing-room. Philip lay in the double bed, propped up on pillows. He looked unexpectedly small, dwarfed by his surroundings. This was the room Charlotte had shared with him. Now it was Philip's alone. The dressing-table had been swept clear of Charlotte's silver and crystal, and held a selection of medicines.

Jill bent over and kissed Philip's forehead. His skin was warm, soft and sweet smelling, like a newly bathed baby's.

He gave her a crooked smile. 'You're looking well. Why don't you sit down – pull up that chair.'

'Jill can't stay long,' Charlotte said. 'Just a short visit.'

He ignored her. He was still looking at Jill. 'It's good of you to come down. I can't think of anyone I'd rather have at the *Gazette*.'

'It won't be for long, I'm sure.'

His eyelids fluttered. 'You must have given up a lot.'

'Not really. To put it bluntly, I got the sack from *Berkeley's*. They didn't call it that, of course, but that's what it was. It was inevitable under the new ownership. So you're helping me out as much as the other way round.'

'Nonsense,' he said, and smiled.

Downstairs the telephone began to ring.

Charlotte clicked her tongue on the roof of her mouth.

'Go on, Charlie,' Philip said. 'Answer it.'

She glanced at him anxiously and left the room. The telephone rang on. Neither Philip nor Jill spoke. Charlotte's feet clattered down the stairs. The bell stopped.

'Fuggle's fighting dirty, Jill,' Philip said.

'You shouldn't be talking about this.'

'I want to. I've got to. It's true, isn't it?'

'Probably.' She leant forward and took his hand, which had been plucking idly and yet obsessively at the coverlet. 'He doesn't know any other way to fight.'

'I don't think Charlotte realises how bad it is. There's only room for one local daily in this area now. The Champion Group is backing Fuggle to the hilt. So it's between us and them. And the one who wins is going to do very well out of it.'

'The *Post* is not going to win,' Jill said.

Philip's fingers tightened round hers. 'I've been a bit slack these last few years. Let things slide a bit perhaps. Between ourselves, Charlotte's income isn't what it was. This damned supertax. So I worry about what would happen if—'

'Don't worry,' Jill interrupted. 'Worrying's not going to help. Just concentrate on getting well. In the meantime I'll keep an eye on Fuggle. Then, when you're better, you can sort him out.'

Philip's eyelids fluttered. 'Funny bugger. Did you know he's married now?'

'I thought he was the eternal bachelor.'

'Everyone did. Used to live with his mother, you know, ghastly woman, probably Ivan the Terrible's first cousin. But she died a couple of years ago and it sent him off the rails. He was very odd for a time.' He was speaking more slowly now, and his articulation was becoming slurred. 'Then, blow me down, he got married. Not a local woman. I've met her once or twice – rather frumpy, no conversation, keeps herself to herself.'

Jill squeezed Philip's hand and released it. 'Go to sleep, I'll see you soon.'

She kissed him on the cheek and slipped out of the room.

On the stairs she met Charlotte, who went up to check that her husband was asleep and then joined Jill in the drawing-room.

'What did you think?' Charlotte asked.

'He's much better than I expected,' Jill lied. 'You're right, I'm sure. Rest is the best medicine.'

She drove back to the flat through the gathering gloom, with the Morris Minor's wipers slipping and slapping across the windscreen. Philip wasn't that much older than she was. Was this what it all came to: a pale, wrinkled face half buried in a mound of snowy white pillows, a shrunken body shrouded by a pink eiderdown? What had Philip done to deserve it? She knew the answer, which was that there was no answer, but that did not make the question any less desperate.

At Raglan Court, the trees of the park huddled around two sides of the little car park, creating pools of almost absolute darkness. Jill hurried into the block of flats, turning on light after light.

It occurred to her as she made her way up to the second floor that she might so easily have said yes when Philip asked her to marry him all those years ago: in that case it could have been she, not Charlotte, presiding over the medicine bottles and the bedpans and all the dreary paraphernalia of a dearly loved invalid's life.

The flat was almost as unwelcoming as the car park. She went from room to room, turning on electric fires and switching on every light she could find. With a conscious effort, she ignored the bottles on the sideboard, filled the electric kettle and plugged it in. She glared round the living-room. *Damn this place.* Not even a comfortable chair to sit and read in.

There was another irritation waiting for her in the kitchen. In the sink was an empty milk bottle. Jill swore. She had used what was left of the milk at breakfast and had intended to pick up another pint on the way home. Going to Troy House had put it out of her head.

There was no help for it. The little general shop near the bottom of Albert Road would still be open. She struggled back into her wet raincoat, tied a scarf over her head, put on damp gloves and went back downstairs and into the car park. It wasn't worth taking the car but the umbrella she had borrowed from Philip's office was still in the Morris Minor. Part of her, a compound of masochism and frustration, almost welcomed the thought of walking through the rain.

She was halfway between the flats and the car when she heard, quite distinctly, the sound of a cough. It seemed to come from the far corner of the car park. She stopped and looked. The shadows were at their deepest there. A tall ever-green hedge ran round the boundary of Jubilee Park, and above it reared the massive branches of a mature oak tree.

It was impossible to see whether anyone was there or not. But she hadn't imagined the cough, she was sure of that. And it had sounded human.

'Hello?' she called. 'Who's there?'

There was no answer. She listened. The rain pattered on the tarmac. In the distance, car tyres hissed on wet roads.

Fear caught her by surprise like a hand on the throat: the idea that someone was watching her, someone had seen her come out of the lighted building, someone who did not want to answer when she called out. She glanced over her shoulder. She was on the verge of sprinting ingloriously to the shelter of the flats. Only pride made her hesitate.

At that moment she heard a car. The twin beams of its head-lights cut across the drive of Raglan Court. Simultaneously metal scraped on metal somewhere near the oak tree.

The car rolled down the slight incline. Its headlights stretched across the tarmac to the corner beneath the oak tree. No one was lurking there. But an iron gate in the hedge gave direct access to the park beyond. It was ajar.

But there was no time to consider the implications. Brakes squealed behind her. She turned sharply, almost losing her balance. The car was coming straight for her. She screamed. The vehicle swerved, its tyres slithering in the wet, and went into a skid.

Time moved more and more slowly. So did the oncoming car. It glided with stately inevitability into the Morris Minor. When the vehicles collided with a metallic crunch, Jill winced as if she had felt the impact herself. The car's engine stalled. The driver's door opened and someone scrambled out.

'Good God, what do you think you're doing?' said a man's furious voice.

'I'm so sorry,' Jill said. Then her brain began to analyse the circumstances of the collision. 'But you were coming into the car park far too fast, especially in weather like this.' Light from the flats revealed the man's profile. 'It's Dr Leddon, isn't it? Oh dear. I suppose we were both a bit to blame.'

'Are you all right? I—' He broke off, frowning, and peered down at her.

'I'm Jill Francis,' she reminded him. 'We met at the Wemyss-Browns' yesterday, didn't we?'

He took off his hat despite the rain. 'Roger Leddon. We're neighbours, of course. Hang on, I've got a torch in the car. Let's have a quick look at the damage.'

'I'll fetch an umbrella – you're going to get soaked.'

He held Philip's umbrella over her while they inspected the cars. Leddon's Ford Consul had a dent on the front of the offside wing. The Morris Minor's bumper was out of alignment and a long scar disfigured the paintwork behind one of the headlights.

'Could be worse,' said Leddon, suddenly cheerful. 'At least we can still drive the wretched things.'

'We'll have to sort out the insurance.'

'We can't stand out here in the rain talking about it. Why don't you come up to my flat and we'll have a drink and work out what we're going to do?'

'I was just going out to get a pint of milk, actually. If I leave it much longer the shop will be shut.'

'I've got stacks of milk. Problem solved, eh?'

Jill allowed herself to be ushered into the building. Leddon's flat was on the first floor. The lights were on, and it was comfortably warm.

'Let me take your coat.'

She was conscious of his physical presence as he helped her out of the raincoat. For an instant she had a mad urge to touch the thick, dark eyelashes fringing the impossibly blue eyes. She sat down on a leather sofa in front of the fire and held out her hands to the warmth.

'Now,' Leddon said, smiling down at her. 'There's a time for everything. And just now it's time for gin. Doctor's orders, eh?'

Chapter Seven

The rain had stopped by the time Amy Gwyn-Thomas set out from her neat little bungalow in Vicarage Gardens. She was conscious of a flutter of excitement somewhere below her breastbone as she turned into Whistler's Lane. Life was full of excitement, full of possibilities, full of interest.

She hurried past Grove House on the corner, hoping she would not bump into poor Dr Bayswater, now so sadly and embarrassingly eccentric. The lane levelled out when it reached the hedge marking the boundary of Jubilee Park and she caught sight of her destination, its chimney stacks poking into the grey murk of the evening sky.

Viney Cottage obtruded like an inconvenient memory on the corner of Fairfield Avenue and Whistler's Lane. The little house was older than its neighbours. It was built of rough-cast stone covered with flaking rendering the colour of dirty sand. Along the front of the cottage and one end ran a narrow, L-shaped strip of garden, filled with brambles, nettles, thistles and two small, dilapidated outbuildings.

Whistler's Lane had once been no more than a farm track leading to the fields south of the town. The laying out of Jubilee Park immediately to the west of it had changed all that. In the first five decades of the century, the fields around Viney Cottage filled with bungalows and semi-detached houses, with neatly clipped lawns and garden sheds, with tarmac and concrete. Doreen Rodley's parents had sold the land behind the cottage to a builder, and there was now a very desirable five-bedroomed house with a hard tennis court where once there had been an orchard and a vegetable garden. But Viney Cottage itself remained, dwarfed and despised by its neighbours, an unwelcome reminder of the past's ability to cling to the present.

Amy tapped on the front door. She heard heavy footsteps on the stairs, and a moment later Joe opened the door. He was a compact, round-shouldered man with thickset eyes. He wore a collarless shirt above brown corduroy trousers held in place with a thick belt. He grunted when he saw Amy, but held the door wide.

'How is she today?' Amy asked.

He shrugged, and in that shrug was all the answer he wanted to give. 'She's waiting for you. Her and her ladyship from up the road. Go on in. I'm off out.'

The stairs were narrow and boxed in so they had moved Doreen into one of the two main downstairs rooms of the cottage. Amy tapped on the door on the right and heard Doreen's voice calling her. She opened the door, and warm air rushed out to meet her.

The curtains were drawn. The room was lit by the glowing coals in the stove and a lamp with a parchment-coloured shade on the table by the window. Two women were sitting at the table. Doreen, who was so slight that she looked like a wisp of smoke, looked up and smiled.

'Come and get warm, Amy. Have you met Mrs Fuggle from up the road? This is Miss Gwyn-Thomas.'

'I don't think we've actually met,' Amy said in the fluting voice she often adopted when talking to strangers. 'But of course I've seen you in town.'

Mrs Fuggle struggled out of her chair and took Amy's hand. 'Pleased to meet you,' she said in a heavy-smoker's husky voice. 'Has it stopped raining yet?'

'For the time being.' Amy gave her what she thought of as her social smile. 'But I suspect it will soon start again.'

She took off her coat and hat and joined the others at the table. Doreen was propped against cushions in her armchair. Amy sat bolt upright on a kitchen chair. Mrs Fuggle perched on the dressing-table stool, which looked too fragile for a woman of her weight. She was a plump, round woman, heavily made up, with tightly permed hair and blunt little features.

'Mrs Fuggle's brought me some magazines,' Doreen said. 'Isn't that nice?'

'It's nice to think that someone's getting some use out of them.'

'Amy works for the *Gazette*,' Doreen went on. 'We've known each other ever since we were four, haven't we, Amy – first day at school. Miss Evans, that was the teacher, she said to me, Doreen, you go and sit next to Amy, you two are going to be friends. And we were.'

The three women smiled, each of them aware in their different ways that the story had been told so many times it had become a formula, a ritual underpinning a friendship.

'Do call me Genevieve,' said Mrs Fuggle, aiming her words midway between the other two women.

Doreen smiled. 'Yes, let's all be comfortable together, shall we? Now, Amy, before you came in, Genevieve was telling me about this game she used to play – well, not really a game, I suppose, more of an experiment, almost.' She paused, smiling, and her eyes glittered orange in the firelight. 'We thought we'd try talking to the spirits. If you wouldn't mind, that is.'

'Have you ever done it?' Genevieve asked, her square, pale face suddenly eager. 'It's ever so easy.'

'Well, I've heard about it, obviously,' Amy said. 'But I've never tried it. Isn't it—'

'It's completely safe. We can stop at any time. I used to do it quite a lot.' Genevieve Fuggle gazed earnestly first at Amy, then at Doreen. 'The thing is it doesn't work very well unless you've got at least three people doing it.'

'It's all right,' Doreen said, patting Amy's hand. 'It's not what you're thinking. Lots of clergymen do it, apparently, and scientists. It's not like black magic or spells or anything. You tell her, Genevieve.'

'We just sit round the table, as we are now,' Mrs Fuggle said in a low, hesitant voice. 'We turn a glass upside down and put it in the middle, and then we put letter cards around it in a circle. I've got some in my bag, actually, Lexicon ones. Then we each touch the top of the glass with our forefinger and we ask questions. We just speak them aloud as you would to someone in the same room. And if there's a spirit there on the other side, he'll answer by making the glass move to the letters. If he wants to.'

'Oh, go on, Amy,' Doreen urged with unusual energy. 'It'll be a lark.'

Genevieve looked sharply at her, and opened her mouth. But she said nothing.

'All right,' Amy said, and she felt a flutter of excitement as though a bird were trapped in her ribcage and beating its wings. 'They say you should try anything once. Can't hurt, can it?'

Now the decision had been made, Genevieve wasted no time. She asked Amy to bring a clean glass from the nightstand beside the bed and laid out the letter cards in a circle around the table.

While they were busy, Doreen said, 'Dr Leddon came this afternoon. He said he was very pleased with me.'

'That's lovely, dear,' Amy said automatically.

'He's such a nice man, and very up-to-date in his methods.

Not like old Dr Bayswater. And he's always got time for a chat.
He said there's been so much rain that the bottom of Lyd Hill
is flooded.' She glanced at Genevieve. 'I didn't see you out
with Macbeth this afternoon. I dare say it was a bit wet for
him.'

Genevieve glanced up. 'He's got a weak chest, and he
catches cold very easily.'

'Macbeth is her Highland terrier,' Doreen explained to
Amy. 'Sweet little thing, but so small if he fell in a pothole
he might not be able to get out.'

'There,' Genevieve said. 'We're ready. Shall we begin?'

With those words, it seemed to Amy that the mood in the
little room underwent a change. The air filled with the sort of
anticipation you get when something is about to happen, and
you do not know whether it will be pleasant or unpleasant.

'Y for yes and N for no,' announced Genevieve. 'Otherwise
the spirits spell the words out. May I move the lamp, dear? I
could put it on the bookcase. The spirits seem not to like bright
light.'

She moved the table lamp on to the low bookcase behind
Doreen. Amy felt a tickle of apprehension in her spine. It was
still light enough – she could see the letters on the cards, the
expressions on the other's faces – but the flickering orange of
the coals now played a greater part, which made outlines blur
and shift, both softening and mottling the colours. Reality lost
its hard edges and became a little more hypothetical than
usual.

Genevieve extended her arm. 'Now we all put our fingers on
the glass.'

Doreen followed suit, and finally Amy.

'I'll begin,' Genevieve said in a whisper, 'as I know the
form.' She raised her voice: 'Is anyone there? Y for yes and N
for no. Is anyone there, please?'

Amy watched the glass gleaming softly on the dark, polished wood of the table. Her fingertip was sweating. She felt the prickle of perspiration under her armpits and prayed that she would not betray any unladylike symptoms of overheating. She glanced quickly at the others, both of whom were staring with rapt concentration at the centre of the table. Suddenly the glass twitched and slid half an inch. Amy and Doreen gasped. Amy nearly took her hand away.

'It's all right,' murmured Genevieve. 'It's starting.'

The glass twitched again, glided two or three inches in a curving path and stopped. A moment later it zigzagged across the table, apparently heading for a destination between the letters K and L, but within a second of reaching the spot it went into reverse. It meandered back to a few inches beyond its starting point and stopped. Another moment passed. Then it slid gracefully, with no hint of hesitation, to the letter Y.

The three ladies sighed.

'Who—' Genevieve broke off and swallowed. 'What is your name?'

The glass slid smoothly towards the S, paused for an instant and then cut across the circle of letters towards the A. It scraped on to M, back to the centre, to M again, to Y and returned to the centre, where it stopped.

'Sammy,' breathed Genevieve. 'We welcome you.'

Sammy did not reply.

'Can it see the future?' Doreen asked. 'Not it, sorry – Sammy, I mean.'

'Sometimes the spirits can,' Genevieve replied. 'Do you want to ask him a question?'

Doreen nodded.

'The spirits don't always answer the way one might like,' Genevieve said.

'I want to ask,' Doreen insisted.

'Very well. We keep our fingers on the glass. Just ask away.'

'Sammy,' Doreen said. 'Will I . . . will I get better?'

There was a long pause. Amy realised she was holding her breath. Only the flames moved. Doreen's narrow face was rigid, the lips drawn back, exposing the teeth. Genevieve Fuggle might have been wearing a mask.

The glass trembled, its rim making a faint scratching sound as it rubbed against the table. Then it slid across to the Y. Doreen let out a long, wavering breath.

'Thank God,' she said, so faintly as to be barely audible. 'Thank God.'

The glass began to travel across the table again. The three women followed its progress: W-H-E-R-E-S-M-I-K-E.

Genevieve gasped and fell back in her chair.

'What is it?' Doreen said, lifting a hand to touch Genevieve's arm.

Amy sat back and dabbed her forehead with an embroidered handkerchief smelling of lily of the valley.

'What's happening?' Doreen said. 'What does it mean?'

Genevieve swallowed twice before she replied. 'Sometimes . . . sometimes they ask questions. On the other side. And . . . sometimes you're talking to one spirit and another will barge in and ask a question – or answer one. It can be a little confusing.'

Amy said, 'Who's Mike?'

Genevieve looked across the table at her. 'I . . . I'm not sure. Not this Mike. But I had a brother called Mike once.' She shivered; her face twisted with emotion, and fissures appeared in the powder coating the skin. 'He . . . he died in the war. But it can't be him because the spirits would know where he was and wouldn't have to ask. I . . . I don't suppose someone could lend me a cigarette, could they? I don't usually smoke, but I feel a bit shaken.'

It was clear that communication with the other world was

suspended, at least for that evening. Amy produced a packet of cigarettes from her handbag. She hated giving them away – it meant one less for tomorrow – but she knew an emergency when she saw it.

'It's never happened to me before,' Genevieve said, sucking hard on the cylinder. 'Not like that. Oh dear, oh dear.' She stubbed out the cigarette before it was half smoked, annoying Amy, who abhorred waste. 'I'm sorry to be so silly,' she went on. 'Just sometimes, when I remember . . . oh, you know how it is. Would you mind if I went home now? Perhaps we can have another session later, another day, next week. I'm rather tired.'

Mrs Fuggle found her coat and hurried away as though late for an appointment with destiny. Amy showed her out and returned to the bedroom.

'She's terribly shy, poor thing, and very nervy,' Doreen confided.

Amy said, 'Living with Ivor Fuggle must be enough to make anyone nervy.'

'You can't say she isn't kind. She never comes here empty-handed.'

Amy hoped that this last remark was not a backhanded criticism of herself.

'Do you want to take some of those magazines on the chair? I've read those. There's *Good Housekeeping*, and *Vogue*, and *Picture Post*.'

A little later, at Doreen's request, Amy made them both some tea. While they drank it, they discussed the identity of Sammy and Mike, the return of Miss Francis, the fire at the *Gazette*, Joe Rodley's habit of going to the pub almost every evening, and Dr Leddon's beautiful hands.

'Anyway, how's your Ronald?' Doreen asked at last.

'He's not my Ronald,' Amy said. 'As you very well know.'

'Ah, but he might be.' Doreen smiled. 'Think of it: Mrs Ronald Prout.'

While Amy was thinking of it, the back door banged. There was the sound of a collision, as if a heavy body had come into unintended contact with a piece of furniture. Joe Rodley had come home.

Doreen's eyes met Amy's. Amy would have been willing to bet they were both thinking the same thing: if only God could have arranged it so that Joe Rodley were more like Ronald Prout.

[Friday, 2 December]

I've done nothing wrong. Not really. So it's not fair. It's as if everyone's ganging up against me.

Or is it just me? Am I going mad? Did I really see him?

I'm afraid. I'm lonely, too. Keep busy, that's the answer. Make myself tired. You don't have time to feel afraid when you're deadbeat, you just sleep instead.

I like the thought of sleeping. I can't remember when I last had an unbroken night.

Chapter Eight

At a little after eleven o'clock on Friday, Jill Francis and Dr Roger Leddon met on the forecourt of Gray's Garage in the High Street. Earlier in the morning, they had left their cars with Mr Gray.

Leddon said, 'I phoned the insurers from the surgery. I think it's going to be simpler if we put both claims on my policy. After all, when you come down to it, I was going too fast and I should have braked sooner.'

'I can't let you do that.'

'Why not? I'm sure the accountant will find a way of setting it against tax. These chaps are full of clever wheezes.'

'No, really.'

'Yes, really.' He grinned at her and she found herself smiling back into those blue, blue eyes. 'I tell you what: if you want to repay me you can buy me a drink or cook me a meal or something. How's that?'

'Done,' Jill said, suddenly happy.

As they walked together into the workshop, she turned her head away so that her face should not betray her. Her reaction embarrassed her, reminded her of the eternal schoolgirl that lurked within.

Gray, a small, bearded man in oil-stained blue overalls, had his head and most of his upper body underneath the bonnet of a maroon Wolseley. He straightened up when he heard their footsteps and wiped his hands on a rag.

'I think that's Bayswater's car,' Leddon murmured to Jill.

Jill looked sharply at him, responding not so much to the words as to the sour note in his voice.

'Well, Mr Gray,' said Leddon. 'What's the verdict?'

'Could be worse, Doc, could be better.' He nodded to Jill. 'It won't take much to straighten your bumper, miss. Paintwork's a longer job. But not more than an hour or two's work. Yours is a bit more time-consuming, sir. Maybe the better part of a day.'

'I shall need my car today,' Jill said. 'Is there any possibility you could do it over the weekend?'

'Anything's possible, miss. Might have to charge more, though.'

'Not to worry about that,' Leddon said.

'When could you drop the car in?'

Jill considered. 'Late this afternoon.'

Five minutes later, she left the workshop with Leddon at her side. They were walking across the forecourt towards the road when an elderly man crossed from the opposite pavement and came towards them, raising his stick in greeting.

'Hello, Dr Bayswater,' Jill said. 'How nice to see you again.'

Bayswater looked appreciatively at her. 'Miss Francis – I thought you'd had enough of us.'

He smiled as he spoke. His face was an anarchic network of lines beneath a shock of dirty grey hair. He looked much as he always had: which was to say that, if he had been only slightly more unkempt, he could have auditioned for a part in *Waiting for Godot*. Not that he would have got very far because, although he looked the next best thing to a tramp, he sounded like a cross between an old-fashioned Hollywood actor and a minor member of the royal family.

Gray, still hovering in the workshop, called, 'Won't be ready till Tuesday at the earliest, Dr Bayswater, maybe Wednesday.

It's your carburettor, look. I've got on the blower to Newport, and they'll send one up, but it won't get here till late Monday. Maybe Tuesday.'

'Damn and blast,' Bayswater said, glancing at his watch. 'I'll have to take the bloody train, I suppose.'

It was a fair walk between Gray's and the railway station. Jill said, 'Would you like a lift to the station?'

The old man smiled at her. 'I was hoping you might say that.'

Leddon coughed. 'If you like I could run you down to the station myself. As a matter of fact, I wanted another word about—'

'What?' Bayswater said. 'Now? Not sure this is the time or the place. I'm in agony, absolute bloody agony. Anyway, Leddon, mustn't keep a lady waiting, must one?'

'I don't want to press you, but it is important. There's the records, you see, as I said the other day, and then there's the question of the land for the new building.'

'Bloody National Health Service,' Bayswater said. 'You know what this is all about? Control.' He glared at Leddon. 'Big Brother.'

'On the contrary, it's all about making things more efficient and being able to look after our patients better.'

'Balderdash. I'm quite sure Hitler and Stalin used precisely the same arguments.'

'That's absurd—'

'So is standing around talking when I've got a train to catch.'

Anger flared in Leddon's face, twisting the features and making them ugly. He took a step towards Bayswater, then shrugged. He gave Jill an apologetic smile, touched his hat to her and said goodbye.

Bayswater stared after him. 'Whippersnapper,' he muttered, his desire to get to the station apparently forgotten.

'He keeps coming round and pestering me – a typical functionary of our brave new socialist world. And who's paying for the workers' paradise, eh? You and me, Miss Francis, the poor damn taxpayers: that's who. Do you know what the NHS alone cost us last year? Nearly £390 million – and that's just for England and Wales.'

'My car's over there,' Jill said. 'The green one.'

Bayswater allowed himself to be shepherded into the passenger seat of the Morris Minor.

'Sorry about that, my dear,' he said as they were driving down the High Street.

She glanced at him and he grinned at her. Jill remembered that Dr Bayswater used to have a considerable reputation in Lydmouth as a ladies' man.

'Fact of the matter is, I've got the toothache,' Bayswater went on. 'Doesn't do much for my temper.'

'Then shouldn't you see a dentist?'

'That's precisely where I'm going. My chap's in Gloucester – these local fellows are only one step up from the toothpullers one used to see at fairs when I was a lad.' He pulled out a pipe and peered into its bowl. 'So you're back in Lydmouth? Come to see the Wemyss-Browns, I imagine.'

'Yes and no,' Jill said. 'I'm the caretaker editor at the *Gazette* while Philip's getting better.'

Bayswater grunted but made no comment on Philip's health. 'Don't mind my asking – just an old man's curiosity – but what were you doing with Leddon back there?'

'It's none of your business,' Jill said with a smile to soften the words. 'As it happens we're both renting flats at Raglan Court. And last night our cars collided in the car park. Hence our morning rendezvous at Gray's.'

'I'd keep your wits about you with that one,' Bayswater said. 'Gray?'

Bayswater waved the pipe. 'Leddon, of course. He's a bit of a slippery Sam if you ask me.'

'I wasn't asking you,' said Jill, turning right down the hill to the station.

'No reason why you should, my dear,' said Bayswater with every appearance of good humour. 'Tell me, what do you think of those flats? I used to have a couple of patients in Raglan Court.'

'Rather impersonal.'

'Rabbit hutches. Just poky little rabbit hutches for the rabbits who will inhabit this brave new world of ours. Fill them with state bureaucrats and let them breed among themselves.'

Jill burst out laughing. 'Actually, it could be quite a nice rabbit hutch as these things go – some of the windows look out over the park and everything is very convenient and well planned. I just wish I hadn't taken a furnished let. There's not a comfortable armchair in the place.'

They neared the bottom of the hill. Jill slowed and turned right into the station forecourt. She pulled over behind the rank of taxis.

'Thank you. If I put my skates on, I'll be able to catch the eleven fifty-three.' He opened the car door and swung his legs outside. He looked back at her over his shoulder. 'One good turn deserves another, eh? I've got a whole house full of comfortable chairs and I can only sit on one at a time. Why don't you come and have a cup of coffee with me tomorrow morning and choose one?'

Jill began to protest but Bayswater ignored her. Once he was outside the car he bent down and looked at her through the open door.

'You haven't anything else planned, have you? So there's nothing to stop a little lady bringing a ray of sunshine into the life of a lonely old man. I'm still in the same quarters – Grove House, corner of Broad Street. Eleven o'clock? Good – that's settled.'

He gave her another of his crookedly charming smiles, touched his hat and walked stiffly into the ticket hall. Jill wasn't sure whether she was irritated or amused by the way he had treated her – or even, God help her, flattered. Perhaps the attentions of any Casanova, even an antique one, were better than none.

She put the car into gear. She was about to pull away when a man ran directly in front of the bonnet, forcing her to stamp her foot on the brake. He was carrying a small suitcase which knocked against the radiator as he passed the car. The man glanced at her for an instant, and Jill had a fleeting impression of a red face, wide mouthed, framed by the brim of a brown trilby and an upturned collar. He ran into the ticket hall, the skirts of his heavy blue overcoat flapping behind him. As he disappeared into the gloom of the hall, he waved an apology at her with a gloved hand.

Jill noticed that the glove was yellow, which later proved to be a circumstance of great significance. She glanced at the clock above the station entrance. The minute hand twitched. According to railway time, it was now 11.53.

A whistle blew.

By now, the first murder had been committed.

Chapter Nine

On his way out, Richard Thornhill went into the CID office. Sergeant Kirby was on his hands and knees underneath his desk.

'What on earth are you doing?'

Kirby's head jerked up, hitting the underside of the desk. A moment later he rose to his feet, red faced and sheepish.

'Sorry, sir. I bust a button off my waistcoat, and I was trying to find it.'

Thornhill eyed the plump, smoothly curving bulge above the waistband of Kirby's trousers. 'You need to take more exercise.'

'Yes, sir. But it wasn't that. I was laughing.' He squinted at the threads dangling from his waistcoat. 'Anyway, it was already loose.'

'Are you going to share the joke?'

'There's been another complaint from Ronald Prout.'

'The Pisser?'

'Yes – and this time our Ronnie's gone to the top.'

'Meaning?'

'The Almighty—' Kirby recollected himself. 'Sorry, sir – the memo came down from the Chief Constable's office. Mr Hendry's taking a personal interest. His daughter and grandson paid a visit to Prout's on Wednesday afternoon, and he had a good moan at them.'

'At least we can't be involved. Nor Divisional CID. Mr

Prout can't expect us to believe that drunken incontinence is a serious crime, even if Mr Hendry's grandson is on his side.'

'No – it's definitely a case for Uniformed with a capital U. They're furious.'

'So what's your joke?'

Kirby grinned. 'They've sent Porter to pay a personal call on Prout. To show him they really care.'

Thornhill kept his face impassive. 'I see. I'm going home for lunch. I'll be back at two.' Halfway through the doorway he turned back. 'And Sergeant?'

'Yes, sir?'

'Do tuck your shirt in.'

He drove home to find Mynott's van outside the house. He parked on the other side of the road and glanced up at his roof. His eyes moved along to the chimney stack at the end, where the unfamiliar shape of a television aerial was outlined against the grey sky. Edith hadn't lost much time in enjoying the fruits of victory. He let himself into the house and followed the sound of voices into the sitting-room.

His armchair had been pushed from the left-hand side of the hearth into the bay window. In its place was a large and shiny cabinet whose open doors revealed a grey screen. Old Mr Mynott and Edith stood with bowed heads before it, as though it were a jealous god in need of placating. Susie was huddled on the sofa chewing the arm of a large golliwog that had once belonged to her brother David.

'Hello, darling,' Edith said over her shoulder. 'Look, isn't it wonderful? It's come already.'

Mr Mynott adjusted one of the controls. 'You should get a pretty good picture here, sir,' he said to Thornhill. 'And I must say your lady wife has made an excellent choice – you won't get much better than this Ekcovision. Seventeen-inch screen, tone control – you've got it all.'

'I'm so glad,' Thornhill said, wondering how much it had cost.

'They're talking about independent television broadcasts in—'

Susie rolled off the sofa and yelped as she hit the floor. Mr Mynott shied away from the wailing child and turned back to the television. Thornhill picked her up and she clung to his neck, and pressed wet kisses on his cheek.

'What's for lunch?' he asked Edith over Susie's head.

'I'm so sorry. I was going to do fish fingers and mash but I just haven't had the time. But there's bread and cheese and fruit. Would you mind helping yourself? I'll come and make some tea in a moment.'

'Daddy,' said Susie, and licked his left ear.

'Yes, darling?'

She put her lips to the ear, so close that they tickled him, and whispered: 'Tocklate.'

'Not on your life,' Thornhill said. Happiness hit him like a shaft of sunshine on a cloudy day. 'You can have some bread and jam, though. Come on.'

Chapter Ten

Jill took Charlotte to lunch at the Coachhouse Restaurant, which was attached to the Queen's Hotel in Framington.

She thought it would do Charlotte good to get right away from Troy House for a few hours; and the restaurant had three stars in the RAC Handbook. It was a good idea, but taken as a whole the outing was not an unmitigated success.

In the first place, it was not an easy matter to prise Charlotte away from Philip, despite the fact that a friend who was a retired nurse had agreed to deputise for her. But Charlotte seemed almost overwhelmed by everything that had to be thought of: medicines, food, emergency telephone numbers; and then a whole range of contingencies such as where the small change was kept if the parish magazine came, or what to do if the plumber at last deigned to call to inspect the leaking tap in the scullery. Her mind chased the contingencies in ever-decreasing circles until Jill succeeded in enticing her into the passenger seat of the Morris Minor.

But as they were driving down the road parallel to the estuary, Charlotte's hands gradually relaxed their grip on her handbag. Her eyes darted from side to side and soon she was giving a running commentary.

'Good Lord, isn't that Mrs Atkins? I'd heard she was moving to Eastbury. But hasn't she aged? The air can't agree with her. And just look at those children over there! What can their mother be thinking of, letting them out dressed like that! By the way, did I see a dent in your car? Is that new?'

'Just a little knock,' Jill said. 'Do we take the next right?'

The Coachhouse Restaurant met with Charlotte's approval, much to Jill's relief. The staff were attentive, the food well cooked and not too foreign, and the helpings generous. As if by mutual consent, they steered the conversation towards neutral topics.

'By the way – how do you like Raglan Court?' Charlotte asked when the coffee arrived.

'Oh, it's very nice. It's certainly very convenient.' Jill chose her words with care, because Charlotte had found the flat for her.

'And I dare say you'll see something of that nice Dr Leddon while you're there.'

'I dare say,' Jill said demurely. 'As a matter of fact, he was responsible for that dent. But he was very sporting about it, I must say. He's going to pay for the repairs – or rather his insurance company will.'

'Really? When did it happen?'

'Yesterday evening. He insisted I needed a drink afterwards. Doctor knows best.'

'Well, he is very handsome,' Charlotte said, following an-other line of thought. 'Where did he take you?'

'We went up to his flat, actually.' She added hastily, 'It wasn't like that. We needed to sort out what to do with the cars, that was all. His was damaged too. And he lent me a pint of milk.'

But Charlotte was not to be deflected. 'What's the flat like?'

'It's the mirror image of mine but on the first floor. He got it unfurnished, and he's made it really quite homely in a bachelor sort of way. Talking of drinks, would you like a brandy?'

'Do you know, I think I might.' Charlotte sounded surprised at herself. 'Will you?'

'Why not?' Jill raised her hand to the waiter.

'I don't know how long Dr Leddon's going to be living there,' Charlotte went on. 'He'll want somewhere larger sooner or later.'

'With a surgery attached?'

'I'm not sure if he wants to live over the shop, as it were. At one point, I heard he was going to build a new surgery on some of the land at the back of Grove House – no, not just a surgery, a health centre as well. Apparently the government gives you money or something. Or is it the Local Health Authority? Anyway, that plan seems to have fallen through for the time being. Money's tight, I suppose. Money's tight everywhere.'

The waiter brought their brandies.

Charlotte took a sip, put down the glass and fiddled with the stem. 'You've talked to people at the office. You'll have gathered that money's rather tight with us.'

Jill nodded.

'Actually, it's rather worse than it seems.' Charlotte lit a cigarette and pushed the packet across the table towards Jill. 'Oh, I know they will have shown you the figures, so you'll be aware that advertising revenue's sinking and so's the circulation. What you don't know is that for the last few years Philip and I have had to subsidise the paper – I mean for the big expenses that in the past we could deal with out of income. We had to have the main office reroofed last year, for example. As for the printing works – all those dreadful machines keep going wrong. And the bills keep coming in and wages go up and up. I'm sure if Philip were well he would know what to do, he'd find a way to cope.'

'I'll see what I can come up with,' Jill promised, wishing she could think of any way to halt what sounded like an irreversible financial decline. Philip had been right: the town was too small for two daily papers.

Charlotte patted Jill's hand with heavily ringed fingers. 'I know you will, dear. I don't mean to complain, truly, but there seems to be such a lot to worry about these days. There's the house, too. It's far too big for the two of us. And now one just can't get servants – even if one could afford to pay them. I haven't dared tell Philip about the crack in the breakfast room. I've an awful feeling the whole wall might fall down.'

'Charlotte, stop worrying,' Jill said. 'Just concentrate on Philip – he's what really matters.'

Charlotte leaned closer and lowered her voice. 'I've had to mortgage Troy House,' she whispered. 'It's that bad.'

Jill concealed her surprise. She said, 'This isn't a time for doing things on a shoestring, is it? If we are to deal with the *Post*, we'll need resources. Have you thought of finding an investor? Someone prepared to make a loan to tide the *Gazette* over?'

Charlotte raised her eyebrows. 'Who would want to?'

'Would you let me make a few enquiries? A private individual, perhaps, rather than a commercial lender.' Jill hesitated. 'There's a friend in London I could try, actually. If you agreed. Of course, even if you said yes, there'd be nothing binding on either side – we'd need to discuss how much the *Gazette* needed and how we'd use the money – and what the security would be and so on. But it would be a start.' Again she hesitated. 'We have to do something, don't we? We can't let things slide.'

'I don't know,' Charlotte said. 'I don't want to saddle us with more debt. I've never owed a penny in my life, and now all this—'

'Think about it,' Jill said gently. 'That's all I ask.'

'I'll think about it.' Charlotte's face wore its familiar mulish expression. 'But I doubt I'll change my mind.'

Jill suppressed the irritation she felt – strange how the older the friends the greater the irritation they tended to arouse – and asked for the bill. Charlotte tried to pay but in this matter at least Jill had her way.

Ten minutes later, they left the restaurant. The Coachhouse shared a car park with the Queen's Hotel and, as the two ladies were walking towards the Morris Minor, the back door of the hotel opened and two men emerged, both smoking cigars. Charlotte was the first to see them.

'Good God,' she murmured, and straightened her spine. Raising her chin, she marched on towards Jill's car. Parked beside it was a steel-grey Humber Hawk saloon, its sides streaked with mud.

Jill saw the men. In the same instant she recalled that the *Evening Post*'s editorial offices were in Framington, and so Ivor Fuggle might also be there; and she realised why the Coachhouse Restaurant had not, after all, been a good idea. Fuggle was walking across the yard with a broad, false smile on his fat red face. Beside him was Cyril George, Lydmouth's most substantial property developer, a man whose company had switched its advertising from the *Gazette* to the *Evening Post* the previous month.

'The snake in the grass,' Charlotte hissed. 'The toad!'

'Mrs Wemyss-Brown,' Fuggle said, clearing his throat, an activity which sounded like shingle shifting on a windswept beach. 'And Miss Francis, too. Enjoying the fleshpots of Framington?'

Charlotte stared coldly at him but did not speak.

Jill said, 'Good afternoon.'

'We were just talking about you, Mrs Wemyss-Brown,' Fuggle said. He paused and smiled. 'Or rather, about Troy

House. Cyril here was saying those older properties up there often have a lot of land attached to them. Of course, most of them have had their gardens chopped up over the years. But not Troy House. You've got a paddock at the back, too, haven't you? Cyril was saying that if ever you and Mr Wemyss-Brown wanted to sell, he might be interested. If ever a property was ripe for redevelopment, eh, Cyril?'

'Thank you, Mr Fuggle,' said Charlotte, 'but my husband and I have no intention of selling at present. Good afternoon.'

'I won't keep you, Mrs Wemyss-Brown.' Fuggle sucked on his cigar. 'I can see you're in a hurry now, but in fact I did want a word about something else. It'll wait. I'll call on you some time.'

Charlotte said nothing. Jill nodded to the two men. As she climbed into the car, she heard them laughing. She reversed at speed across the car park, forcing them to step back. As she pulled out on to the road, she glanced in the rear-view mirror. Ivor Fuggle had raised a hand in farewell. He was still smiling.

Jill was furious. The anger was for Charlotte, rather than for herself; and an altruistic anger was often more intense because it was so wholly righteous, never adulterated with the knowledge of one's own fallibility or one's own guilt. Three years ago, Ivor Fuggle would not have dreamed of talking to Charlotte Wemyss-Brown like that, and Cyril George would not have colluded with him.

Times had indeed changed. The old certainties were shifting and crumbling. The world was evolving, so was this country, so was London; and Jill had thought that Lydmouth was somehow immune. But now Fuggle and George were the people who mattered. Charlotte Wemyss-Brown was coming perilously close to being a figure of fun.

Neither of them spoke until they had left the outskirts of

Framington behind. Canada geese flew low over the estuary. Everything was grey – the river, the sandbanks, the sky.

Charlotte said, 'I never thought I'd want to kill anyone. Not that I do, of course.' She gave a high, nervous laugh and stared out of the window. 'Just a figure of speech.'

For a moment Jill did not reply. The car meandered into the centre of the road. A lorry rounded the bend in front and came towards them, its horn blaring.

'Charlotte,' she said, swerving towards the nearside kerb, 'I'm going to London on Monday, come what may. I'm going to see if I can raise a loan.'

'No you're not. I told you – I don't want to plunge into debt.'

'I'm not asking you to plunge into debt.'

'Then what are you proposing to do?'

'I'm going to get a loan. A personal loan – something to tide us over.'

'You can't do that. Don't be silly.'

Jill glared at her. 'I'm not being silly.'

'It's terribly sweet of you, but why should you?'

'Because you and Philip were kind to me when I needed help. But it's not just that. It's because I can't bear to think of someone like Fuggle lording it over Lydmouth. I've got to do something.'

'If you get a loan, I won't take it.'

'Then I won't take my salary. I'll work for free instead. That'll save you something.'

'Don't be ridiculous. If you do anything as nonsensical as that, I shall have to sack you.'

'I won't go.'

Jill glared at Charlotte, and Charlotte glared at Jill. Then, simultaneously, they burst out laughing.

'We'll show them,' Charlotte said. 'There's life in the old dog yet.'

Chapter Eleven

For the price of a couple of cigarettes, Charlie Dyke, a beat constable on the graveyard shift covering the southern part of Lydmouth, agreed to wake Peter Porter in time for the early shift on Saturday morning. It was a weight off Porter's mind.

One problem solved – another to go: the sergeant had told Porter to call at Prout's Toys and Novelties on his way off-shift and question Mr Prout about the Pisser.

'You mustn't call him the Pisser, mind,' the sergeant had said. 'It wouldn't be nice.' He gave Porter a nudge and grinned broadly. 'Remember – Mr Prout's got friends in high places. So you'll have to be diplomatic.'

Porter made his way to St John's Passage. He had known Ronald Prout for years, though he doubted Mr Prout knew him. The late Mrs Porter had been a Baptist, and Porter had often accompanied his mother to the chapel on the corner of Broad Street and Chepstow Road.

In Lydmouth's Baptist circles, Mr Prout was a figure of some distinction, and not just because he was the chapel's organist and director of music. Many of the ladies had hoped that he might one day be tempted into matrimony, either with themselves (if they were single) or with their daughters (if they were not). The men, who formed a minority in the chapel's congregation, were on the whole less enthusiastic about Mr Prout. But they treated him with respect. No one denied that he was shrewd, and he could be waspish when annoyed.

A bell dangled over his head as Porter pushed open the door of the shop. Nostalgia shot through him as he glanced at the shelves of train sets, brightly coloured cars, games, dolls, toy soldiers, cap guns, and cowboy equipment. At the back of the shop was a curtain consisting of strips of coloured nylon, which shivered as Mr Prout appeared. He wore a maroon bow tie, a mustard-yellow moleskin waistcoat, and a suit with a Prince of Wales check, in the top pocket of which was a handkerchief that matched the tie. His large, muddy green eyes, hugely magnified by the thick lenses of his black-rimmed glasses, stared accusingly at Porter.

'Yes, Officer?'

'Mr Prout, sir, I've come about the . . . the trouble—'

'Trouble? Is that what you call it? Trouble, eh? A drunken lout has persistently been using my letter box as a public urinal – and you call it *trouble*.'

'Sorry, sir, I didn't know quite how else to—'

Mr Prout took a step forward and laid his hands, palm down, on the counter. On each of his little fingers was a gold signet ring.

'Then let me assist you, Constable. You've come – and I hope with good news – about the persistent vandalism which has been directed against my property, a campaign that has been not only destructive, but time-wasting and obscene.'

'Yes, sir.' Porter put his hands behind his back and laced his fingers tightly together to stop them trembling. 'How . . . how many times is it now?'

'Four. It is becoming an epidemic of malevolent incontinence. I have already given all the details to your colleague, including what these attacks have cost me in terms of time, cleaning materials and lost profits. So – have you made an arrest?'

'Not exactly, sir.'

Prout leaned across the counter and the overhead light gleamed on his glasses. 'What is your name, Constable?'

'Porter, sir.'

'Well, Porter, you have some explaining to do. In the first place, *why* have you not made an arrest?'

Porter opened his mouth but no words emerged.

'I take it that your guilty silence means that you haven't the foggiest idea,' said Prout, in an unexpectedly gentle voice. He leaned a little closer across the counter. 'Then I suggest you remind your superiors that I am a citizen of good standing who pays his rates. That I number among my friends several councillors, one of whom is a member of the Standing Joint Committee. Furthermore, one of my most valued customers is the daughter of your own Chief Constable. What do you want me to tell her the next time she visits with Mr Hendry's grandson? That Lydmouth is at the mercy of a hooligan with inadequate bladder control? That Police Constable Porter is a blithering ass who couldn't arrest an infant riding a tricycle without lights?'

As Prout was speaking his voice remained level. Porter knew that the sarcasm was designed to be withering, and he was duly withered. Yet a part of him was not entirely cowed. He suspected that he was receiving no more than he deserved, because he had been taught to believe this was usually the case. But still there burned within him a dangerous desire to show Mr Prout that he was wrong – not for his own sake but for the honour of the force in which he served.

'We haven't yet made an arrest, sir,' he said, his words falling into the pool of silence left by the impact of Mr Prout's invective. 'But I can tell you that we hope to do so soon. Very soon.'

Mr Prout stared at him. Then, like a rainbow after a

thunderstorm, he smiled, threw back his puny shoulders and poked his thumbs in the pockets of the mustard-yellow waist-coat. 'Good,' he said. 'When? And who is it?'

'I can't tell you any more, sir. It's confidential.'

For an instant Porter stared at Mr Prout while the panic rose higher and higher until it threatened to smother him. Visions of disgrace paraded through his mind. He sketched a salute and blundered out of the shop. The bell pinged. Mr Prout chuckled.

Chapter Twelve

On his way home that day, Richard Thornhill remembered that he had promised to buy a block of vanilla ice cream. He parked on the High Street just beyond the Rex Cinema, and went into the little general shop beside the Gardenia Café. Dr Bayswater was at the counter, asking indistinctly for a tin of sardines and a packet of Sugar Puffs. The old man was carrying a string bag that contained a badly wrapped bottle of Cutty Sark whisky.

'Ah – Thornhill,' he mumbled. 'Can't talk properly – two damned fillings.' He patted the whisky. 'I've prescribed myself a combined anaesthetic and disinfectant.'

'Very wise,' Thornhill said.

The old doctor paid for his purchases. He lingered while Thornhill was buying the ice cream. 'Went to my dentist in Gloucester,' he confided. 'Had to go by train, which was terribly tiresome.'

'Something wrong with the car?'

'Something wrong with that bloody man Gray, if you ask me. Perfectly simple repair job and he takes for ever. Still, not a wasted day, unexpectedly. I saw something most interesting. Very curious indeed.'

'What was that?' Thornhill asked, because it seemed to be expected of him.

Bayswater tapped his finger against his nose. 'My lips are sealed.'

Thornhill smiled at him. 'Then why mention it in the first place?'

'You know how it is. Sometimes one can't resist teasing people's curiosity. But, believe me, it's absolutely fascinating.'

They left the shop. Bayswater raised his hand and ambled down the pavement. At the pillar box on the corner he stopped and pushed a letter in the slot. Thornhill crossed the road. He almost collided with Jill Francis, who was coming out of Gray's Garage.

'Good evening,' he said, raising his hat.

'You're very formal these days.'

'I'm sorry.' He forced himself to say the name. 'Jill.'

'Richard.'

He stared at her, his eyes narrowing. He thought that her features had grown a little sharper in the intervening three years since he had seen her last, and that the wrinkles at the corners of the eyes were deeper. She was in the wrong place, at the wrong time. She shouldn't have come back to Lydmouth. He wondered why he had wanted her, or at least his idea of her, for so long. Why did he still want her? What on earth was the point of it?

He cleared his throat. 'I was sorry to hear about Philip Wemyss-Brown.'

'Yes.' She looked at him as though he were a biological phenomenon of only moderate interest.

He said, 'How is he? Is there any news?'

Jill shrugged. 'He's getting better. Slowly. But it'll take time.'

'So you'll be running the *Gazette* for the time being?'

'Probably.' She flicked a strand of hair underneath the band of her hat and looked coolly at him. 'Nothing is absolutely certain, though. One can take nothing for granted, can one?'

'You must notice some changes here.'

'Yes and no.' Her voice sharpened. 'It's still the same dingy, parochial little town, isn't it? Just rather more crime-ridden than it used be.' She nodded over the road at the boarded-up window of the *Gazette*'s storeroom. 'So was it arson the other night?'

'I don't know.'

'It can't have been anything else, can it? Are you likely to catch who did it?'

Thornhill took refuge in formality. 'I'm afraid I can't comment. In any case, I'm not involved in the investigation.'

'Does that mean Divisional CID are handling it?'

'For the moment, yes.'

'Is that an indication of how you rate it? So it's not important enough for the Central Office for Serious Crimes?'

He shook his head, knowing silence was safer.

'No need to answer that. But can you at least ask the officer in charge to—'

'No, I'm afraid I can't,' he snapped. 'If you phone headquarters they'll put you through to someone who can help. Now – I mustn't keep you any longer. Good evening, Miss Francis.'

Her eyelids flickered, a momentary tightening of the skin. He knew that he had reached her at last. For an instant he was filled with triumph, as sour as indigestion. Unsmiling, she nodded goodbye and crossed the road.

Thornhill walked back to his car and drove home without noticing what he was doing or where he was. The anger was mixed with pain now. She deserved it, he told himself, she needs to be taught a lesson, she was asking for it. The trouble was, he didn't believe himself. If anyone needed to be taught a lesson, it was himself.

Unhappiness takes many forms, and for years he had grown used to the dull ache of his desire and Jill's absence. Now she was back, and the knowledge that she was in Lydmouth had

stripped away the comfortingly familiar cocoon of his misery
and left him naked and unprotected. It would have been
simpler if she had been dead. Or if he had been dead.

He let himself into the house. He heard the chatter of the
television behind the closed door of the sitting-room. He went
through to the kitchen and tossed the block of ice cream into
the freezer compartment of the refrigerator, another recent
purchase, which squatted on one of the marble shelves in the
walk-in pantry. The table wasn't laid. There was no sign of a
meal.

Once more, his temper rose. Edith, Elizabeth and Susie
were in the sitting-room, gathered round the TV set with silly
smiles all over their faces. They formed a tableau, a flesh-and-
blood equivalent of those meretricious advertisements you saw
everywhere nowadays: the family clustered round the television, happiness oozing out of every pore, their problems
solved, heaven on earth and goodwill to all men thanks to
the square-eyed technological miracle that squatted in their
home.

When he came in, Elizabeth did not look up. Edith raised
her head and said, 'Hello, darling.' Susie staggered across the
carpet, bounced off the sofa, seized his hand and tried to drag
him towards the television.

'Where's supper?' Thornhill said.

'I'll get down to it in a moment,' Edith replied, without
turning her head.

'This is absurd. You're allowing that damned box to rule
our lives.'

He detached his wrist from Susie's slightly sticky grip
and left the room, slamming the door. His anger collapsed
like a punctured balloon. He sat down at the kitchen table
and spread out the *Gazette* in front of him. He stared at
the smudged black print and listened to Edith's footsteps

approaching down the hall. A moment later he sensed her standing in the kitchen doorway. He did not look up.

'What was that all about?' she demanded.

'Where's supper?'

'I just wanted to see the end of the programme. And the children were having such fun. Anyway, does it really matter if supper's a little late? It's Saturday tomorrow, and you're off duty this weekend.'

He looked at her. She was well built, with softly rounded curves. The years had treated her kindly, and so had three children. Thornhill knew that many men envied him.

She said softly, 'You're looking at me as if you hate me.'

'Oh, don't talk nonsense.'

She pulled out a chair and sat down opposite him. 'You could have started supper yourself if you were in such a hurry. Or at least laid the table.'

'Yes,' he said stiffly. 'I suppose I could. But usually you do it. It's . . . it's your job.'

'Sometimes I wish it wasn't.'

He said nothing.

Edith sighed. 'This is ridiculous.'

'I quite agree.' He turned a page of the newspaper.

'I mean, we can't go on like this. Most of the time you're at home, you're like a bear with a sore head. It's not fair on the children. Or on me.'

'I'm sorry,' he said. 'But you must realise that it isn't easy for me, either.'

Edith let a silence lengthen between them. Then she said, very quietly: 'You have to choose, Richard. We can't go on like this. What is it you really want? A divorce?'

Chapter Thirteen

M ost people had gone home. Jill jotted down two appointments for the following week, closed the desk
diary and slid it into a drawer of Philip's desk. Next door
the tapping of Miss Gwyn-Thomas's typewriter stopped. Jill
heard the murmur of voices. Howard Mork was making the
rounds, collecting the last of the post.

'And if it's raining when you get outside, don't let them get
wet,' Amy said.

But Amy was alone when Jill came out. 'Such an obliging
boy, Howard,' she said, setting her hat carefully on her
permed hair and adjusting it in the mirror. 'Do you know,
he just offered to walk home with me and carry my bag.'

'You've made a conquest.' Jill worked her fingers into her
gloves.

'Oh, it's not like that, I'm sure. Howard's far too young. He
was only being helpful. Anyway, I turned him down.' In the
mirror over her desk, Amy's lips curved into a smile. 'Mr
Prout's collecting me, as a matter of fact.'

Jill wished her goodnight. On her way out, she put her
head into the reporters' room, which, like the editor's office,
was on the first floor. One young woman, a trainee, was still
there, industriously transcribing shorthand notes. For an
instant, Jill saw her former self in the girl: young and
desperately keen to succeed; and before her the future,
a vast unknown, full of possibilities. At present the girl

worked with more industry than judgement, but she would learn.

'I'm off,' Jill said. 'How was the Transport Committee?'

'Nothing was really decided, I'm afraid. They were meant to be making up their minds about the bypass, but they just went round and round in circles. I think some of them didn't want to make up their minds – they just like the sound of their own voices.'

Jill laughed. 'Council meetings never change.'

'There was one thing, though.' The young woman blushed. 'Afterwards, when I was in the Ladies, a couple of the secretaries came in. They couldn't see me. One of them said to the other that her husband had just phoned, and that there were going to be twenty redundancies at Broadbent's.'

'Twenty? That sounds serious.'

'And at Broadbent's, too.'

'Worth checking – see if you can confirm it.'

Five minutes later Jill let herself out of the side door of the *Gazette* and set off for Raglan Court. It was already dark. She was annoyed to find that she was a little nervous, alert to footsteps and shadows, hurrying from one street lamp to the next. She had not forgotten the watcher in the car park at the flats the previous evening. Not that she actually knew there had been a watcher – only a cough in the darkness and a grating of metal as though someone had slipped through the gate to the park.

On her way back, she visited the shop at the bottom of Albert Road and bought milk, bread and a tin of baked beans. She wasn't hungry after that substantial lunch in Framington but she knew she should eat something.

When you lived by yourself, it was frighteningly easy to let things slide. Sometimes Jill glimpsed a possible future that terrified her, one in which she was no longer able to persuade herself that things mattered, that it was important to get out of bed in the morning, important to wash one's body and feed it and water it. Gin, she thought, that's what I need. Immediately afterwards, she wondered whether she was becoming – had already become? – one of those women who drink alone and try to conceal the bottles they put out for the dustmen.

She let herself into the flat, turned on the living-room fire and went into the bedroom to take off her hat. The doorbell rang. Roger Leddon was at the door, looking charmingly apologetic.

'You must think I'm a perfect pest.'

'Not at all, Doctor.'

'I just wanted to tell you that the insurance company's being wonderfully straightforward about the whole thing. No problems. And do call me Roger, please. Anyway, I'm sorry to bother you. I'll—'

'You're not bothering me. Would you like a drink? I owe you one.'

He smiled again. She had never seen such beautiful eyes in a man. He followed her into the flat.

'I'd avoid the armchairs, if I were you,' she said as she rummaged for glasses. 'The chairs at the table are more comfortable.'

Leddon glanced at the armchairs and cocked an eyebrow. 'They look as if they were designed with a race of Martians in mind.'

'Not just any old Martians, either. The dwarf mutations with enormous bottoms and very short and very spindly legs.'

'Like Humpty Dumpty before the fall?'

Jill laughed, suddenly happier than she had been since returning to Lydmouth. She brought the drinks and fetched an ashtray. While they drank, they chatted in a wary, slightly self-conscious way, as people do when they are faced with the task of discovering whether an initial liking may turn into something more extensive, more durable. She learned that Leddon had trained at Guy's and until recently had been a partner in a big practice in Leicester. She gave him an edited version of her job with *Berkeley's* and how she came to be caretaker editor of the *Gazette*.

'How does it feel?' he asked. 'Coming back, I mean.'

'I don't really know yet. Early days.'

'It can be unsettling,' Leddon said. 'I went up to Guy's a couple of months ago and looked up a few people I used to know. I wished I hadn't, if the truth be known. I didn't feel I belonged there any more.'

'The difference is, I've got a job to do here.'

'And old friends, of course.'

'Yes.'

'Including Dr Bayswater?'

Jill remembered the scene in the garage that morning. The question was not as casual as it sounded. 'He wasn't someone I knew well. But doing my job, and in a town like Lydmouth, we tended to run up against each other quite a lot. And Dr Bayswater's been here since the year dot. He knows everyone.'

'So I'm finding.'

'What do you mean?'

Leddon delayed answering, offering her a cigarette, taking one himself and lighting them both. At last he exhaled a lungful of smoke. 'When I bought his practice, I rather understood he was going to move away from Lydmouth. But he's hanging on. It's rather like having the ghost of Christmas past peering over your shoulder.'

'Does it matter? I've been hearing golden opinions about you.'

He smiled. 'That's always nice to hear, even if it isn't true. But it's not just the fact that he's staying in Lydmouth. Why shouldn't he, after all? Even his little eccentricities aren't important. You've heard about the rats, I take it? No, the real problem—'

'The rats?'

'Sorry – I don't mean to gossip. I thought you'd have heard.'

'I gathered he's become a little cranky.'

Leddon threw back his head and laughed. 'That's one way of putting it. He's got various bees in his bonnet. Have you noticed how people often become rather odd when they retire? It's as if they've had to conform all their lives and suddenly the barriers are removed and a great tide of idiosyncrasy floods out. Do you know his house? There's a huge garden at the back, must be at least an acre and a half, perhaps two, all gone to rack and ruin. Every evening he feeds the wildlife. He's got a row of bowls and tins underneath the veranda at the back, and he fills them with milk and bread. I've never seen it myself but I'm told that feeding time is quite extraordinary. You get all sorts coming along. Hedgehogs and cats, of course. There's a fox and a badger. But – most of all – there's an awful lot of rats. The whole area's riddled with them.'

'Surely it's a danger to public health?'

'Not an easy thing to prove.'

'But why is he doing it?' Jill asked.

Leddon shrugged. 'He's not trying to be a latter-day St Francis. He told me he was contemplating a paper on the social aspects of cross-species feeding habits.'

'I didn't know he was interested in wildlife.'

'Nor did he, I suspect, until he retired and found that he had time on his hands.' Leddon hesitated. 'I think he wants recognition as a scientist, perhaps, as much as anything. I imagine that a psychiatrist might see it as a desperate bid for immortality.'

Dr Bayswater had no children. Jill shifted on the hard chair, uncomfortable with the idea that the childless might need to find another way to ensure they were remembered for a generation or two after their deaths.

'It's up to him if he chooses to make a fool of himself,' Leddon continued. 'The snag is, it affects me. When I bought the practice, we had a sort of gentlemen's agreement about the house and garden.'

'You were going to buy those too?'

Leddon shook his head. 'I didn't want the house – it's one of those enormous old places, all very well for a Victorian GP with five children and a couple of live-in servants. No, he was going to divide the garden in two. Part of it he'd sell with the house. The other part, the bit that fronts on Whistler's Lane, he was going to sell to me. I want to build a surgery and a decent modern health centre. It's an ideal site. Central location, lots of space, and everyone knows where it is because it's where Bayswater's been practising for years.'

'Wouldn't it be hideously expensive?'

'The Executive Council and the Health Authority like the plan, and if they're happy, so's the bank. I had a word with a couple of chaps on the Planning Committee, and they didn't think there'd be a problem, either, not in principle.' Leddon glanced sideways at her through his long, dark lashes. 'But Bayswater changed his mind. His so-called research was more important than honouring his agreement with me. Which leaves me having to pay the earth in rent for a glorified scout hut on Chepstow Road. The patients don't like it, and nor do I.'

'Perhaps he'll come round. His experiment isn't going to last for ever.'

'I sometimes think he'd make it last until kingdom come just to spite me. He should be passing on practice records to me, but he's even dragging his feet about that.'

'Why doesn't he like you?'

'I suppose I've been a little more outspoken than was altogether tactful.'

They sat in silence for a moment. The flat had warmed up. Jill sipped her gin, willing herself not to gulp it.

'I'm sorry to go on about it.' Leddon had a way of squeezing his eyes when he looked at you so the skin of the corners wrinkled in a most attractive fashion. 'You must be bored stiff.'

Jill shook her head. 'He's not a bad man,' she said. 'Just naturally bloody minded. And it sounds as though you've rubbed him up the wrong way.'

'He couldn't be much more unpleasant if he thought I'd murdered his grandmother.'

'My impression was that he really cared about the welfare of his patients. Especially the poorer ones. Do you know, before the National Health Service, he'd often not charge for seeing people he thought couldn't afford it. He just wouldn't send in his bills.'

'That's another reason why he doesn't like me,' Leddon said, his mind following a track that diverged slightly from Jill's. 'He sees me as the Lydmouth representative of the National Health Service, and therefore as someone who needs to be tarred and feathered and run out of town.'

'I think you should try and talk to him. Not about the rights and wrongs of it, all that Big Brother nonsense. But about the patients. About how much better off they would be if there was a new health centre here. If you go in with all guns blazing, he'll just blaze back. If you appeal to his generosity, though, he might just come round.'

'I can't see that happening, I'm afraid. He's too entrenched.'

By the sound of it Bayswater was not the only one who was entrenched. The problem with trench warfare was that the most likely outcome was a costly stalemate. She said, 'No harm in talking to him, surely?'

Leddon smiled. 'I've a feeling I'd only make matters worse. But thanks for letting me unload my troubles. You've no idea what a pleasure it is, and a relief.' He looked at his watch. 'I'd better be off.'

There was a hint of uncertainty in his voice, and Jill knew that if she offered him another drink he would accept. At that moment, though, the telephone began to ring, postponing the necessity of making a decision. She stood up to answer it, and Leddon took this as a signal for his departure. Jill picked up the phone.

'Hello, dear? Is that you? It's Charlotte,' said Charlotte unnecessarily. On the telephone, her voice became a caricature of what it normally was, making it sound as though she were addressing a mass meeting of the Mothers' Union. 'I just wanted to thank you for lunch. I did so enjoy it – such a break. Philip sends his love, by the way – he's sitting up now and feeling much better.'

Leddon smiled at her, mouthed his thanks and slipped out of the room.

' 'Bye,' Jill said, and waved.

'Who was that?' Charlotte demanded. 'Who were you talking to?'

'Roger Leddon. He just dropped in for a moment. About the car insurance.'

'So it's *Roger* now, is it? Has he gone?'

'Yes. He was telling me about Dr Bayswater.'

'Not much love lost there, I'm afraid. Understandably enough. You've heard about the health centre, I assume?'

'And about the experiments.'

'Oh dear, yes. Dr Bayswater was always contrary. Consistent in that, at least. Encouraging the vermin that everyone else is trying to put down. Absolutely typical. Still, at least he's not nasty, only a little odd. Unlike some people I could mention.'

Jill had wondered how long it would take Charlotte to get round to this subject. 'I'm sorry Fuggle was at the hotel this afternoon. I should have remembered that the *Post*'s offices are in Framington.'

'Nonsense,' Charlotte boomed. 'Why should you? Why should we let that man make our lives a misery? But heaven knows, he deserves his come-uppance. If you ask me, Philip would be fit and well today if it weren't for him.'

Jill doubted that. Philip had never shown the slightest interest in his own health. And now he was paying the price.

'Such a vulgar man, too,' Charlotte was saying. 'My grand-father would have horse-whipped him. And a jolly good thing too. In my opinion, whipping's too kind for a man like that.'

Chapter Fourteen

Later that evening, Peter Porter walked home from the table tennis club and took the route through Temple-fields. He had done well in the club tournament and was now almost certain of a place in the quarter-final. He had also solved the problem of how to wake up early. All in all, he would have felt happy if he had not told that stupid lie to Mr Prout.

In Mincing Lane, music wafted out of the King's Head. The curtains were still open and he could see men and women in the public bar. Most of them were gathered round the piano, singing the rude song about someone called Dinah, a favourite of the police rugby XV at the end of a long evening when there were no ladies present. The air was thick with cigarette smoke and everyone seemed to be having a wonderful time.

Porter lingered at the window, both attracted and repelled by what he saw. He wished that he had that marvellous ability to enjoy himself, to forget, at least for a while, the crushing weight of being Peter Porter. But he knew the King's Head wouldn't suit him. He didn't enjoy that sort of fun. It was as if there were something missing in him.

Two men were sitting at the table near the window, facing each other but both with their eyes fixed on the glasses in front of them. For an instant, Porter took them for father and son. Then he recognised their faces. The one on the right was Joe Rodley, the lorry driver who lived in that old cottage near the

park. The one on the left was Howard Mork, the lad whose
dad ran the men's outfitters in the High Street, and who
worked at the *Gazette*. They looked a pair of miserable
buggers, Porter told himself, and then mentally apologised
for swearing to the deity whom he still believed was invisibly
monitoring his every word, every thought and every action.

He walked back to his lodgings. Miss Mynott was in the
kitchen, smoking a cigarette and doing the accounts, while a
saucepan of milk warmed on the stove.

'Do you want some cocoa, Peter? There's milk in the
fridge.'

It was pleasant to sit with her at the table and drink cocoa.
She asked him about his day and listened, running her fingers
restlessly through her hair, while he told her about the table
tennis tournament and about Mr Prout.

'Sleep on it,' she advised him. 'Everything looks better in the
morning. Then ask your sergeant, or whoever it is, whether
there's any news about the Pisser.'

Porter winced, hearing a lady use a word like that.

Miss Mynott appeared not to notice. 'Then you go and see
Prout. If you're lucky, there'll be good news you can tell him,
and if you're not, just say that you are afraid you were
mistaken, and that a promising lead has come to nothing. It'll
be easy. You'll see.'

Porter was not convinced. No conversation with Mr Prout
was going to be easy. On the other hand the sound of Miss
Mynott's voice and the very fact that he was sitting here
sipping cocoa in a warm kitchen, just like a normal person
with a real home, were soothing in themselves.

'There's something I wanted to ask you, actually,' Miss
Mynott said. 'You know Mr Frederick?'

'Who?'

'The man you met the other day – the engineer who's been

staying here. He left this morning, which means we've got a room free again. I don't suppose any of your colleagues are looking for one? I'd prefer a long-term let.'

Porter promised to enquire. He helped Miss Mynott wash up, and then went upstairs, trying to tread quietly because he knew Mr Mynott went to sleep early, and loathed being disturbed. When he was ready for bed, he took down the suitcase from the top of the wardrobe and found the ball of string.

He opened the window and, shivering in the cold air, leaned out. Breathing heavily, he unrolled the string from the ball, watching the ghostly white thread curl and twist in the light breeze. When he judged that the end was a foot or two above the ground, he lowered the sash almost to the sill and backed towards the bed, still clutching what was left of the ball of string. He wriggled out of his dressing-gown and kicked off his slippers.

The cold was intense. Porter had climbed into bed before he realised it would be necessary to cut the string from the rest of the ball, which meant getting out of bed again, crossing the freezing linoleum to the wardrobe and finding his nail scissors. At last he slid back under the mound made by four blankets, an eiderdown and a bedspread. Using his teeth and his free hand, he tied the end of the piece of string to his left thumb. Thornhill's original plan, he knew, had called for him to use his toe, but he decided that toes were only suitable for summer conditions.

He set the alarm clock. He turned on his side, curled into a ball and willed his body to become warm. His last conscious thought was that Mam would have made him a hot-water bottle.

Suddenly, brutally, he was fully awake again. There was no interval between deep sleep and full consciousness. His thumb ached with the aftermath of acute pain, and his hand was hanging out of bed.

The room was not entirely dark. The glow of the street lamp filtered through the crack between the curtains. Charlie Dyke had pulled the string. It was time to get up. But Charlie needn't have pulled so hard.

Porter rolled out of bed, crossed the room to the window and threw up the sash. Gasping at the cold, he leaned out, meaning to wave an acknowledgement to his colleague. But no one was there, only the string, still dancing in the breeze. He heard hurried footsteps, though, and glimpsed a figure turning into St John's Passage.

The revelations hit him like a series of punches: it was still evening; it was not time to get up; someone had played a trick on him.

For the first time it occurred to him that the string plan, brilliant though it was, had a flaw. Because his room was at the front of the building, so was the piece of string, dangling down, white against the black of the shop window. It was asking for trouble – he saw that now. Mr Thornhill's window must have been in a less obvious place.

He was well and truly awake now and, still with the string attached to his thumb, he groped for cigarettes and matches on the dressing-table. A smoke would calm him down and help him sleep. He was about to close the curtains when he heard a second set of footsteps outside. He looked down at the street.

Dr Leddon was walking rapidly along the pavement on the opposite side of Broad Street. His hands were deep in the pockets of his dark overcoat. For an instant Porter saw his profile in the light from the street lamp. He had a distinctive way of wearing his trilby, tilted far back on his head as if he were someone in the films. The doctor turned into Albert Road, and his footsteps dwindled into silence.

Leaving the window slightly open, and the string still dangling down to the street on the principle that lightning was unlikely to strike twice on one night, Porter stubbed out his cigarette and went back to bed. It was still warm under the covers. He felt sleep glide over him, a glorious tide of unknowing. He had nearly drowned in it when there was another interruption.

Outside, someone screamed.

At first Porter thought it was a cat or an owl. Immediately afterwards, however, there came the sound of running footsteps, drawing closer, and more howls, but quieter now and lower in pitch too.

Groaning, Porter wriggled out of bed and crossed the freezing linoleum to the window once again. He drew back the curtains, raised the sash and leaned out. No one was there. The howling had stopped. A moment later he could not hear the footsteps, either.

Porter yawned. He stumbled back to bed, the string trailing after him. He slithered under the bedclothes and turned on his side. The thumb to which the string was attached found its way first to his cheek and then to his mouth.

The fog swirled up from the river and fingered its way through the streets and alleys of Lydmouth. Silence enveloped the town. Police Constable Peter Porter slept.

[Saturday, 3 December]

Yesterday was the worst day of my life. Afterwards, I tried to sleep, and before the tablets worked, I – oh God, it was like one of those nightmares when something horrible happens and you try and escape from it, only to find that you're facing something even more horrible.

And it's not over. There's so much I have to do. So much I don't know.

Please God, tell me, what am I going to do?

Chapter Fifteen

Children may know less but sometimes they understand more. Over breakfast on Saturday morning, Elizabeth and Susie seemed oblivious of the strain, but Thornhill thought he sensed a constraint in their dealings with him, a wariness that had not been there before. They hadn't heard what Edith had said, of course, but neither of them was stupid. They were well aware, in their different ways, that their parents were treating each other with exaggerated politeness.

At breakfast, Edith announced that she and the girls were going shopping. Self-consciously noble, Thornhill volunteered to do the washing up. The female part of his family left him to it, rather to his surprise. When he was alone he piled dirty crockery in the sink and scowled at it. The frying pan resisted his efforts to clean it. He spilled sudsy water all over the scullery floor and broke a teacup.

Now what? He had the entire weekend at his disposal. There were plenty of jobs he should do – the shelves in Elizabeth's room, the window that needed reglazing in the side door, that suspicious damp patch that required investigation in the box-room ceiling, and of course the dining-room, which had been in the process of being redecorated since they moved into the house all those years ago. There were more jobs waiting for him outside: all the tedious, back-breaking tasks involved in settling a garden down, albeit rather late, for winter.

Instead, at a loose end, Thornhill wandered through the

house. He was not used to being alone here and it increased his uneasiness. Strange how that one word, divorce, had changed everything. It was as if Edith had put a marker down to show how far the discontent they shared had reached. Until then, it had been possible to fool oneself that their life together wasn't really so bad. But once the marker was there, planted in plain view, they could see exactly how bad it had in fact become. The question was: would it stay that way?

He moved aimlessly from room to room, pausing longest in his son's bedroom, empty until its owner returned from school for the Christmas holidays. He missed David more than he cared to admit. He had not wanted the boy to go to boarding-school, but Edith had overruled him. Thanks to a legacy from her mother and the generosity of her Uncle Bernie, Edith was increasingly financially independent.

First the school, now the television: the message was clear – he now lacked the power that most of his colleagues took for granted, control of the family purse strings. If Edith wanted to leave him, he thought it probable that she could, in the sense that she could afford to do so. If necessary Uncle Bernie would help her financially. And Edith was more than capable of earning her living, if she wanted to. She had trained as a teacher before their marriage and had continued working until she was heavily pregnant with David.

To distract himself, Thornhill decided to go to the library. In the old days, when he still had leisure, he had been a voracious reader, mainly of fiction and poetry. Sheltering beneath an umbrella, he walked quickly through the drizzling rain. Mist still clung to the higher ground on either side of the river. The town was trapped in an eternal twilight.

As he walked, the word *divorce* blinked on and off in his mind like a neon sign. If Edith left him, it wouldn't be good for his career. Senior police officers were meant to give the appearance of being happily married. Fornication, adultery and marital catastrophes made the Standing Joint Committee morally queasy. Police authorities were conservative animals by their very nature, especially somewhere like Lydmouth, where appearances mattered because everyone was aware of everyone else's business.

He was alive to the irony in the fact that it had been Edith who had raised the idea. Three or four years ago, he had seriously contemplated leaving his wife and family, and probably leaving the police force as well, in order to live with another woman in the hope of eventually marrying her. And what made the irony even more exquisitely uncomfortable was the fact that the woman in question had recently returned to Lydmouth and was showing every sign of disliking him intensely.

The library was crowded. He met too many people he knew, from the vicar's wife to the increasingly evil-smelling factotum at the Bull Hotel. All of them wanted to ask him how Edith and the children were. In the end he seized a copy of *Lucky Jim* and the latest Agatha Christie novel and nearly fled down the steps into the relative anonymity of the High Street.

He walked briskly down to the *Gazette* – the window of the printing works was still boarded up; he made a mental note to check the progress of the investigation with Divisional CID – and turned into Broad Street. He glanced across the road at Grove House on the corner of Whistler's Lane, wondering what Bayswater had found so fascinating the previous evening.

'Sir! Chief Inspector!'

Thornhill was approaching Mynott's electrical shop and there, standing on the pavement, was the massive shape of PC Porter. He watched the young man's face brightening as he drew nearer. He was uncomfortable with the unconditional loyalty that Porter gave him. He knew he wasn't worthy of it.

'Morning, Peter. How did the string trick work?'

'Well, sir. Very well in one way, but I suppose I'd have to say it wasn't quite as straightforward as I'd hoped. You see' – he jabbed a thumb upwards – 'my room's just up there and—'

'And someone pulled the string as they were passing by, just for the hell of it, eh?'

Porter nodded. 'Late last night. I was asleep. But it worked perfectly when Dyke pulled it this morning. The only thing was' – he bit his lip – 'I'd forgotten I'd swapped. I wasn't on earlies because I took George's turn on Tuesday. I'm not on duty till two o'clock. So I thought I'd go up to the cemetery and see—'

The shop door opened and Miss Mynott appeared in the doorway. 'Peter,' she said. 'Have you got a moment?'

'I've got *hours*,' Porter said with a touch of pride.

'It's very odd. Mrs Frederick rang again. She talked to Mr Frederick's manager, and he was really quite surprised that he hadn't seen him yesterday.' Miss Mynott saw Thornhill standing to one side. 'Oh – I'm sorry, I didn't realise—' Recognition flooded her face. 'It's Mr Thornhill, isn't it? Are you enjoying your television?'

'I haven't watched it myself,' Thornhill said. 'But I don't think my family can imagine life without it.'

She wasn't listening. 'It's been one of those mornings. Has Peter told you? We've lost a lodger, and the phone hasn't stopped ringing.'

Thornhill realised that she knew what he did for a living. He said, 'What exactly is the problem? The man hasn't arrived home?'

She nodded. 'Mr Frederick was going to catch the London train yesterday morning. He must have left about nine-thirty. Apparently he never got there. His firm thought he might have gone home, even though he said he'd come in on the Friday afternoon, and his wife thought he might have stayed another night down here. Then his boss phoned his wife, and they realised something was wrong and they both phoned us.'

'Was he going directly to the station?'

'I presume so.' Miss Mynott looked at him with bright eyes. 'He didn't say he was going anywhere else on the way.'

If he left at that time and walked down to the station, he wouldn't have caught a through train to London. Thornhill, who had suffered from the shortcomings of the timetable himself, knew that Frederick would have had to change at Gloucester and at Swindon and he would have arrived at Paddington only half an hour before the through train that left Lydmouth about midday.

'Had he any friends in Lydmouth?'

She shook her head. 'Not that I know of. He asked if he could borrow the phone book the other night but he didn't say why.'

'Luggage?'

'He took it with him. All he had was a small suitcase.'

'What about his room? Was anything left behind?'

'No. I changed the bed and cleaned it yesterday evening. It was all very clean and tidy. The only thing I found was a receipt. It was in the armchair, between the cushion and the arm. He bought something at Butter's the other day, and it was for that.'

'Might it have been their phone number he wanted?'

'Why? Their shop's only round the corner.'

'What had he bought?'

'A pair of gloves. Very expensive. They were kid leather – Mr Frederick thought they were the cat's whiskers. But they weren't what I would have chosen. Mustard yellow – you could see them a mile off. Still, there's no accounting for taste, is there? Maybe they'll tone down when he's worn them a bit.'

Chapter Sixteen

On the other end of the line Mr Gray sighed. 'No, Miss Francis, no can do. Not today. I'm sorry, I know I said I would, but I've got to go out on a breakdown. Monday, though, that's another matter. No problem at all if you can wait till Monday.'

Jill glanced at her watch. It was a little after 10.30. She had plenty of time before her cup of coffee with Dr Bayswater. 'I'll be in London on Monday,' she said, looking out of the window to assess what the weather was up to. 'I'm not sure when I'll be back – it may be after you've closed.'

'Do you want me to bring the car to Raglan Court, then? We could leave it at the back and put the key through your door.'

Jill agreed, her attention partly distracted by the sight of Ivor Fuggle walking slowly out of the park with a cigarette in his gloved hand.

'Have no fear, Miss Francis,' Gray said. 'It'll be as good as new.'

She said goodbye and put the receiver down. Fuggle turned into the cemetery. Jill picked up her handbag and let herself out of the flat. The shortest way to Grove House was to turn right into Albert Road and then right again into Broad Street at the end. Instead she turned left. The mist was beginning to clear and it had stopped raining for the time being.

At the entrance to the park Jill hesitated for a moment and

then walked briskly into the cemetery. She acted on impulse, without a clear idea of what she intended to do. After all, Fuggle was not the sort of man you could plead with. He would certainly be open to an appeal to his self-interest, but she could not at present see a way of doing that.

The cemetery, with its cropped grass and its regimented rows of graves, was not an attractive place, though in summer, when the sun was out and the trees were heavy with foliage, it could at least be peaceful. In winter, it was bleak and utilitarian: here, one felt, lay the dead, stripped of their essentials, not awaiting resurrection but undergoing a slow dissolution in a great corporeal waiting-room.

She saw Fuggle immediately. He was in the section to the right of the broad central path, the area containing the more recent graves. He had his back to her. Jill walked slowly towards him, picking her way among the headstones, her shoes making no noise on the damp grass. As she drew nearer, her anger increased. Suddenly it occurred to her that, because he was a ruthless opponent, there was nothing to be gained from not being frank. Just as pleading would not make him less ruthless, telling him exactly what she thought of him could not make him more. So at least she could afford the luxury of being honest with him.

When she was within ten yards of him, though, she stopped. There was something very odd about Fuggle's pose. He was standing beside a grave with his feet apart, his head bowed. She could not see his face but she imagined he was staring fixedly at the low hummock extending from the headstone. But he was not entirely motionless. The shoulders, which were hunched higher than usual, were shaking.

Ivor Fuggle was crying.

Jill turned and walked away from him as quickly as she could without actually breaking into a run. His mother, she thought, it must be his bloody mother. Until then, she had not even wondered why he was in the cemetery. The strength of her dislike – no, hatred – had blinded her to anything other than her own emotions.

She came out of the cemetery and turned right into the park. The only person in sight was a woman walking a very small dog in the distance. Moisture dripped from bedraggled trees. In the children's play area, the swings were looped over their frames and the great green slide was streaked with rust. Untidy drifts of rotting leaves lay in streaks of orange and brown on the grass and the paths. It looked as though the park were going rusty.

She found herself thinking not of Ivor Fuggle but of Richard Thornhill. She just couldn't understand the man: after all that had happened between them, he had simply cut her off; he hadn't once tried to get in touch with her; he hadn't even found time for a postcard. But at least the three-year silence had given her the opportunity to see him for what he really was: a narrow-minded, provincial policeman with many admirable qualities, no doubt, but not really one's own sort.

Suddenly it felt colder. Jill clutched her coat to her throat and hurried up a path on the left, which curved towards one of the smaller gates leading to Whistler's Lane. She was going to be early but she didn't think Dr Bayswater would mind. She came out of the park into the lane, which wound its way down to Broad Street. Grove House stood on the corner of the two roads, with its long garden running up the lane.

She tried the iron-shod front door, which was recessed in a porch the size of a small chapel and flanked by Early English windows filled with stained glass. She tugged the bell-pull but could not hear an answering jangle inside the house. She glanced up at the arch of the frame above the door and saw, at its apex, a dense cluster of cobwebs attached both to the stone of the arch and to the door. Even three years ago, Jill recalled, Bayswater had not used the rooms at the front very much; he had lived mainly at the back, near his surgery at the side.

She returned to Whistler's Lane. The high, grey wall of Grove House reared above her. The nearest window was twelve feet or more above the ground. There was a gate marked 'Surgery' in the garden wall. She turned the handle, and the gate swung inward.

Immediately inside was a pint of milk, awaiting collection. She picked it up, wincing as the condensation on the bottle marked her glove. A flagged path led to the half-glazed door of the surgery. The blinds were lowered over the windows, and a couple of slates had slid down to the guttering. The path continued round the corner of the surgery and into the garden beyond.

It was not so much a garden as a wilderness – an L-shaped enclosure, unusually large for a town house and crammed with vegetation, most of it the sort that gardeners spend their lives fighting against. There were huge clumps of bramble, plantations of nettles and thistles, forests of ash and sycamore saplings. At its heart a weathered sundial streaked with bird droppings stood at the junction of four paths.

Jill took the one that led up to the back of the house. She came to the flight of steps rising to the veranda, a wooden superstructure built over a sloping bank. At one end was a small, partly glazed loggia. On either side of the steps, at the foot of the bank, was a row of bowls, an ill-assorted mixture of china, earthenware and enamel.

She mounted the steps carefully, because they were slippery with green slime. On the veranda, three wicker chairs rotted quietly against the wall of the house. Jill turned towards the loggia.

That was when she saw the rat. It was a large grey creature with a very long tail and it was standing, with the air of one who had every right to be there, in front of the loggia and looking at Jill. She gave a gasp, not quite a shriek, and the rat ambled to the edge of the veranda, slipped between two of the railings and disappeared.

Jill gripped her handbag strap more firmly and forced herself to walk resolutely towards the loggia. She despised the sort of woman who recoiled from mice and spiders. The fact that she did so herself in no way altered her opinion.

The loggia was little more than a porch. In the centre of the space was a bamboo table which had once been painted white. An assortment of tools was scattered on top – among them a screwdriver, a hammer and a saw – together with an ashtray and a pair of binoculars. Beside the table was an armchair with a sagging seat. She hoped it wasn't the armchair that Bayswater intended to lend her. Because of the sloping foundation of the veranda, an occupant of the chair would be able to look down and see the line of feeding-bowls.

Jill called out Bayswater's name. There was no answer.

A French window, which was closed, separated the loggia from the room behind. Jill could not see into the room because a pair of red velvet curtains were in the way. She tapped on the glass. After a moment, she tried the handle. The window opened into the room, snagging on the curtains. There was a flurry of movement inside, little more than a rustle. She could not tell whether it had been caused by a human or some other animal.

'Hello?' she said, and her voice sounded unnaturally high and breathless. 'Anyone there?'

Her heart was beating more quickly than usual and her mouth was dry. She pushed her way past the curtain and entered the house. It was dark. A triangle of grey light from the

French window illuminated a slice of the room – part of a carpet, the corner of a table, the arm of a chair.

'Dr Bayswater,' she called. 'It's Jill Francis. Are you there?'

The room was cold and it smelled unpleasant. It seemed to her that the big, church-like house was holding its breath, waiting for her to do something. But was there another human in the house, also holding his breath?

Or a human with no breath at all?

Jill wanted to slip away and walk down to Broad Street, where there were people and cars and lorries – even a public telephone box. Instead, she tugged gently at one of the curtains. It slid halfway across the window and then stopped.

Even so, there was more than enough light to see the room as a whole. It was furnished as a study, with bookshelves, a large, roll-top desk, a work table and filing cabinets. There was a single leather armchair and beside it, on the edge of the desk, was a bottle of whisky. Jill's eyes drifted down to the floor. Then, as part of her had known she would, ever since she had smelled the room, she saw Dr Bayswater.

The milk bottle slid from her gloved hand. It fell with a clunk to the carpet, rolled a few inches to the edge and clattered on to the border of bare boards between carpet and wall. The aluminium top gave way, and the bottle belched spurts of milk over the dark-stained wood. Jill glanced at it: for a split second she envisaged herself searching for cleaning materials, on her hands and knees swabbing up the mess, buying a replacement pint of milk.

Reality instantly blotted out this oddly seductive fantasy. She crouched beside Bayswater. He was lying on his side, half shielded by the desk, with his legs drawn up like those of a sleeping child. He wore a dressing-gown and pyjamas. She removed the glove from her right hand and touched his cheek.

He needed a shave. The skin was very cold. Only one eye

was visible and that was open. There was a draught from the French window and strands of hair, grey, greasy and badly in need of cutting, twitched lethargically.

Jill forced herself to push up the sleeve of the dressing-gown and touch the skin beneath. The veins on the inside of the wrist were gnarled and prominent, like the roots of an old tree. She felt for a pulse she knew she would not find.

How old had Bayswater been? In life, he had been vigorous enough to make him seem younger than he probably was. Now he looked half as old as time.

She straightened up. For the first time, it occurred to her that the room was in a dreadful mess that went far beyond the grime and clutter one might have expected in an old bachelor's living-quarters. There were papers scattered, seemingly at random, over every horizontal surface, including the carpet. Three desk drawers were hanging open.

A phone, she thought. A phone.

Jill looked wildly around her. To her relief, she saw it almost immediately on top of a low bookcase to the left of the fireplace. Reaching the telephone was less easy because it involved clambering over the body and squeezing between it and the unforgiving metal of one of the filing cabinets. When she lifted the Bakelite handset, it seemed much heavier than usual.

She glanced down, suddenly anxious that she might be treading on some part of Bayswater, an outstretched hand, perhaps. She wasn't: but there was something beneath the sole of her left shoe. She bent down.

Partly concealed by a fold of the dressing-gown was a glove. With the tip of her shoe, she nudged it away from the body so she could see the whole of it. She began to tremble. A chill crept like poison through her body.

Her hand was trembling so much she could hardly use the

phone. Instead of dialling 999, she dialled the four-figure number, once so familiar, of the police station in the High Street. The phone rang at the other end.

A new and bizarrely irrelevant terror came over her. She might have to talk to Richard Thornhill. Even now, even in this situation, she wasn't sure she could bear to do that.

'Lydmouth police station. Good morning.'

A man's voice, with a local accent; sounding bored. Jill was irrationally disappointed. Now it wasn't Richard, she wished it had been. Not that someone of his seniority would be answering the phone.

'Yes?' demanded the voice. 'Who is it? Are you there, caller?'

Jill licked her lips. She stared down at the thing on the floor. She could not find the right words. The wrong ones would have to do.

'I've found a glove,' she said unsteadily. 'A yellow, right-hand glove. I think it's made of kid leather.'

Chapter Seventeen

By five minutes past two on Saturday afternoon, the queue from the Rex Cinema stretched down the High Street almost as far as Gray's Garage. The doors would open at ten past and the lights would go down at half-past.

Amy Gwyn-Thomas was near the head of the queue. Usually, she preferred the evening performances on the grounds that there were fewer children. Today was an exception, however, because this would be the first showing in Lydmouth of Alfred Hitchcock's *To Catch a Thief*, starring Cary Grant and Grace Kelly.

Amy had been deeply attached to Cary Grant for more years than she cared to remember. He appeared in her mind more frequently than any other star of stage or screen. He seemed equally at home there whether she was waking or sleeping. At one time she had thought that Philip Wemyss-Brown looked rather like Cary Grant, but now she realised she had been mistaken.

But Ronald Prout was another matter. Lately she had devoted a good deal of thought to the question of whether he resembled Cary Grant, and if so how much and in what way. She had concluded that, although the physical resemblance between the two men was not immediately obvious to the casual onlooker, there were striking similarities in their mannerisms, and in their moral and intellectual qualities.

She was waiting for Mr Prout now. She was keeping a place

for him – he had worked over the lunch hour; he was now snatching a quick sandwich and making quite sure that his assistant understood her job properly. But Amy was not alone in the queue, because she was with Doreen and Joe Rodley. Doreen was in her wheelchair. Joe stood with his back to the women, smoking and glowering at the traffic. He was in a bad temper, which was not unusual, especially when he was out with his wife.

'It's not that he doesn't love me,' Doreen had once explained to Amy. 'If anything he's too fond of me, he's like a great big soppy boy sometimes. It's that he doesn't like to see me in this wheelchair. Also, he hates the fuss of it all, and the thought that everyone's looking at us. Just like a man.'

Also in the queue, four or five yards behind them, was Howard Mork, standing by himself and all dressed up in his ridiculous finery – suede shoes, tight trousers, a long jacket with padded shoulders and his hair slicked back in a way that made it seem as though a duck were squatting on his head. Amy confided to Doreen that she felt sorry for these Teddy boys, though many people she knew found them frightening. It seemed to her they were desperate to be noticed. She waved to Howard. He waved back and coloured deeply.

'He's nothing but a big baby,' Amy murmured to Doreen. 'He's ever so obliging, though, I'll say that for him.'

At last she saw Mr Prout walking briskly up the High Street on the other side of the road. With his hat tipped back, his overcoat unbuttoned and a cigarette in his hand, he looked quite the man about town. He strode jauntily across the road. A moment later he joined them, earning several scowls from the people behind them in the queue. The four of them exchanged greetings, though Joe's sounded less of a greeting and more of a growl.

'I don't suppose any of you heard something last night,' Mr

Prout said, smiling round at them. 'No? I fancy those who live in Broad Street will tell you another story.'

'Whatever do you mean?' Amy asked.

He smiled at her in a way that instantly and unmistakably brought Cary Grant to mind. 'At one point, late last night, there was a good deal of screaming and shouting,' he said. 'There were running footsteps.'

'Whose?' demanded Joe. 'Spit it out or let's talk of something else.'

'You'll remember that my shop has been the victim of several attacks of hooliganism? The police seemed unable to resolve the matter. Worse than useless. So I decided that I would take the administration of justice into my own hands.'

Amy squealed and put her arm through his. 'Oh, Ronald – but it must have been dangerous.'

He patted her hand. 'Don't you worry, my dear. I gave the miscreant a lesson he won't forget in a hurry.' He glanced at Doreen and Joe, drawing them into his audience again. 'I worked on the theory that the person responsible had been drinking, and would leave the pub at closing time. Also, that Friday, being pay day for most people, was the evening he was likely to get most drunk. With that in mind, I laid an ambush at the shop.'

'Oh, Ronald!'

'So did you see the bugger?' Joe said.

'Joe!' said Doreen. 'Language!'

'No – not exactly,' Mr Prout replied. 'You see, the blinds were down – if I'd had them up it would have given the game away. And though I tried to get a glimpse of him when he was running off, it was too late. However, I'm pretty sure he won't be back.'

'But what did you do?' Amy said.

'I shall have to choose my words carefully. Mixed company,

you know. Let me put it this way: he tried his usual trick of using my letter box as a public urinal. But I was lying in wait for him. I was sitting on a low stool just inside the door. The shop was in darkness behind me.' He paused, savouring the memory. 'In my hand was a fish slice.'

'You hit the bugger with it?' Joe said. 'Well, I'll be damned.'

'Joe!'

'With a fish slice!' Joe began to laugh. 'Who'd have thought you had it in you?'

Neither of the men kept their voices down. The tribulations that Mr Prout had suffered because of the Pisser were no secret. The news of his counter-offensive spread up and down the queue, the progress of the story marked by a trail of sniggers and titters, and by people craning their heads to look at Mr Prout. Doreen was the first to notice the approach of a police constable.

She nudged Amy. 'Look, isn't that Peter Porter? He's put on a bit of weight lately, hasn't he?'

'He was never exactly a Slim Jim,' said Amy with the calm superiority of one who has always prided herself on her slender figure. A sudden anxiety struck her. 'Do you think he's heard about last night? About the . . . about the fish slice?' She had a feeling that the police disapproved of those who took the law into their own hands.

Ronald Prout preened himself as PC Porter approached, for he was not a man who suffered from self-doubt. But Porter passed the little group without a second glance and stopped a few yards farther down the queue beside Howard Mork.

'Do you know where your dad is, son?' Porter asked, raising his voice to a bellow because of a passing car.

Howard blushed again. He mumbled something in reply. What with the blushing and the acne and the tendency to mumble when embarrassed, Amy thought, he had a lot of growing up to do.

She called down the line, 'Speak up, Howard. Otherwise the constable can't hear you.'

Howard cast her a desperate glance and stared up at PC Porter's red face. 'My dad's up at the cemetery,' he said in a clear, defiant voice. 'Like he always is on Saturday afternoons. He goes up to see Mum.'

Chapter Eighteen

'It's like that damned fairy story,' Vincent Drake said. 'You know – Cinderella, the one who lost her slipper.'

'Who's got the other glove?'

'Exactly. It's a damn silly question by the sound of it, but it's one we need to ask.' He peered into his teacup, as though the answer might be lurking in the big black tea leaves floating at the bottom. 'I'm sorry, Thornhill – I think you'd better take this one. I know you're meant to be off duty this weekend but there it is. More tea?'

Thornhill shook his head; he had never acquired a taste for China tea. They were sitting in the study of Drake's house, a modern building just outside Lydmouth on the Chepstow Road. Drake had spent many years serving in India and the room was littered with mementoes, from the brass coffee table in front of the fire to the carved Malay heads glaring down at them from the top of one of the bookcases. Drake had phoned Thornhill at home and broken the news. Thornhill had called at Grove House to talk to Brian Kirby and then driven here to report.

He said, 'I left them dusting for prints. It's a pity, though – Bayswater's char seems not to be very keen on housework. So there's an awful lot of fingerprints around.'

'This Francis woman,' Drake said. 'Have you talked to her yet?'

Thornhill swallowed. 'Not yet, sir. She's made a preliminary statement to Sergeant Kirby.'

'Shame it had to be a journalist who found him. Would you say she's reliable?'

Yes and no, Thornhill thought, no and yes. 'She seems to have kept her head. She didn't panic, and she didn't touch anything unnecessarily. She didn't notice the blow to the head. There was very little blood, and the damage was on the side of the head resting on the carpet – the left side. Kirby said that it looked as if someone had hit him from above, as if perhaps he'd been sitting down when he was attacked.'

The DCC grunted. 'We'll have to wait for the autopsy. We'll get the inquest adjourned, of course. They've moved the body, I assume?'

Thornhill nodded.

'This business with the Mynotts' lodger.' Drake poured himself more tea. He squinted into the cup and then added a drop of hot water. 'Are we absolutely sure it's connected?'

'The only link we have so far is the glove, sir. I understand that PC Porter managed to track down the manager of Butter's, Mr Mork.' Thornhill didn't mention where Mr Mork had been found, meticulously manuring the minuscule flower beds that traced the shape of the letter M over his wife's grave. 'He definitely sold a pair of yellow kid gloves to the Mynotts' lodger, Mr Frederick. There was a label inside them – Thidwich of Regent Street. Not cheap – they were the only pair he had in the shop. Sergeant Kirby showed me the glove found beside Bayswater. It looked brand new to me. Apart from the fact that one of the fingers is chewed.'

'Chewed?'

'Yes, sir. I understand that Bayswater's house is infested with rats, and that's probably the reason for that.' Thornhill paused. 'Sergeant Kirby says there are similar marks on Dr Bayswater.'

'Good God,' Drake said. 'Biting the hand that feeds, eh?

One sees that sort of thing in India, of course, but here – well, it makes you wonder. So what have we got? A retired GP dead in suspicious circumstances which may amount to murder. The television engineer who leaves his lodgings in Lydmouth to go back home to London, and his wife and his employer say he never got there. And the yellow glove found by Dr Bayswater's body may or may not have belonged to this television chappie – Mr Frederick?'

'Sergeant Kirby's sent someone down to the station to see if Frederick was seen there.'

'Time of death?'

'We don't know yet. But I saw Dr Bayswater myself early yesterday evening.'

Drake raised his bushy eyebrows. 'You actually talked to him?'

'Yes, sir. Briefly. He'd been to Gloucester to see his dentist for a couple of fillings.' Thornhill frowned, digging into his memory. 'He'd had to go on the train because his car had broken down. But he seemed quite cheerful. He'd seen something that interested him, he said, I assumed as a medical man. He'd just bought a bottle of Scotch, too. He was going to dose himself with it.'

'He went by train? In the morning?'

'He may well have done. So it's possible that he travelled on the same train as Frederick.'

Five minutes later Thornhill drove back to the centre of Lydmouth. The ambulance had long gone but two police cars and the SOCOs' van were still parked outside Grove House. PC Porter was on duty, patrolling from the front door on Broad Street round to the side gate on Whistler's Lane and back again.

Word had travelled quickly. Knots of bystanders stood watching, smoking and talking; most were on the opposite pavement of Broad Street but some were in Whistler's Lane itself, only a few yards away from the door in the wall. Most of them were boys and young men. Thornhill parked in front of the van. Porter saluted him.

'Are you all right by yourself?' Thornhill asked. 'We've got the ghouls out, I'm afraid.'

'Just local folk, sir,' Porter said. 'No one I don't know. Besides, there's not a lot they can do or see unless they get a ladder. The door in Whistler's Lane is the only way in and that's bolted, with a man on the other side.'

Thornhill nodded. Kirby knew his job. So, in his own way, did Peter Porter. Four years ago, Porter had been something of a laughing stock in the police canteen. Gradually, though, the laughter had become friendly as well as mocking. Porter would always be slow moving, both mentally and physically, but his knowledge of Lydmouth and its surroundings was encyclopedic, his good nature was apparently inexhaustible, and his prowess as a second-row forward in the Lydmouth Police Rugby XV had become legendary throughout the county and beyond.

Thornhill knocked on the door in the wall and was admitted by an anxious probationary constable. He walked round the surgery extension and followed the path to the veranda. A member of the scene-of-crime team was hunched behind a camera in the loggia.

'We've finished in the room, sir,' he called. 'Sergeant Kirby's in there.'

Thornhill found Kirby looking through the desk. He was wearing his hat, a muffler and a heavy overcoat. When he turned towards Thornhill, his face caught the light from the lamp on the desk. The skin was pale and there was a sheen of sweat on his forehead. It was very cold.

'Anything interesting, Brian?'

Kirby shook his head. 'I'm trying to work out why the place was searched. If it was searched.'

'What do you mean?'

Kirby gestured at the desk, at the papers scattered round the room. 'It's hard to see any rhyme or reason. It's as if someone was just trying to make a mess. See that drawer? It was hanging open, and some of the files have been pulled out and chucked on the floor. But the rest of the files are still in there, and it looks as if they haven't been disturbed at all.'

'So someone was trying to create the impression that the room had been searched?'

'Maybe.'

Thornhill poked a gloved finger into one of the desk's pigeon-holes. He extracted a ball of grey fluff wrapped like a cocoon round a rusting paper clip. 'Was anything taken?'

'I can't find a cheque book, sir. And there's marks in the dust on the mantelpiece – looks like an ornament used to stand there.'

'Find the char. She should know what's missing.'

Kirby grinned wanly. 'I wouldn't bank on it. Judging by the rest of the house, her heart's not really in the job.'

'Was anyone else working for him?'

'No – he used to have a receptionist, but that stopped when he retired.' He glanced at the window. 'I don't think he's had a gardener for some time.'

'Next of kin?'

'There's an ex-wife in Southern Rhodesia. Porter thinks there's a sister – she came and spent a few days here a couple of years ago. Lives in Birmingham.'

Kirby took Thornhill round the rest of the house. It was a large place, built for a family in the days when families weren't small. There were six or seven bedrooms, most of them now shut up, not counting the attics of the servants. Bayswater's own room was at the back of the house, overlooking the garden. A damp patch was spreading over the wall by the window and there was no obvious form of heating. The high, single bed was unmade, and the sheets needed changing.

'You'd think he could have afforded to make himself comfortable,' Kirby said. 'Or perhaps he liked it like this. Reminded him of his bleeding boarding-school.'

'Or perhaps he just wasn't interested.'

Thornhill led the way back downstairs. Apart from his bedroom, Bayswater seemed to have spent most of his time either in the study or in the kitchen. The evidence suggested that he cooked for himself and ate mainly out of tins. The place was at least superficially clean – the charwoman kept down the more obvious forms of dirt – but it had the neglected feel of a house that nobody thinks of as home.

The two men went into the loggia. By now the light was fading.

Kirby stared out at the abandoned garden and gave a bark of laughter. 'Imagine searching that. We'll need a troop of boy scouts armed with machetes.'

Thornhill peered into the gloom. 'What's that? Beyond the end of the veranda.'

'A shed. It's the only part of the place that looks well cared for. It's a sort of workshop.'

'Let's have a look. Have you got a torch?'

'No need. Bayswater ran a power line down from the house.'

They went down the steps and followed the path to the shed tucked away at the far end of the veranda. There was a padlock on the door but it hung open.

'Was it like this?' Thornhill asked.

'Yes, sir. We found a bunch of keys in Bayswater's pocket,

and one of them looked as if it might be the padlock key. I've not checked yet.'

Kirby opened the door and switched on the light, a bare bulb dangling over the work table that filled one end of the shed. The place smelled strongly of creosote. In contrast with the house itself, everything was clean and orderly. The floor was swept. The tools had been put away, the larger ones hung from nails fixed to the wall above the spotless workbench. Thornhill thought about the tools that had been discarded on the veranda.

'What did he do here?'

'Not a lot, as far as I can see.' Kirby pointed out a couple of magazines on a shelf under the bench. '*Furniture Maker's Monthly*. I think he planned a hobby for himself but hadn't actually put the plan into practice yet. He was working on the veranda, of course. Some of those steps are rotting away, and so are some of the railings.'

'What were the tools left up there?'

'On the veranda?' Kirby stared, his face all glare and shadow in the harsh overhead light. 'A hammer, a screwdriver, a saw, maybe one or two others.'

'We need to find a blunt instrument somewhere,' Thornhill said. 'I wonder if all the tools are here. See if you can find out before we get the results of the autopsy.'

He drove home through the deepening twilight earlier than he had expected. It was often the way with a case, that after the initial flurry of activity there was a lull – a time for gathering information, for waiting for results. The fog was growing thicker, and the car's headlights were reflected in a million shifting water droplets, a dazzling opacity.

The house in Victoria Road was empty. Thornhill remembered belatedly that Edith had taken the girls to a birthday party. He fetched a beer from the larder and went into the sitting-room, where he made up the fire. He glanced from the library books on the table to the blank screen of the television.

He switched on the set, just to see what was on. He might as well find out what all the fuss was about.

Chapter Nineteen

Upstairs in Troy House, Philip Wemyss-Brown lay sleeping. In the drawing-room, Charlotte handed Jill Francis a martini with dry vermouth and a dash of orange bitters. In the old days she had enjoyed mixing cocktails – enjoyed making them more than drinking them. She drew the curtains against the darkness and poured herself a small dry sherry. It would have been warmer in the kitchen, but Charlotte liked to use the drawing-room. It preserved the illusion of ordered normality.

'Are you feeling any better, dear?' she enquired. 'You still look dreadfully pale.'

'I'm perfectly all right now.' Jill sipped her drink. 'Will you tell Philip?'

'At some point I shall have to.' Charlotte's forehead wrinkled. 'I just don't want to give him a shock – any sort of shock. It's not as if they were particularly friendly but Philip's known him for years.'

'Was anyone friendly with him?'

'With Dr Bayswater?' Charlotte snorted. 'He never seemed to bother much with that sort of thing. Some people don't need to, do they? He was more self-sufficient than most, I suppose. He used to have a dreadful reputation as a ladies' man when he was younger, but of course that's rather different.'

'Need it be?' Jill said.

'Oh yes – certainly in his case. Not that he couldn't be charming if he wanted to, but he just wanted women for one thing, and it wasn't the pleasure of their company. That's why his wife left him. They divorced before the war and she married this frightfully nice chap whose people farmed in quite a big way near Hereford. They went to Africa. I believe they've bought a tobacco farm.'

'If he was murdered,' Jill said slowly, 'could it have been a jealous husband?'

'I doubt it, dear. I don't think he's been up to that sort of thing for some time. Since the end of the war, perhaps. He still had an eye for the ladies, but that was it. Just an eye.' Charlotte looked at Jill, and there was a spark of the old malice in her face. 'I thought you would have noticed.'

There was a ring on the front doorbell.

Charlotte scrambled to her feet, spilling a few drops of sherry on her cardigan. 'I do hope that hasn't woken Philip. Who can it be?'

She went into the hall. Jill heard the door open and the murmur of voices, Charlotte's and a man's. A moment later she returned to the drawing-room with her visitor behind her.

'It's Mr Fuggle,' she announced in a colourless voice.

'Evening, Miss Francis. Didn't expect to see you here.'

'What a surprise.' Jill looked up at him. 'I didn't expect to see you, either.'

'I just wanted a word with Mrs Wemyss-Brown.' He chuckled, his little eyes flitting around the room. 'I can come back later if it would be more convenient.'

'Anything you have to say to me, you can say in front of Miss Francis,' Charlotte said.

Fuggle sat down without being asked. 'Well, in a sense what I want to say concerns you both, so maybe it'll save time in the long run.' He stretched out his legs. 'My employers asked me to come and lay a little proposition before you. Mutually beneficial, you might say. I know life hasn't been easy recently, what with Mr Wemyss-Brown and so on. And obviously the *Gazette* hasn't been doing as well as it used to. Now, you're the major shareholder in the *Gazette*. The Champion Group would like to make a very substantial offer for your holding.'

'I'm not interested, thank you, Mr Fuggle.' Charlotte, who had remained standing, took a step back towards the door. 'I mustn't keep you any longer.'

'No, hear me out at least. The Champion Group is aware of the situation. The board feels that there's no reason why they shouldn't help you and help themselves at the same time.'

'How very generous of them.'

'They've authorised me to say that they are willing to pay you not only a very substantial capital sum but also an annuity. They'll guarantee an income for life, secured on both you and Mr Wemyss-Brown. They can't say fairer than that, can they? You'd get financial independence and peace of mind. You'd no longer have to worry about the paper. The Champion Group would take over the worry of running the *Gazette*.'

'You make it sound as if you'd be doing us a favour.'

'Not me – the Champion Group. It makes sense for them financially, naturally. They're not fools. They've got their own shareholders to satisfy. As we all know, the newspaper business is changing. This is the shape of things to come. A place this size can't really support two competing papers.'

'You'd close down the *Gazette*,' Charlotte said in a flat voice.

'No.' Fuggle spread his hands and beamed like a vicar welcoming a new parishioner. 'I don't know for sure how they'd arrange it, but my bet is they'd merge them. They'd probably keep both names on the masthead for the time being.

Then everyone would be happy. I dare say we'd find room for at least some of your staff. The Champion Group employs a lot of people. Maybe Mr Wemyss-Brown would like to keep his hand in? I can't promise anything, but I might be able to swing a seat on the board as a non-executive director.'

'No,' Charlotte said. 'No, I'm not going to sell the *Gazette* to you.'

A handbell tinkled faintly above their heads. Charlotte looked up at the ceiling and for an instant the mask of determination slipped from her face.

Jill said, 'Would you like to see what Philip wants? I'll show Mr Fuggle out.'

Charlotte nodded and almost ran from the room. They listened in silence to her footsteps on the stairs.

Fuggle sighed. 'You really should help her see sense, Miss Francis. As a friend, I mean. For her sake, and for his. All this worry and uncertainty can't be good for them.'

Jill said, 'I think Mr and Mrs Wemyss-Brown will make up their own minds.'

Fuggle stood up. He was still wearing his overcoat, which made him look even broader than he was. 'I hear you had a bit of shock this morning, Miss Francis. I didn't like to mention it when Mrs Wemyss-Brown was here. I didn't know if you'd told her.'

'How very sensitive of you.'

'I wouldn't be surprised if this makes the nationals, would you? Well-respected GP bludgeoned to death in his own study. Well-known journalist stumbles on the corpse. They like a nice murder that involves the middle classes. Especially when there's a pretty woman in the picture.'

'I didn't realise it was murder,' Jill countered. 'Who told you that?'

Fuggle smiled and moved towards the door. In the hall he

picked up his hat from the chest and settled it on his head. 'That's one lead for Monday's paper. The sackings at Broadbent's will be on the front page too, I shouldn't wonder.'

'Very likely.' Jill slipped past him, catching a waft of his smell, a rank blend of old sweat and old alcohol, tinged with stale tobacco. She opened the front door.

'Two almost identical front pages in a town like this,' Fuggle murmured as he crossed the threshold. 'It really doesn't make sense. Think about it, Miss Francis, and help Mrs Wemyss-Brown do the same. Look at your balance sheet, look at your advertising revenue. Look at poor old Philip up there. And you can't fight a run of bad luck, that's what I always think. There's Philip ill, Cubbitt getting himself beaten up, and now that fire in your print works. Whatever next?'

Jill said, 'You're letting cold air into the house. Please leave.'

He smiled down at her, exposing his perfect false teeth. 'It's not a question of which of us is going to fold, Miss Francis. We both of us know that.'

A flurry of rain swept into the house. Fuggle slowly descended the steps.

As she was closing the door, he turned back and looked up at her in the doorway. 'It's just a question of when it happens, Miss Francis. And how.'

Chapter Twenty

The fog thickened steadily throughout the evening. It lay on the river like ghostly froth; it flowed through the streets and clogged up the alleys and lanes; it stole shape and substance from the town and left nothing worth having in return.

Despite the fog, despite Doreen's phoning her to say there was no need, Amy Gwyn-Thomas came to Viney Cottage just before eight o'clock. She felt that if she let the weather stop her she would never do anything, and she was looking forward to a nice chat about Cary Grant and poor Dr Bayswater, and perhaps a game of cards as well. Joe was going out. 'He needs a bit of independence,' Doreen had confided to Amy in the ladies' lavatory at the Rex Cinema. 'It's no fun for him at home, not with me like this.'

Amy was a little put out to find that Genevieve Fuggle was already at the cottage, warming her hands in front of the open doors of Doreen's stove. Amy enjoyed playing the Good Samaritan as much as anyone, but it was not a role she liked to share. If she wasn't even going to be useful, she thought, she might as well have spent the evening beside her own fire rather than venturing out into the cold and the fog.

'I'm off out, then,' Joe Rodley said, putting his head into his wife's room. 'I left the kettle on.'

The front door banged. Off drinking again, Amy thought, drowning his sorrows.

Genevieve had brought a box of chocolates – which must have cost seven and six if they'd cost a penny – and the women nibbled as they drank tea. They talked about Dr Bayswater and the mysterious circumstances of his death. Genevieve said little – when Doreen asked her whether she was feeling all right, she said she was just tired, as she had spent some of the day painting an old table and tidying the garden. Amy said that no one had much energy at present, which was probably due to the weather; they all needed bucking up.

Later, Amy suggested a game of cards. To her annoyance, Genevieve said flatly that she didn't want to play. She was too tired; and also it didn't seem quite right, not with the death of Dr Bayswater. Doreen at once agreed.

Amy was vexed. She was annoyed that Genevieve had objected to her proposal, and a little resentful of the fact that Doreen had supported her so readily. Did their behaviour imply that they thought her suggestion had not been in the best of taste? If Genevieve's so tired, Amy thought, why doesn't she just go home?

But Genevieve stayed, rubbing the thick tweed of her skirt with the heel of her left hand, to and fro, to and fro. Amy loathed people who had nervous movements. They showed a lack of self-control. The more she watched Genevieve, the more irritated she became.

In the end Amy could bear it no longer and said she must be going. She wanted an early night, she explained – Ronald was playing at the early service at the Baptist chapel and she had promised to join him on the organ stool and turn the pages of his music for him. There was a pleasure in this, and also in the surprise and unhappiness that Amy fancied she saw on Doreen's face.

'You're coming round next week?' Doreen asked.

'All right. If you want. Let me see.' Amy frowned, creating

the impression that she was consulting an enormous mental diary bulging with important appointments. 'How about Thursday evening? I think that's free.'

'That'll be lovely, dear.'

'Mind you, I'm not sure I am free, but if I am, I'll pop in.' Amy smiled grimly at Mrs Fuggle. 'So nice to see you again, Genevieve. I do hope you feel more rested soon. Perhaps the chemist would give you a tonic?'

She said goodnight and left the cottage. The fog had become even thicker. She walked down Whistler's Lane, feeling she had won a small but significant moral victory over Doreen and Genevieve. When she got home she would have a nice cup of Ovaltine and look at those magazines Doreen had given her.

On the corner of Fairfield Drive there was a telephone box. As Amy was passing it, the phone inside began to ring. Automatically she glanced in its direction. In the dimly lit interior, a man snatched the receiver from its rest and the ringing stopped.

The man had his back to her but there was something familiar about his stance. Amy paused, a tremor of surprise interrupting her thoughts about the beastliness of the fog and the hurtfulness of Doreen's behaviour. She took a step to the right, so she could see his face in profile.

The man was Joe Rodley. That was doubly puzzling. Why wasn't he sitting in a nice warm public bar with a glass of beer in front of him? And why should someone ring him in a public phone box rather than on the Rodleys' own telephone, which sat on Doreen's bedside table?

Sunday, 4 December

You get used to anything, they say. Even this? I'm so scared. She's calling, and I'd do anything to stop her.

Be quiet, be quiet. Sleep now. Just leave me alone.

Does he suspect?

I must think sensibly. Terrible accidents, that's what they were. It's NOT my fault. It needn't be the end of the world, not if I keep my head.

I made two mistakes. What happened to the bag? What happened to the other glove? Have they found them? And if they have, will they know what they mean?

Especially the glove.

Chapter Twenty-One

The bells of churches and chapels summoned the faithful and the conservative to church. At Police Headquarters, Detective Chief Inspector Thornhill acknowledged the greeting of the man on the desk and went upstairs to the CID office. In the doorway, he met Sergeant Kirby going hurriedly in the opposite direction, his right hand clutching his stomach and a greenish pallor on his face.

'Won't be a moment, sir,' Kirby said, darting across the landing to the lavatory. 'Murray's report's just come in.'

The lavatory door slammed behind him. Thornhill went into the office, which was almost empty. Murray had driven up yesterday evening and conducted the autopsy in the morgue at the RAF hospital on Chepstow Road. According to Kirby, the pathologist hadn't been best pleased to have his weekend interrupted; but his daughter was being confirmed this morning, which had given the case an urgency for him it might not otherwise have had.

The fog still held the town in its grip and the long office was even gloomier than usual. The artificial light from Kirby's lamp served to emphasise the dullness of the day rather than dispel it. Thornhill slid the report out of the envelope and stood by the window to read.

Murray was a Scot, agreeably laconic. Dr Bayswater had been killed by several blows from an unidentified blunt instrument to the left-hand side of his skull. They had probably been administered by a right-hander, who may have been standing above his victim. It was difficult to establish the angle of the attack or the sequence of the blows with any certainty, because they had overlapped. The weapon had a rounded edge and a squared end. The estimated diameter was approximately five-eighths of an inch. It may have been an iron bar or some sort of tool.

Some sort of tool?

The body was still in the grip of rigor mortis when Murray had conducted his examination. Taking into account such factors as body weight and the temperature of the room, Murray believed that Bayswater had probably been killed between 9 p.m. on the Friday evening and 3 a.m. on Saturday morning. He appeared undernourished; otherwise he had been in reasonable health. He had not eaten since the Friday morning but he had had a substantial whisky a few hours before death.

Kirby came back in the room. In the interval he'd combed his hair and straightened his tie.

'You all right, Brian?'

'Fine, sir.'

Thornhill wondered whether to send him home. But Kirby should be capable of assessing his own health. Brian was hungry for promotion, and the last thing he would want was to spend the crucial first few days of what might be a major murder inquiry on sick leave.

'Right,' Thornhill said. 'So Murray doesn't leave us much farther on. You've talked to the charwoman?'

'She was off shopping in Gloucester yesterday. She lives off Mincing Lane in one of those new council flats. I'm seeing her this afternoon.'

Thornhill glanced at his watch. 'We'd better talk to Miss Francis, too, if she's at home. Take her through what happened on Friday and Saturday morning.'

Kirby nodded, his face averted. There was a silence, which lasted slightly longer than was comfortable. Thornhill had never known quite how much Brian Kirby knew or suspected about Jill and himself. He didn't want to know, either. Some things were better not talked about.

He dropped the report on Kirby's desk. 'You've dealt with the sorting office?'

'Yes, sir. They'll redirect all Bayswater's mail here. I've been on to the telephone exchange as well. And I talked to Birmingham yesterday evening and they sent a couple of officers round to the sister. We found a will in Bayswater's desk and according to that she's his heir.'

'Really?' It was always worth considering the obvious person with the obvious motive.

Kirby gave him a faint grin. 'Nothing for us, I'm afraid, sir. Mrs Enid Andrews, OBE. She's a magistrate.'

'That's not necessarily a guarantee of innocence.'

'She was dining with a colleague on the bench and his wife on Friday night, and he drove her home. It was after midnight by the time he dropped her off.'

'How did she take the news?'

'Hard to tell, apparently. One of the old school. Trained never to show emotion before the lower orders.'

'What about Bayswater's house?'

'We went over it till midnight. I don't think we learned anything we didn't know. He was always a bit eccentric, wasn't he, but since he retired he was growing worse. You know that shed of his? We found a detailed plan of it, on graph paper, measured to the last inch. He was going to build an extension, at right angles to the veranda. Like a hide. So he could study the wildlife and their feeding habits.'

'What did he think he was up to?'

Kirby searched his desk for cigarettes. 'There's all these

letters, all these articles he wrote. Stacks of them. Mainly for scientific journals who didn't want to publish them.'

'About rats and so on?'

Kirby lit a match and squinted through the smoke at Thornhill. 'I don't think he minded what it was about. As long as someone printed it. There's some about the wildlife, some about diet, some about psychology. He was a wee bit barmy, if you ask me. But then, it's surprising how many people are, isn't it? They just go quietly round the twist and nobody notices.'

It was a sad epitaph, Thornhill thought. The old doctor had often been difficult to deal with but he deserved a kinder label than barmy. But what had aroused his curiosity on Friday evening? *My lips are sealed.* Had Bayswater been too scrupulous to betray somebody else's secret? Or had he merely been trying to make the hobby of his dotage seem more important than it was?

Thornhill said, 'We'll need to take prints of his known visitors in the last six months, just to be on the safe side.'

Kirby groaned.

'There can't have been that many. The charwoman can help with a list, and perhaps Leddon. Bayswater must have had some friends. And you'd better take the charwoman down to the house and have her see if she can identify what's missing. This morning, if possible – the sooner the better. Then there's the glove.'

'Mr Mork says it's a whopping coincidence if it wasn't one of the pair he sold Frederick the other day. Same size and everything.'

'Prints?'

'Nothing usable. Frederick still hasn't turned up, by the way. I phoned the wife this morning. She's so worried she can't think straight.'

'We have to treat the cases as linked, at least for the time being. We're absolutely sure he caught the train?'

Kirby nodded. 'The eleven fifty-three. The direct train to London. Caught it by the skin of his teeth, apparently. The ticket collector noticed him running for it, and one of the porters too. We're trying the train staff but we haven't had any luck with them yet.'

'You'd better circulate a description at the stations where the train stopped, up to and including Paddington. You know what he was wearing?'

'Miss Mynott said he had a jacket with a houndstooth check, grey flannel trousers, some sort of striped tie, she thought blue and green, a dark blue overcoat and a dark brown trilby. And the gloves, of course. He was carrying a small blue suitcase.'

'What was he doing here exactly? Working for the Mynotts?'

'Selling televisions.' Kirby opened his notebook. 'His firm makes them on the cheap and flogs them to small retailers. They do servicing as well, which was why he stayed for a couple of nights.'

'So he left the Mynotts at about nine-thirty,' Thornhill said. 'If he'd crawled on his hands and knees, he'd still have been early for the eleven fifty-three. So what did he do in the meantime? We'll need a house-to-house – find out if anyone saw him between Mynott's and the station on Friday morning, and if so when. If we don't have any luck between the shop and the station we'll widen the net. The roads up to the park, Chepstow Road, around the church.'

'It's a lot of ground to cover, sir.'

'Not with Div. CID and Uniformed to help.'

'They won't like it.'

'We have a link to a probable murder inquiry. They'll have to lump it.'

Kirby was making notes. He looked up. 'Aren't you off duty this weekend, sir?'

'Not now.'

Thornhill thought he saw a shadow passing over Kirby's face; if there was kudos attached to this case, Brian wanted as large a share as possible. Moving towards the door, he said, 'If Frederick hasn't turned up by tomorrow morning, I want you to go up to town tomorrow. Have a word with his employer. Talk to his wife. We want to know what sort of a man he is. It would be useful to have a recent photograph as well. Let the Met know you're coming up, of course. Is there anything else I should know?'

'Have you heard about the Pisser, sir?'

Thornhill paused, hand on the edge of the door. 'Heard what?'

'We don't know officially,' Kirby said, and for a moment his face filled with his old good humour. 'But Dyke says it's all over town. Mr Prout lay in wait for him on Friday night. Sure enough, the Pisser turned up and put his prick through Prout's letter box. He was just about to leave his usual visiting card when Prout leapt up and whanged him with a fish slice.' Kirby threw back his head and laughed. 'And the poor sod ran through the town squealing like a pig.'

'Prout?' Thornhill raised his eyebrows. 'I wouldn't have thought he'd got it in him.'

'Nor did most people. But Joan's health visitor – she sings in the chapel choir – says she wasn't surprised. According to her, Ronald Prout is a holy terror if you get on the wrong side of him.'

Chapter Twenty-Two

The memory of Dr Bayswater's body jostled Jill's thoughts, demanding her attention.

She refused to think about it. Not that her other thoughts had much to recommend them. Sunday was her least favourite day. If you weren't a regular churchgoer, if you didn't like cooking and eating Sunday roasts, and if you didn't have a family to share it with, then there wasn't a great deal you could do with a Sunday. Shops, cinemas and theatres were shut. Even the radio was affected by the solemnity of the day.

This Sunday was worse than most. Nothing had gone right since her return to Lydmouth. She had known the *Gazette* was in a bad way, like its editor, but in neither case had she realised quite how bad. Nor had she realised the strength of Ivor Fuggle's ambition or the emotions that fuelled it. It was as if he were hell-bent on avenging himself for slights and snubs spread over an entire working lifetime.

The sight of Richard Thornhill had made matters worse. She had known that she did not want to see him – who would want to see someone who had tempted you into folly and then ignored you? – but she had not realised that her dislike still had such a power to disturb her. Nor did this soulless flat make matters any better. She was convinced that its owner must be a man, for no woman would have furnished the place with such a callous disregard for convenience, comfort and taste. She

could not even drive away from it all because the car was still at
Gray's Garage.

She pulled the table over to the window, unzipped her
portable typewriter from its case and tried to work. Usually
the business of putting words on paper calmed, absorbed and
distracted her; but not today. Her attention wandered, time
and again, to the view from the window – the gates of Jubilee
Park and the driveway of the cemetery at right angles to them.
Even in the fog, and the grey drizzle that came with it, there
were people about – walking dogs, returning from church, or
simply walking, aimlessly.

Suddenly, once again, she saw Dr Bayswater, shockingly
vivid, projected on the screen of her mind. She saw the way his
hair twitched in the draught like grey, submerged seaweed.
The unexpected prickliness of his cheek – did hair continue
growing after death? The frayed cuff of the pyjama jacket and
knotted veins of the wrist. The single eye. Those were the
things that really made this dreary, foggy Sunday so insup-
portable, those and the knowledge that however much she
thought about it, however much she wanted to make time go
backwards, she couldn't bring the old man back to life.

She was still looking out of the window when a car turned
into the driveway of the flats. A few minutes later her door bell
rang. When she opened the door, she found Richard Thornhill
outside, with Sergeant Kirby standing a pace or two behind
him. They must be missing their Sunday lunches, Jill thought,
cooked by their doting wives.

'Good afternoon, Miss Francis.' Thornhill had removed his
hat. 'I hope this isn't an inconvenient time. I wondered if we
could have a word.'

Jill wondered why, if he was so concerned about her convenience, he had not phoned beforehand. He knew where she
lived: he could find out the phone number. But she knew the

answer because as a journalist she often used the same tactic: if you wanted to interview someone, you generally got better results if they didn't have time to prepare themselves.

She held open the door and they trooped into the living-room. She noticed them both giving the room a practised, professional glance; and no doubt in the process comparing it unfavourably with the comfort of their own homes. Their presence unsettled her.

'Will this take long, Chief Inspector?' she said.

'We need to talk to you about yesterday,' Thornhill said, sidestepping the question.

'I've already told Sergeant Kirby everything I know.'

'It can be useful to go over these things again. When one's had time to think about things. Time to remember.'

'Then you'd better sit down.' Her voice sounded un-gracious even to her ears, and automatically she said, 'You can leave your coats on the hooks in the hall. And do smoke if you want.'

All three of them sat at the table where Jill had been working. Then Kirby stood up.

'Excuse me, miss—?'

'It's in the hall. Second door on the left.'

Jill winced mentally at the thought of the nylons hanging to dry over the bath and the untidy cluster of cosmetics on the window sill. Kirby hurried from the room. The bathroom door closed. The bolt slammed home.

Thornhill said, 'I'm sorry to intrude – you're obviously working.'

'It doesn't matter,' Jill said, wondering why he had to be so pompous about it. 'Can we get on with this, or do you have to wait for Sergeant Kirby to come back?'

He avoided looking at her. 'We may as well begin now.' He took out a notebook. 'First, I wonder if you can come down to the station tomorrow and make a formal statement. This is really just a preliminary session.'

'I'm afraid tomorrow won't be convenient,' Jill said. 'I won't be in Lydmouth.'

He uncapped a fountain pen and, with his eyes on the blank page of his notebook, said, 'On Tuesday morning, then?' He took her silence for assent. 'Tell me about Dr Bayswater. Was he someone you knew well?'

'As you may remember, I ran across him a good deal when I was living in Lydmouth,' Jill said crisply. 'But we were not sufficiently friendly to keep up the friendship when I left.'

He refused to meet her eyes, though she knew the thrust must have gone home. 'So you hadn't seen him for over three years?'

'No, not until I happened to bump into him at Gray's Garage on Friday morning.'

'How did he seem?'

'He said he was in agony – he had toothache. His car wasn't ready, and he was rather put out about it because he wanted to go to Gloucester to see his dentist. He didn't trust the local people, he said.' She heard the sound of the lavatory flushing. 'He was going to catch a train instead, and he was running a bit late, so I offered to run him down to the station.'

'Something wrong with your car? Is that why you went to Gray's? I noticed it wasn't in the car park here.'

So he'd taken the trouble to make a note of the car she was driving. Was that from professional habit or personal interest? She said, 'I'd taken the car in for an estimate for insurance purposes. It was only slightly damaged – it was quite drivable.' She heard her voice running on, and realised she must be more nervous than she thought. 'Someone ran into it behind the flats.'

'Who?'

'Dr Leddon. He was with me at the garage – anyway, I needed my car on Friday, so I told Mr Gray I'd drop it in later.' She licked her lips. How absurd to feel guilty. 'It should be ready by Monday.'

'And Dr Bayswater's car?'

The lavatory was flushed again.

'I think Mr Gray had found that he needed to order a part from somewhere. Which meant he couldn't repair it until Tuesday or Wednesday.'

'What did you talk about – with Dr Bayswater, I mean?'

'This and that.' Jill shook a cigarette out of the packet on the table. 'Dr Leddon was there – at the garage, that is. They had a few words about the practice. Dr Bayswater invited me for a cup of coffee on Saturday morning. I'd mentioned that there wasn't a comfortable armchair in this flat, and he said he'd see if he could find one I could borrow.'

'So that was the reason you went to Grove House yesterday morning?'

Jill lit the cigarette. 'Yes. That, and to renew a friendship. Though of course I wasn't sure if it was a friendship in the first place. And things can change a great deal in more than three years, can't they?'

His eyes narrowed, and for a moment she thought he was about to say something that wasn't one of his carefully scripted questions.

For the third time the lavatory was flushed.

Jill said, 'Ought you to see if Sergeant Kirby is all right, Chief Inspector?'

'I don't think that will be necessary.'

The bathroom bolt shot back. They heard Kirby's footsteps in the hallway. Both Thornhill and Jill sat back in their chairs, as though to put as much distance between themselves as possible. Kirby mumbled an apology and sat down, swaying slightly in the chair. He made notes while Thornhill continued the questioning, taking Jill through the events of Saturday morning, over ground that Kirby had already covered with her.

'One last thing,' Thornhill said. 'Would you mind if we took your fingerprints for the purpose of elimination? Sergeant Kirby will show you what to do. It won't take a moment.'

They were in the middle of this when the door bell rang. Kirby answered it, moving slowly into the hall as though the pull of gravity had unexpectedly increased in his immediate vicinity. Jill heard Roger Leddon's voice. The young doctor followed Kirby into the living-room.

'Hello, Jill.' He grinned. 'Helping the police with their enquiries?'

She smiled back, grateful for the uncomplicated friendliness rather than the words.

'I just dropped in to see if you'd care to share an omelette this evening,' he went on. 'I'm told I make rather a fine omelette, and it seems a shame to make one just for me.'

'Thank you,' Jill said, deriving a furtive enjoyment from the knowledge that Thornhill was hearing this. 'I'd love to.'

'Not interrupting, am I?' Leddon asked, eyeing the inkpad on the table.

'Not at all, sir,' Thornhill said. 'We were just about to leave. But, since you're here, I wonder if we could talk to you for a few minutes.'

'What – now?'

'If it would be convenient.'

Leddon shrugged. 'As convenient as it ever will be, I suppose. What do you want to talk about exactly?'

'We understand you saw Dr Bayswater on Friday.'

Leddon gave a laugh, which to Jill's ears sounded false.

'That's correct. In the morning, at Gray's Garage. Miss Francis was there too. That was the last time I saw him.'

'And occasionally you must have visited him at his house, I assume?'

'Very occasionally. Less so recently.' Leddon frowned. 'We weren't close, Inspector. He sold me his practice, that's all. But we weren't colleagues, not in any real sense, let alone friends.'

'I see. Nevertheless, you won't mind if we take your finger-prints for the purpose of elimination, just as we've taken Miss Francis's?'

Leddon's eyes dropped to the pad. 'I suppose not. Looks frightfully messy, though.'

'So is what happened at Grove House,' Thornhill said. 'In your flat, if you don't mind. Shall we go now? I don't think we need bother Miss Francis any longer.'

The three men said goodbye and left the flat. Sergeant Kirby was the last through the door and he glanced back at Jill, giving her a wan smile.

She washed the ink from her fingers with some difficulty, and went back to the typewriter. It was even harder to concentrate than before. Richard Thornhill intruded into her mind, with his long, narrow face set in an expression she couldn't read. He had been intolerably formal with her, she told herself, making it tacitly clear that he had no wish to see her, and nothing to say to her that could not have been said by Sergeant Kirby. So why hadn't he delegated the interview?

But she knew him well enough, or thought she did, to realise he wasn't happy. Good, she told herself, I hope he's miserable. I'm a ghost from his past and I've come back to haunt him.

This line of thought was somehow less satisfying than she had anticipated. She stared out of the window. The fog had cleared a little. Her view took in part of the park, and she recognised a woman she had seen on her first evening in the

flat, the one with the miniature terrier, zigzagging in a seemingly aimless fashion in and out of the shrubbery that
bordered one side of the children's playground. The woman
seemed to tire of this and dragged the dog towards the gates of
the park.

There was very little one could see of her even as she drew
closer, because she wore a heavy mackintosh, wellington boots
and a sou'wester tied under the chin. Despite the notice
prohibiting dogs, the woman turned once again into the drive
of the cemetery, towing the little animal behind her. Jill
thought it was a Highland terrier. Where the hell was the
pleasure in having a dog? Both the terrier and its owner looked
as if they were going walkies in purgatory.

Jill gave up the pretence of work. She washed some underclothes in the bathroom. The window was open and Kirby had
done his best to clean up after himself. Afterwards she drank a
cup of tea she didn't want, wrote a shopping list, and completed three clues in the previous day's *Manchester Guardian*
crossword. Restlessness filled her. She needed exercise, and
she needed company. It was better to be out than in, even in
this miserable weather. While it was still light, she would walk
through the park to Troy House and see whether there was
anything she could do for Charlotte.

Once outside, however, Jill did not go at once into the park.
On impulse, she turned into the cemetery. There were three
people above ground, all female and old, each hovering beside
a grave, but no sign of the woman with the little terrier. She
followed the path to the block of more recent graves, where the
headstones were unweathered, and passed the neatly tended
grave of Howard Mork's mother, who had died aged forty-
three.

According to Charlotte, Ivor Fuggle had had some sort of a
breakdown after his mother's death. She herself had seen him

weeping at her grave. If knowing thine enemy was a sound principle, then knowing something about your enemy's mother might also have something to be said for it.

The late Mrs Martha Jane Fuggle, widow of George Albert Fuggle, was at the end of a row. She had been eighty-two at the time of her death. Underneath her name and dates were the words 'Not dead merely sleeping'.

At the foot of the grave was a small, rectangular bed of earth, empty now for the winter apart from a vase containing Michaelmas daisies and sombre chrysanthemums, gleaming with moisture. Between the headstone and the little flower bed stretched a low, grassy mound. It reminded Jill of a sleeping body under an eiderdown. In the middle of this mound, roughly where the heart would be, was a very small, very fresh turd.

A cat, Jill wondered – or possibly a tiny dog like a Highland terrier?

Chapter Twenty-Three

In the early evening Thornhill sat in front of the television with Edith and the girls, just as happy families were supposed to do according to the television advertisements. Susie climbed on to his lap, buried her face in his waistcoat and fell asleep. Her warmth and her weight became uncomfortable but he would not have dreamed of moving. The firelight gleamed on her hair, bringing out the red highlights. Where had they come from? No one he knew on either side of the family had red hair.

His youngest child was a mystery to him in other ways, constantly surprising him as the elder two never did. He thought that might be one reason why he loved her so much. Another reason, of course, was that she loved him so fiercely and was too young to feel any hesitation in showing it.

At a quarter to six, Edith prised Susie away from her father and put her to bed. She made scrambled eggs for supper – they rarely ate much on Sunday evenings – and Thornhill had a couple of slices of the beef he had missed at lunchtime. Elizabeth chattered about her homework, or rather justified the fact that she had done only the barest minimum that weekend. Afterwards, while Edith encouraged her up to bed, Thornhill washed up for the second time that weekend. He was becoming a domestic paragon, and was glad his colleagues were not there to witness it.

The telephone rang while Edith was upstairs, and

Thornhill, still wearing his apron, went to answer it. It was Joan Kirby.

'I'm sorry, Mr Thornhill, but Brian's going to be off work for a day or two. It's this tummy bug – he's got it coming out of both ends now, and a temperature. I called the doctor and he says we just have to let it run its course. But he's as weak as a kitten. He really shouldn't have come into work today.'

There was a note of grievance, only partly veiled, in the thick Midlands voice. Since her marriage, Joan had left the police and gradually she had developed a grudge against an organisation that failed to value her husband as she believed he deserved.

Thornhill said, 'Tell him to stay in bed until he's better. That's the important thing. We'll manage without him.'

Joan sniffed, perhaps catching the implication that Kirby was not indispensable to his employers. 'He was worried about going to London. He said it was important.'

'Someone else will go. Just tell him not to worry. When did he come home?'

'About an hour ago.' Joan sounded suspicious. 'Why?'

'It's not important.'

'He needs me. He's calling.'

Thornhill said goodbye and put the receiver down. If Kirby had been home only an hour, he had probably been to see Bayswater's charwoman, as he had intended.

In the hall, he met Edith coming down the stairs.

'Who was that?' she asked.

'Joan Kirby. Brian's ill – some sort of gastric bug. He's been looking seedy for a day or two.'

Edith wrinkled her forehead. 'Rotten for him, I know, but it's bad timing, isn't it?'

Thornhill recognised the question for what it was, a sort of olive branch. 'We'll cope. I think Joan holds me personally responsible.'

'She'll be better when she's had her baby,' Edith said, with the comfortable assurance of a woman who had produced three. 'The first child is always the hardest, and at present she's like a bear with one cub. Shall I make some tea while you say goodnight to Elizabeth?'

He went upstairs. Saying goodnight to Elizabeth was never a short process – when it came to inventing delaying tactics she showed an ingenuity that she never revealed in her homework. He looked in on Susie on his way down and kissed the soft, sweet-smelling hair.

He found Edith in the sitting-room with the tea. The television was off. He felt happier than he had felt for days, since he had heard that Jill Francis was returning to Lydmouth. At least there were the children, he thought; there were always the children.

The fragile truce between Edith and himself lasted for the rest of the evening. Neither mentioned the subject of divorce. They tiptoed round each other's feelings, as though both of them had splitting headaches and were on the verge of nervous breakdowns. He told her about Mr Prout's exploits on Friday night, which elicited a gurgle of amusement.

'By the way,' he said. 'What do you think of that new doctor – Roger Leddon?'

'He seems very nice. Lovely hands – and he's very gentle with the children. Have you met him?'

'In connection with the Bayswater business.'

'Ah.' Edith contemplated the blank grey rectangle of the television screen. 'I don't think they got on very well. That's what people say, anyway.'

'What was the reason?'

'Dr Bayswater didn't need a reason half the time. You know

what he was like – if he took against someone, that was that. He could be terribly rude. But he liked you, didn't he?'

'In his way. Not that I saw much of him after he retired.'

'You could never tell how he was going to react. Dr Leddon wants to change things, and they say he didn't like that. And someone told me – I think it was Amy Gwyn-Thomas – that they had a disagreement about some of the diagnoses that Dr Bayswater had made.'

'What did Leddon feel?'

'It can't have made life easy for him, in all sorts of ways. The practice records are in a frightful state and some of them seem to be missing. And then there's that business about a new surgery and a health centre. Dr Bayswater was going to let Dr Leddon build on part of his garden. At the last moment he changed his mind, which made things very difficult.' Edith hesitated and then burst out, 'I don't know any of this for certain, Richard. It's only what people say. You don't think—?'

'I don't think anything at present.' He smiled at her. 'I wish I did.'

Edith picked up her knitting. The silence lengthened from seconds to minutes. Thornhill stretched his hand to the bookcase and took Housman's *Last Poems* from the shelf. The book lay unopened on his lap.

'Oh, by the way,' Edith said. 'If you don't mind, I thought I might go up to town for the sales after Christmas. Just for a night or two.'

'And the children?'

'We can arrange something about that. If you can take some leave then, perhaps you and David can do something together. You wouldn't mind, would you?'

'No,' said Thornhill. 'I wouldn't mind at all.'

Monday, 5 December

How can I compete with the dead?

I dreamed of her last night. She was calling me: come and join us, there's only you left now. And she laughed, in the way she had, the way that made me feel so small, so unimportant, so scared, as if I wasn't one thing or the other, just some sort of freak like something in a circus.

The dreams are bad but being awake is worse. The fear sits inside me like a stone imp.

It occurred to me last night, as I was lying in bed, will it start to smell soon? I suppose it must. But I've a feeling there's something one can do – I'm sure I read something once, in an account of a murder trial. A man had put down quicklime, which dissolved the body, or most of it.

But would it also destroy the smell? How do I find out without anyone noticing? And if it would help, then I'd have to buy some quicklime, presumably quite a lot of it. Perhaps if I went to London.

Still no news about the bag or the glove. Of course, they might have found them but decided to keep quiet about it, biding their time. Funny to think that little things like that, like a glove or a bag, could put you in the dock, could bring you to the gallows.

That was my other dream. I was standing on the gallows, and the chaplain wanted me to kneel and pray. But I wouldn't. I couldn't.

What would I have to say to God? After all, I'm one of His ghastly mistakes.

Chapter Twenty-Four

On Monday morning the fog still sprawled over England, muffling sounds. To Jill Francis, sitting in a second-class compartment of a train rushing eastwards across the country, it was as though they were travelling through a grey tunnel with a leaky roof. She had caught an early train which, though it meant changing twice, would get her to London in time for a little light shopping in Bond Street before lunch. Borrowing money was rarely easy, and she wanted to look her best for it.

It was still raining when the train reached Paddington. Jill found a phone box, assembled a pile of change and dialled the *Gazette*. She asked for her secretary.

'Just a couple of things, Amy. Mr Gray should have left my car at Raglan Court this morning. I wonder if you'd collect it for me and leave it at the station car park? I'm not sure what time I'll be back, and I don't want to have to walk home in this weather. I left a spare car key in the centre drawer of my desk. The insurance will cover you.'

Amy twittered happily at the other end of the phone.

'There was another thing I wanted to ask. Ivor Fuggle's mother. What was she like?'

'Old Mrs Fuggle?' On the other end of the line, Amy considered the question, sucking air through her teeth, a sound which the intervening technology converted into a noise like the last of the bath water whirling down the plug hole. 'A bit of a battleaxe when she was in her prime. I never knew the husband, he must have died long before the war. She kept house for Ivor for as long as I can remember. Though when she got older, it may have been the other way round. She didn't get out much.'

'Where did they live?'

'Where Mr and Mrs Fuggle live now – the dormer bungalow at the end of Whistler's Lane – you know, just beyond the park.'

'So what happened when she died?'

'He went potty,' Amy said simply. She added, with a trace of regret in her voice, 'Well, perhaps not entirely. But he certainly behaved very oddly for a time. He wouldn't change anything in the house, or throw away her things. He even tried to get in touch with her.' Amy's voice dropped to a thrilling whisper, further distorted by the telephone line. 'On the other side.'

'He went to a *medium*?' Jill failed to keep the amusement out of her voice.

'A lot of people do,' Amy replied, piqued. 'It's quite respectable these days, if you do it in a scientific way. He was in Bournemouth in the summer and he went to see a lady who lives there. Just the once, and I don't think it was a success. But there was one good result. That's how he met his wife. She took him to the seance.'

'Amy – how do you know all this?'

'Oh.' Amy gave a little laugh, high pitched and rather breathless. 'Actually, I know Mrs Fuggle a little – that is, Mr Fuggle's wife, rather than his mother. An old friend of mine's housebound and she lives in Whistler's Lane, and Genevieve Fuggle sometimes drops in as well. I met her there the other evening. Doreen knows her much better than I do, of course, and sometimes she's mentioned things to me.'

The pips went. Jill had no more change.

'Quick – what's the new Mrs Fuggle like?'

'She seems very kind. Rather shy. There was a photo of her in the *Post* the other day. I'll see if I can dig it out.'

Jill knew she should tread warily, warned by the sixth sense that any journalist develops. 'And is she still interested in . . . in psychic research?'

'Yes – as a matter of fact she is. Of course, she hasn't much else to do. Mr Fuggle's hardly ever there – he works very hard. It's not as if she's got children, just her little doggie, and he's very sweet if you like dogs, which I can't say I do particularly, but hardly a—'

Jill plunged into the flow of words. 'Her dog. What sort is it?'

'It's a Highland—'

At that point the money ran out and the line went dead.

Jill replaced the receiver. Was the new Mrs Fuggle jealous of the old one, even after death? Was that the reason for the turd on the grave of Ivor's mother? How terrible to be jealous of the dead, who were invulnerable for all eternity.

She did not have to queue long for a taxi. In Praed Street, her driver stopped for a moment to allow another taxi driver out of a side street and into the stream of traffic. Jill glanced out of the window. Standing on the pavement was a bedraggled queue waiting for a bus. With a jolt of surprise she recognised one of the people.

Near the end of the line, sheltering under an umbrella, was Detective Chief Inspector Richard Thornhill.

Chapter Twenty-Five

Peter Porter knew that Mrs Rodley had talked to the dead because he played for the Police Rugby XV. For home matches they used the pitch on the George V Sports Field. The sister of the groundsman was Mrs Rodley's District Nurse. The groundsman was one of those people who seem never to stop talking, even when no one is listening.

The very idea of contacting the dead filled Porter with fear and longing. What would it be like? Listening to the radio or using a walkie-talkie? Or talking on the telephone? Or perhaps you didn't hear the voices of the dead, not as you did those of living people, but instead the words floated like clouds between your minds.

That, too, was a worrying possibility. What if his mother, being dead, could slip in and out of his thoughts at will? In that case she would know that it was he, not the grocer's boy, who had stolen half a crown from her purse in October 1938. Even worse, she would also know about certain nocturnal emissions which brought him a strange, guilt-ridden pleasure more intense than any other emotion he had known.

Charlie Dyke opened the gate at Viney Cottage. Porter hesitated on the pavement. He glimpsed Mrs Rodley sitting at the window of the room on the right of the front door. Because of the window pane, he couldn't see her clearly: her face loomed grey and insubstantial against the darkness of the room behind her; it was as though she were half dead already, which in a way she was.

Dyke knocked on the front door.

'She's waving to us, Charlie,' Porter said, watching a claw-like hand frantically gesturing at the window. 'She wants to say something.'

'Go and see what she wants, then.'

'Door's open,' she mouthed at Porter through the glass. 'Come on in.'

The cottage was as hot as a greenhouse, filled with a steady, airless heat. Mrs Rodley was sitting in a wheelchair drawn up to the table at the window. She was a small woman, with a pleasant open face and skin like tissue paper. Porter remembered her when she worked in the greengrocer's at the bottom of Lyd Street. Late one afternoon, when he was standing outside on the pavement looking at the river, she had been clearing the display in front of the shop. She had popped a very ripe Victoria plum in his mouth, and he still remembered its blinding sweetness.

Dyke explained why they were there. Doreen Rodley watched him without interrupting. She had been very pretty once, Porter thought, and even now, sitting there with the light behind her, she was a good-looking woman.

'So why have you come up here?' she asked when Dyke had finished. 'This man you're looking for – it's not exactly on his way to the station.'

'Because Mr Mynott thinks he may have crossed the road and gone into Whistler's Lane. He's not sure – he was dealing with a customer and he wasn't really watching. He must've gone somewhere, though, because he left Mynott's at around nine-thirty and the next time anyone noticed him was when he caught the eleven-fifty-three train to London.'

'Maybe he wanted a walk, a breath of fresh air before he went back to London.'

'Not much of a day for a walk.'

Mrs Rodley glanced at the blanket covering her legs and gave an almost imperceptible shrug. Dyke looked away. Peter Porter remembered how the juice of the plum had trickled over his chin, down his neck and under the collar of his shirt.

'There was someone come by, as a matter of fact,' she said, sounding surprised. 'A man. It could have been Friday. Or it might have been Saturday or Thursday. No, I think it was Friday, because I was waiting at the window for the District Nurse.'

Dyke leaned forward. 'Someone you didn't recognise?'

She nodded. 'Not that I was looking particularly. Not at him.'

'What time was this?'

'I don't know. Must have been before half-past ten as that's when the nurse came. She was here when he went back, I can tell you that. She was in the kitchen making me a cup of tea, and I was here by the window.'

'So you definitely saw him going back?'

'Yes – I wondered if he was an insurance agent or something like that. He was quite smart.'

'Can you remember what he was wearing?'

Mrs Rodley screwed up her face. 'A dark coat, I think. And a hat, of course. I think he was carrying something – a small suitcase, maybe. And gloves, I noticed those.'

'Gloves,' PC Porter echoed. 'What colour?'

She looked at him with surprise, as she might have looked at a large dog who had suddenly revealed a gift for human speech. 'Yellow ones.'

The two police officers exchanged glances. Dyke tried to get Mrs Rodley to be more precise, both about the man's appearance and about the times he had passed Viney Cottage. But it was no use. The more they questioned her, the vaguer she became. As they were leaving, Dyke paused in the doorway.

'Is your husband at home, Mrs Rodley? I don't suppose he saw this chap?'

She looked up sharply, a flush staining her cheek. 'Joe was at work on Friday.'

'Of course. Where does he work?'

'At Broadbent's. Assistant transport manager.'

Dyke said they would come back later, if she didn't mind. The two policemen said goodbye and left.

As Porter turned back to close the garden gate he saw Doreen at the window, watching him. She looked worried, he thought, and hoped she wasn't, because of the plum; but maybe it was just the glass that made her look that way. He raised a hand, and she waved back. She was nice. Perhaps he could ask her about talking to dead people.

'At bloody last,' Charlie Dyke said. 'I thought we'd never get a sniff of him.'

'Poor old girl,' Porter said, still thinking about talking to dead people, and the plum, and how pretty Mrs Rodley used to be. 'Stuck there all day can't be much fun. Especially now.'

Dyke looked at his watch. 'Only a couple more houses to go. We'll do those before we report.'

They stopped at the wrought-iron gates leading to the house next door to Viney Cottage. It was a modern house, with a balcony stretching between the bay windows on the first floor and a double garage.

Dyke glanced back at the cottage. 'Bit of an eyesore in an area like this. All these posh houses around it – you'd have thought someone would have made the Rodleys an offer they couldn't refuse, if only for the land.' He frowned. 'What did you mean? *Especially now.*'

Porter said, uneasily, because he was uncertain where his loyalties lay, 'My mate at table tennis was talking about the lay-offs at Broadbent's the other night.'

Charlie cocked an eyebrow. 'Oh aye?'

'He said Joe Rodley had been sacked – made redundant, whatever they call it. There was a whole lot of them. And they got their cards and a week's wages.'

Chapter Twenty-Six

Thornhill sat on the upper deck of the bus rumbling down Praed Street and relished his anonymity. He was a damp stranger among other damp strangers. He could go anywhere, be anyone, and no one would care.

The trip to London was a luxury, he thought, one of those slightly shameful private indulgences like the second glass of whisky after the guests had gone. He had cleared it with Drake, of course, mentioning Kirby's illness, the fact the department was short staffed, the fact that so many officers were engaged in the house-to-house enquiries, the delicate nature of the case and the crucial importance of establishing the nature of the link between Frederick's disappearance and Bayswater's death as soon as possible. Drake had raised no objection, but still Thornhill felt slightly – very slightly – guilty. It was one thing to convince Drake but another to convince himself.

He called first on Frederick's employers, because they were nearer than his home. Redwood and Nephew were based in a cul-de-sac east of Kilburn High Road. The reality was less imposing than the letterhead Miss Mynott had given Thornhill. The firm occupied a lock-up yard with workshops roofed in corrugated asbestos on two sides and offices on the third.

A large, motherly secretary took Thornhill's coat and showed him into the office of Mr Redwood Junior. He wore a brown pinstripe suit whose jacket bulged before him like the

breast of a pigeon. His black hair swept back from a widow's
peak and glistened with grease.

'Thanks, Mum,' he said to the secretary.

Mr Redwood was younger than he appeared at first sight,
probably in his late twenties, but he dressed and moved as if in
late middle age, perhaps to reassure the customers. He offered
Thornhill a cigarette, a cigar, a cup of tea and a cup of coffee,
all of which Thornhill declined.

'No sign of him, I suppose, Chief Inspector? It's not like
him, you know.'

'He's a reliable sort of chap, then?'

Redwood nodded. 'Sound as a pound. My uncle took him
on five or six years ago when he was setting up. He's a damn
good salesman. People trust him.'

'What exactly is he selling?'

'We build televisions. We let others do the retailing, though,
but each retailer markets them under their own name. The
way it works is this: say you're an electrical shop and you're
selling televisions. You stock Pye, of course, and Ekco and
Sobell – all the big makes. Problem is, they don't come cheap. I
mean, you can get a television for fifty or sixty pounds, but if
you want something reasonable quality you have to pay a lot
more.' He flicked his fingers at the pile of trade journals on the
corner of his desk. 'Have a look through these – you can pay
well over a hundred guineas if you want. You're paying for the
name, of course. We assemble our own sets, using the cheap-
est and the best components we can find – we're not tied to
one supplier, you see – and then we approach an electrical
shop and say, "Look, how would you like to be able to sell a
good-quality twenty-one-inch television? It's got thirteen-
channel tuning, automatic picture control and a couple of
high-quality loudspeakers. And it's all in a handsome walnut-
veneered cabinet which will look good in anyone's home.

What's more," we tell them, "it will have your name on the set, not Pye or Ekco, and you can sell it for a fraction of the price while increasing your profit margins." We even throw in after-sales service – within reason, that is. The sets just walk off the shelves. Everyone wins – us, the retailer, the customer.'

Thornhill said, 'I thought he was an engineer.'

'He is.' Redwood beamed. 'But he's also a salesman – got it down to a fine art. He goes and talks to them, you see, gets to know them for a day or two. But the thing is, as he's an electrical engineer by trade, he really talks their language. He used to be a wireless operator in the RAF, did you know that? He's Dutch, actually, though you wouldn't know it to hear him. He came over in the war and then he married an English girl and settled down.'

'He didn't know anyone in Lydmouth? Nothing he said gave you the idea he might have anything else he wanted to do there?'

'No and no.' Redwood sighed. 'I hope this won't jeopardise the order. I talked to him on Thursday night on the phone, and he reckoned Mynott's would be good for half a dozen of our mid-range sets.'

'What's he like, Mr Frederick? How does he get on with people here?'

'He's well liked. He's the steady type. I've seen him get a bit uppity at the Christmas knees-up when he's had a few drinks, but apart from that he's as gentle as a lamb.' Redwood looked at Thornhill with guileless brown eyes. 'I hope nothing's happened to him. We'd miss him. We'd all miss him.'

Outside it was still raining. Thornhill walked back to the High Road and caught a Tube train up to Queen's Park. Another train took him to Willesden Junction. Mr and Mrs Frederick lived in a little Victorian terraced house not far from Harlesden High Street. The house was set back from the pavement behind a low wall. On the ground floor, flanked by a pair of grimy laurel bushes, was a bay window. Thornhill rang the bell and watched the net curtain twitch. A moment later the door was opened by a small, dark-haired woman with red-rimmed eyes.

Thornhill touched his hat. 'Mrs Frederick? I'm Detective Chief Inspector Thornhill from Lydmouth. You talked with my sergeant on the phone.'

She took him into the front room. It was very cold – the grate was empty and spotlessly clean. On the tiled hearth stood a paraffin heater, a blue flame flickering behind the little window, filling the chilly air with the pungent smell of burning oil. Thornhill thought that they would have been more comfortable and certainly warmer in the kitchen, but Mrs Frederick had her pride.

Two aspidistras stood sentinel on the window sill, matching the laurels outside. There was a piano which had lost its candle holders, a three-piece suite in need of reupholstering, a worn carpet which had once been patterned but had been ineffectually dyed a deep red, a radio and many family photographs. But there was no television.

Still standing, she said, 'Is there any news?'

'I'm afraid not.'

'It's not like Paul,' she burst out. 'He's usually so . . . oh, do sit down, Mr . . . I'm sorry, I didn't catch your name.'

'Thornhill.'

Somewhere in the house a baby began to cry. Thornhill saw her stiffen, and turn towards the door.

'Is that your baby, Mrs Frederick? I can come back a little later if it would be more convenient, or you could bring the baby in here with you.' He tried the effect of a smile. 'I'm quite used to babies.'

She smiled back, transforming her face, and hurried out of

the room. She returned with a baby in her arms. Thornhill felt himself on familiar territory and asked the questions he thought mothers liked to be asked. Mrs Frederick told him that the child was called Margaret, after the princess, that she was seven months old and remarkably advanced for her age, and that right from the start she'd slept like a lamb for most of the night, which was a great blessing. Margaret condescended to hold Thornhill's forefinger, which was a sign of remarkable precocity.

By the time these formalities were out of the way, Mrs Frederick had become calmer. Thornhill led her gently through the obvious questions. Had Mr Frederick any friends or business contacts in the Lydmouth area he might have wished to visit? Had he seemed his normal self when he left on the trip? Had he any financial worries?

'Only this house,' Mrs Frederick said. 'We're buying it – we've got a mortgage. It's such a worry having that amount of money hanging over you, but Paul says it will be worth it in the long run. By the time the little ones are grown up, it'll be all ours.'

Thornhill asked whether Frederick liked his job.

Mrs Frederick nodded vigorously. 'He's doing ever so well. Mr Redwood told me himself on the summer outing. Paul thinks he might be made sales manager one day, even a partner. It's the new thing, television, you see, and it's going to get bigger and bigger and we're in on the ground floor.' It was clear that she was quoting, and her face was pink with vicarious enthusiasm.

Thornhill said, 'It would be helpful if we could have a list of the clothes your husband had with him.'

She stared at him with huge eyes, all excitement gone. 'You mean . . . you mean in case he's had an accident, or lost his memory – or something.'

'We have to think of everything, Mrs Frederick.'

He took out his notebook and wrote as Mrs Frederick listed the clothes. Each item had a history, a personal significance. There was the dark blue overcoat that they had been lucky to find in the sales. The tie, which had something to do with his old squadron, recently purchased to replace an older one. The jacket with a houndstooth check which her brother had passed on to Paul because he had grown too plump for it himself.

Thornhill closed the notebook. 'It might be useful to have a recent photograph.'

She brought out an album from the home-made bookcase to the left of the fireplace and opened it on the coffee table. As she turned the pages, the Fredericks' married life flashed before Thornhill in an unbroken parade of smiles.

He frowned. 'I didn't realise he had a moustache.'

It wasn't any old moustache, either, but an RAF handlebar moustache, the tips of which trailed beneath the line of his jaw.

'Oh, he hasn't, not now. He shaved it off in the summer.' She gave a nervous giggle. 'I was glad to see it go, to tell you the truth. It was so prickly.'

'So he's clean shaven? Have you got a photograph of him without a moustache?'

She shook her head. 'I tell you what I have got, though. There's one of him in uniform, just before the end of the war. He hasn't got the moustache in that.'

'But surely he's changed since then?'

'Not very much – everyone says how young he looks. I'll show you.'

She left the room, the baby tucked in the crook of her arm. She returned with a brown envelope and shook out the miscellaneous photographs it contained, mostly of herself as a girl. One of them, however, was of Frederick in a flight sergeant's uniform.

'He looks like someone,' Thornhill said.

'The film star – John Wayne.' Mrs Frederick smiled. 'Everyone says that.'

'May I borrow that one, then, please, and one of the more recent ones with the moustache?' He would ask Miss Mynott which was the better likeness.

'Of course you can.'

He studied the older photograph. Frederick was sitting on a bench, his right arm along the back, with a cigarette in his mouth. The sun was out and casting long shadows, so it was either early in the morning or late in the day. In the background was an ornate church with a tower at the side, in which was inserted a great door.

'Where was this taken?'

'I don't know. Somewhere in London, probably. I think he was stationed at Northolt then.'

There was nothing more to say. Thornhill stood up. His eye caught a picture postcard on the mantelpiece, half concealed by the clock. It was a colour photograph and there was something familiar about it, enough to make him take a step or two towards it. Two towers, one lower than the other, with a stretch of crumbling wall between them.

'Isn't that Lydmouth Castle?'

Mrs Frederick nodded. 'Yes – it came today. It's for the children. Paul always sends a card for the children.'

Thornhill said calmly: 'But you didn't mention it.'

'There didn't seem any point. He must have sent it before he disappeared. You can read it if you like.'

Thornhill picked the card up and turned it over. It was addressed to Master Ian and Miss Margaret Frederick. On the left-hand side was the message:

> *Thursday*
> *It's very foggy. See you soon.*
> *Lots of love to you and Mummy from*
> *Daddy xxx*

She pointed at the card. 'See – Thursday.'

'Yes, indeed,' Thornhill said. 'Still, would you mind if I took this as well? You can have a receipt, of course, and you'll get it back. It's just possible we might need a sample of his handwriting.'

Ten minutes later, he left the house, with the postcard and the photographs in his briefcase. As the bus carried him to Paddington he wondered about that postcard. It had been postmarked in Gloucester, the 6 p.m. collection on Friday, 2 December.

Did the postmark suggest that Paul Frederick had left the train at Gloucester? Bayswater had been in Gloucester on the same day. There was no evidence that the two men had previously met. But had they met on Friday? Had something happened between them?

At the station, he hurried on to the concourse and glanced up at the clock. He would be just in time for the 3:19. The train was already waiting at Platform 3. He phoned Edith and walked briskly along the line of carriages, looking for an empty non-smoking compartment.

Twenty yards ahead of him, a lady opened the door of a smoker and, as she climbed aboard, glanced over her shoulder. Their eyes met. It was Jill Francis.

Chapter Twenty-Seven

The last house in Whistler's Lane was a pre-war dormer bungalow on the left-hand side, with the corner of the park on the right. After the bungalow, the lane narrowed and became a muddy footpath running between two field boundaries. An iron finger-post pointed the way to March Hill.

Dyke turned into the bungalow's drive but Porter lingered. The hill was just visible through the murk, a deeper grey than its surroundings. From the summit there were views over Lydmouth and, according to legend, six counties. Perched on the crown of the hill like a tuft of hair on a bald head was a densely packed grove of Scots pines, planted in commemoration of Queen Victoria's Diamond Jubilee in 1897. Everyone knew that lovers went there on summer evenings.

Dyke, halfway up the drive, called back: 'What you gawping at? Come on.'

Porter pushed aside the thoughts of young women dappled with sunlight under the trees. He followed Dyke, glancing at the Fuggles' large and gloomy garden. The grass was trim and the flower beds clear of weeds but the trees and shrubs were large and lank, as if no one bothered much with pruning. The patched tarmac drive led past the side of the house to a small barn of crumbling stone at the end of the garden. The barn's roof was made of weathered pantiles that had settled over the years into a shape resembling a tent with slack guy ropes.

'Probably a farm up here in the old days,' Dyke said. 'Let's get this over with, eh? It's going to piss with rain in five minutes, I can feel it in my bones.'

He rang the front-door bell and they waited. There were box-like bay windows on either side of the door. Thick net curtains shrouded the rooms within from prying eyes.

Dyke pressed the bell again. A moment later he walked to the corner of the house. 'Someone's in – look, there's a window open down there. We'll try the back.'

They followed the drive that skirted the left-hand side of the bungalow. The kitchen was at the back, and there were no net curtains here. Dyke knocked on the door and then tapped on the window pane. Still there was no answer. While they waited, Porter turned his back to the house and surveyed the garden. It looked like a nice little vegetable patch beside the barn. He could never see the point of flowers – he'd left those to Mam – but a vegetable garden was something different. You could eat a potato. But a rose just went and died on you.

A dog barked near by, a high yapping, angry and alarmed. Porter caught a movement out of the corner of his eye. A very small terrier scampered towards them. A lady appeared in the open doorway of the barn with a paintbrush in one hand and a cigarette in the other.

'Morning, ma'am,' Dyke called. 'Mind if we have a word?'

The woman balanced the paintbrush across the top of a tin standing on a kitchen chair just inside the door. She took a few steps towards them. She seemed uncertain, as if sleepwalking. She wore a shapeless tweed coat with a rip in one arm and a button missing, wellington boots and a beret. Her round face was off-white, almost grey.

The terrier circled Porter, snarling and snapping at his ankles. Dyke seized the dog by the collar.

'Be careful! Be careful! He's very delicate!'

'Don't worry, ma'am. It's Mrs Fuggle, isn't it?'

'Yes, Officers,' she said in a voice that trembled a little. 'But do be careful with Macbeth.' She dropped the cigarette and scooped up the little animal. She cradled him in her arms. 'There, there, sweetie. It's all right now.'

Macbeth licked his mistress's hand and stared at the police officers with hot little eyes.

Mrs Fuggle cleared her throat and went on more firmly: 'Now – what can I do for you?'

'We're looking for a gentleman who's gone missing,' Dyke said.

'I've not seen anyone.' She waved in the direction of the garden and the vegetable patch. 'I've been out here most of the time, or in the kitchen.'

'Not today. Were you here on Friday?'

A twitch ran over her face, as though large invisible fingers had squeezed her features together and then released them. 'Yes, I suppose I must have been.'

'We think the gentleman came up Whistler's Lane in the morning. Maybe about ten o'clock, or a bit later. And then he went back down about three-quarters of an hour afterwards.'

'I didn't see him.'

'Are you sure? We think he came up this end of the lane.'

'A lot of people do. There's the footpath up to March Hill. We get all sorts coming up here.'

'It wasn't a day for walking, though.'

She coughed, and the phlegm rumbled deep inside her chest. 'There's people that walk in all weathers. Anyway, I wouldn't have seen him even if he had come. I wouldn't have been at the front of the house.'

Porter wandered towards the vegetable garden, which took him past the open door of the barn. He missed Mam's garden, especially the vegetables. He stared approvingly at the Fuggles' carefully tended patch. Not a weed in sight.

'Lot of work, look,' he said, half to himself, filling a pause in the questioning. 'Worth it, though. Can't beat the flavour.'

Dyke sighed.

Mrs Fuggle said, 'Is that all? I'm hoping to get that table finished before lunchtime.'

Porter turned. The two leaves of the barn door were propped open. Inside was a pine kitchen table. Two of its legs were now a deep rich purple.

He ambled closer. The colour reminded Porter of something. He found himself thinking of Miss Stevens, a teacher at his infant school. He remembered her reading a book whose cover was a similar colour to this. It was a story about a dragon, and he had assumed that the cover of the book was that colour because it had been dyed in the blood of the dragon. He stretched a hand out towards the glistening surface.

'Careful,' Mrs Fuggle said sharply, darting towards him. 'It's wet.'

She shooed him outside. Porter glanced over her shoulder into the little barn. It was used as a garage, judging by the puddle of oil on the floor, and also as a garden shed and as a wood store. Someone had been sawing kindling and chopping logs.

'You've got a nice pile there,' he said, feeling that a compliment was in order to make up for his clumsiness with the wet paint. 'That should keep you warm for most of the winter.'

'Yes, I hope it will,' Mrs Fuggle said, and started coughing.

'Ash and oak, by the look of it – and is that a bit of beech? No, it's—'

He broke off. A car was coming up the lane, drawing steadily closer.

The three of them turned to look. A grey Humber Hawk nosed into the drive, the driver revving the engine unnecessarily. It rolled towards them and came to a halt five yards away from the barn. The driver's door opened.

'Ivor, you're home early. I—'

Fuggle hauled himself out of the car and looked from Dyke to Porter. He ignored his wife. 'What are you two doing here?'

'Asking about some man,' Mrs Fuggle said.

'What's that?'

Dyke said, 'It's a missing-person inquiry, sir. We believe the gentleman walked up Whistler's Lane on Friday morning. Mrs Fuggle didn't see him. I don't suppose you did?'

'Not unless I had telepathy or whatever you call it. I was in Framington all day.' Fuggle frowned at his wife. 'You all right, Genevieve? You look peaky.'

She gestured at the half-painted table in the barn. 'I feel a bit wobbly, that's all. I think it's the paint fumes. I . . . I was trying to get it finished before the rain started in earnest. Why have you come back?'

'I left the notes for this afternoon behind.' Fuggle turned back to the two constables. 'So who's this missing person?'

'A man called Frederick, sir,' Dyke said. 'That's his surname – a television engineer from London. He'd been staying in Lydmouth for a couple of days. They expected him back in London on Friday.'

Fuggle glanced at his watch. 'No sign of him here.' He turned back to his wife, pointedly ignoring the two policemen. 'I'd better pick up another can of oil while I'm here. The pressure's down again. It's leaking like a blasted sieve.'

'Should you ask the garage to have a look?'

'I don't want to spend money on this old heap – the new one's due for delivery before Christmas.' Fuggle started to walk towards the house, then stopped and looked back. 'Make me a cup of coffee while I'm here, will you?' He glanced at the two police officers. 'Haven't you fellows got work to do?'

Chapter Twenty-Eight

It was a little after three o'clock when Amy Gwyn-Thomas left the *Gazette*. It was now raining hard, but she was well wrapped up, and she was not the sort of person, thank heavens, who minded a little bit of bad weather. With her mackintosh flapping around her calves and her big brown umbrella sheltering her from the rain, she strode along Broad Street and turned up Albert Road.

The little outing afforded her several small pleasures. She liked the break in routine and the fact that Miss Francis had trusted her enough to send her up here. And she was especially pleased that she would be able to drive Jill's car – the next best thing to brand new and such a pretty shade of green – through the centre of Lydmouth. She would be sure to pass several people she knew and would be able to honk the horn at them.

Amy had only recently passed her test and was still in the honeymoon stage of the driver's development, keen to display her prowess. She did not have many opportunities to do this in the normal course of things because she could not afford to run a car herself, and to her great regret Mr Prout had never asked her whether she would like to drive his, though she had thrown out a number of hints to that effect.

She was walking on the left-hand pavement. After a few minutes, the houses gave way to the hedge that bounded the side of the park. Raglan Court was now in sight, a stark grey oblong against the lighter grey of the sky. Amy liked Raglan

Court. Such a smart location, and the flats attracted a very nice class of person. She glanced up at the rows of windows, wondering which belonged to Miss Francis's flat, and which to Dr Leddon's. Not for the first time, she contemplated the intriguing possibility that they would fall in love with each other.

In the car park behind the block, she saw the green Morris Minor in the corner near the private gate to Jubilee Park. She walked round to the driver's side and opened her handbag. She was aware in some corner of her mind of movement, or fluttering, and would have assumed, if she had thought to analyse it, that it was made by reflections shifting in the car window.

Amy took out the key and inserted it into the lock. She opened the door. Inside the car there were sounds of scrabbling and rustling, together with a blur of movement.

She did not quite believe what she saw. In the well in front of the driver's seat, below the steering wheel, were two grey objects, moving rapidly. There was also something quite still, something bloody and torn, with glimpses of bone, and other things less easy to identify.

Her mouth fell open but no sound came out. She took a step backward.

A large grey rat jumped from the door sill to the ground and ran towards her. Immediately after it followed another, even larger. They had sharp little skulls and tails as long as themselves. Amy threw herself backward, slipped, and fell heavily. Her head smacked against the corner of the right-hand post of the gate to the park.

She waited, silent, half stunned, hardly aware of the blinding pain in the back of her skull, waiting for the rats to sink their teeth into her. She heard footsteps pounding towards her and someone shouting.

At last she screamed.

Chapter Twenty-Nine

'Richard,' Jill Francis said, 'I'm sorry but this is quite absurd. You can't pretend nothing ever happened. And nor can I. Neither of us wants to turn the clock back but surely we can have a civilised conversation occasionally? It's going to make things awfully complicated if we can't.'

As she spoke, she thought how tart her voice sounded: like a vindictive Sunday school teacher's.

He glanced up at her, standing above him in the doorway of the railway carriage, and gave a ghost of a shrug. 'All right. After you.'

He followed her down the corridor of the train until they came to an empty compartment.

'Do you mind a smoker?' she said over her shoulder.

He slid the door open. 'Not at all.'

There was a moment's awkwardness while they settled themselves in the compartment. For an instant their shoulders brushed in the confined space as he removed his raincoat. They jerked apart, as though by magnetic repulsion, and he apologised. Jill chose a window seat. Richard sat diagonally opposite, by the door to the corridor.

'I take it you've been working in town?' she said.

'Yes. And you?'

'In a manner of speaking.' She smoothed a wrinkle in her glove. Perhaps this was a mistake, sharing a compartment – she felt unhappy enough as it was. 'Something to do with the *Gazette*.'

Once upon a time, when they were younger and perhaps less wise, she would have been able to tell him everything, about the humiliation of asking an old friend for a loan and watching the friend's face change. Her trip to town had been a disaster.

What she really wanted to do now was to ask Richard what he had meant by not coming to see her or even phoning or writing. They had been friends and lovers once and he had no right not to keep in touch with her. He had humiliated her. She would never forgive him for that. The least he could do was say sorry. God, how tired he looked.

'Jill,' he said.

Her head snapped up. 'Yes?'

He smiled. She had always liked his mouth. He said, 'I know it's not easy, and you must think—'

The compartment door slid back and there was a sudden draught of cold air.

'These seats free?' enquired a man wearing a yellow check overcoat over a pea-green tweed suit. 'Yes? Good – come along, dear. In here.'

He chivvied a nervy, dun-coloured little woman into the compartment. The newcomers settled in the two empty corners. They brought with them more than the normal complement of bags, hats, coats, newspapers and magazines. They had hardly had time to stow away their belongings before the last two seats in the compartment were taken by a soldier on leave and an elderly lady. The corridor filled with standing passengers.

A whistle blew, and the train slid along the platform. Having lectured his wife on the weather, British Rail and the short-comings of the station buffet, the man in the pea-green suit opened his newspaper and began to read. Every few minutes he would emerge from the pages of the *Daily Express* and share a titbit of news with his wife.

When the ticket collector came, he mentioned that the train was especially crowded that day, because one carriage was missing. Jill glanced at Richard and they exchanged the fleeting smiles of comrades in adversity. It was infuriating, she thought. But with luck their fellow travellers would be getting out at Reading or Swindon.

The man in the pea-green suit finished the *Express* and began to read *Punch*, showing the cartoons to his wife and, where he thought it necessary, explaining the jokes to her. There were few things quite as tiresome, Jill thought, as hearing cartoons laboriously explained by someone whose sense of humour you did not share.

She tried to read. No one left the compartment at either Reading or Swindon. The train picked up speed again, travelling through thickening fog.

'No, dear,' the man in the pea-green suit said impatiently. 'It's the dentist's waiting-room. That's why extraction is funny.'

Richard looked up from his newspaper and glanced directly at Jill. His right eyelid drooped.

The wife murmured something inaudible.

'That's right,' her husband said. 'He's a coal miner, you see.'

Jill gave a little snort of laughter, as much hysterical as amused, which she swiftly turned into a cough. Richard smiled, and she saw the amusement in his eyes.

Her heart gave a treacherous twitch. The last three years were neither forgotten nor forgiven. But nor, it seemed, was what had gone before them. Nevertheless the pull on her emotions was merely a reflex, she told herself, no more than that – the sentimental equivalent to the pain an amputee feels in a lost limb.

The train rattled through a world of mist and steam and

smoke. Their fellow passenger spread his tweed-covered thighs wide and lit a pipe that filled the compartment with an internal fog smelling of old soap and fresh tar.

'Filthy day,' he observed with apparent satisfaction, and consulted his watch. 'We're running late, a good five minutes. Never used to happen before the war.'

Once again, their eyes met across the compartment, hers and Richard's, making them conspirators, separating them from the couple between them.

It's like a force, Jill thought, which attracts or repels. In a way, it's nothing to do with him or me. It just is. Surely he can feel it?

Richard looked down at the newspaper folded on his knee. He was doing the crossword in *The Times*, filling in an answer every now and then with a silver propelling pencil. She hadn't known that he did crosswords. Was it something new? What else about him didn't she know? A man could change in three years, fall in and out of love.

The mist grew even thicker, merging imperceptibly with twilight. They stopped at stations made unfamiliar and ghostly. She wasn't sure whether to be sorry or glad that the other people stayed in the compartment, preventing conversation.

The man in the pea-green suit fell asleep and snored; his wife prodded him occasionally with her foot, which changed the rhythm of the snoring without stopping it for more than a few seconds. Meanwhile she knitted a short-sleeved jersey in a virulent shade of green. The clicking of her needles kept time with the rattling of the wheels on the rails.

By the time the train was running down the valley to Lydmouth, the last of the daylight was gone. Somewhere in the darkness beyond the window was the invisible river, the spire of St John's and the castle ruins on their low hill.

Somewhere in that same darkness, almost certainly, was the killer of Dr Bayswater.

The train slackened speed. She and Richard stirred in their corners and collected their belongings, watched incuriously by the knitting woman. The train hissed and panted to a stand-still.

'Lydmouth!' a porter shouted, his voice sounding faint and muffled, distanced by the fog.

The man in the pea-green suit woke up with a start and consulted his watch. 'Lydmouth? That means we're running nine minutes late now.'

Richard left the compartment first, holding the door for Jill. She followed him along the corridor. The door to the platform was already open, and a stout lady was clambering down. The journey was over, and with it their chance of exorcising the ghosts that lay between them.

Jill said with sudden urgency: 'Richard—'

He turned and looked at her. His eyes widened, as though he were surprised by what he saw. 'Jill.'

'We must talk.'

'I know.'

He swallowed, his Adam's apple bobbing in his throat. He jumped down to the platform and held out his free hand to her. She looked down at his face.

A young man burst through the ticket barrier, running for the train.

A child shrieked, 'Daddy!'

Richard swung away from her, leaving her hand dangling foolishly in midair. A tiny girl was sitting in a pushchair, not ten yards away from them. She had red-blonde hair and pale freckled skin. Her face was ablaze with joy and she was waving two clenched fists above her head. On one side of the push-chair was an older girl, Elizabeth, whom Jill had known slightly in the old days but would not have recognised now; and on the other side was Edith Thornhill, her face impassive.

'Daddy!'

Richard glanced back at Jill, and his face was as expressionless as his wife's.

How can I ever compete with that, Jill wondered, with the little girl in the pushchair, the little girl who looks as though she's just seen an angel?

'Miss Francis!'

Jill looked up. The young man was pounding down the platform towards her. With a shock, she recognised Howard Mork, hatless and coatless, his long jacket hanging open from his padded shoulders, the two sides flapping behind him like poorly co-ordinated wings. Despite his exertions, his face was very pale, throwing the acne into even more vivid relief than usual.

'Miss Francis,' he called. 'Miss Francis, something awful's happened.'

Chapter Thirty

'Oh, it's you,' said Mr Prout. 'I suppose you'd better come in.'

He pressed himself against the wall to give PC Porter the space he needed to manoeuvre himself into the narrow hall. The bungalows in Vicarage Gardens were ideally suited to those with slender figures. Mr Prout smoothed his gleaming hair in the mirror over the table.

'In there, Officer.' He indicated a door on the left.

The room was crowded with dark furniture that belonged to another house, another era. Both bars of the electric fire were on and it was very warm. Amy Gwyn-Thomas sat nearby in an armchair, with a rug drawn over her. Dr Leddon, bag in one hand and hat in the other, was just inside the door.

He nodded to Porter. 'Evening, Constable.'

'She's all right, is she, sir?' Porter blurted out.

'She'll do.' Leddon glanced back at Miss Gwyn-Thomas and gave her a smile that made her eyelashes flutter. 'I'd keep your feet up, if I were you, and have a nice quiet evening. You should be as right as rain in the morning. But give me a ring if you're not.'

He left the room, and Porter heard Prout in the hall saying, 'I say, Doctor, I don't suppose anyone's been to see you in the last few days with a damaged you-know-what?'

Leddon laughed and murmured something in reply that

Porter could not catch. Then the front door opened and closed behind him.

Clutching his helmet, Porter advanced slowly into the room, plotting an anxious course between a nest of occasional tables and a revolving bookcase, on which stood a lady and gentleman made of china and wearing old-fashioned clothes.

'How are you, miss?' he enquired in a hushed voice.

'Bearing up. You took your time getting here, I must say. You'd better sit down.' Amy's head swivelled on the end of her long neck, drawn by the sight of a car pulling up outside the house. 'Who's that? Oh – one of the station taxis, I think – and, look, Ronald, it's Miss Francis. And Howard. Isn't that kind? He must have met her at the station.'

'I don't know what the lad's doing here now,' Mr Prout said. 'He'll only get in the way.'

'Just trying to be helpful,' Miss Gwyn-Thomas said, unusually sharply.

The door bell rang. Mr Prout ushered Miss Francis and Howard Mork into the room, making it even more crowded than it was already.

'How are you, Amy?' Miss Francis said.

Amy told her, at length.

'Such a beastly thing to happen.' Miss Francis flashed a smile at PC Porter. 'Hello, Mr Porter. You've come to sort this out, I hope. I must say it goes a long way beyond a practical joke.'

'Yes, miss. I was about to . . . to establish what had happened.' He unbuttoned his pocket and drew out his notebook. 'That is, if Miss Gwyn-Thomas feels up to it, of course.'

'I'd like to hear myself, if you don't mind,' Jill said. 'Howard told me the outline in the taxi.'

PC Porter was not entirely clear how Miss Francis contrived it, but somehow she made everything simple. Howard and

Mr Prout were dispatched to the kitchen to make tea on the grounds that they had already heard the story. Porter found himself sitting down, minus his overcoat and helmet. One bar of the electric fire was switched off. Best of all, perhaps, Miss Francis relieved Porter of the necessity of asking most of the questions.

Not that Miss Gwyn-Thomas needed much prompting. 'I went to collect the car after lunch, Miss Francis, and Gray's had left it outside the flats, all just as you said.' She gave a little shudder. 'There wasn't a great deal of light – it's such a gloomy day and the car was in that dark corner near the gate to the park. Otherwise I might have seen what was inside before I opened the door. Anyway, there were two rats – and they were eating something under the steering wheel. Huge long tails, as long as they were. I've never seen rats so close, nor such big ones.' She screwed up her face and her hands twisted the top of the rug into a tight little roll. 'Then they jumped out of the car, actually coming towards me. I thought they were going to attack me. I'm afraid I rather lost my head.'

'I'd have screamed blue murder,' Jill said. 'And probably fainted.'

'I didn't actually faint but I jumped backwards. I wasn't thinking straight – I thought they were coming to attack me. I must have slipped and fallen. Then I heard someone running behind me, and Howard came up.'

'What was he doing at Raglan Court?'

Porter saw Miss Gwyn-Thomas hesitate, saw her eyes meet Jill's.

'He'd gone out to post some letters, and then he said he felt a bit faint, so he thought he'd better walk around a little and get fresh air. Anyway, he was very kind and helpful. He stopped a passing car and the driver kindly took us down to the *Gazette*. And we phoned Ronald, and he brought me home and called

Dr Leddon.' She frowned, and looked down at her hands. 'I'm sorry to make such a fuss about it.'

'Don't be silly,' Jill said. 'You're not making a fuss. You're being perfectly splendid.'

'Ronald – Mr Prout, that is – phoned Gray's as well. Mr Gray said one of his mechanics left the car at Raglan Court at about two-thirty. And he swore there weren't any rats in it then, dead or alive.'

'Who knew you were collecting the car?'

'I told the girls in reception when I went out.'

'No one else? And not before then?'

As Amy was shaking her head, Mr Prout backed into the room, towing a tea trolley. Howard shambled after him, his arms swinging by his sides.

'I used the Royal Doulton,' Mr Prout said. 'And I hope everyone likes ginger biscuits. You've told the constable everything, then?'

Miss Gwyn-Thomas gave a start and looked at PC Porter, almost as if she had forgotten he was in the room. 'Yes. Unless he has any questions, that is. You'll have a cup of tea, won't you, Constable?'

Porter cleared his throat, about to say yes please, if it wouldn't be too much trouble. But Mr Prout interrupted before he could speak.

'It can't be a coincidence, can it? Two nasty practical jokers at work. The one I had to deal with, because the police seemed incapable of it themselves, and now this horrible attack on Amy. It must be the same person.' He stared challengingly at Porter, who looked down at his notebook. 'Rats,' Prout went on after a moment. 'Funny, though. They sort of remind you of Dr Bayswater, don't they? Him and his rats.'

Chapter Thirty-One

'Mr Drake rang,' Edith said as they walked through the station yard to the car. 'He said he's in a meeting till seven, but would you drop in and see him at his office afterwards?'

Thornhill looked at his watch. 'Time for some food first.'

He was grateful for the presence of the girls. Edith had said nothing about coming to meet him when he phoned her from Paddington to say which train he would be on. He was also grateful for whatever crisis whisked Jill Francis away after only the briefest of greetings between her and Edith. The two women had never been intimate when Jill lived in Lydmouth before, but they had known each other reasonably well. Thornhill sometimes wondered whether they had known each other too well.

When they reached home, Edith made high tea for all of them. They ate macaroni cheese, followed by apples from the garden, their skins already leathery but the insides surprisingly juicy and sweet. It was a silent meal.

Thornhill peeled an apple for Susie. For once he succeeded in removing the skin in one unbroken curling line, an achievement that made her crow with pleasure. He sliced it up and fed her the pieces one by one.

'I'm a bird,' she said, opening her mouth wide for the next piece. 'I'm in my nest and you're giving me wiggly worms.'

'It was quite a coincidence bumping into Miss Francis on the train,' he said to Edith, elaborately casual. 'I wonder what she was doing in London.'

'You didn't ask her, then?' she said.

'No opportunity. The train was terribly crowded – the ticket collector said they were a carriage short.' He stretched the truth a little: 'I met her in the corridor when we were getting off at Lydmouth.' He tried a smile. 'Who was the lad who rushed up? Someone at the *Gazette*?'

'His name's Howard Mork.' Edith soaked up knowledge about Lydmouth and its inhabitants without obvious effort, as though she inhaled it in the very air she breathed. 'His father manages Butter's. They came down from London a couple of years ago but the mother died rather suddenly. What were you and Miss Francis talking about?'

'Just saying hello,' Thornhill said. 'There wasn't time for anything else.' He glanced up at the clock on the mantelpiece. 'I'd better be off.'

He left the house with relief. He felt a little annoyed about the whole business – he had done nothing yet somehow he was being made to feel guilty. He drove down to headquarters, where he had time to go through his in-tray. After seeing the charwoman yesterday afternoon, Kirby had drawn up a surprisingly short list of the items possibly stolen from Dr Bayswater. Thornhill was studying it when Drake appeared in the doorway of his room.

'Come into my office,' he said. 'Bloody awful day. I think we deserve a drink.'

In his office, the DCC produced whisky from one desk drawer and a couple of glasses from another. He poured a generous two fingers into each of them and the two men raised their glasses in a silent toast. They had never had an intimate conversation in their lives, and perhaps never would, but for all that Thornhill liked Drake and trusted him as much as he trusted any man.

After a moment, Drake said, 'Well – what did you get?'

'By all accounts, Frederick was a model employee. Good job, with prospects, taken out a mortgage. Happily married with a couple of little children. He'd come over from Holland in the war and joined the RAF. Neither the employer nor the wife knew of any connection with Lydmouth or any friends he might have in the area. There's one thing, though – she had a postcard from him this morning. It had been posted on the day he vanished, the Friday. In Gloucester, the six o'clock collection.'

'So either he left the train at Gloucester or he gave the card to someone else and asked them to post it there? Someone he met on the train, perhaps. Bayswater? What did the card say?'

'Nothing, really. It was addressed to the kids, one of whom's a baby and the other one's not much older. There was a picture of Lydmouth Castle on it.'

Drake contemplated his glass. He looked tired. 'According to Carney, all the reasonably fresh prints in Bayswater's house are from people we can account for, people who had legitimate reasons to be there, people like the char.'

Sergeant Carney ran the Fingerprint Department in the basement.

Thornhill said, 'What about Leddon's?'

'His were there, but you'd expect that.'

'No trace of Frederick's?'

'No. Have you heard about the house-to-house?'

'I've just been reading Dyke's report.'

'Damned odd, eh? What was Frederick doing up Whistler's Lane on Friday morning? Doesn't make sense.'

'Stretching his legs?'

'Hardly the weather for it.' Drake straightened the blotter, which was already precisely aligned with the desktop. 'And then the witness says she saw him again, coming back down, perhaps three-quarters of an hour later. Her name's Doreen Rodley.'

'I've not come across her.'

'She's an invalid – housebound for the last nine months or so.'

'She might have been making it up,' Thornhill said. 'It happens. Anything for a bit of excitement.'

'Unlikely. She mentioned the gloves. It's not generally known that Frederick's are yellow.'

'No, sir. But some people know.'

Drake's face was red, weathered and expressionless, just like the skin of the apple Thornhill had peeled for Susie. 'Anyway, it's all we've got to go on so far. We've found no one else who saw him up there. Not yet.'

'Mrs Frederick gave me a couple of photographs of her husband, and what seems like a pretty detailed list of his clothes. I'll get copies made.' Thornhill hesitated. 'We've still heard nothing from the railway police?'

Drake shook his head. 'And there's no evidence that he came back to Lydmouth from Gloucester, by train or any other way. Circulate his description to Gloucester. Bayswater's too. Perhaps someone saw them there. Get someone to talk to the dentist.' He picked out a sheet of paper from the sheaf of notes in front of him. 'You've seen Sergeant Kirby's list of missing items?'

'Yes, sir.'

'We know Bayswater usually carried a wallet inside his jacket pocket, which he left in his desk at night-time. It's not there, and we can't find his cheque book, either. But other bank books are still there, and also several gold sovereigns. A silver cigarette box is missing from the mantelpiece.' He looked up, running his thumb along his brush-like moustache. 'Any thoughts?'

'The obvious one: everything was in the study, sir – which suggests the intruder didn't go elsewhere in the house.'

'We haven't found a weapon yet, either.' Drake glanced down at the notes again. 'I gather a pair of pliers may be missing. Medium to large. Murray says it could have been something like that that killed him.'

'And if the tools were lying on the table on the veranda, the killer could have snatched the pliers on impulse.'

'All a bit speculative,' Drake said. 'And God knows how Frederick comes into this. He was long gone by the time Bayswater died. Unless he came back to Lydmouth.'

Thornhill coughed. 'It's possible the cases are separate. Frederick might have done a bunk – dozens of men do every year and there's no reason why he shouldn't be one of them. He could have lost his glove on the train, and Bayswater could have picked it up. Found it in his pocket when he got home and left it on his desk. Maybe it was knocked to the floor in the struggle. It's perfectly plausible. And if that's what happened, then Bayswater's death isn't connected with Frederick.'

'In that case, where does that leave us?'

Thornhill swallowed, and a sense of almost physical unease crept over him. 'There was bad blood between Dr Leddon and Dr Bayswater. Bayswater was blocking Leddon's plans for building new premises, and making life generally awkward for him. It wasn't necessarily personal – he was conducting a one-man war against the National Health Service, and Leddon happened to be the obvious target. Leddon felt cheated, and I think he may be having a hard time financially because of it. Suppose he decided to go and reason with Bayswater, and it turned into an argument that got out of hand. Leddon had the motive and the opportunity. And if the pliers were on that table, then he had the means as well. Afterwards, he tried to disguise it – make it seem as though Bayswater had surprised a burglar who had lashed out. It hangs together.'

Drake shook his head. 'But it's entirely circumstantial.' He looked curiously at Thornhill. 'You couldn't hang a dog on that evidence.'

Those last words, and the look on the DCC's face, lingered in Thornhill's mind. They were still there when he left Drake's office ten minutes later. Was he allowing his dislike for Leddon to influence the conduct of the case?

In the CID room, Porter was talking earnestly to the duty officer. They broke off as Thornhill entered.

'Something's come up, sir,' the duty officer said. 'Could be the Pisser again, or it could be quite different.'

'Nasty business, whoever done it,' Porter said.

Thornhill gazed from one man to the other. 'What's a nasty business?'

Porter explained that during the day someone had left two rats and a dead rabbit in Miss Francis's car at Raglan Court. Amy Gwyn-Thomas had blundered into the trap and fallen, hurting her head. He, Porter, had interviewed her at her home, where she was receiving medical attention.

The duty sergeant said, 'Anyone could break into those Morris Minors if they had a mind. Practically asking for it.'

'Rats,' Porter said slowly. 'I wonder if they were Bayswater's.'

'Why should they be?' Thornhill said sharply.

Porter blushed. 'No reason, sir, really, just Mr Prout said perhaps that's where they'd come from, the rabbit too, maybe. It's true there are an awful lot of rats in that garden.'

'But it's unlikely anyone could have got in there without our knowing since Saturday morning,' Thornhill said. 'If someone took them beforehand, that would mean—'

He broke off. It would mean the attack on Jill's car had been planned for some time, and not been the result of a moment's impulse. But was that making it too complicated? The idea was only a few steps removed from the sort of paranoid logic that saw everything as part of a gigantic, complex and hostile conspiracy.

St John's clock was striking eight as Thornhill left head-quarters. It was still misty, and the street lamps threw out fuzzy globes of discoloured light in the moisture-laden air. The fog made everything unreal, or rather real in a different way, so different rules applied. On impulse he drove up Albert Road. There was no harm in paying a call on Jill to see whether she was all right. In a way it was no more than his duty. She might be able to provide more information about the booby-trapped car.

He parked on the road outside the flats. He rang Jill's bell and waited with a strange mixture of fear, guilt and excitement for her to answer it. The door opened and there was Roger Leddon.

The doctor's eyes widened. 'Inspector – what can I do for you?'

'Is Miss Francis here?'

'Yes – you'd better come in, I suppose.'

Thornhill looked past the doctor to the closed door of the living-room. He said, 'Actually, sir, I also wanted a word with you as well. About Friday evening – could you tell me your movements from about six o'clock onwards?'

Leddon frowned. 'Why?'

'Just for the purpose of elimination. We're asking everyone whose fingerprints we've found at Grove House.'

'Of course mine were there.'

'Of course. So what were you doing on Friday evening?'

'Is this really necessary now? After surgery and a couple of house calls I had a drink with Miss Francis. Here, in this flat. I left about seven-thirty, perhaps a little later, and went upstairs. I cooked a bite to eat, read for a while and then went to bed. All very humdrum, I know, but there you are.'

'Thank you, sir,' Thornhill said. 'We may need to talk to you again, but that's fine for now. If I could just have a word with Miss Francis, I won't keep you much longer.'

Leddon ushered him into the living-room. Jill was mixing drinks at the sideboard. She had changed for the evening, into a dress that outlined her figure. She looked up at Thornhill, her face unreadable. A surge of desire ran through him.

'I've just heard about your car,' he said gruffly.

'That's what Howard came to the station for,' she said. 'To tell me. You remember? The boy on the platform.'

'How's Miss Gwyn-Thomas?'

'It was most unpleasant for her at the time, obviously. She's coping very well, though. Would you like a drink?'

Thornhill shook his head. 'Have you any idea what's behind this?'

'The rats? They're either a nasty little practical joke, which seems unlikely, or part of a campaign of intimidation.'

'Directed at you personally?'

'At the *Gazette*, of course.' She looked at him, her expression half amused, half challenging.

It was quite clear what she was implying, though neither of them was going to spell it out. If there was a campaign against the *Gazette*, then the obvious suspects were Ivor Fuggle and the *Post*. But suspicion was one thing, and proof was another. He had no doubt that the *Post*'s lawyers would be delighted to deal with any hint of slander or libel.

'Anyway,' she went on, 'Mr Porter has all the details. He wrote everything down in his notebook.'

There was nothing more to be said, not with Roger Leddon standing in the doorway. Thornhill wished them goodnight.

Leddon showed him out, an affable smile plastered across his handsome face. When Thornhill reached the car, he looked up at the windows of Jill's flat. The curtains were drawn.

What had he expected to see? Jill looking down and blowing him a surreptitious kiss?

He wondered what they were saying now, Jill and Leddon, whether they were discussing him, or whether his visit had been so insignificant to them that they had simply ignored it. Unhappiness lay sour and inert inside him like indigestion. He climbed into the car.

You're a fool, Thornhill told himself, a bloody middle-aged fool.

[Tuesday, 6 December]

I couldn't stop myself. I knew I might be caught. But after all these years of being careful, suddenly everything's different. Who cares, after all? – you might as well be hanged for a sheep as a lamb.

I didn't like writing that word. Hanged. Do it again. Hanged. HANGED.

That's what they do to murderers. Get used to it, it's only a word. Every time you say something or do something, it loses a little bit of its meaning. Hanged. Make the word stale by using it again and again, squeeze its meaning out of it, like squeezing air from someone's lungs, life from someone's body.

Hanged. Hanged.

Someone said today – on the radio? In the paper? – that the Forestry Commission are so keen to get rid of grey squirrels that they've doubled the rate they pay to pest officers. They pay two shillings a tail now. I wonder what they'd pay for someone like me. I wonder what my tail would be worth.

When do the tails begin to smell? I'm so worried about the smell. I can't smell anything yet. The cold must slow things down. If I can't add something that would take away the smell, perhaps I could cover it up somehow. There must be a way.

Have they found the bag and the glove? The biggest worry of all.

Chapter Thirty-Two

On Tuesday morning the alarm went off at seven o'clock. It was still dark outside. Jill lingered in the warmth of the bed. Her mouth was dry. She could not remember her dreams but she knew they had made her uneasy. She had slept heavily – the barbiturates had seen to that – but not well. She rolled her head from side to side on the pillow, trying to shake out some of the grey cotton wool that filled it.

The memory of the previous night insinuated itself into the forefront of her mind like a gatecrasher at a party. She had nearly allowed herself to be seduced. Roger Leddon was very good looking, very charming. They had both had enough to drink for desire to be heightened and inhibitions lowered. It had been nice to be wanted, too. If she were going to be brutally honest with herself, she would have to admit that she had liked the idea that a good-looking man found her attractive, especially one who was a little younger than she was.

So what had stopped them? It had been partly his impatience. He had been in too much of a hurry. But there had also been something he had said just before he lunged at her, something which had made her wonder whether she really liked him very much.

'You can see he's a family man, can't you? Monochrome sort of chap.'

'Who?' Jill had asked, though she guessed the answer

because they had been speculating about the lines of enquiry the police were following.

'The chief inspector. What's his name – Thornhill.'

There was no reason why she should take exception to the remark, which was arguably no more than the truth, and in any case she no longer had a reason to care what anyone thought of Richard Thornhill. Perhaps she would ask Roger Leddon for coffee this evening, just to show there were no hard feelings. Or perhaps not.

Jill counted to three and sat up, gasping at the cold, and reached for her dressing-gown. The more awake she became, the more the gatecrashers from yesterday's memories flocked into her mind. First the fruitless journey to London, followed by the equally fruitless attempt to talk to Richard. She remembered how Edith Thornhill had looked at her on the station platform at Lydmouth. There had been hatred in her face, Jill was sure, and she knew that Edith could be an implacable enemy. Jill was not used to being disliked and she found it uncomfortable. Then the booby-trapped car – the very thought of which made her feel physically ill. Looming in the shadows of yesterday's party was Fuggle, as implacable as Edith, though for different reasons. That was the trouble with a town the size of Lydmouth: emotions grew to strange, contorted shapes.

Jill left the flat at a quarter past eight – when she had phoned Charlotte the previous evening with the news that her trip to London had been fruitless, she had arranged to call in on her way to work. She walked across the park, where the mist hung in the air and moisture dripped from spectral trees.

At Troy House, Charlotte opened the front door almost as soon as Jill rang the bell. She looked pale and shrunken; her clothes sagged on her, which seemed against nature. Charlotte's majestic plumpness was evident in every photograph ever taken of her and should be an inalienable part of her birth-right.

The first thing she said was: 'What's this I hear about rats in your car?'

'Who told you?' Jill said, taken by surprise because she had hoped to keep this from Charlotte.

'Amy. She phoned last night to see how Philip was.'

Jill stepped into the house and unbuttoned her coat. 'It was unpleasant for her, obviously, but probably just someone's idea of a joke.'

Charlotte led the way down the hall to the kitchen. 'Non-sense,' she threw back over her shoulder with a touch of her old authority. 'It was a piece of carefully planned malice, aimed at either you personally or the *Gazette* – quite possibly both.'

'It could have been kids messing around.'

'You must feel very vulnerable living all by yourself. I wonder if you should move in with us for a while.'

'No, thank you,' Jill said rather more emphatically than good manners allowed. 'It's very thoughtful of you, but I'll be fine, I promise you.'

'It's Fuggle, of course,' Charlotte said, banging the kettle down on the stove. 'One way or another he's behind it. Who else could it be?'

Jill sat down at the kitchen table and rummaged in her handbag for cigarettes. 'You may well be right,' she said wearily.

'So you admit it?'

'You mustn't worry. If it is him, it shows how desperate he's getting.' Jill hurried on, aware her logic was not irreproachable. 'He's not stupid enough to do anything really serious.'

Charlotte sniffed. 'I wouldn't bank on that, dear. The fire at the printing works was serious. So was what happened to Johnny Cubbitt.'

'All we have to do is keep our nerve. I'm not going to let him bully me.'

Charlotte sighed, and as the breath left her so did her determination. She took one of Jill's cigarettes without asking and leaned across the table for a light.

'How's Philip?' Jill asked.

'Every day he's a little bit stronger. Dr Leddon's very pleased with him.'

'I'm so glad. Is he awake? May I go and say hello to him?'

Charlotte hesitated an instant too long. 'Yes, of course you may. He'd love to see you, I'm sure. And if you don't mind staying a few minutes, I could pop out to Roby's for a few things. We're very low on sugar and flour. They don't deliver any more, it's so annoying.' She inhaled another lungful of smoke. 'And I've run out of cigarettes. But perhaps I shouldn't go – Philip might need me.'

'I think you should go. A change of air will do you good.'

Twenty-five minutes later, having lost and found her purse, powdered her nose, changed her mind twice about going out, and changed it back again, Charlotte at last left the house. Philip's illness had worn away at her powers of decision as the ebb and flow of tides wear at the rocks of a beach.

Jill went upstairs and sat in the easy chair beside Philip's bed. He wore crisp clean pyjamas and was propped against snowy-white pillows. His hair had been brushed, his face had been shaved. He was pink and plump and outwardly placid, like an enormous middle-aged baby. But he was still the same old Philip underneath, a journalist to whom muck-raking came as easily as breathing. In a couple of minutes he had winkled out of her everything of importance about the current state of the *Gazette*.

'Charlotte told me about trying to borrow money. But she said you came back from London empty handed.'

'Randolph Haughton would help if he could. It's just that he's feeling the pinch a little at present.'

'With his income?'

'He's got a lot of expenses,' Jill said defensively. 'His uncle died and the death duties are crippling. But he did say he's going to have a word with Bernie Broadbent and see if they can put something together.'

Philip sat up. 'Well, that's hopeful. When will we hear?'

'I'm going up again on Thursday.'

Philip sank back against the pillows. 'What about collateral? It would be much easier if we could go to the bank.'

'But we can't. Not with the *Gazette*'s balance sheet over the last few years. Beggars can't be choosers.'

'Everything's going to pot,' he said quietly. 'This business with the rats – it's foul.'

'Don't worry. We've got through worse things than this. Leave it to Charlotte and me. Just concentrate on getting well – that's your job.'

Philip looked at her with watery eyes. 'Jill, if I wasn't . . . if I wasn't here, you'd keep an eye on Charlotte, wouldn't you?'

'Of course I would,' Jill snapped. 'But don't talk like—'

'She looks as tough as old boots,' he interrupted. 'But she's not, you know.'

'You're as tough as old boots too,' Jill said. 'And don't try to pretend otherwise.'

'I could have another heart attack at any time. Do you know what one of the nurses called me when she thought I wasn't awake? A cardiac cripple. The point is, Charlotte would be better off without me. She's just fading away with the strain. It's not fair to her.'

'Of course she wouldn't be better off without you,' Jill snapped. 'Don't be so bloody stupid.'

Philip grinned, which threw her off balance. 'I always liked seeing you get cross.' Neither of them spoke for a moment, and then he went on: 'I know it would be awful for her at first, but in the long run it would be better.'

He spoke with such authority that when Jill opened her mouth she found she had no words to say. Was that what love meant, she thought, knowing when it was time to leave?

The telephone began to ring. Glad of the diversion, Jill stood up. Still smiling as though relishing the memory of a joke, Philip waved her out of the room. Downstairs, Jill picked up the receiver and recited the Troy House number.

At the other end of the line, a man cleared his throat, a grimly familiar gurgle. 'Is that Miss Francis, by any chance? I'd like a word in Mrs Wemyss-Brown's shell-like ear, if I may.'

'I'm afraid she's out, Mr Fuggle.'

'You won't mind taking a message, I'm sure. After all, my dear, it concerns you.'

Fuggle paused, but Jill said nothing.

'Ask her from me if she's decided to sell yet,' he said.

'I will.'

'It's a generous offer, as I'm sure you know. Tell her I can't be sure how long it will remain open. These things are not up to me. I'm just the messenger boy, in a manner of speaking.'

'I'll tell her.'

'You've got that, have you? I can't be sure how long the offer will stay open.'

'I've got it. But she won't change her mind.'

'You can't be sure. Let's face it, my dear, we can't be sure of anything. Even life, eh? It's so uncertain these days, isn't it?'

Chapter Thirty-Three

PC Porter was not having a good morning. Perhaps Mr Thornhill's trick with the piece of string had something to be said for it after all, and he should have given it another try. Today he was on earlies again. He had failed to wake in time, with the result that he had been forced to shave in cold water, forgo breakfast and run through the dark, freezing streets all the way to headquarters, where he was greeted with a mug of cold tea and a reprimand that could have stripped paint from a Sherman tank.

At 9.30, there was a call from old Davies at the cemetery. Davies lived in the cottage by the gates and was responsible for maintenance and gardening as well as keeping an eye on the place. He told the duty sergeant that there had been a bit of trouble at one of the graves. Someone had scattered the flowers and daubed white paint over the headstone. The grave was one of the newer ones. It belonged to Ivor Fuggle's mother.

The duty sergeant covered the mouthpiece for a moment. 'Oh, bugger,' he said.

Davies had notified Mr Fuggle's wife, and it was she who had insisted he phoned the police.

'Off you go, chum,' the duty sergeant said to PC Porter afterwards. 'Fuggle's going to bust a blood vessel.'

'What do you reckon, Sarge? Who did it?'

'Eh? Maybe it's our old mate the Pisser. Maybe it's God

Almighty showing his disapproval. How the hell should I know?'

Porter cycled up to the top of Victoria Road. It was raining again, a steady, penetrating drizzle, and the cemetery was sodden and bedraggled. Davies took him down to inspect the desecrated grave.

'Shall I clean her up?' Davies asked.

'You'd better leave it for now,' Porter replied. 'Can we go somewhere dry and talk about this?'

They plodded back through the rain to the cottage by the gates. Porter hung up his helmet and cape in the porch. He sat in the warm, dry kitchen and wrote while Davies made tea and talked. Things were going very pleasantly until there was a loud rap on the window, so unexpected that Porter spilt sugar over his notebook. He looked up and saw the engorged face of Ivor Fuggle glaring at him on the other side of the glass.

When Davies opened the door, Fuggle pushed past him and stamped into the kitchen, shaking himself like an angry rain god. 'My wife phoned me and I came straight over from Framington,' he barked. 'I've just been to see the grave. It's bloody unbelievable. There's no respect any more, even for the dead.' He glared at Porter. 'And what are you lot doing about it? Sweet Fanny Adams, I'll be bound.'

'Well, sir,' Porter began, turning another page of his note-book. 'We're still—'

'No, you listen to me for a change. I want the CID involved, I don't want this left to some bumbling bobby.' Fuggle turned back to Davies and stabbed a finger at him. 'Leave the grave as it is. Don't clear up the mess, not yet. I've got a photographer on the way. This is going to be on the front page of the *Post*, you'll see.' He put his face very close to Porter's. 'I've a good mind to put your picture there too. It was you yesterday, wasn't it? Pestering my wife.'

Porter cycled back to headquarters and blurted out what had happened to the sergeant, who said, 'Oh Christ, so you've put your foot in it with Ivor Fuggle, have you? That's all we need. And now Mr Thornhill wants you upstairs. Get your skates on.'

Porter expected another reprimand to be waiting for him. But he found the chief inspector putting on his overcoat, with his mind on other things.

'I want you to take me back to Whistler's Lane,' Thornhill said. 'You can tell me what's been happening at the cemetery on the way.'

Porter wasn't sure whether to be flattered or alarmed. He knew Sergeant Kirby was on sick leave still but there were others Thornhill could have taken, including Dyke.

'I've ordered a car from the pool,' Thornhill said. 'A police car. I want this to look official.'

The rain had stopped for a while. They drove up to Whistler's Lane and Thornhill told Porter to pull up outside Viney Cottage. Joe Rodley answered the door. He was un-shaven and his eyes were bloodshot.

Thornhill introduced himself. 'I hear you and Broadbent's have parted company.'

Rodley shrugged. 'What's it to you?'

'We'd like to have another word with Mrs Rodley, if we may.'

'She's got a headache. Can't see no one.'

'Joe,' Mrs Rodley called, 'it's all right. It's not that bad.'

'Don't tire her,' Rodley said in a hoarse whisper. 'She won't rest when she should.' He paused and then added unexpect-edly, 'Please.'

The hallway was warm but Mrs Rodley's room was like the Western Desert at noon. Doreen was still in bed. There was a tray on the bedside table with the remains of her breakfast – a pot of tea for one, fragments of eggshell and two abandoned toast soldiers.

'Hello,' she said to Porter. 'I didn't think you'd be back so soon. Who's this?'

'I'm Detective Chief Inspector Thornhill, Mrs Rodley. We can come back later if this isn't a good time.'

She shook her head and her husband gave an angry sigh. 'It's all right, Joe. I get bad days sometimes, that's all, and to tell the truth I'm better off with a distraction.' She smiled at the three men and Porter remembered the way she had smiled all those years ago when she gave him the plum. 'So go on, then,' she said. 'Distract me. Sit down if you like, and Joe will take your coats.'

'There's no need, thanks,' Thornhill said. 'We won't be long. I just wanted to talk to you about the man you saw on Friday.'

Porter waited, conscious of Joe's hot eyes resting on him while Chief Inspector Thornhill took Mrs Rodley step by step through the information she had given Porter and Dyke the previous morning. He tried to make her be more precise about the time, and to describe the man more fully, but she told him nothing they did not already know. She would have told them if she could, Porter thought – he sensed that she had warmed to Thornhill, to the gentleness of his manner. He could not have explained how he knew this or why he was so certain, but he knew he was right.

The two police officers left the cottage and returned to the car. Porter started the engine and waited for Thornhill to tell him where to go.

The chief inspector said, 'Have the Rodleys any other source of income, do you know?'

'Doubt it, sir. I think the cottage is theirs. It was her dad's.'

'So things aren't going to be easy now Joe's lost his job? All right – drive on.'

They parked outside the Fuggles' dormer bungalow and walked up the drive. There was no sign of the Humber. A dog began to bark.

'That's her little terrier,' Porter said. 'If she's not in the house, she'll probably be in that barn or in the garden somewhere. They've got a lovely vegetable patch.'

Thornhill glanced at Porter but said nothing. He rang the front-door bell. The dog's yapping grew louder and more furious. They heard footsteps on the other side, the rattle of bolts and a key turning in the lock. The door opened a few inches and then stopped. It was on the chain, which wasn't something you often saw in Lydmouth.

'Yes,' said Mrs Fuggle. 'Who is it?'

Porter said, 'Hello, Mrs Fuggle. It's PC Porter again. You remember? I came to see you yesterday.'

The door closed in their faces. The chain rattled. The door opened more fully, and Mrs Fuggle waited for them to speak. Her hair was in curlers and covered in a headscarf. She wore a flowered nylon housecoat over her dress and a pair of unexpectedly frivolous pink slippers. She had put the terrier on his lead and looped the end over the newel post at the foot of the stairs. The dog strained towards the two police officers with such angry urgency that he nearly throttled himself.

'Mrs Fuggle? My name's Thornhill, Detective Chief Inspector Thornhill. May we come in?'

All this while, the dog yapped. Mrs Fuggle remained in the doorway.

'His name's Macbeth,' Porter said. 'He's a good guard dog, isn't he?'

Both Macbeth and his owner ignored this friendly overture. 'Well, what do you want this time?' Mrs Fuggle demanded.

'We're interested in tracing a man who may have come up the lane on Friday morning,' Thornhill said.

'I told him.' Mrs Fuggle nodded at Porter. 'I didn't see a thing.' Behind her, Macbeth took another step towards self-strangulation. She stepped back and unlooped the lead from the newel post. She lifted Macbeth, still barking, into her arms. 'Like I said, I was either in the kitchen or in the garden at the back. If he did come up here, I wouldn't have seen him.'

Her blunt-featured face was expressionless, the skin covered with a layer of make-up so thick it was like a mask. She scratched the top of Macbeth's head. Porter extended a hand towards the animal.

'Good doggie,' he said.

Macbeth sniffed the fingers and gave them a brief lick.

Mrs Fuggle stared at Porter. 'Have you been eating chocolate or something?'

'Do you get many walkers up here at this time of year?' Thornhill asked. 'Or anyone using the footpath at all?'

She glanced at him, her former hostility returning. 'How should I know? I'm not nosy like some. Listen, why are you pestering me? I've already told you twice – I didn't see this man. How many more times have I got to say it?'

Thornhill thanked her and said goodbye. He and Porter returned to the car. Instead of opening the door, however, Thornhill turned to the left and walked to the stile at the top of Whistler's Lane. The stile marked the point where the tarmac ended, beyond which the lane reverted to its older, more rural form – a muddy path between high hedgerows, its surface strewn with fragments of stone and hollowed beneath the level of the neighbouring fields by generations of passing feet. The weather had turned the path into a natural drain, carrying the rainwater down from the higher ground until it glided into the grille of a culvert just below the stile.

'It's a nice walk in summer,' Porter said, trying to introduce a cheerful note. 'But you'd need wellingtons now.'

Thornhill glanced at him. 'Was he wearing wellingtons?'

'Who?'

Thornhill sighed. 'The man we're looking for. Frederick.'

Porter thought for a moment and then said, 'No. Leastways, if he was, no one's mentioned it.'

'Exactly. So if he did go up that path, he'd have come back down with wet and muddy feet, maybe wet and muddy trousers as well.' Thornhill walked back to the car, saying over his shoulder, 'Or maybe he didn't go up that path at all. We'll try the other houses again, the ones between the Fuggles' and Viney Cottage.'

It was a waste of time. Either the houses were empty, or their residents hadn't seen anything on Friday morning. At last they went back to the car. Thornhill stared at the rain running down the windscreen. Porter thought longingly of a cup of tea.

'We'll go to the cemetery now,' Thornhill said. 'We've still got to catch our hooligan.'

'Maybe it's the Pisser,' Porter said.

'If it is, then Mr Prout's exploit with the fish slice wasn't quite as effective as he'd hoped.'

Porter started the engine and put the car in gear. 'Have you asked Dr Leddon, sir?'

'How does he come into this?' said Thornhill. 'Are you suggesting we ask him if anyone's been to see him with a damaged penis? He wouldn't tell us even if someone had.'

Porter let out the clutch with an uncharacteristic jerk. He reversed into the Fuggles' drive so that he could turn the car round.

'It wasn't that, sir.'

'Then what did you mean?'

'I thought maybe Dr Leddon might have seen the Pisser.'

They drove down Whistler's Lane in silence for a moment. Then Thornhill said, 'I don't understand. Seen him when?'

'On Friday night, sir.'

'What time was this?'

'I don't know. Maybe around midnight.'

'Why didn't you tell me before?'

'I didn't realise it was important, sir.'

They reached the bottom of Whistler's Lane and turned into Broad Street.

'Stop the car,' Thornhill said. 'I want to get this straight before we go any farther. Tell me exactly what happened.'

Porter pulled over to the kerb and switched off the engine. In fits and starts, he reminded Mr Thornhill about the piece of string and how he had dangled it outside the window and gone to bed; and how – here Porter was careful to make it clear that Thornhill was in no way to blame for this – someone had tugged the string late in the evening, waking him. Porter thought he had seen somebody turning into St John's Passage, but he couldn't be sure. While he was out of bed, smoking a cigarette and just about to close the curtains, he had heard a second set of footsteps and seen Dr Leddon walking along the opposite pavement and then turning up Albert Road.

'Which way was he coming from?'

'From the war memorial, sir.'

'You actually saw him that far along Broad Street? So he might have come down the High Street?'

Porter shook his head. 'When I looked out he was between Whistler's Lane and Albert Road.'

'So he could have come from Bayswater's? From Grove House? Can't you see the importance of that, man?'

Porter stared unhappily at his hands, which were clamped to the steering wheel. 'Yes, sir.'

'You're absolutely sure it was Leddon?'

'Oh yes, sir – I could see him under the street light, and

anyway he's got this way of wearing his hat, sort of tilted back on his head.'

Thornhill nodded. 'If only you could put an exact time on it. Are you sure you didn't look at your watch? Or hear the church clock striking?'

Porter shook his head. Then he brightened. 'I think I heard the Pisser just afterwards, though.'

'You heard the Pisser, too,' Thornhill said in a very quiet voice. 'You mean you looked out, and there he was?'

'No, sir, not that. Mynott's is only round the corner from St John's Passage, look, and I heard this awful shrieking, like a cat or something, just after I got back into bed. So it must have been when Mr Prout hit his . . . his you-know-what with the fish slice.'

'How long after you saw Leddon?'

Porter wrinkled his forehead. 'I'm not sure, sir. About five minutes? I heard the yelling and someone running. I got out of bed, but I couldn't see no one.'

'So what did you do then?'

'I went to sleep, sir.'

Chapter Thirty-Four

At half-past ten on Tuesday morning, Jill Francis left the *Gazette* and walked up the High Street to Police Head-quarters. She asked for Detective Chief Inspector Thornhill, explaining that he wanted her to make a formal statement.

'He's not available, miss,' the man on the desk said. 'But that don't matter. He'd get someone else to do it anyway.'

She felt simultaneously diminished, relieved and annoyed. A youthful constable showed her into a small office on the ground floor and fetched her a cup of weak, milky coffee that tasted as though it had been made in a tea urn. After one sip she pushed aside the cup and lit a cigarette.

After a while, a detective sergeant and a stenographer, neither of whom she knew, joined her and took her through the process of making a statement. Yet again she described how she had found Dr Bayswater's body on Saturday morn-ing. Repetition had drained significance from the memory, leaving behind a sludge of unease. She spoke mechanically, with most of her attention elsewhere.

Was Richard Thornhill unavailable because he was in the building but did not want to see her? She pushed the question from her mind and found Ivor Fuggle filling the resulting vacuum. She knew from experience how ruthless he could be in pursuit of a story. Now, when the stakes were even higher, she had little doubt that he was capable of going one step farther.

Since Philip was ill and Charlotte a mere shadow of her former self, only she herself stood in Fuggle's way. The thought made her anxious, then angry. It was quite simple, she told herself: if she carried on as she was doing, Fuggle would win in a matter of weeks, perhaps, certainly months. It followed that there was simply no point in pursuing a purely defensive strategy. Both she and the *Gazette* were too vulnerable; and time and money were running out. Their only hope lay in attack.

'We'll have it typed up and ask you to come and sign it,' the sergeant said in a hard, monotonous voice like a dentist's drill. 'You're not intending to leave Lydmouth in the next few days? It's possible we may need to have a word with you again.'

'I'm going up to London on Thursday,' Jill said. 'Otherwise, I'm staying here.'

She walked back to the *Gazette*. She felt grubby, in need of a bath. Why was it that officials always made one feel guilty, or at least on trial for unknown crimes? The sergeant had been perfectly polite yet somehow she had come away feeling that she was in some respect responsible for Bayswater's death.

What would Philip do now, if he were well enough? She knew the answer immediately. When she got back to the office, she went up to see Amy.

'How are you feeling?'

'I'm fine,' Amy said, lifting her chin and straightening her spine as though on parade. 'One can't let a few rats upset one. Can one?'

'I've got a couple of meetings before lunch, haven't I? Would you reschedule them for this afternoon? When you've done that I'd like you to make coffee for us both and come into my room. There's something I want to talk to you about.'

Amy's face portrayed surprise, pride and curiosity in a swift sequence of emotions. Jill smiled at her and went into the editor's office, closing the door behind her. She took off her hat and coat and sat in the armchair by the window.

Glistening umbrellas paraded along the pavement below, concealing their owners. Everyone concealed something. Whether intentionally or unintentionally didn't matter. No one was invulnerable. Fuggle must have a weakness somewhere. It was simply a matter of finding it.

There was a knock at the door and Amy came in with a tray.

'I found that picture in Wednesday's *Post*,' she said. 'The one with the photo of Mr and Mrs Fuggle.'

While Amy was pouring the coffee, Jill studied the photograph. *The* Post's *editor Mr Ivor Fuggle and his wife Genevieve share a joke with Lady Ruispidge.* There was no doubt: Mrs Fuggle was the woman she had seen with the terrier.

She gave Amy a cigarette. 'I want to pick your brains,' she said as she leaned across with the lighter. 'I think you know more about Lydmouth than anyone else on this newspaper. And you've got a pretty good idea of the state we're in.'

Amy nodded, her eyes bird bright. 'It's the *Post*, isn't it?' she said in a husky, conspiratorial voice. 'I know things are very difficult.'

'Of course they are. The trouble is, they're even worse than we thought.' She sipped her coffee. 'This mustn't go beyond you and me, but I'm very much afraid that some of our problems at present have been caused by Ivor Fuggle. I don't mean the straightforward rivalry between us and the *Post* – it's not doing us any good, but that's nothing new, and at least it's all above board in its way. I mean the other things.'

'The rats?' Amy breathed.

'Yes, and the fire in the printing works, and Mr Cubbitt getting beaten up by an anonymous drunk and also, oh so conveniently, having the offer of a job from one of the *Post*'s sister papers. And here's something you don't know about:

Fuggle's been talking to Mrs Wemyss-Brown in what I can only describe as a threatening way. He's trying to browbeat her into selling out, probably at an absurdly low price.'

'He's a horrible man,' Amy said with a shiver. 'But I'm not at all sure what we can do unless we catch him red handed—'

Jill shook her head. 'He's not a fool. He's not going to do the dirty work himself.' She took a deep breath, hating herself and hating Fuggle for the depths he was forcing her to plumb. 'You said his mother had the reputation of being a bit of a battleaxe, and she was housebound. What actually happened when she died? Was it at the house?'

Amy nodded. 'They say he went in with her morning cup of tea before he went to work and just found her there. Stiff and cold.'

'And afterwards?'

'He had some sort of a breakdown – he was on sick leave for a couple of months at least and he used to go and moon around her grave in the cemetery. It was very strange.' Amy hesitated and then added, 'I suppose he'd never had to live on his own before.'

'It's not easy,' Jill said.

'No.' Amy's eyes met Jill's and a spark of understanding passed between them. 'Well – I always think women cope with these things far better than men. He just couldn't stand his own company for very long. It's funny, isn't it, you wouldn't think a man like that would be afraid of being left alone. And Mr Fuggle always seemed so certain of himself. I suppose some men—'

Jill refused to let the conversation be diverted into generalities. 'So he went to Bournemouth and that's where he met Miss . . . Miss whoever it was who became his wife. How did they actually meet?'

'Genevieve – that's Mrs Fuggle, of course – told Doreen

that they happened to share a table at teatime, and they got talking. She's been interested in spiritualism for years. Mr Fuggle must have liked something about her even if he didn't think much of the seance – they kept in touch after he came back to Lydmouth. Doreen says it all seemed to happen very quickly.'

'Where does Mrs Fuggle come from?'

'Do you know, I'm not quite sure. I think she was living in Bournemouth, not just staying there. It was a private hotel, you see, that's where they met. She was probably getting the off-season rate. You know how they like to fill these places during the winter. You can find some real bargains.'

Jill thought of the grim shapeless woman dragging her horrible little dog through the park and into the cemetery. She thought about the miniature turd on the grave of Mr Fuggle's mother. She said, 'Is she happy, do you think?'

Amy became a little pinker than usual. 'Well, I'm sure I wouldn't know. As I told you the other day, I have met her once or twice at Doreen's but Genevieve's not easy to get to know. Not the sort to wear her heart on her sleeve.'

'I really meant is she happy with her husband?'

'Yes,' Amy said, drawing the word out. 'I rather thought you did.' She lowered her voice and hissed, 'Separate rooms, I believe. I don't think Mr Fuggle is very active in that department. Anyway, that's what Doreen thinks, and she should know if anyone does.'

'But they get on all right?'

'She's always very keen to make sure things are just so at home for him. I wondered if she was a bit scared of him. Not that she'd complain, even to Doreen – she's a very private woman, terribly shy.'

Jill poured them more coffee. 'Had she lived in Bournemouth long?'

'I don't know.'

'Is there any way we can find out the name of the hotel?'

Amy shook her head. 'Apart from asking her, which I suppose wouldn't do at all.'

'Marriage certificate?'

'No, that wouldn't help. She came to stay in Lydmouth for over a month before the wedding. That bed-and-breakfast in Castle Street – do you know it? It's the house with the wisteria all over the front.'

'At least we can find out her maiden name. Where were they married? At the registry office?'

'In the Baptist chapel.' Amy sat up sharply. 'Now there's a thought. Ronald played the organ at their wedding. I've a feeling she wrote to him about it before she came to Lydmouth, so that must have been from Bournemouth. There was a bit of a fuss, I think – there was a hymn Mr Fuggle wanted because it had been a favourite of his mother's but Genevieve thought it was unlucky for some reason. I'll ask him if you like – I'll pop round to the shop at lunchtime.'

Chapter Thirty-Five

I n Lydmouth, as in so many places, it wasn't what you knew that counted but who; and often it wasn't what they said that mattered but what they didn't say. A silence was better than a nod or a wink, a nod and a wink were better than words, and anything was preferable to committing yourself in writing.

By the end of the morning, Richard Thornhill had the following items of information about Roger Leddon at his disposal. He had an uncomfortably large overdraft. Shortage of suitable accommodation meant he was spending a small fortune leasing surgery premises whose nature and location were not ideal. He had been forced to negotiate an extension to his overdraft in order to pay the last quarter's rent on the Raglan Court flat.

In the last few months, Leddon had held a number of informal discussions with the Family Doctor Service's Executive Council, the Local Health Service and the Planning Department of the District Council. These had concerned the possibility of a new, jointly financed surgery and health centre in the southern part of Lydmouth.

Finally, Wilfred Shipston, the solicitor who had drawn up Dr Bayswater's will and who had been appointed executor, had hinted broadly that Dr Leddon had already expressed a strong interest in buying a substantial part of the land attached to Grove House.

After lunch, Thornhill drove to Chepstow Road and parked

on the tarmac apron in front of the surgery building. This was little more than a large, rectangular shed with clapboarded wooden walls dark with creosote. At one end, a flue belched smoke into the sky. On the left was a small parking area empty of cars.

Thornhill went inside. He passed through a vestibule into a long waiting-room where nobody was waiting. In one of the farther corners was an L-shaped counter behind which a receptionist was filing cards. Next to her enclosure was another door, presumably leading to the doctor's room.

'Good afternoon,' Thornhill said.

After a calculated pause, the woman looked up, an index finger marking her place in the card file. She was small, and as thin as a greyhound. She wore glasses with heavy, angular frames that extended at the outer corners in a manner that reminded Thornhill of the tail fins of American cars.

'We're not open. Surgery times are in the lobby. Afternoon surgery begins at three-forty-five. Are you registered with us? I can make you an appointment if you want.'

'I don't want an appointment,' Thornhill said. 'I want to see Dr Leddon.'

'I'm afraid you'll have to wait your turn like everyone else.'

Thornhill laid his warrant card on the counter. 'I'm not a patient. I'm a police officer.'

He watched her face change as she saw the card and heard his words. Her eyes widened. Her cheeks twitched. Then came a tentative smile. He was used to seeing how announcing his profession affected people, even the innocent, and if he were honest, he would have to admit that part of him relished it.

He nodded at the closed door beside the counter. 'Is he in?'

'No, no I'm afraid he's not. Is there anything I can help with?'

'When is he due back?'

'It could be any time. He just popped out for a bite of lunch. If you like I can take a message or—'

'I'll wait, thank you,' Thornhill said.

He sat down, took a newspaper from the pocket of his raincoat. The receptionist offered him tea, which he declined. He stared at the newsprint but his mind drifted back to Edith and what she had said the other night. If either of them had summoned up the courage to raise the subject of divorce, he had always assumed it would be himself. He felt she had, in some mysterious way, contrived to outflank him.

A few minutes later he heard the sound of a car pulling off the road.

The receptionist looked out of the window. 'It's doctor,' she said, her thin face glowing, and the omission of the definite article bestowed on her employer a quality not far removed from divinity.

Thornhill folded his newspaper. 'Thank you.'

He went outside. Leddon was standing by the open door of his car, leaning inside to pick something up from the back seat. He straightened as he heard Thornhill's footsteps approaching.

'Oh – it's you.'

'Good afternoon, Doctor.'

'What can I do for you?'

'I understand you want to buy some of Dr Bayswater's garden?'

'Who told you that?'

Thornhill said, 'I imagine it will be a weight off your mind if that land behind Grove House becomes available.' He glanced back at the ramshackle building behind them. 'That can't be very satisfactory for anyone.'

'I appreciate your concern, Chief Inspector, but if you'll excuse me I haven't got all day to stand around chatting. And if there's something you'd like to say, why don't we go inside? It won't have escaped your notice that it's raining.'

'This won't take long. It's just that I was curious about your movements on Friday evening.'

Leddon turned aside to slam the car door. 'I've already told you. For most of the evening I was by myself in my flat. From about seven-thirty onwards. Dreary but unfortunately true.'

'So you didn't go out at all? You're sure?'

The doctor was already walking towards the door of the surgery. 'I told you. No.'

'Would your answer be the same if I told you that we have a highly reputable witness who saw you in Broad Street on Friday evening, at about a quarter to eleven? According to the witness you were walking along the pavement between Whistler's Lane and Albert Road.'

Leddon stopped. White faced and wide eyed, he stared at Thornhill.

'The witness is prepared to swear to this in court.' Thornhill was now enjoying himself, as one does when duty and pleasure march together. 'So in the light of that, I wonder if you wish to modify your earlier statement.'

The younger man swallowed and licked his lips. Thornhill heard a car drawing up behind him. He glanced over his shoulder. It was a grey Humber Hawk. Ivor Fuggle rolled down the driver's window.

'Chief Inspector,' Fuggle said. There were white blotches on his cheeks and forehead. The hand on the steering wheel was trembling. 'I want a word with you. And there's no bloody time like the present, is there?'

Chapter Thirty-Six

In 1893 Amy Gwyn-Thomas's mother had been encouraged or compelled to embroider a text in coloured wools. A wavering border of alternating flowers and crosses enclosed a text in mauve letters which staggered from left to right. SOW A KINDNESS: REAP A BLESSING.

Framed in dark-stained pine, the text had hung over her mother's bed – first as a child, then as a married woman, and at last as a widow living and dying in a high, narrow bed in her unmarried daughter's spare room. Now her mother was dead, and Amy had redecorated the spare room, disposed of most of her mother's clothes and put the embroidery in the bottom of a drawer beneath several layers of spare blankets.

The text, however, which Amy had known all her life, was not so easily disposed of. It surfaced regularly in her memory as a moral promissory note on those occasions when she did someone a good turn.

SOW A KINDNESS: REAP A BLESSING.

In the early evening of Tuesday, 6 December, Amy called at Troy House, determined to sow as many kindnesses as possible in the time at her disposal before joining Ronald Prout outside the Rex Cinema for the eight o'clock performance.

Since Philip's illness, Amy had become one of the Wemyss-Browns' most regular visitors. Her philanthropy was motivated by the memory of an unrequited passion for Philip, by a generalised and not entirely altruistic loyalty to her employers, and by the hope of a future harvest of blessings. There was also the undeniable pleasure of knowing oneself to be useful, always more agreeable than being used.

'Now why don't you have a nice sit-down?' she ordered Charlotte. 'Put your feet up for five minutes. I'll put the kettle on.'

'I've just had some tea, thank you.' Nevertheless Charlotte stood irresolute, poised between the chair and the sink. 'Anyway, Amy, it's awfully kind of you, but should you be here? I'm sure Dr Leddon wouldn't approve after that horrible business yesterday. You should be taking it easy.'

Amy flashed a smile at her as water sprayed over the floor. 'Whoops!' She tightened the tap. 'It's all right, I feel much better now. Of course, it was a shock at the time but everyone's been so nice about it that I've managed to put it behind me. Least said, soonest mended – that's what Ronald says. Mind you, he was absolutely furious. He says it simply wouldn't have happened if magistrates weren't so wishy-washy nowadays. He's all for corporal punishment himself.'

'Yes,' said Charlotte, turning away and wondering how many more samples of the wisdom of Ronald Prout she would receive this evening. 'I'm sure he's got a point. I don't think I will have any tea, thanks – do have some yourself if you'd like to.'

This was not what Amy had in mind at all. Instead she washed up two cups and saucers that were already clean. She offered to prepare the invalid a meal, and also to change his sheets. Charlotte declined both offers with unexpected vigour. Philip was dozing, she said, and she didn't want him disturbed.

'I know!' Amy said. 'I'll do a little dusting. It's so easy to let things slide when you're pressed for time, isn't it? Why don't I do a little dusting in the drawing-room?'

'That would be very kind,' Charlotte said with indecent eagerness. 'Do you know, I might sit down after all.'

Amy enjoyed the excitement of finding the dusters and the polish. She put on a housecoat which was too short and too wide for her. Charlotte provided her with dusting gloves and a dustpan and brush.

The big drawing-room was at the front of the house. The air struck cold after the warmth of the kitchen. Amy flicked on the light. The chandelier blazed with a harsh, unforgiving glare. The curtains were open. The panes of the bay window were black mirrors, reflecting herself as an array of dark ghosts hesitating in a series of doorways. She took a step towards the window, meaning to draw the curtains, not so much to shut out the darkness as to prevent her seeing these fragmented versions of herself.

What happened next happened so quickly that the events trod on each other's heels. It was only afterwards, when Amy was questioned about it again and again, that she was able to establish their probable sequence.

First, a jagged star appeared in one of the black mirrors – the upper of the two central sashes of the window. This was accompanied by the shockingly abrasive sound of breaking glass. Then came the tinkle of the fragments falling on tables and chairs and rugs, a variety of hard and soft landings. A current of cold air rushed like a wraith across the drawing-room, through the door and into the body of the house.

Glass sparkled like frost, like diamonds, at Amy's feet. Among the glass, by the carved wooden leg of the Victorian armchair, was a curious anomaly – a brightly coloured label. Amy was not close enough to read the words on the label. But there was no need. She recognised the design immediately – the brightly coloured sun containing a smiling human face. The words said: KIA-ORA SUNCRUSH ORANGE DRINK.

All these things happened in an instant, and then they lodged somewhere in her memory. At the time, she barely noticed them, which was hardly surprising. Her attention was entirely diverted by the sheet of flame erupting from the rug on which she was standing.

Wednesday, 7 December

Fear feels like grief, and grief feels like hunger, a sort of aching absence. But how can nothing feel pain?

I wish I knew why it had to be like this. I never wanted to hurt anyone or to be hurt. I never wanted to live like this. All I ever wanted was to be myself. Surely everyone deserves that?

I think it's beginning to smell. I'll have to do something soon.

Quicklime – but imagine, going into a chemist's and asking for half a hundredweight of quicklime – and of course it might do only part of the job. What about acid? I remember reading about Haigh a few years ago. He put that old woman in a forty-gallon drum of sulphuric acid. But of course there's the same problem. I don't know where I could find that without arousing suspicion.

How very odd. I was beginning to feel quite panicky then. Unreal. This can't be me. A few minutes ago, when I had written the words above, I thought I'd go and make myself a cup of tea in the kitchen. On the way, I remembered a film I'd seen at the Rex – The Wooden Horse. Suddenly – and it was like a revelation – it showed me the answer to my problem.

So simple. Earth and patience.

Everything must have looked terribly bleak for those men in their prisoner-of-war camp. But they were very patient. They burrowed their tunnel, inch by inch, very slowly, very patiently, so as not to alarm the guards, and took away the earth in little bags and scattered it over the parade ground.

I shall do the same but in reverse. Little by little, I'll BRING the earth. I will be patient. Gradually everything will be covered. There's no hurry, not really, not if I don't panic. It's so cold and dreary. Anyway, no one goes there but me. So there it is.

Earth and patience.

Chapter Thirty-Seven

It was mid-morning but the lights were on. The huge, ribbed radiators below the windows pumped out heat that sent the layers of smoke swirling in grey arabesques beneath the high ceiling. The fug was filled with the steady rumble of men's chatter, so different from women's.

Jill Francis was five minutes early. The room was already crowded, far more so than usual. In view of the circumstances, Drake had brought forward the press conference to Wednesday. A stringer based in Swindon waved at her and indicated a vacant seat beside him. They had known each other slightly in London before he lost his staff job on the *Daily Express*. She went to join him, squeezing past Fuggle's chair.

Fuggle's face was redder than usual and he had cut himself shaving. Jill looked down on him as she passed, at the wisps of greasy hair surrounding the pink, gleaming bald patch. For an instant, in the grey haze of the room, he looked like quite a different form of life: something glimpsed beneath the shifting surface of a sunless sea; shapeless and malevolent, like a jellyfish.

Her acquaintance leaned towards her. 'What the hell are they getting up to in this town? Is it something in the diet or just inbreeding?'

Before Jill could reply, the door opened and Drake came into the conference room, followed by Thornhill.

The man beside her gave a low whistle. 'They must be in a

flap,' he murmured. 'Two top brass. And we don't usually get Brer Fox himself.'

'Brer Fox?' Jill said, momentarily diverted.

'Drake – the Deputy Chief Constable. Was he after your time here?'

'I left just after he came.'

'Everyone calls him Brer Fox because of his colouring. Don't you think he looks like a fox? He acts like one sometimes, I'll tell you that.'

The briefing began. Talking in a quiet, clipped voice, Drake outlined the official view of recent events, emphasising his points occasionally by tapping the sheet of paper in front of him with a pencil. Jill noticed that the lead of the pencil never broke. She found herself looking at the pencil, at that black point, rather than listening to what Drake was saying. At last he finished, and called for questions.

Ivor Fuggle grunted and thrust his heavy shoulders forward. 'You told us nothing we don't already know, Mr Drake,' he said. 'We need to reassure our readers that they can sleep sound in their beds at night. Surely that's what you'd like us to do? But how can we do that if there's every chance some homicidal maniac will chuck a Molotov cocktail through their front window or hit them over the head with a blunt instrument?'

'As I already told you, Mr Fuggle,' Drake said, 'we are doing everything to catch the person or persons responsible.'

'I'm sure we all hope that Mr Wemyss-Brown's going to get better soon,' Fuggle said, glancing piously at the ceiling with its moulded, nicotine-stained plaster. 'But the fact remains he's a very ill man, and a shock like that could have killed him.'

'We're aware of that. We're following a number of leads.'

'But it's not good enough, is it? My readers don't want

leads, they want results. And that's what the police are failing to provide. What about poor Dr Bayswater? Or the vandals who go round beating people up and urinating through their letter boxes? And folks are not even safe if they're dead, are they? I noticed you didn't mention what's been going on at the cemetery—'

'The desecration of the grave belonging to your mother, Mr Fuggle?' Drake interrupted. 'I can assure you we're investigating that as well.'

'No doubt just as successfully as the rest. When are you going to call in the Yard?'

'If and when that proves necessary, you can rest assured that the press will be informed.'

'We need them now. So why don't you call them now?'

'That's a decision for us.' Drake stared round the room, his chin lifting. 'There will be time for more questions later but I know Detective Chief Inspector Thornhill has another matter he'd like to raise with you first. In this force, as you know, we place great importance on co-operating with the press. Chief Inspector?'

Thornhill stood up. 'As some of you will be aware, we are trying to trace the whereabouts and last known movements of a recent visitor to Lydmouth. He lives in London, and his wife has reported him missing. He is believed to have left Lydmouth by train on Friday morning but we are keen to establish where he went and whom he met before he caught the train. There's also a possibility that he left the train at Gloucester or at another station on his way to London. Our Photographic Section is making copies of a photograph of him, and we will be sending these out to you very shortly, together with a description. We'd be grateful if you'd ask your readers to get in touch with us if they saw this man on Friday, or have seen him since then. His name is Paul Frederick, and he lives in London. He is a radio and television engineer who was working here for a couple of days. Any questions?'

Jill raised her finger. 'Do the police believe that Mr Frederick may be linked in any way to these other incidents?'

'It's too early to say, Miss Francis.'

'Bloody incompetence,' Fuggle muttered. He raised his voice: 'My readers are beginning to believe that the police have lost the ability to do their job. There's not much law and order here, is there? Judging by our mailbag, they think there's an epidemic of crime and it's spreading. And it's hard to say they're wrong, eh? It's like Dodge City around here, and no sign of Wyatt Earp.'

'Mr Fuggle, we—'

'Once folks get the idea they can get away with anything, then what's to stop them trying? What's your comment on that, Chief Inspector? Do you think the public have lost faith in their police force?'

'I'll take that,' Drake said, glaring across the table. 'What we have here is a handful of incidents, some of them very serious, some less so. We have every hope that we can bring the culprits to book. The one thing we don't need, Mr Fuggle, is irresponsible reporting in the press. Believe me, that's what can really damage public confidence.'

There was a short, uncomfortable silence, and then the man from the *Citizen* chipped in to ask whether the police had any evidence connecting Paul Frederick with Gloucester. Other questions followed, which added little to what had already been discussed.

Neither Fuggle nor Jill said anything more. Jill felt weak, as though recovering from an illness. At first she blamed the stuffiness of the room, but then it occurred to her that shock might be responsible. If the fire had spread more quickly, if Philip had tried to do something about it, if Charlotte had been sleeping – things had been bad enough as they were, but they might have been much worse. Philip and Charlotte could have died last night. So, for that matter, could Amy.

On one level of her mind she continued to be aware of the questions and answers bouncing to and fro across the table. But the words had lost their significance and become mere sounds that followed an alien and inexorable pattern of their own: a logic terrifying in its inhumanity, like shingle shifting on a shore as the sea sucked at the land. Monsters lurked in the sea, monsters like jellyfish, monsters like Ivor Fuggle.

She tried to focus on safe, external details – the rasp of the match as Fuggle lit his fourth cigarette in the last half-hour; the clock on the wall whose minute hand staggered slowly down the right-hand side of the dial; Richard Thornhill's fingers twisting a fountain pen; the network of scars and scratches on the old mahogany table around which they sat. The world went on, these things said, even a world where Molotov cocktails were thrown through drawing-room windows, where old men were bludgeoned to death in their own homes.

When the briefing was over, she was one of the first outside. Sheltering under her umbrella, she waited on the pavement. Despite the cold and the rain, the air refreshed her. She heard behind her the sound of a man clearing his throat and bringing up what sounded like a bucket-load of greasy sludge.

'Still here, Miss Francis?' Fuggle loomed over her, bowing his head so that the spokes of his umbrella clashed with hers. 'Not a very edifying session, was it? Too many questions unanswered.'

'Oh yes, I quite agree,' Jill said, fired with the flaring energy of anger. 'For example, is it possible that you had something to do with the arson attack on Troy House last night?'

Fuggle glanced round, as though fearing or perhaps hoping for witnesses. 'I can't think what on earth you mean.'

'You know perfectly well. You're the only person who stands to gain from all this. People could have died, do you realise that? As it was, Miss Gwyn-Thomas—'

He placed his gloved hand on her arm and gave what at first appeared to be a friendly squeeze. But the grip tightened and tightened. For an instant Jill saw him for what he truly was, with all pretence of civilised behaviour stripped away. She snarled at him and wrenched her arm away.

'Dear me, Miss Francis. What an extraordinary accusation. Now, where was I between six and seven yesterday evening? Let me think. Oh yes – I have it. The Chief Constable was having a little cocktail party and he was kind enough to ask me to drop in. So at the time in question I was probably chatting to Mr Hendry. Or if it wasn't him it was Sir Anthony Ruispidge, or Lady Ruispidge, or Mr and Mrs George or Mr Shipston or possibly the vicar. I'm sure any of them would be happy to vouch for me.'

'You know quite well what I mean,' she hissed, aware that she sounded pettish, even childish. 'I'm not suggesting you did it yourself. I'm suggesting that you hired someone to do your dirty work for you, just as you hired someone else to set fire to the printing works at the *Gazette* and beat up poor Mr Cubbitt. It's working out very well for you, isn't it? You're not just trying to damage the *Gazette*, you're also trying to attract readers and advertisers.'

'My dear young lady—'

'I'm not your dear anything.' Nor did she feel young or ladylike. 'You're spreading fear and hysteria throughout the town and undermining the morale of the police, just so you and the *Post* can pose as a bastion of law and order. It's . . . it's cheap and nasty, Mr Fuggle, just like you.'

He looked surprised, and shocked. She felt a brief stab of satisfaction. She had at least given him something he was not expecting. Even as she watched, though, she saw a smile beginning to spread across his fat red face. Was he bluffing or had she made a terrible mistake?

She wheeled abruptly away and strode down the High Street through the rain, careless of puddles, careless of passers-by. If she stopped moving, she thought, her legs might no longer be able to bear her weight: she would crumple to the pavement in an untidy, rubbery blob of something not quite human and not quite inanimate.

She saw Sergeant Kirby coming the other way. He was very pale, she thought, and his cheekbones were more prominent, which made him look somehow younger. He raised a hand and opened his mouth as if about to greet her, and then looked surprised as she swept on.

Hatred corroded the emotions. She had not realised she could hate anyone as much as she hated Ivor Fuggle. She hated him partly because he wanted to hurt those she was fond of and partly because she was afraid of him. Her hatred stripped him of his humanity.

The consequence of this was what truly shocked her most of all: he had made her feel that perhaps it would be preferable to be a puddle on the pavement rather than a thinking, feeling, upright human being. She could cheerfully murder him.

Except, she told herself, for her it would hardly count as murder, any more than causing the death of those rats he had put in her car. It would merely be a necessary killing, not murder: so the normal rules of civilised conduct would not apply. You cannot murder something that isn't quite human.

Which led in turn to the consequence that shocked her most of all: to the niggling fear that to have reached this stage was to be no longer quite human oneself.

Chapter Thirty-Eight

Brian Kirby's hand trembled as he put the coffee cup down on the desk. He took out a cigarette and patted his jacket pockets, searching for matches.

'You shouldn't have come in,' Thornhill said.

'I'm fine, sir. Maybe I look a bit seedy, but that's all.'

Thornhill grunted. He could send Kirby home but he wouldn't be doing anyone any favours. CID was short handed enough as it was. As for Kirby, he wouldn't do his chances of promotion any good if he was skulking at home looking pale and interesting when all hell was breaking loose.

'How's Joan?'

'Blooming,' Kirby said, sounding disgruntled. 'Ten days to go, according to the quack. But she'll be glad when the baby comes. It's the waiting. Tell you who doesn't look very well, though. Miss Francis. I passed her on the way here just now and she looked like death warmed up.'

Thornhill's internal organs appeared to lurch as if they had hit an air pocket. 'Looked all right at the press conference. She's got a lot on her plate at present.'

'She wasn't at Troy House last night, was she?'

'Not until after the fire.'

'Didn't any of the neighbours notice something? It wasn't exactly the middle of the night.'

Thornhill shook his head. 'It's not that sort of neighbour-hood. Everyone else in the road seemed to have their curtains drawn. Anyway, most of them were in their kitchens at that time, at the back of their houses.'

'Fire at the *Gazette* – a fire at Troy House. Poor old Cubbitt getting beaten up the other month. The rats in Miss Francis's car. It all points one way.'

'It won't work, Brian. As far as we can tell, at the precise time the Molotov cocktail went through the window of Troy House, Fuggle was haranguing Mr Hendry over a glass of dry sherry four miles away.'

'So? He's got someone else to do his dirty work.'

'Maybe. But the question is who, and how do we prove it? In your absence, we've got a little farther with the Bayswater business, though. Porter saw Leddon walking up Broad Street on the night that Bayswater died.'

'Porter! Then why—?'

Thornhill held up a hand like a constable halting a flow of traffic. 'Don't ask. We've also confirmed that Leddon's financially over-stretched, and that he believes the long-term solution to all his problems involves buying the garden at Grove House and building a new surgery there. We knew that already, of course, but we now know he's already been on to Shipston about it. I rang Bayswater's sister Mrs Andrews this morning. He's been in touch with her too.'

Kirby's eyes gleamed. 'Looks good.'

'It would be if we had the weapon with his prints on. And if we had an explanation for that yellow glove. No sign of Frederick. The photo in the papers may jog somebody's memory but we still haven't got a link between him and Bayswater. And there's another thing: have you heard about the cemetery?'

Kirby shook his head.

'Someone vandalised the grave of Fuggle's mother. White paint on the headstone – plants pulled up. He's livid, as you might expect. He hasn't any idea who is responsible but that doesn't stop him blaming us.'

'I can't see Miss Francis or Mrs Wemyss-Brown doing it somehow.'

'Porter's got a theory.'

Kirby burst out laughing.

Thornhill said, 'Does the name Howard Mork mean anything to you?'

'Don't think so.'

'He's one of these Teddy boys – you must have seen him about, you can hardly miss him. His dad's the manager of Butter's. They moved down from London a couple of years ago, and the mother died – her grave's up at the cemetery quite near Mrs Fuggle's. Bit of a wild lad, by all accounts – drinks too much, and with the wrong people, the sort of lad who's always on the edge of trouble.' Thornhill hesitated. 'And he works at the *Gazette*.'

'Is that all Porter's got on him?'

'Mork was up at Raglan Court when Miss Gwyn-Thomas found the rats in Miss Francis's car the other day. He claims he felt a bit faint and was having a walk to get some fresh air. Not one of those stories that inspires confidence. Maybe you could have a word with him, Brian. Porter reckons he might be the Pisser as well.'

Kirby stubbed out his cigarette and cleared his throat. 'With respect, sir, at a time like this, when we've got a case of probable murder and a couple of outbreaks of arson, surely a kid like this isn't—'

'That's the trouble with Lydmouth at present,' Thornhill said, suddenly angry. 'There's just too much going on – too many lines of enquiry. If Howard Mork's a loose end, I want him bloody well tied up and accounted for.'

Chapter Thirty-Nine

Amy Gwyn-Thomas felt aggrieved. Yet again, she had borne the brunt of attacks meant for others. First the rats in Miss Francis's car and now the Molotov cocktail in Mrs Wemyss-Brown's drawing-room. It wasn't fair. And here she was, parked in a hospital bed with nothing to do while her visitors chatted to one another and ignored her completely.

It seemed to her that no one really appreciated the quiet heroism of her conduct. She had suffered minor burns on the arms when smothering the flames with the Wemyss-Browns' rugs. She had kept her head, phoning the police and Jill Francis, soothing Charlotte, and preventing Philip from storming outside after the person who had thrown the bomb through the window.

Charlotte had been to visit earlier in the day, and now Jill was here, but so too was Mr Prout. It was very nice to have visitors, but if only they had had the good sense to space themselves out. As it was, Miss Francis was perched on the end of the bed, chatting with Ronald Prout, and she herself might not have been there. It was infuriating.

'Yes, I found it in the end,' Ronald Prout was saying, leaning back in the visitor's chair and crossing his legs. 'Though I say it myself, Miss Francis, my filing system's pretty good and I knew I'd find it sooner or later. Mind you, it was up in the loft and it wasn't easy.'

'That's wonderful,' Miss Francis said. 'Thank you so much.'

Ronald stuck out his chest and smirked. 'Anything to oblige.' He felt in his jacket pocket and produced a brown envelope, which he handed to her. 'That's not the original envelope, I'm afraid.'

Miss Francis opened it and took out the single sheet of paper. She quickly scanned the contents. 'Oh, well done. This could be very useful.'

The smirk became more pronounced and so did Amy's dislike of it.

'May I see it?' she demanded.

Miss Francis turned towards her. 'Of course you may. Are you sure we're not tiring you?'

'I'm fine, thank you.'

The letter which Mr Prout had found was written in an upright, easily legible hand. The future Mrs Fuggle, who signed herself Genevieve Ellwood, wondered whether Mr Prout could suggest suitable alternatives to 'The Voice that Breathed o'er Eden' and 'O Father All Creating' because she didn't care greatly for either of them; she thought they were rather trite choices, like Lohengrin's Wedding March.

What cheek! Amy almost said it aloud. She often thought about the music she would like for her own wedding and had already settled on the Lohengrin; and both the condemned hymns were on her short list.

At the head of the sheet of paper was a printed address: *33 Yorkley Grove, London N.* This, however, had been scratched out and Miss Ellwood had written *The Longbeach Hotel, St Michael's Road, Bournemouth* instead.

Miss Francis smiled. 'I wonder if that London address is where she lived before she came to Bournemouth. It's worth a try, isn't it? And thanks to Mr Prout we've now got a maiden name for her.'

Ronald bobbed his head in acknowledgement of the compliment.

'I must be going,' Jill said. 'I'm sure you and Mr Prout have lots to talk about.'

But Ronald was rising to his feet as well. 'I fear I must be leaving, too. I don't like to leave my staff without supervision for too long, and we mustn't tire Amy.' He glanced at the window. 'Dear me – it's still raining.'

'Would you like a lift?' Miss Francis asked him. 'I've got the car outside.'

With indecent haste, Mr Prout said that Miss Francis was too kind. They bade Amy goodbye and soon she was alone with the empty teacups: marooned on a shameful island of silence in the middle of a sea of chatter from the other patients and their visitors.

She got out of bed, pulled on her dressing-gown and walked slowly down the long room to the row of metal lockers near the door. The ward sister was writing up her notes in her little office on the other side of the doorway. Amy opened her locker and took out her clothes.

'Miss Gwyn-Thomas.'

Amy turned and faced the sister, a middle-aged woman as broad as she was long, who looked as if she had recently eaten a lemon.

'What on earth are you doing?'

'I'd have thought that was quite obvious,' Amy said. 'I'm discharging myself.'

Chapter Forty

A little after nine o'clock, they found Howard Mork in the public bar of the King's Head on Mincing Lane. Porter was not surprised to see that he was playing shove-halfpenny with Joe Rodley.

The rain had stopped. The two police officers stood outside and looked through the half-glazed door. Kirby was in civvies but Porter was in uniform. The only other people in the room were two old men, who avoided looking at the policemen and stared with fixed interest at their glasses of mild and bitter. The landlady, Mrs Halleran, was serving in the saloon bar, where somebody was playing the piano.

The two officers watched the game for a few seconds. Neither Howard nor Rodley appeared very interested in it. Porter noticed they were drinking pints with whisky chasers. A coin chinked against one of the glasses. Howard flicked it again and it snagged in a puddle of beer on the table-top.

'Who's he with?' Kirby murmured. His face was haggard and his movements sharp and sudden.

Porter told him, adding the fact that Rodley had recently lost his job at Broadbent's.

'Drowning his sorrows, eh? So he's the one whose wife saw Frederick in Whistler's Lane on Friday morning?'

Porter nodded.

Kirby said, 'Just follow my lead, okay?' He led the way

across the room and came to a halt beside the table where the two men sat. 'Howard Mork? We want a word with you, son.'

The boy looked up, seeing Kirby and then Porter in his uniform. His eyes danced from side to side. 'All right.'

'Outside, I think.'

Mork pushed back his chair, but Rodley laid a hand on his arm.

'All friends here. Why don't you stay in the warm?'

'I wasn't asking you, Mr Rodley.'

'You know my name, but I don't know yours. I know young Peter Porter there, but who are you?'

'This is Detective Sergeant Kirby,' Porter said.

'All the more reason to stay in the warm.'

'Come on, Mork,' Kirby said.

'He can't make you, Howie, not unless he arrests you. And you don't have to answer anything he asks you. That's the law, that is.'

The boy looked from Kirby to Rodley.

'Look, son,' Kirby said. 'I want to talk about your mother.'

Porter saw Howard wince.

'I can do it in front of your chum here or we can do it in private. So what's it to be?'

Kirby laid his hand on Howard Mork's shoulder. The boy stood up and allowed himself to be steered, swaying, towards the side door, which led to a covered passage running from the street to the yard at the back. Joe Rodley raised his glass, as if in a toast, and drank deeply.

Porter followed Kirby through the door and into the passage. At the end, as Howard Mork stumbled into the yard beyond, Kirby paused and turned back to Porter.

'Stay here. I don't want to be disturbed.'

'But Sarge—'

'You heard.'

Mork meandered into the middle of the little yard. Kirby went up behind him. Porter watched. The only light came from the bare bulb in the passage and the faint, artificial glow reflected in the sky. The cobbled yard was dotted with puddles.

The boy stopped but did not turn round. Kirby put his hand in his pocket and jingled his change. A few seconds crawled by. Kirby's hand whipped out of his pocket. His arm drew back. Metal glittered in the cracks between the fingers. His fist crashed into the side of Howard Mork's head, an inch above the right ear.

The boy yelped with pain. He staggered and slipped on the cobbles, then fell to the ground, grunted and wrapped his arms round his head. Kirby kicked him somewhere in the area of the kidneys.

'Sarge,' Porter said in an anguished whisper. 'Sarge.'

'Shut up,' Kirby hissed. 'Just do as you're told, or I'll have you thrown off the fucking force.'

Porter leaned against the wall. 'I don't understand,' he muttered.

'What's new?' Kirby bent down and gripped the collar of the long jacket with its padded shoulders. 'Listen, son, you're in trouble. You're really in trouble. Did you know that?'

Howard said nothing.

Kirby pulled harder so the head and shoulders left the ground. 'I don't think you're listening to me.' He slapped the left ear. 'Can you hear me better now? Can you?'

'Yes,' Howard sobbed.

Kirby hit him again. 'Yes, what?'

More sobbing. 'Yes, sir.'

'Good. Good boy. That's what I like to hear, a bit of politeness, eh?' Kirby took the lobe of Howard's left ear between finger and thumb and forced the boy to look at him. 'The other thing I like is a straight answer to a straight question. You got that?'

Howard tried to nod.

'What was that? I didn't hear you.'

'Yes.'

'Yes, what?'

'Yes, sir.'

'Good. Do you know Ivor Fuggle?'

'No. No, sir.'

'Not to speak to – do you know what he looks like?'

'Yes. Yes, sir.'

'When did you last see him?'

'The other day. At the cemetery.'

'What was he doing up there?'

'Standing by his mother's grave. It's near my mother's. He was just standing there. I don't know – praying or something.'

Howard tried to stand but Kirby would not relax his grip on the boy's ear.

'Listen carefully, son. You heard what someone did to Mrs Fuggle's grave?'

'Yes, sir.'

'It was you, wasn't it?'

'No – I promise. I never did. Let me go, you—'

Kirby kicked him. The boy squealed and lay still, moaning.

'You work for the *Gazette*, Fuggle's the editor of the *Post*. He's doing his damnedest to put the *Gazette* out of business. That means he'll put you out of a job because who else would want to employ someone like you? I think you know more about Mr Fuggle than you're letting on. And I don't think you like Mr Fuggle. And I reckon that's why you vandalised his mum's grave.'

'I never,' Howard whimpered.

'You like vandalising things, boy. You come down from London with all your nasty London habits, eh? Like pissing through people's letter boxes when you've had a skinful, eh? Maybe you like a bit of arson in your spare time, too?'

'Please, sir, please.'

Kirby bent down so his face was inches away from Howard's. 'Do you want to tell me about it now?'

'But there's nothing to tell.'

Kirby slapped him casually with his left hand. 'Liar.'

Porter heard a door opening and the sound of the piano increased in volume.

Kirby straightened up. 'I'll be back, Howard. You'll tell me next time.' He squeezed the ear until the boy cried out again. 'See you later, chum.' He pushed past Porter and sauntered through the alley to the street.

'Sarge.' Porter hurried after him. 'Sarge, why did you—?'

Kirby stopped to light a cigarette. 'Listen, Pete, you just keep your mouth shut and leave the talking to me. There's ways and ways of doing things. If you want results, sometimes you can't afford to go by the book. A short, sharp shock – that's what the likes of young Mork need.'

'Yes, Sarge – but you hurt him.'

Porter was used to the casual violence that went with his job. Everyone knew that the best way to deal with some kids was a quick clip round the earhole. Or that the tricks you'd learned in the privacy of the rugby scrum came in handy when you had a few Saturday night drunks to deal with. But all that was very different from Kirby's cold and calculated infliction of pain.

In the light of the match the sergeant's face was like a skull.

'Of course I bloody hurt him. That's the point. Wouldn't get results otherwise. That's what we do in the Smoke. Put pressure on them. Put pressure on them until they crack wide open.'

'But he hasn't.'

Kirby put his face very close to Porter's. 'Just you wait. He will.'

Thursday, 8 December

I found the bag. It had caught on the branches of one of the bushes in the park. I must have looked there half a dozen times already but I'd missed it. I hadn't realised I'd thrown it so high.

Last night he cried. It's weak, unmanly. And stupid. And to cry for a reason like that. After all, what does it matter now?

Earth and silence. That's what we all come to in the end. After that, who cares?

Chapter Forty-One

Susie Thornhill had kept her parents up half the night. Red faced, running a slight temperature, full of undeniable but inexplicable anguish, she wailed and hiccupped and moaned for what seemed like hours on end. She spilt warm milk over her bedclothes and clung with irrational tenacity to the notion that a family of ghosts lived under her chest of drawers. She was a formidably obstinate child, and opposing her was tiring in itself.

Now she was sleeping the sleep of the unjust while her parents faced each other across the breakfast table. Elizabeth had gone to school.

'Have you thought any more about it?' Edith said suddenly.

'About what?'

'About whether you want a divorce.'

'For God's sake.' Thornhill pushed back his chair, and the legs scraped on the linoleum. 'This isn't a good time.'

'I know it's not a good time,' she said. 'But then it never is, is it?'

'Do you want a divorce?' he asked.

She took her time pouring herself a second cup of tea. 'I've seen the way you look at that Francis woman. She's come running back to Lydmouth, hasn't she? I thought she would sooner or later. Or that you'd go to her.'

'She's got nothing to do with it. You're imagining things. I've hardly exchanged two words with her.' He knew he sounded petulant. 'Anyway, the point is, you're the one who mentioned the word divorce.'

Edith stared coolly at him. 'If that's what you want, you can have it.'

'Edith—'

From above their heads came the sound of a thin, reedy crying. Susie had woken up.

'I hope she's all right,' Thornhill said, hardly missing a beat as the conversation changed gear. 'Do you think we should call the doctor?'

'Not yet. See how she is later in the day.'

For an instant their eyes met and Thornhill saw his own concern mirrored in her face.

'Edith, I—'

She stood up. 'I'd better see what's wrong.'

'Yes, of course.' Thornhill glanced at his watch. 'I must go to work.'

'When will you be back?'

'I don't know.'

She stared at him, shrugged and left the room without another word. Thornhill fetched his coat, hat, gloves and briefcase. Upstairs, Susie's cries continued. For a moment he tried and failed to imagine a life where he no longer came home to his family every night.

He left the house and drove to the High Street. For once it was a dry morning, with a promise of sunshine to the south where the clouds were thinning to a pale blue-grey like watered milk. He wondered briefly what men would do without work – without the daily escape, the physical separation from home and family, the ability to step into different worlds with different inhabitants. Simultaneously it occurred to him that for thousands, perhaps millions, of women such a form of escape was not available: that their home was their prison. Was that part of the reason that Edith had brought up the subject of divorce?

At the station, he discovered that the Photographic Section had sent up the photographs of Paul Frederick. Thornhill told the stenographer to type up the envelopes and the accompanying letters for the press and bring the letters to him for signature. He worked on the files in his in-tray for nearly an hour until there was a tap on his door and Kirby came in.

'Morning, guv.'

Thornhill said, 'How did you get on last night?'

'I had a chat with Howard Mork. Found him in the King's Head – it was only about nine o'clock but he was already as drunk as a lord.'

'Any luck?'

Kirby shrugged. He looked much more like his normal self. 'Yes and no. He could have done the grave, I reckon, and I think he's the Pisser too. He didn't actually admit it, mind, but I don't think there's much doubt. If I see him again, he'll probably cave in. He's that type. Puts up a brave front at first, but he can't keep it up.'

'Are you sure about him?'

'As sure as you ever can be. He's a proper tearaway, that one, and thanks to Fuggle his job's on the line. The bleeding hearts will say it's not his fault, of course, that it's all the fault of his mum dying and him and his dad coming down from London.' Kirby hissed through his teeth, as though reducing internal pressure. 'There was something else. Guess who his drinking partner was? Joe Rodley.'

'That's interesting. Awkward customer – I met him at Viney Cottage on Tuesday.'

'Porter said they'd laid him off at Broadbent's.'

'That's right. Can't be easy for them – you know the wife's an invalid?'

Kirby smiled. 'You wouldn't have thought money was short, not the way he was drinking last night. Cocky bastard, too, bit of a barrack-room lawyer. Might be worth having a word with him, too.'

'You think he's up to something?'

'Where's the money coming from? They were on chasers and all. My granny used to say rotten apples always stick together at the bottom of the barrel.'

There was another tap on the door and the stenographer poked her head into the room. 'Sorry, sir – I'll come back later.'

'No, now's fine.' Thornhill waved her into the room. He said to Kirby, 'Okay, have a word with him. Go cautiously, though.'

'I will, sir.' Kirby grinned wolfishly. 'You know me – gentle as a lamb.'

He slipped out of the room. Thornhill heard him whistling in the corridor and wondered why he was so cheerful. The stenographer laid the letters, the envelopes and the photographs on his desk in three neat piles.

'What do you think of him?' Thornhill asked, angling one of the prints towards her.

'Rather a dish, isn't he? Bit like John Wayne.'

'That's what his wife said.'

'Must be awful for her.' The stenographer wrinkled her face in sympathy. 'Shall I wait while you sign the letters, sir?'

'Leave them. I'll ring when I'm ready.'

Thornhill wondered whether the stenographer thought of coming to work as an escape. She was unmarried, but perhaps that had nothing to do with it. The thought lurked in the back of his mind as he dealt with the rest of his in-tray and then worked his way through the pile of letters, scrawling his signature at the foot of each one.

He hesitated when he came to the letter addressed to Jill at the *Gazette*. The nib dug into the paper as he signed his name. It was tempting to add a postscript, just a few bland words. Even better would be to talk to her. What was she escaping from? Loneliness? A home with another man? The idea of her living with someone, barbed as a fish hook, twisted in his mind. He pushed the letter and the photograph into the envelope. In his imagination, he heard himself saying, casually, to the stenographer: 'Leave that one with me – I'll drop it in as I'm passing.' And he saw himself, equally casually, bumping into Jill in the front office of the *Gazette*.

The phone rang. The dream shattered, exposed for what it was, something tawdry and insubstantial.

'Gloucester CID for you, sir,' said the clerk on the switchboard. 'Detective Inspector Grimes. Shall I put him through?'

A moment later, Thornhill heard the familiar voice of his former colleague, Dracula Grimes, on the other end of the phone.

'Drac,' he said. 'What can I do for you?'

Grimes laughed, a little smugly. 'It's more a matter of what I can do for you, Richard. A little birdie told me you were looking for a yellow kid glove for the left hand. One of my WPCs has just found one.'

Chapter Forty-Two

J ill Francis calculated that if she hurried there should be time for a little research. Her meeting with Bernie Broadbent and Randolph Haughton was not until three in the afternoon, at the latter's Mayfair flat.

Besides, she needed the distraction. Too much depended on this meeting. If she were lucky, she might hear news of potential investors willing to bail out the *Gazette* or, even better, Randolph and Bernie might be willing to do the job themselves. She shut her mind to the prospect of what might happen if she were unlucky. The two men came from different parts of her life. Both were old friends. The trouble was, old friends sometimes became more old than friendly. Life moved on.

When she left the train at Paddington, she took a taxi to Yorkley Grove, which lay in the patchwork of streets north of the Euston Road. The street ran north–south, and at the southern end stood the remains of a bombed church with a jagged, blackened tower topped with the amputated stump of a spire. On the opposite corner a block of council flats gleamed in the thin sunshine like a beached white whale. The name and the location had led Jill to form a mental picture of gracious terraced houses with tall windows facing each other across a broad, tree-lined avenue. Instead she found a brave new world of glass and concrete, muddy lawns and high-rises interspersed with the soot-stained houses and faded shops of an earlier era.

Sweet wrappers and chip papers danced in the gutters. In the little churchyard, a pair of tramps smoked and played cards in the smoke-blackened angle where the tower met the wall of the nave. They glanced at her, and one of them wolf-whistled.

Jill hurried up the road. On the right, about halfway up, a terrace of little houses had survived from before the war. At one end of it was a pub called the Wintour Arms and at the other a general shop with a window display consisting largely of dead flies and sun-bleached packets of suet. In the shop, an old man in a greasy brown coat was filling in his football pools behind the counter. Jill went in to buy a packet of cigarettes that she did not need.

'I wonder if you can help me,' she said as she took her change. 'I'm looking for someone who used to live around here during the war. At number thirty-three.'

The shopkeeper grunted. 'Thirty-three? That was down there.' He nodded in the general direction of the bombed church and the new flats with their streamlined balconies. 'Shame. Used to be a lovely street before the war.' He sucked at his moustache, which was worn long so the fringe drooped over his upper lip. 'Then the council moved in all the riff-raff. Bloody shame.'

'I don't know if you knew my friend,' Jill persisted. 'Her name was Ellwood, Genevieve Ellwood.'

The old man shook his head, his eyes drifting down to the pools form. 'She didn't live here before the war, I can tell you that. That's when the rot set in, you know. Most of the old people left, and we had all sorts and sizes turning up instead. Half of them thought you kept your coal in the bath, and the other half was foreigners. Even a couple of wogs. I ask you.'

Jill said, 'Is there anyone else who might have known her?'

'You could try Maisie at the Wintour, I suppose. Doubt she'll be any good, though.' He leaned closer, bringing with him a smell of old fish and overflowing ashtrays. 'Losing her marbles, eh?'

She thanked him and went outside. The Wintour Arms was encrusted with glazed tiles the colour of elderly uncooked beef. She glanced at her watch and pushed open the door of the saloon bar. Had she done the same in Lydmouth, all conversation would have stopped. Here in London, it merely faltered, then resumed a little more loudly than before. When she asked for Maisie, the barman nodded towards a corner table where two women, one old and one young, were engaged in an animated argument.

Jill went over and introduced herself.

'I'm Maisie Lawrence,' the older woman said, and when she nodded her head, the artificial cherries in her hat bobbed up and down. The face was weathered and almost perfectly round, studded with tiny, bright eyes and a snub nose. 'Who are you looking for, dear?'

'How did you know I was looking for someone?' Jill asked, momentarily diverted.

'People usually are when they want to talk to me. People I don't know, I mean.'

'Gran's the oldest inhabitant,' the younger woman said. 'In a moment she'll tell you she was born in this pub.'

'Mind your sauce. You know what the trouble is with young ladies these days? Too much education. It's not good for you.' She glanced up at Jill and added, 'This is my granddaughter Marlene.'

'Why not?' Marlene said, but without anger.

'It just teaches you to be cheeky. Can't see the point of it myself. Not for a girl. Because you just go and get married and have babies.'

'I want a job. I don't want babies.' Marlene looked up at Jill, her eyes assessing but not unfriendly. 'Hadn't you better ask this lady what she wants? Or rather who.'

Maisie turned to Jill. 'You got kiddies, dear?'

'No.'

'There you are,' Marlene said. 'And I bet she's got a job.'

'As a matter of fact I have,' Jill said. 'And that's why I'm here. I'm trying to trace someone, Miss Genevieve Ellwood. And the last address I have for her is Yorkley Grove – number thirty-three.'

'Jenny? Genevieve Ellwood?' Maisie tapped the rim of her empty glass with a long fingernail coated with chipped varnish a jaunty shade of pink. 'Yes, dear. My memory's not what it was. But I do remember Jenny.'

Jill said, 'Why don't we chat over a drink? May I get you something?'

Maisie's face brightened. 'Port and lemon, please. Since you're asking.'

Marlene sighed. 'Oh, Gran.'

Nevertheless, Marlene accepted a Babycham. Jill ordered gin and French. Soon a festive atmosphere enveloped the table at the corner. This was partly to do with the alcohol but more to do with Maisie, who proved to be the sort of person for whom any gathering of people, however small, has the makings of a party. But extracting useful information from her was a frustratingly slow process. At last Jill managed to steer the conversation back to Genevieve Ellwood.

'Jenny was a Nippy in the Lyons Corner House in the Strand,' Maisie said. 'Lovely girl, always good for a giggle. Is she all right?'

'As far as I know,' Jill said. 'I've not actually met her.'

'Not sure I'd want to meet the brother again, not that I will. He was a dreary old sod, excuse my French—'

'Gran!'

'Well, he was, dear.' Maisie smacked her lips. 'They were as different as chalk from cheese. Jenny always had a smile on her lips and a song in her heart. But Mike looked as if he was on his way to a prayer meeting. As for the mother, well!' She took a genteel sip of her drink. 'Thought she was too good for Yorkley Grove, and that's a fact. Stuck-up old cow.'

'You shouldn't be talking like this,' Marlene interrupted. 'Maybe this lady's a friend of theirs.'

'Not exactly,' Jill said, glancing at the clock behind the bar. 'I'm a journalist trying to trace her. There may be a small legacy involved.'

Maisie's eyes widened. 'A lost heir,' she breathed. 'How romantic.'

'It's not like that,' Marlene said.

'How do you know?' Maisie demanded.

Marlene scowled at her grandmother. 'Because it never is.'

'Had they lived here long?' Jill asked, her eyes straying to the clock over the bar.

'Two or three years? They used to have a house in Tufnell Park, I think. But they just had the first floor of number thirty-three. Old Mrs Hutt, she was the landlady, she was a funny old bat too – she once—'

'The son – Mike, was it? – what did he do?'

'Clerk in one of the ministries. Couldn't join up – he had a dicky heart or something.'

'What happened to them?' Jill spoke quickly, trying to accelerate the interview. Time was running out and it wouldn't be easy to find a taxi in Yorkley Grove. 'Where did they go?'

'Poor old Mike never went anywhere. Nor did Mrs Ellwood – she died of pneumonia, must have been '43 or '44 – the winter, anyway. So there was just the two of them. Not that they were here for long after that. Mike was killed in the V-2 attack.' The old woman winced, squeezing her eyes shut. 'We copped a direct hit. Were you in London during the war, dear?'

'Some of the time.'

'They sounded like a blooming express train coming down on your head. I wasn't here that night, mind, not when ours come down. I'd gone to visit my friends in Camden Town, the Newleys. When I got back, my house wasn't there any more. Nor was half of Yorkley Grove, come to that, or half the folk who lived here. Including Mike Ellwood.'

'I'm sorry.'

'These things happen.' For a moment Maisie's face became as bleak as a winter landscape. 'Poor girl came back later that night and there was nothing left for her. No home, no family, no nothing. Poor kiddie. I don't think there was even enough for a proper burial.'

She sniffed, took a handkerchief from her enormous handbag and blew her nose so loudly that a momentary silence descended on the bar. Marlene touched her grandmother's hand.

'I went off and stayed with my daughter in Stoke Newington,' Maisie went on. 'I only came back here when they gave me the flat. It's a nice flat, but it's not the same place it was. There's no one I know any more. Not except old droopy-drawers in the shop.'

'Where did Genevieve go?'

'I don't know. Someone said she was ill. In any case, she didn't stay here. Nothing left to stay for, was there? I never saw her again. It's like that, a bomb in the neighbourhood. It's not just the bricks and mortar that go, or the people. It's like your whole life's blown up. Not to mention your past and your future.'

'Did anyone talk to her before she went?'

Maisie shrugged. 'How do I know? I remember thinking afterwards, well, you can't blame her for going. She wanted a fresh start. She didn't even tell her fiancé where she was off to. Maybe she didn't know herself.'

'Her fiancé?'

'Tony – nice man. He came back looking for her when he was demobbed. But she was long gone.'

Chapter Forty-Three

'It was left at a newsagent's in Westgate Street.' Dracula's long fingers lifted the spoon and plunged it into the mug of tea. The hot, milky liquid turned into a whirlpool. 'Just inside the door. There weren't any customers at the time, and the owner had just nipped into the back room for a pee. He didn't think anything of it. Why should he? He's used to people leaving stuff on the doorstep when the shop's closed. He's been collecting jumble for the scouts for the past fortnight. So when he gets a suitcase full of clothes with "Jumble" chalked on the side he just naturally leaves it in his shed with all the other stuff.'

'What colour is it?'

'Blue. No labels or other identifying marks. They started sorting the jumble yesterday evening. One of our WPCs has got a nephew in the scouts, and she was giving them a hand. Smart girl. She thought the clothes looked too good for jumble. Anyway, there was an overcoat, and the lining of one of the pockets was torn. The glove had fallen through.'

'A mustard-yellow kid glove.'

Detective Inspector Grimes nodded. 'Like I said, she's a bright girl. Left-hand glove, too – she remembered that.'

'Send her down to Lydmouth when she wants a move,' Thornhill said.

Grimes shot him a dark, suspicious glance. 'You all right?'

'Yes – fine, Drac.' Thornhill's voice sounded falsely jolly to himself.

'Lot on your plate at present. That's the trouble with this job: it's like the number nineteen bus – all the crimes come at once.'

Grimes looked like Bela Lugosi, which was why his nickname was Dracula. It was also perhaps an ironic comment on his temperament, which had nothing to do with vampires. He had worked in Lydmouth for many years before being made up to inspector and moving to Gloucester. His sympathy was kindly meant but it made Thornhill feel uncomfortable.

'Do you mind if we take a look?' he said.

Carrying his tea, Grimes led the way down to the evidence room, a glorified cupboard which opened out of the CID office. The open suitcase sat on a plain deal table with its contents in a heap beside it. Thornhill poked at the pile with his forefinger: a pair of pyjamas with a jaunty blue stripe, slippers and a dressing-gown with a brown check; a linen bag containing a pair of socks, a pair of underpants and a vest, all used; a maroon jersey and a sponge bag with shaving tackle, toothbrush and soap; a dark brown trilby hat and a matching overcoat. In his mind he itemised what wasn't there.

'And what about the glove?' he said softly.

With the air of a conjuror revealing a rabbit, Grimes lifted the hat. Underneath was a left-hand glove in yellow kid leather.

'It's a match?' Grimes said.

Thornhill peeled back the lining of the glove and found the label: Thidwich of Regent Street. 'Yes. And your WPC found it in the overcoat?'

Grimes showed the hole in the lining. 'Easily missed, if you were in a hurry.'

'You checked the labels in the clothes?'

Grimes hesitated for a moment, perhaps to make the point that this was his patch, and he was doing Thornhill a favour.

'Of course. It's all mass-produced stuff, apart from the gloves. No name tags or laundry labels.'

Thornhill examined the overcoat, outside and inside, inch by inch. It came from Burton's, as did probably half the overcoats in the country. There was little sign of wear. It smelled of cigarettes and hair oil. On the inside hem, almost entirely concealed by the hang of the lining, he found a smear of grease with half a dozen white specks in it.

'What's this?'

'Oil?' Grimes said. 'He probably brushed up against a motorbike or something. No saying when it happened.'

'And the white stuff?'

Grimes fetched a magnifying glass and examined the stain more closely. 'I reckon it's sawdust. Can't be certain but the lab would know. They could probably tell us what the wood is too. What's all this about?'

Thornhill glanced over his shoulder. 'The Bayswater case.'

'They're connected?'

'Keep it to yourself, Drac, but under Bayswater's body we found the matching glove, the other half of the pair. So on the one hand we've got a missing person, a man with no connection to Dr Bayswater, a man last seen leaving Lydmouth on the eleven fifty-three train last Friday. And on the other hand we've got his glove turning up the following morning under Bayswater's body. Bayswater died some time late on Friday evening or early on Saturday morning. Now we need to know if anyone saw Paul Frederick in Gloucester. Or noticed any strangers travelling from Gloucester back to Lydmouth.'

Grimes nodded. 'Bus station, railway station, taxis, and so on. Not a problem.'

'I'll give you a photo of Frederick. The only other thing we know is that his family had a postcard from him – which someone posted in Gloucester on Friday.'

'You must have an idea of what it all means.'

'It means that Frederick's done a bunk. But it seems he did it before somebody killed Bayswater. If, on the other hand, he didn't do a bunk, then maybe he's been killed as well, and someone else left his clothes for the boy scouts. Or rather some of his clothes – he was wearing the hat and overcoat and the gloves when he was last seen on Friday morning. But the other clothes he was wearing aren't here.'

Grimes looked sorrowfully at Thornhill and chewed his lower lip. 'So it looks like maybe you lost a body rather than a person? I don't envy you.'

Thornhill shrugged. 'It's progress in one way, but not in another.'

'Progress? Is that what you call it? Two murders on your plate instead of one?'

Chapter Forty-Four

'**M**y dad will kill me,' Howard Mork said with a tremor in his voice.

Amy tried and failed to imagine Mr Mork killing anybody. He was a mild little man with protruding ears. On the other hand, so was Dr Crippen.

'I'm sure he wouldn't. Anyway, he doesn't know.'

'He will if they arrest me. That sergeant's really got it in for me.' The boy's eyes were huge with fear. 'I bet he's going to frame me for killing old Bayswater. What's to stop him?'

'Nonsense. This is Lydmouth, not the Wild West.'

'The police do frame people. They do it all the time.'

'Only in films, Howard. Look, this is very upsetting for us all. And the police have to do their job, they have to ask everyone questions.'

'But he was really nasty. He—'

'I know,' she interrupted. 'Sometimes they seem a little . . . well, brusque. It's nothing to worry about, though. You must try to keep a sense of perspective.'

She settled her hat on her head and examined the result in the large, cracked mirror above the fireplace in the front office. Apart from the caretaker and the cleaner, she and Howard were the only people left in the building. She was in a hurry to be gone. Thank heavens she had discharged herself from hospital yesterday. If she hadn't, she might still be there, mouldering away under the baleful eye of that tyrannical ward sister. But she felt fine now – apart from a headache and the burn tingling on her left wrist.

'Miss Gwyn-Jones?'

She turned towards the boy. 'Yes, Howard.'

He was blushing. 'Would you like me to walk back with you to your house – see you get there safely, I mean?'

She blinked, surprised both by the offer and by the fervour in Howard's voice, and unexpectedly touched.

'So many things have happened to you, and I thought you might feel . . . it might be better if . . .'

His voice trailed away and he looked down at his shoes, which were in need of cleaning. He was carrying a large brown envelope under his left arm and he picked nervously at the flap with the fingers of his free hand. Amy felt embarrassed – even a little frightened. Knowing that someone expected you to feel afraid was not only humiliating: it could sometimes create a fear that was not there before.

'No, I'll be fine, thank you,' she said, more sharply than she had intended. She cast around for a way to change the subject. 'What's that you've got there?'

'It's for Miss Francis,' he said. 'It came this afternoon. Someone from the police station brought it over.'

He held it out to Amy, who saw Miss Francis's name on the front of the envelope and the words 'Private and Confidential' in the top left-hand corner.

'Why didn't you bring this upstairs immediately?' she snapped.

'Sorry – I thought that because Miss Francis wasn't here it was—'

'You thought wrong, I'm afraid. Now go upstairs right away and leave it on her desk. I know she's had to go to London today but it's possible she'll look in at the office on her way home.'

'Yes, miss. Sorry.'

He shuffled towards the door.

Amy called after him, 'And don't worry about your father. I'm sure everything will be all right.'

He looked back at her from the doorway and shook his head. 'It's all wrong.'

Amy left the *Gazette* by the side door. In the High Street she hesitated on the corner. If she turned left, she would go home to her warm little bungalow in Vicarage Gardens. Alternatively she could follow her conscience, turn right, and walk up to Viney Cottage.

If it hadn't been for Howard, she would probably have turned left. The conversation had unsettled her. She was aware that she had not been particularly kind to the boy. If you sowed unkindnesses you didn't reap any blessings. The last occasion she had seen Doreen, on Saturday evening, she hadn't sown many kindnesses either. And she had half promised to drop in at Viney Cottage.

Amy crossed the road, passed the grimly Gothic façade of Grove House with its darkened windows and turned into Whistler's Lane. At least it was still dry. She met nobody coming down the lane. As she drew level with the boundary of the park, however, she saw ahead of her the figure of a man. He was staggering from street light to street light, weaving to and fro across the pavement as though adrift in the Atlantic Ocean and under the influence of a Force 8 gale.

She slowed her pace because she did not want to catch up with him. The farther he went, the more the suspicion grew: that the man was Joe Rodley, already, at not much more than six o'clock in the evening, dreadfully drunk. When he turned in at the gate of Viney Cottage, the suspicion hardened into certainty.

At this point, Amy Gwyn-Thomas seriously considered

turning back. But she was not a woman who changed her mind lightly. Besides, there was nothing much on the radio this evening and Mr Prout was conducting choir practice at the chapel. There was also the matter of sowing kindnesses and it looked as if Viney Cottage would be particularly fertile ground this evening.

At the cottage door, Joe glanced over his shoulder and saw her. He waited for her to draw closer. Without a word, he opened the door, nodded to her and stood back against the wall. As she slipped past him, she smelled the tang of spirits on his breath.

The bedroom was hot and stuffy. Doreen was sitting at the window, and although she smiled her face was worried.

'How are you, dear?' Amy said, advancing towards her.

'Not so bad, thank you.'

'She'll soon be as right as rain,' Joe said behind her.

Startled, Amy turned.

'What she needs is a doctor who knows something about it. Not these bloody sawbones down here. I'll take her to London, and have her sorted out there.'

'Joe,' his wife said, 'would you like to put the kettle on? I'm sure we'd all like a nice cup of tea.'

'Tea? We should be celebrating. You can't celebrate with tea.'

'I'd still love a cup, Joe, and I'm sure Amy would too.'

Amy said, 'Oh yes, please. If you want to go and lie down, I could make it myself.'

The good humour dropped away from him like a cloak. 'What do you mean?'

'I thought perhaps you seemed—' Amy hesitated, frightened by what she saw in his face. 'You seemed a little tired – that's all.'

'You're a liar.'

'Joe—' Doreen began.

He ignored her. 'You think I'm drunk. Go on, admit it.'

'Since you insist, I did wonder if you might have had one too many.'

'What would you know about that?' He let go of the door handle and moved unsteadily towards her. 'Yes, I've had a drink – and why not? I can handle it. The trouble with you is that you don't know anything about men – real men.'

Amy glared at him. 'I think I know quite enough.'

He raised his fist and Amy flinched. 'You stupid woman. Why don't you bugger off? I can look after Doreen. Just you stop interfering.'

'I'm not—'

'Christ knows why Prout's sniffing after you. It's probably your money. Can't think of any other reason, and ten to one he's a pansy anyway. Personally I'd sooner go to bed with Nelly the fucking elephant.'

Amy was shaking with rage and humiliation. She heard a strangled sound behind her. Joe Rodley's face had changed – all the anger had been wiped away; his attention was diverted from her. She looked over her shoulder. Doreen was holding on to the table with one hand and the chair back with the other. She was trying to lever herself to her feet. Her face was white and contorted.

Without a word, Joe pushed past Amy and settled his wife back in her chair. As he did so, strange crooning sounds came from his mouth, like those of a man trying to soothe a sick animal. He knelt at her feet and put his arms around her waist. Eyes closed, Doreen lay back against her chair.

Amy cleared her throat. 'Is there anything I can do to help?'

Joe glanced back at her. 'Go away, you cow,' he said wearily. 'Just go away.'

Chapter Forty-Five

J ill Francis no longer felt quite the same about her car.
Unless you inspected it carefully, the green Morris Minor
looked much as it had done on her return to Lydmouth a
little over a week ago. Since then, however, it had survived a
collision with Roger Leddon's car and an invasion of rats. It
was true that the damage from the accident had been repaired
and the interior of the car had been thoroughly cleaned. But it
was impossible to remove all traces of recent events and to
expunge the memories.

That evening, when the train reached Lydmouth at last, she
walked out of the station and made her way towards the car,
which she had parked in the rank of spaces behind the Station
Hotel. Before unlocking the door she peered into the interior in
case it contained another unwelcome surprise. As she was
fumbling for her car key in her handbag, she heard the sound
of raised voices behind her.

Despite her tiredness, she turned, drawn to whatever was
happening outside the hotel by the reckless and insatiable
appetite of a journalist. Three men had emerged from the door
to the hotel's bars and were clustered under the street lamp
immediately outside. The first she recognised was PC Porter,
who would have been unmistakable even if he hadn't been in
uniform.

But why was he doing nothing about the other two men?
One of them was gripping the other's neck and pushing him

up against the lamp-post. The victim struggled, and the light fell more clearly on him: Howard Mork, surely? An instant later, she realised that his assailant was Brian Kirby.

Jill walked rapidly towards them. They looked round at the sound of her heels on the pavement. Kirby released his grip and stood back, slipping his hands in the pockets of his overcoat.

'What on earth's going on?' she demanded.

'I'm afraid it's none of your business, Miss Francis,' Kirby said.

'Of course it's my business, Sergeant. Howard Mork is one of my staff.'

'I can't discuss an investigation with you. As it happens we've said all we need to now, but I dare say we'll be asking Mr Mork a few more questions later.'

Kirby nodded to her and turned away. Porter followed him across the car park, glancing back at Jill. A man can change a great deal in three years. There was a quality about Brian Kirby that hadn't been there before – envy, perhaps, a sense that the world had ill used him. His body had become heavier, and his mind more sullen. With age, Jill thought, characters seemed to go through a process of natural selection, and the surviving traits hardened and often turned into caricatures of their former selves; and they were not necessarily the more desirable traits, merely the less vulnerable.

Howard Mork was still leaning against the lamp-post, with his face turned away from her.

'Are you all right? Did they hurt you?'

He bowed sideways like a tree in a gale and vomited on the pavement.

'Did they hit you?'

'No, Miss Francis,' Howard gasped. He found a hand-kerchief in his trouser pocket, wiped his mouth and dabbed ineffectually at the right-hand sleeve of his jacket.

'Is it just the drink?'

'Yes. Sorry.'

Jill was relieved. A drunken teenager was a relatively easy matter to resolve. 'Are you going to be sick again?'

'I don't think so.'

'Then hop in the car. We'll go back to the *Gazette* and clean you up.'

He shambled obediently after her and sat in the passenger seat of the Morris Minor. His knees nearly touched his chin. In time, the rest of his body would catch up with his height, but at present he resembled a sartorially ambitious stick insect.

The windows of the *Gazette* were in darkness. Jill parked outside the gates to the yard and let them into the building by the side door. She suggested that Howard clean himself up in the lavatory while she made him some tea.

As the kettle was boiling, she read the neatly typed memo from Amy Gwyn-Thomas, which brought her up to date with the main events of the day. She was beginning to realise why Philip had set such store by Amy, despite her unfortunate mannerisms. When her loyalties were engaged, she was a formidably efficient secretary.

Howard came out of the lavatory as she was pouring the tea. She gave him three spoonfuls of sugar and told him to take the tray along to her office. She made him sit in one of the armchairs beside the gas fire. He looked alarmingly young, clean and bewildered. Jill lit a cigarette and, after a moment's hesitation, offered him the packet.

'Feeling better?' she asked.

He nodded. 'Sorry – sorry about everything.' His voice was still slurred but his co-ordination was much improved. 'What . . . what are you going to do?'

'I think that depends on you,' Jill said. 'What were those policemen up to?'

'Asking questions.'

'I gathered that. What about?'

'It's the one in plain clothes – he keeps asking me . . . asking me about all the things that have been going on here.'

'Sergeant Kirby? So he's talked to you before?'

Howard nodded. 'Him and Mr Porter came to the King's Head last night. I was having a drink with a friend, and they pulled me out for questioning.'

'And where did they find you tonight?'

'I was in the Station Hotel. I thought . . . I thought—'

'You thought they wouldn't come looking for you there?'

'Yeah.' The boy sniffed and sucked on his cigarette. 'They're picking on me. That sergeant is. Last night, he . . . he hit me. Several times. Once it really hurt – I think he put coins between his fingers.'

'Leave any marks?'

'No. It was just here.' He touched the spot above his ear where the hair concealed the skin beneath. 'And he kicked me and slapped me around a bit.'

'Why? He must have had a reason.'

'He thinks I did it. Everything. So he tried to make me admit it. He reckons I did those things to Mrs Fuggle's grave.'

'Why would you want to do that?'

The boy glanced at her, his face suddenly sly. 'Because of the *Gazette*. Because Mr Fuggle wants us closed down.'

'Desecrating his mother's grave's not going to stop him.'

'I know. But you try telling that sergeant. And he thinks I done other things, too.'

'Like the arson here and the attack at Troy House?'

'No! Me? Of course I wouldn't do something—'

'Then what did he think? You were the Pisser?'

Howard's face showed a different sort of shock now – that a

lady who happened to be his employer had said the word 'Pisser'.

Jill said, 'Well? Are you the Pisser?'

He said nothing.

'Look,' Jill said. 'I want to help you, Howard, but I can't if I don't know what you've done and what you haven't done. No one else is here – this is all between ourselves. If it was you peeing through people's letter boxes, I don't suppose you'll be doing it again. All you need do is nod your head. Are you the Pisser?'

She stared at him, trying not to laugh.

After a long moment, he dipped his head.

'Good. Now we know where we are. So what's wrong with the Baptists?'

'Mum was a Baptist.' He sniffed, and a tear gleamed on his cheek. 'Fat lot of use they were. Told us to pray, and God would listen. Bloody liars.'

'Anything else you'd like to mention while we're at it?'

Howard stared at his long, thin legs in their tight trousers.

'Mrs Fuggle's grave?' Jill prompted.

He shook his head vigorously.

'As far as I'm concerned your job's perfectly safe. The arson?'

He lifted his eyes to hers. 'No.'

'I didn't think so but I had to be sure. And you had nothing to do with Mr Cubbitt getting beaten up, either?'

There was another shake of the head. He looked across the table at her. His eyes were half closed and he licked his lips.

'But perhaps you know something?' Jill waited for a reaction that failed to come. 'Or suspect something? What is it, then?'

The boy knotted his fingers together and squeezed. 'I pulled the string.'

'What string?'

'It was hanging out of a window one night.' He was talking quickly now, as if it was a relief to get the words out. 'One of the windows above Mynott's shop. I think that policeman lives up there – Mr Porter. I pulled the string and woke him up.' A slow smile spread across Howard's face. 'I reckon it was like his alarm clock, see? Friend of mine used to do that to stop him from being late for school. In London that was, Clapham.'

'You miss it? London, I mean?'

He stared at her. ' 'Course I do. Things was different then.'

He must have lost almost everything, Jill thought – home, friends and then his mother. All he had found instead was a lowly job at the *Gazette* and the dubious friendship of Joe Rodley. *Rodley*: the thought of him nudged her memory. Had the string been a diversion as much as a confession?

'I know you didn't attack Mr Cubbitt, Howard, but is there any chance you might have an idea who did?' Once more she waited, and once more he said nothing. 'I was wondering about Joe Rodley.'

'Joe's been good to me. He's my friend.'

'I know he's your friend. But sometimes friends can do foolish things. That's their business, of course, but I don't think it's right that you should have to suffer for what they do. I'm not trying to make you –' she sought in her mind for the right euphemism and at last settled on one that seemed suitably childlike '– tell tales on him. But for your sake, I need to know.'

He struck a match but failed to light the cigarette in his mouth. He mumbled, 'He's the only person round here who talks to me.'

'Now that's not true. People talk to you here, at the *Gazette*. Miss Gwyn-Thomas was telling me only the other day how useful you've been.'

He lowered his head and lit the cigarette. Jill wasn't sure but she thought he was blushing. The thought of Amy arousing passion in this unlikely quarter was so astonishing she had to bite back a laugh. Then she felt humbled. So that explained why Mr Prout had been the Pisser's principal target among the Baptists, and why Howard had been so providentially on hand when Amy discovered the rats in Jill's Morris Minor. He had followed Amy because he was in love with her.

Howard looked up. 'He's not been short of a bob or two lately. Joe, that is. And that's surprising.'

'As he's got a sick wife and he's just lost his job?'

'Yes – and there's something else. I had a drink with him the day after Mr Cubbitt was hurt. His knuckles were bruised, I noticed them, and he was clumsy rolling his fags. I asked him what he'd been doing and he said he'd ridden home on his bike after having a few drinks, and he'd fallen and grazed them on the road.'

Neither of them spoke.

Howard looked at her. 'It might have been true.'

'It might have been true,' Jill echoed.

They sat in silence for a moment.

He burst out, 'My dad will kill me.'

'Why?'

'He's always going on about something. About me. Says I'm a disgrace to him and Mum.' A tremor entered the boy's voice. 'He doesn't understand. There's nothing to do down here. Not that he cares. After work he just sits in that bloody flat upstairs reading his books. It drives me nuts.'

'What do you want to do? I might be able to help you find a job in London.'

Howard's face brightened. 'Could you? The only thing is, I wouldn't like to leave the *Gazette*. I . . . I like it here.'

Jill doubted the attraction would survive for very much longer. She said, 'That's fine, of course – you can stay here. Let me know if you change your mind, though.'

He was very nearly sober by the time he left and considerably happier. Jill let him out of the side door and went back upstairs. In her office, she skimmed through the mail on the desk and found a large brown envelope with her name typed on the front. The envelope almost certainly contained the photograph of the missing man, Paul Frederick. Jill began to tear it open, then stopped. Instead she snapped open her briefcase and thrust the envelope and the rest of the mail inside. She would look through it all at the flat.

Before she went home, she had one more call to make. She drove up to Troy House. She could have phoned Charlotte but she had the sort of news it was better to announce in person. She parked on the road outside, making sure the Morris Minor was under a street lamp, and tapped on the front door rather than use the bell because she knew Charlotte would worry about its waking Philip. A curtain twitched in the newly mended bay window. It twitched almost as soon as she knocked, which suggested that Charlotte had been sitting or standing in the bay and waiting for her for some time.

Jill had expected they would sit in the kitchen, which was warmer and perhaps safer. Instead, Charlotte ushered her into the drawing-room. The fire was lit and the lamps on either side of the fireplace were on. On the side table by Charlotte's chair was a newspaper and a yellow-jacketed Gollancz novel. She was doing her best to pretend that life was normal: that she was capable of rising above the facts that her husband was lying in a drugged sleep upstairs, her family's newspaper was on its last legs, and someone had recently chucked a Molotov cocktail through her drawing-room window. Charlotte offered first tea and then cocoa. Jill declined both but, glancing at the drinks trolley, said she wouldn't mind a small brandy and soda instead.

Charlotte clicked her tongue against the roof of her mouth. 'You drink too much, dear.'

'It's been a long day.' Jill sank into an armchair and opened her handbag. 'I'm sorry I wasn't here earlier. I had to sort something out at the office.' She took out her cigarettes.

Charlotte uncorked the brandy bottle. 'And you smoke too much, too.' Liquid gurgled in the glass. 'Well? What did they say?'

Jill said, 'They won't help.'

For an instant Charlotte's face crumpled. Then she sponged away the wrinkles and handed Jill the brandy. She sat down on the other side of the fireplace, her hand groping for a cigarette.

'I'm sorry,' Jill went on. 'It was always a long shot, but it was worth trying.'

'It was the only thing left to try,' Charlotte said. 'I thought perhaps Bernie Broadbent – after all, Randolph Haughton's not a local man, I know, but Bernie—'

'Bernie never mixes sentiment with business.'

'Yes, but I'd have thought he'd have welcomed the chance to invest in the *Gazette*.' She tapped ash from her cigarette. 'And we could have opened doors for him, perhaps. After all, money doesn't buy everything, even these days.'

The trouble was, Jill thought, even if Charlotte still had the things that money couldn't buy, she didn't think Bernie wanted them, or not any more. 'He spends most of his time in London now. I don't think he's very interested in Lydmouth.'

Charlotte stared at her. 'How very sad.' Frowning, she threw the half-smoked cigarette on the fire and heaved herself out of the chair. 'I'd better see how Philip is. Would you excuse me?'

'I should leave – it's quite late.'

'No – don't go yet. As a matter of fact there's something I wanted to ask you.' Charlotte opened the door, then stopped and glanced back at Jill. 'I suppose I'll have to tell him.'

'What about? That Bernie and Randolph refused the loan?'

'Yes. I'm not looking forward to it. It will just make him worry all the more.' She sighed. 'Anyhow, it can wait till morning. He's almost certainly asleep.'

Charlotte left the room. Jill put down her drink and opened her briefcase, which was on the carpet by her feet. She reached, as she had known she would, for the large brown envelope. If it was the photograph of the missing man, there was absolutely no reason why Richard Thornhill should have enclosed a personal note with it. But it wouldn't hurt to make sure. She ran her finger under the flap and pulled out the envelope's contents.

There was a letter, typed and impersonal, no doubt identical to those that had gone to every other newspaper on the list, right down to the neat signature: R. M. Thornhill. She wondered what Richard's middle name was; in the days of their intimacy she had never thought to ask.

As for the photograph, it was a good-quality print, about ten by eight inches, showing a handsome young man in RAF uniform, a flight sergeant. He was sprawling on a bench, a cigarette drooping from one corner of his mouth. Behind him and to the left was a church with a slim spire and a jumble of pointed windows and doorways.

The door opened and she looked up.

'Fast asleep.' Charlotte gently closed the door and came to warm her hands by the fire. 'He should go right through now.'

'You make him sound like a baby,' Jill said, meaning the words as a pleasantry and immediately wishing she could bite them back.

'He's like one. Most of the time, anyway.' Charlotte turned away from Jill and picked up a china milkmaid on the mantel-piece.

'Would it help if I moved in for a while? You must be exhausted. I could at least give you a break occasionally.'

'No.' The older woman put the milkmaid down at the other end of the mantelpiece and then moved it back to its original position. 'Sorry, I didn't mean to sound so abrupt. It's very kind of you but we manage.'

'The offer stays open. Let me know if you change your mind.'

'Yes, dear. Do you know, I might have a little brandy myself. Dr Leddon said a modest nightcap has much to recommend it. On medical grounds, that is.'

'I'm sure he's right.'

Charlotte moved towards the drinks tray. Brandy bottle in hand, she laughed in an arch, strained manner. 'Such a nice man.'

'He seems very pleasant.'

'And quite an asset to Lydmouth,' Charlotte went on, with the next best thing to a simper. 'In all sorts of ways.' She splashed soda into the glass and walked back to the warmth of the fire. Her eyes fell on the photograph on the arm of Jill's chair. 'May I?' She picked it up and studied it. 'Ah – I thought so.'

'Thought what?'

'The style; quite unmistakable.' But Charlotte's attention was elsewhere. She took a deep breath and put the photograph back on the arm of the chair, from which it fell to the carpet. 'There's something I want to ask you.'

'Fire away,' Jill said, stooping to pick up the photograph.

'Philip and I think . . . well, he had a long talk with Dr Leddon this morning and he thinks it may be some time before Philip's well enough to return to work.' She moistened her lips. 'If he ever does.'

'I'm sure he—'

'I'm not sure of anything these days. The point is, Philip's very worried about the effect of all this uncertainty on the paper – editorially, I mean. He'd feel so much happier if you'd agree to take over permanently. It would make it easier for everyone.'

'Including you?'

'Yes. I don't pretend it's an easy decision. But I'm sure it would be for the best. On the other hand, it may not be what you yourself want – I'm sure you've got far more interesting plans.'

'Let's assume I haven't,' Jill said lightly. 'Just for the moment. What then?'

'Philip would know that the *Gazette* was in safe hands. Both of us feel there's no one who could do the job as well as you. And it would make it quite clear to the *Post* and everyone else that we're not intending to go under.'

Jill wasn't so sure about that. 'Of course I'll do it. On the understanding that when Philip wants his job back I'll resign.'

Once again, Charlotte's face crumpled. Then she touched Jill's shoulder with a heavy, beringed hand and forced herself to smile. She looked again at the photograph in Jill's hand. 'Who's this dashing chap? He's awfully like some film star, isn't he – some American?'

'John Wayne, I think. Imagine him in a cowboy hat. His name's Paul Frederick, and I saw him running to catch a train at the station on Friday.'

'Why have you got his photo?'

'Because no one's seen him since. Are you sure you want me to take the job?'

'Oh yes.' Charlotte sipped her drink. 'If I can't stop Philip worrying so much about everything, it's going to kill him.'

Friday, 9 December

The smell is worse. Don't panic. Pretend everything is normal. Though in a way nothing has been normal for a very long time. It's not a word that suits everyone, is it?

I can't stop thinking about what might happen. I'm lying in the bath or trying to go to sleep and all I can think of is the drop. The fall with its obscene ending. The full stop. Is there a snapping sound? Would it be like the breaking of a twig or a branch? Do you hear it in that endless moment between living and dying?

What if it doesn't kill you right away, if they make a mistake, if you find yourself strangling on a string, gasping for air? I read somewhere that in the old days they used to pull your legs, dragging you down, so that finished you off. But I don't know if they still do that. I'm sure they wouldn't just leave you. But I suppose they might pull you up and try all over again. 'Sorry – better luck next time.'

But that wouldn't be fair, would it, to try again? Surely you should hang only once? Then your debt is paid.

If they mess it up, then it should be their problem.

Chapter Forty-Six

Routine, really: that was the nature of the job. You didn't depend on brilliant intuitions or flashes of good fortune. You had to work at it instead and then, in the long run, you made your own luck. Brian Kirby understood that, which was one of the things Thornhill liked about him.

On Friday morning, Kirby banged on the door of Thornhill's room and came in without waiting for an answer. His face was flushed. He had pushed his fingers through his hair so it stood up in a tangle of greasy spikes.

'Want to hear the news about Leddon, sir?'

Thornhill laid down his pen. It was clear from Kirby's expression that it was the sort of news that Leddon wouldn't want him to hear.

'I rang the Leicester nick – mate of mine is a DC there and his wife's a nurse, so I reckoned between them they might be able to find out if there was anything we should know about Leddon. And there bloody is something.' Kirby beamed. 'This smarmy bastard's got a wife. Not to mention two kids and one or two unpaid debts.'

'Then why isn't the family here with him?'

'Separated. The word is, he had a fling with a patient. He wants a divorce but the wife's a Catholic so she won't play ball. But the news got around, which is why he had to make a new start. He's paying for their upkeep still, so no wonder he's poor.'

'Well done, Brian.' Thornhill felt an unholy joy spreading through him. 'So we know he's even more strapped for cash than we'd thought he was. But it's not a crime to conceal the fact that you're married.'

Kirby stared at him for an instant too long. 'As long as you don't try to marry again.'

'Just so.'

The telephone began to ring at this moment. Thornhill snatched at it.

'Thornhill.'

'Good morning, Chief Inspector,' said Jill Francis.

'Good morning.' He shot a glance across the desk. 'What can I do for you?'

'I want to ask you how you justify the extraordinary behaviour of certain officers under your command.'

'One moment, please.' Thornhill covered the mouthpiece with the palm of his hand and said to Kirby, 'Thank you, Brian – that's all for now.'

Eyes bright with curiosity, Kirby left the room.

'I don't think I understand what you mean, Miss Francis.'

'Howard Mork.'

'What about him?'

'He's one of my staff. Two of your officers have been harassing him.'

'There's no reason why they shouldn't ask him questions. If that's what you mean.'

'I'm not talking about asking questions. I'm talking about behaving like playground bullies. I'm talking about the use of violence.'

He sat up sharply and drew a notepad towards him. 'That's a very serious allegation, Miss Francis.'

'I wouldn't be talking to you if I didn't believe it to be true.'

'I appreciate that.' That was what really terrified him. He knew her well enough to realise that if she believed such a thing was true, there was nothing on earth he could do to prevent her from speaking out. Only an act of God would stop her. 'You'd better tell me who the officers concerned are.'

'Sergeant Kirby and PC Porter.'

Before he could stop himself, Thornhill sucked in his breath. 'And what are they meant to have done?'

'Look, Chief Inspector, I don't think you quite understand the gravity of this. It's not a question of what somebody else alleges them to have done. It's a question of what I saw happening with my own eyes.'

'Then will you tell me exactly what you saw, please?'

'I was in the station car park yesterday evening and I saw Kirby, Porter and Howard Mork outside the Station Hotel. Kirby had his hand round Mork's neck and was pushing him up against a lamp-post. He appeared to be trying to throttle him.'

'How can you be sure? There can't have been much light.'

'I told you – they were under a lamp-post and perhaps thirty or forty yards away from me. There was quite enough light to see what was going on.'

'What happened next?'

'I went over and asked what they were doing. Sergeant Kirby said it was none of my business.'

'And?'

'And what? As soon as they realised they had a witness, they stopped harassing him and sidled off. I took Howard Mork back to the *Gazette* and cleaned him up. He was sick, which I imagine had something to do with the investigating technique of your officers.'

Thornhill said coldly, 'On the other hand, I assume he'd been drinking so it may have had something to do with that.'

'I wouldn't be too sure. Anyway, I haven't finished. This is not the first time that my employee has had to put up with physical violence from your officers. They attacked him on Wednesday night, too.'

'Is Mr Mork intending to make a formal complaint?'

For a moment she said nothing. He fancied he could hear her breathing, the sound magically transmitted a few hundred yards up the High Street. Then came the rasp of a match.

'I don't know,' Jill said. 'But what I do know is that this sort of behaviour can't be allowed to continue. I'll do whatever is necessary to make it stop. I will, and so will the *Gazette*. Do you understand?'

'Oh yes. I understand.'

'Richard?'

The use of his Christian name took him by surprise. The balloon of his anger suddenly subsided. 'What?'

'Something very strange is going on in Lydmouth. Some of it probably doesn't matter very much – but some of it does. Have you come across a man called Joe Rodley?'

'I know who you mean.' He tried to keep the surprise out of his voice as he struggled to keep up with her. 'What about him?'

'Well, that's the point, isn't it?'

Without warning Jill put the receiver down. Thornhill slammed the useless handset on its rest. This business was bad enough without her threatening to complain about Kirby and Porter – *Porter?* – and making enigmatic remarks about Rodley. He wondered whether she knew that Leddon was married, and with children. Should he tell her? Whether she already knew or not, she'd think it was none of his business. She never bloody picks the right man, he thought, and the thought saddened him, for her sake.

He pushed back his chair and stood up. He found Brian Kirby in the CID room, going through a file with Sergeant Carney of the Fingerprint Department. Carney was nearing retirement, and he stooped over the file, peering at it through thick glasses. He glanced up at Thornhill, his expression both naked and surprised, like that of a recently clipped old English sheepdog.

'Been through the whole house now, sir,' he said, straightening up and tapping the report with a long, nicotine-stained forefinger. 'We haven't been able to identify all of them, but that's only to be expected. We reckon all the more recent ones are accounted for.'

'That page covers the veranda,' Kirby said. 'And that's the room where he died.'

Thornhill ran his eyes down the list. Jill Francis, the cleaner, Bayswater himself, Leddon, a jobbing builder who had helped Bayswater build the shed at the end of the veranda.

'What you'd expect, really,' Kirby said. 'Though it's a relief to know there aren't any jokers in the pack.'

'My office, Sergeant Kirby,' Thornhill said, turning on his heels. 'Now.'

He left the suddenly silent room. A moment later, Kirby joined him in his office.

'What's up, guv?'

Thornhill sat down. 'Howard Mork.'

Kirby frowned. 'What?'

'Don't come the innocent with me, Brian. I know you and Porter have been talking to him. That's not the problem.'

Kirby stared at him. His eyes were round and glassy.

'It's your method of interrogation. We have a highly

respectable witness who says you appeared to be using physical force on Mork.'

'Miss Francis.'

'The source has nothing to do with it at present. What concerns me is whether this is true.' Thornhill paused. 'I gather PC Porter was with you. I shall be talking independently to him.'

Kirby shrugged. 'It's a storm in a teacup, guv. You know how it is.'

'No, I don't know how it is. You'd better tell me.'

Kirby, who was still standing because he had not been asked to sit down, raised himself on the balls of his feet as though trying to make himself taller. 'Some of the people we deal with . . . I mean, they're not like you and me, sir. You have to use the sort of language they understand. Sometimes you can go on till you're blue in the face without getting anywhere. But as soon as they realise you're someone to be reckoned with, they'll talk all you want.'

'Not here, Sergeant. Not in Lydmouth. Not while you're under my command.'

Kirby stared at him. 'But everyone does it sometimes, sir,' he said. 'It's just one of those things. I dare say it's always been like that. We don't hurt them, sir, it's only that some of them need to be shown who's boss. And there's no way to reason with them because they're too stupid.'

'As far as I can tell you've achieved absolutely nothing by bullying the lad, apart from causing us problems. It won't do, Brian. I don't know if this will go farther or not, but one thing I do know is that you'll be doing things entirely by the book from now on, that is if you want to continue doing them at all. Off you go.'

Thornhill saw something he'd never seen before: Brian Kirby blushing from a cocktail of emotions that probably ranged from anger to embarrassment via shame and hurt pride. He left the room without another word, closing the door behind him with a little more force than was necessary. Marriage mellowed some men and soured others. It seemed to have soured Kirby. He had sought promotion before he married Joan but not like this. Now he constantly wanted to prove himself. The irony was that in doing so he had alienated the very person whose support he needed.

Thornhill picked up the internal phone and asked for PC Porter. The constable was not in the building so Thornhill left a message that he wanted to see him as soon as he came in. He wondered whether he should talk to Drake about suspending Kirby from duty but decided that that would be too much, too soon. In his memory he again saw Kirby in the CID room poring over the report with Carney. He had been cheerful, pleased to see Thornhill, pleased to share this latest snippet of information. Thornhill wondered whether he would ever see Kirby look like that again.

His mind slid sideways from Kirby's face to the report on his desk. He picked up the phone again and asked for the Fingerprint Department. Sergeant Carney answered.

'Have you got a copy of that report on Bayswater's house?'

'Yes, sir.'

'You said you'd found Dr Leddon's fingerprints in Bayswater's study. What were they on?'

Carney said in his slow, country voice, 'There was a partial on the door handle from the veranda, sir. And a good one on a whisky bottle.'

'Nothing on a glass?'

'No. But the sink in the scullery was full of dirty crocks soaking in water, including a few glasses. It might have been one of those.'

'Okay – thanks.' Thornhill was about to put the receiver

down when another thought struck him. 'Wait a moment, Sergeant. The print on the whisky bottle. Can you remember what sort of whisky it was?'

'Cutty Sark, sir. Only just opened, by the look of it.'

There was a knock on the door.

'Come in,' Thornhill called.

Peter Porter edged his large body into the room.

'Cutty Sark,' Thornhill said to him. 'Good God.'

Chapter Forty-Seven

'A good journalist never divulges his sources,' Amy Gwyn-Thomas said. 'Or her sources.'

Ronald Prout looked less impressed than she had hoped. 'That's all very well, but I don't see how you can be so sure.'

'I am sure. You can take my word for it.'

The bell pinged and Mr Prout turned aside to deal with a customer, a woman searching for a tractor for her son's birthday. Amy pretended to examine a doll's layette. She had taken her lunch break early and, at Jill's suggestion, had dropped into Prout's Toys and Novelties to put Ronald's mind at rest about the Pisser.

At last the woman left with a Dinky toy in a brown paper bag. Amy decided that it was time to mould the truth into a more acceptable form.

'My source told me the person concerned was frightened off after what you did with the fish slice. That's why there won't be any more incidents.'

Mr Prout nodded curtly, his expression contriving to imply that no other explanation was worth serious consideration. Then, to her relief, he smiled.

'So that's that, is it?' he said. 'Do you know, I think I shall almost miss the . . . the attacks. They added a touch of excitement to life.'

'We all like that, I suppose,' Amy said a trifle wistfully.

'Of course, I don't mean it, not really. The inconvenience,

the worry – not something one would wish to repeat. I tell you one thing, though. Whoever the culprit is, I'm pretty sure he's going to come to a bad end.'

'I don't know about that, Ronald.' Amy felt a tide of maternal feeling wash warmly over her as she thought of Howard's misplaced but endearing devotion. 'It might be just a phase he's going through. I wouldn't be at all surprised if he grows out of it.' She smiled. 'Whoever it is.'

Amy left the shop soon afterwards and walked back to the High Street with the intention of having a bowl of soup and a roll for lunch in the Gardenia Café. As she drew level with the zebra crossing. Mr Gray began to cross from the garage on the other side. Two cars and a lorry came to an unanticipated halt. Amy glanced automatically at the nearest vehicle.

It was a police car. Peter Porter was driving. In the back were Detective Chief Inspector Thornhill and Dr Leddon.

Amy hesitated, and began to walk to the *Gazette*. What, she wondered, would Miss Francis make of that? Surely the police couldn't have arrested that nice Dr Leddon?

Chapter Forty-Eight

The car turned left off the High Street and then right into the yard at the back of Police Headquarters.

'No, sir,' Thornhill said. 'You're free to go at any time. You haven't been arrested, let alone charged.'

'In that case—' Leddon began.

'Yet,' Thornhill added.

'What?'

'You haven't been charged yet. Which is not to say you never will be. The fact remains that sooner or later you'll have to answer some very awkward questions. If you want to be arrested first that's your business, but I really wouldn't recommend it.'

Leddon turned his head and looked out of the window. Porter slipped the car into a vacant slot, parking with geometric precision so the car was aligned with the white lines on the tarmac. He sprang out and opened the rear nearside door for Leddon.

Rather than take Leddon upstairs for a chat in his office, Thornhill told Porter to take him to one of the interview rooms in the basement. These little hutches, with their concrete floors and dented metal tables, were not comfortable places. Thornhill thought they reeked of fear and anxiety.

He left Leddon stewing in one of them, under the eye of Porter, while he went upstairs to the CID room. Even in informal interviews like this, a witness was often advisable, and

in normal circumstances his first choice would have been
Kirby. Brian was in the room, his head studiously bowed
over the typewriter on which he was picking out a report with
two fingers. Thornhill called out a young DC named Kear. He
knew that within minutes of their leaving the room, everyone
would know where they had gone, and why.

'I'll ask the questions,' he told Kear on their way downstairs.
'I want you to make notes. Watch his hands and his face. Sit to
one side so he can't see us both at the same time.'

Thornhill wondered fleetingly whether this tactic was a form
of psychological warfare, in its way as intimidating as Kirby's
more physical tactics. It was an unsettling thought and he
pushed it aside. Regulations covered physical violence but
they had nothing to say on the relative positions of chairs in an
interview room.

They found Leddon sitting at the table with a lighted
cigarette in his hand and the half-smoked butt of another in
the empty tobacco tin that did duty as an ashtray.

'I hate to state the obvious, Chief Inspector, but I'm a busy
man. I haven't had my lunch yet and I've got a number of
house calls I need to make immediately afterwards.'

'We'll try not to keep you any longer than we need, Doctor.'

He introduced Kear and began the questioning. At first he
took the increasingly restive Leddon over familiar territory:
notably his troubled relationship with Dr Bayswater and the
awkward fact that, contrary to his original statement, he had
been seen in the vicinity of Grove House at about 10.45 the
previous Friday evening.

'We've discussed all this before. You can dislike a man
without having to kill him – I should have thought that was
obvious.'

'But it wasn't just dislike, sir, was it? We understand that
he was making your life difficult in a number of ways, in

particular by refusing to sell you some of his garden for a new surgery.'

'He reneged on our agreement. That's one reason I disliked him.'

'I see. But now he's dead, we understand that there's every possibility that you will be able to buy the land after all.'

'That may be true. But I had no way of knowing that beforehand. I had no idea who Bayswater would leave the house to. I didn't even know he had a sister.'

It was a reasonable point, though not a conclusive one. Thornhill let the silence develop.

'Then why lie about Friday evening, Dr Leddon?'

'I've explained all that. It was foolish of me – a reflex – but I couldn't see the point of being involved. I didn't want to waste my time or yours.'

'We're the best judge of that, sir.'

Leddon ignored him. 'Besides, you must realise that a doctor is in a very delicate position in the community. We're like clergymen or judges. We have to be whiter than white. The trouble with cases like this is that suspicion can cling to the wrong people for no good reason. And it does cling.'

'In cases like this, Doctor? You've been involved in scandal before?'

'Of course not. I'm just telling you what any doctor in general practice would tell you.'

'So you haven't had personal experience of scandal, sir?' Thornhill repeated.

'I don't like the tone of this.' Leddon stood up abruptly. The chair behind him, a lightweight affair of canvas and tubular steel, rocked and slid a few inches across the floor. 'I'm leaving now. Unless you plan to arrest me.'

Thornhill remained seated. 'I suppose it all depends on your definition of scandal. If a married doctor, a family man, had an affair with one of his patients: would that constitute scandal?'

The blood drained from Leddon's cheeks. The shadow of his stubble darkened against the pallor. He licked his lips and began to say something, stopped and sat down on the edge of the chair.

'I . . . I've done nothing wrong. I want to make that quite clear.'

'I don't think I said you had. But in any case, according to you, that's not the point: mud sticks, isn't that what you were saying? Even when it hits an innocent target. I was under the impression that you were a bachelor. I imagine most people in Lydmouth are. Tell me, why didn't you bring your family with you?'

Leddon made a performance out of finding and lighting a cigarette. 'My wife and I are estranged. I don't think I need go into the reasons for that – it's nothing to do with you. You'll appreciate . . . you'll appreciate that it's not the sort of thing I want to advertise. Some of my patients are very old fashioned in their views.' He sucked hard on the cigarette and went on in a softer voice, 'Is there any reason why this need go any farther? After all, it's not relevant to your investigation, surely?'

'We don't know that, yet.'

'I can assure you—'

'You assured us you didn't go out on Friday night,' Thornhill said gently.

'I've explained—'

'You've explained very little, I'm afraid. If you explained some more, it might help convince us that you have nothing to do with this. If you co-operate with us, we have every reason to co-operate with you.'

'I am. I will.'

'Then when did you last see Dr Bayswater?'

'On Friday morning, at Gray's Garage. Miss Francis was there.'

'I know you saw him there. But I think you saw him after that as well. In the evening.'

Leddon shook his head. 'Look, I did go out for a walk – I admit it. There was no point in my going to see him, though, and I didn't. Nothing you can say can make me pretend otherwise.'

'Even the truth, Dr Leddon?'

'I don't know what you mean.'

'We have a piece of evidence that suggests you were not only outside Grove House on Friday evening but that you were inside it too.'

'Nonsense. If you mean fingerprints or something like that it simply won't hold water. Of course I've been to Grove House on many occasions. The last time was a few days before the old man died. I was trying to change his mind, though I might as well have saved my breath.'

'When you were there, you had a drink,' Thornhill said. 'Was that before or after he died?'

Leddon hesitated. 'I don't want to say any more. If you're going to arrest me, you should get on with it, and then I want to see my solicitor before I say anything else.'

'We have a witness who met Dr Bayswater in the High Street after he had returned from Gloucester on the day he died. It was late in the afternoon, and he'd just bought himself some whisky, a bottle of Cutty Sark. We found the bottle in his study after his death. It had been opened, which must have happened in the last few hours of his life. But the really interesting thing about that bottle, Dr Leddon, is that it has your fingerprints on it.'

Chapter Forty-Nine

By the time Jill returned to Raglan Court, it was already dark. The longest night of the year was not far away. She parked the car in the wedge of light near the back door of the flats. It would be safer there.

Despite the darkness and the fact that she was nervous – or perhaps partly because of all this – she decided to stretch her legs in the park. She had been cooped up all day in smoky offices, her muscles tight with tiredness and tension. She needed exercise, and even a four-minute walk was better than nothing.

Since twilight, the fog had begun to seep back over the town. She locked the car and made her way into the park by the main entrance. The broad path from the double gates was well lit by lamp-posts. At least four people and two dogs were in sight. Away from the main path and the lamps there were swathes of darkness on either side, but they were too far away to be worrying. There was nothing to be frightened of. She wasn't alone.

The path led to a junction with other, lesser paths. Here, about 150 yards away from the gates, there was an octagonal bandstand where the town band played concerts on summer evenings. It was still visible, but now mist blurred the outlines of the ornate iron railings that ran round the perimeter of the low platform. Jill walked briskly to the junction, circumnavigated the bandstand and began to retrace her steps towards the gate.

In the interval, someone else had come into the park from Albert Road. Gradually Jill drew nearer to the newcomer, whose outline emerged in fits and starts, wraith-like, as the distance shortened. The wraith turned into a sturdy woman attached to a little dog, which was yapping with piercing ferocity.

'Good evening, Mrs Fuggle,' Jill said when they were close enough.

The woman mumbled something and would have hurried past, but the terrier plunged towards Jill, snapping his jaws. Mrs Fuggle pulled him aside and wound the lead round the nearest lamp-post. With her eyes on the ground, she waited for Jill to pass on.

'I'm Jill Francis of the *Gazette*,' Jill said, refusing to move. 'I don't think we've met, but I know your husband through work.'

'Of course. Not . . . not a pleasant evening, is it?'

'It gets dark so early at present,' Jill said, moved as much by the woman's evident misery as anything else. 'I was so sorry to hear about what happened in the cemetery.'

'Yes – well. Be quiet, Macbeth, you silly dog.' Mrs Fuggle jerked the terrier's lead and the tiny animal's yapping became a yelp. 'We must be on our way. Goodbye.'

She hurried towards the bandstand, despite Macbeth's attempts to remain beside the lamp-post. Jill looked after her. The poor woman was a nervous wreck. Was that Ivor Fuggle's doing?

Mrs Fuggle stopped and half turned, so Jill could see her shadowy profile. 'I wonder if it could have been one of our neighbours. In the cemetery, I mean.' She coughed and then added in a hoarse whisper: 'It's funny how you get bad feelings among neighbours, isn't it?'

She receded into the mist. As Parthian shots went, it

had been a particularly ambiguous one. Joe Rodley was the obvious candidate, but why should he want to desecrate the grave of a former neighbour? And why now?

Shivering, Jill walked back to Raglan Court, back to a briefcase full of work, a portable typewriter and an unappetising supper whose centrepiece was likely to be a tin of pilchards. She let herself into the flat and went round turning on lights and fires and drawing curtains. She poured herself a glass of sherry – one needed some sort of appetiser for those pilchards – and sat down to smoke a cigarette and skim through the *Evening Post*.

Judged by his own lights, Ivor Fuggle was doing a good job on behalf of the shareholders of the Champion Group – both the shrill tone of his editorial and the content of many of his stories were designed to appeal to the baser part of human nature; and you couldn't ignore the lucrative implications of the increasing number of advertisements that a few months before would have appeared only in the *Gazette*. Jill folded the paper and put it on the arm of her chair, fighting the temptation to have another cigarette.

By chance it was open at the page with the photograph of Paul Frederick. There was something odd about it, Jill thought, something she could not put her finger on. Had Charlotte glimpsed the same thing yesterday evening just before she offered Jill her husband's job? *The style; quite unmistakable.* Jill glanced at her watch. Not a bad time to phone Charlotte. She went to the telephone and began to dial the number of Troy House.

As the dial was whirring back on the second digit, the doorbell rang. Jill put down the receiver. When she opened the door, Roger Leddon was standing there, looking gaunt and rather handsome, with the beginnings of blue stubble on his cheeks.

'I was wondering if you'd like to have dinner with me?'
He smiled at her. 'Actually there's something I wanted to
say.'

She allowed herself to be persuaded. They went up to his
flat, where he heated baked beans and burned the toast. In the
meantime they drank half a bottle of burgundy. The rest of the
burgundy slipped away while they nibbled the more edible
parts of the meal. Afterwards, Leddon fetched fruit and cheese
and another bottle.

'I shouldn't have any more,' Jill said. 'Nor should you.'

'Nonsense. Speaking as a doctor, I can hardly overempha-
sise the importance of relaxation after a hard day's work.' He
withdrew the cork with a pop. 'Come on, half a glass won't
hurt. It helps the digestion too.'

As he leaned across the table to refill her glass, his hand
brushed hers. Their eyes met. Roger Leddon smiled and Jill
found herself smiling back.

'I wish—' he began, and then broke off and took a sip of
wine.

'Wish what?'

'I wish I'd done things rather differently.'

Jill began to peel an apple. 'That sounds enigmatic.'

'There's something I need to tell you. I'm afraid I haven't
been altogether frank.' He pushed away his plate and reached
for his cigarettes.

'You don't have to tell me anything.'

'I'd like to.' He dropped a dying match into the ashtray and
a wisp of smoke spiralled upwards; for an instant before it
dissolved, it twisted into an inverted hook, a question mark.
'For me, coming to Lydmouth was making a fresh start in all
sorts of ways. I wanted to be my own boss – run my practice in
the way I thought it should be run. And there were personal
reasons, too. When . . . when I first came here, people

assumed I was single. And for a number of reasons it seemed wise to go along with it.'

'You're married?' Jill wondered why she didn't feel surprised.

'I wasn't planning to keep quiet about it. It just sort of happened. It was all Bayswater's fault, as a matter of fact. Something I said when I first came over to have a look at the practice here led him to think I was a bachelor. After that it was simpler to play along, especially –' he hesitated '– especially because my wife and I aren't getting along too well at present. In fact we're separated. And that was the problem, you see. Something like that, it's a black mark against you in a town like Lydmouth. I couldn't afford it, not when I was trying to establish myself here. You understand?'

He tapped ash from his cigarette and waited. Jill sipped her wine but did not speak, though she understood perfectly. Lydmouth had more than its fair share of Mrs Grundys, ready and willing to sit in judgement on the private lives of other people.

Leddon picked up the bottle. 'Anyway, it seemed easier to let things slide, just for the moment, and I thought I'd let the fact that I was married emerge gradually after I'd settled in.' He screwed up his face until he looked like an exceptionally handsome monkey. 'But settling in is taking rather longer than I'd anticipated. I over-estimated Lydmouth's ability to absorb newcomers.' He topped up her glass. 'I imagine you've noticed that too. And now poor Bayswater's dead, and what with all this other trouble in the town, the fact that I failed to mention I was married looks bad. I can't help feeling that the police are building a case against me.'

'For what?'

'I had a rather uncomfortable interview with that chief inspector today. They'd found out about Thelma.'

Thelma, Jill thought – *Thelma.* Now she had a name.

'That wouldn't matter normally,' Leddon continued, 'not in itself, but the trouble is they think I'm the most likely person to have wanted Bayswater dead so Thelma's existence sort of confirms their general opinion that I'm an all-round bad hat.'

'They think you killed Bayswater?' Jill said slowly, and the aftertaste of the wine turned sour in her mouth. 'I know they've been talking to you, but they've been talking to everyone.'

'The thing is, they reckon I've got the best motive. He reneged on his agreement to sell me that land, which has left me in limbo. A bloody expensive limbo. Except for that land, I had everything else lined up. We . . . we had our professional disagreements too. This is something I haven't told anyone else, but I wasn't very happy when I went through some of his more recent diagnoses.'

'He was behind the times?'

'It was partly that. But it was also that he'd succumbed to the disease that afflicts a lot of chaps in my profession. He'd grown too convinced of his own infallibility. And because of that, there's at least one person in this town who'll never walk again. I told him so once, to his face. He didn't like it.'

'Why are you telling me all this, Roger?'

The cigarette smouldered between his fingers, the coil of ash on the end growing longer and longer. The room was so quiet that Jill heard the sound of his breathing. Why, she wondered, why do I always choose the married ones?

'I want things to be straight between us,' he said to her. 'I owe you that. I should have told you earlier. And listen, there's a bit more.'

'About Thelma?'

'I mean about Bayswater, and the police. It's not just that they think I have a motive. There is other evidence.'

'You were alone here at the time. They can't argue with that, surely?'

'I'm afraid I wasn't completely straightforward about that, either.' He gazed at her with clear blue eyes that seemed the colour of honesty itself. 'I did go out last Friday night. Quite late – it was after ten. I was thinking about this business of the Grove House land. You remember we were talking about it? I thought I'd do as you suggested and go and see Bayswater, have one last try at persuading him to see sense. The trouble is, someone saw me in Broad Street, not far from Grove House. So Thornhill nailed me in one lie. I told him I'd just gone out for some air, for some exercise before bed. It seemed pointless making things unnecessarily complicated – pointless for them as well as for me.'

Unnecessarily complicated?

'What do you mean?' Jill said, suddenly sober. It occurred to her that it was just possible that she had been getting tipsy with a murderer.

'To make matters worse, when Thornhill hauled me in today, it turned out he'd got hold of another bit of awkward evidence. I didn't think I'd have to worry about fingerprints.'

Jill kept her voice light. 'If you went to Grove House, surely you must have realised you'd left your fingerprints there – and you knew the police were fingerprinting everyone for the purposes of elimination?'

'That's the point. They knew I'd been to Grove House relatively recently, so they were expecting to find my prints there. The problem was, old Bayswater wanted a whisky. Not that he offered me one. But as I was leaving he asked me to pass him a bottle that was on the desk. As my bloody luck would have it, it turned out that someone had seen him buying that very bottle early the same evening.'

'Which meant if your fingerprints were on it, then almost certainly you must have paid him a visit during the evening?'

Leddon nodded. 'I can see it looks bad. That's why I hoped we'd never have to bring it out into the open. After all, it was only going to waste everybody's time. Anyway, they positively grilled me.'

'Are you surprised?'

He grinned at her. 'I've no right to be, have I? I've been damned stupid, that's the long and the short of it. But honestly, I was only there for about five minutes – must have been around half-past ten – and Bayswater was alive and well when I left. And just as obstinate as ever.'

Jill thought of the slovenly old man she had found on Saturday morning. She said, 'What happened?'

'When I got there, he was reading. Some textbook – you know he had this bee in his bonnet about making a great contribution to medical science? He was in his pyjamas already. He let me say my piece and then he said I might as well go because he wasn't going to change his mind, and would I kindly pass him the whisky on my way out. Short, sweet and rather unpleasant – that was about the sum of my relationship with Dr Bayswater.'

'No sign of the room being searched?'

He shook his head. 'I almost forgot – you found the body, didn't you?'

'I try not to remember.'

He reached across the table and patted her hand. 'Sorry.'

'Not your fault.' She stood up, suddenly in need of exercise, and went to warm her hands at the electric fire. 'They've not arrested you – that must be a good sign.'

'I hope so. It may just be they realise I've got nowhere to run to or maybe they're waiting for a little more evidence.' He got up, glass in hand, and came to stand near her. 'My guess is that they think he was killed with one of his own tools. You know he fancied himself as something of a handyman?'

Jill nodded.

'There were some tools on a table on the veranda. Not that I could see them very clearly.'

'It could have been a hammer or something like that,' Jill said quietly. 'It suggests that if he was murdered, it was done on the spur of the moment.'

'Try not to think about it,' Leddon advised. 'What about another glass of wine?'

'Not for me, thanks. I should be going.'

'No hurry.' Leddon came another step nearer. He smelled of tobacco and wine. It occurred to Jill that it would really be very pleasant just to rest her forehead against his chest and feel his arms around her and not have to say anything or do anything.

He said, 'At the start of this evening I was going to ask you a favour.' He waited for her to say something, and when she didn't he continued, 'I wondered if you might like to say that you saw me last Friday night – we might have passed in the hallway or something – and you could tell them that I seemed quite normal. Not like a man who'd just committed murder.'

'I'm glad you didn't ask me.'

'Yes. I'm glad I didn't ask. It wouldn't have done any good, anyway, would it?'

'Probably not.' Jill was aware that she'd had a little more wine than was altogether wise. 'Anyway, I really must go. Where did I leave my bag?'

He was very close to her now. She felt his hand on her shoulder and his arm encircling her. She leaned against him. Just for a moment, she told herself, it can't hurt. He dropped a kiss on her hair. She ran her fingers slowly down the tweed of his jacket. She felt very tired.

It was bad enough when men were married. The trouble was, they so often felt obliged to lie as well – not just to their wives but to their lovers. Off the top of her head, she could think of only one exception to this general rule among the people she knew. Richard Thornhill. But in his case, there was the further problem that he was the one person in Lydmouth, or indeed anywhere else, that she definitely did not want to think about.

Roger Leddon squeezed her more tightly and began to manoeuvre himself so they were chest to chest. His right hand stroked the back of her head.

'Roger?' she said, raising her face.

He lowered his head and kissed her. At the last moment she moved slightly so the kiss fell chastely on her cheek rather than on her lips.

She pulled away from him a little but not out of his embrace. 'I was wondering – you said that because of Dr Bayswater, someone in Lydmouth wouldn't walk again. I hadn't realised he was such a bad doctor.'

'He wasn't – most of the time, anyway. But when you combine outdated knowledge with an absolute conviction that you're always in the right, you occasionally make mistakes. As that poor woman has found to her cost. Not that she knows that he's responsible – not exactly. Though I had to say that I thought she'd been misdiagnosed. He put it down to stress-related hysteria, you see, but it's Pott's disease – a tuberculous abcess on the spine. The irony is, you can treat it these days. But if you leave it too long, the damage it does to the spine is irreparable.'

Jill edged a little closer and received a kiss on the other cheek. 'Who was it, as a matter of interest?'

'I couldn't possibly say. My lips are professionally sealed.'

They're certainly not sealed in any other way, Jill thought, as she felt him nuzzling her forehead. He reminded her of a greedy horse in search of sugar lumps. Looked at objectively, the physical mechanics of love and lust had a ludicrous quality.

She went on: 'I don't suppose it was Doreen Rodley? I know you can't possibly answer but she's the only woman I can think of who fits the bill.'

'I couldn't possibly comment. On the other hand I could possibly say you've got an uncanny genius for speculation.'

She let him kiss her once on the lips and then broke away. The last she saw of him that evening was when he was standing in the doorway, his face flushed with wine and lust, his tie askew and his hair rumpled. He looked out of place and rather pathetic, like a teddy bear left out in the rain.

[Saturday, 10 December]

Not well today. Fluey, temperature's over 102°. I shouldn't have gone out — that made it worse.

I shouldn't have read the papers either. I saw his face. Strange — they used a photograph of him as he used to be. It's a message. He's calling, calling, calling. Tap, tap, tappity tap. He was a wireless operator once, flying high as a bird in the sky.

High as a bird, higher than someone swinging in a prison yard, strangling at the end of a rope.

Tap, tap, tappity tap.

Chapter Fifty

On Saturday morning the postman brought an unscheduled letter from David Thornhill. Like every other boarder at Ashbridge School, he was obliged to write to his parents after chapel on Sunday morning. But this letter had been written on Thursday evening.

It was short and businesslike, a politely phrased request for a loan to deal with some unexpected expenses and carry him over to the end of term. All his parents had to do, David said, was pop a postal order in an envelope and send it to him; he would do the rest. He would pay them back with some of the money he confidently expected to receive at Christmas. As an afterthought he hoped everyone was well. After his signature there followed a rather lengthier afterthought in the form of a postscript in which he considerately listed some of the Christmas presents he would be pleased to receive this year.

It was not in other respects a particularly informative or affectionate letter, but it had a benign influence on the Thornhill family. The letter was passed round as they were eating a leisurely breakfast of porridge followed by scrambled egg and bacon. Edith pored over it with the concentration of a textual scholar, wringing every drop of meaning and speculation from it. Richard was happy too, because he missed his son and a letter was better than nothing. Elizabeth was happy because she was a greedy child and loved Saturday breakfast and also because her mother was taking her out to buy new shoes. Susie was happy because, all things being equal, she generally was.

After Elizabeth and Susie had left the table, their parents remained, eating toast and drinking coffee.

Thornhill reached for the marmalade and said, 'He sounds quite cheerful, doesn't he?'

Edith looked up from the letter. 'Yes – how much do you think we should send him?'

'So you think we should send him something?'

'Oh, I think so. After all, it's nearly Christmas, and I expect he'd like to buy his friends presents and things.'

Thornhill grunted.

Edith went on, 'I thought perhaps ten shillings.'

'Isn't that—' Thornhill broke off. 'No – I think you're right.'

Edith smiled at him. 'You're in a good mood.'

'It's been a hell of a week. It's nice just to be at home for a few hours.'

'If he's happy, that's the main thing,' Edith said, apparently apropos of nothing.

Thornhill knew, decoding the shorthand of marriage, that her mind had moved back to David, and that in her words there was even an acknowledgement that sending him away to boarding school, which had been at her insistence, had drawbacks as well as advantages for all concerned. Also implicit was a hint that what united David's parents might be more important than what divided them.

'I think he's settled in astonishingly well,' Thornhill said, tacitly conceding that sending their son to boarding school had not necessarily been a mistake.

Edith said nothing but smiled.

'Have you told him about the television yet?'

She shook her head. 'I will when I write tomorrow.'

'He'll love it,' Thornhill said, and hoped his voice did not sound suspiciously hearty.

'You don't mind? I thought you did.'

'About the television? I know I was against it at first, but I'm beginning to think it has its virtues. It certainly keeps them quiet, and it must have some educational value.'

'Richard,' Edith said, 'I've been thinking.'

He looked up. As Edith opened her mouth to continue, the telephone began to ring in the other room.

'I've a horrible feeling that's for me,' Thornhill said. 'I hope not.'

He went into the dining-room, picked up the receiver and recited his phone number.

'Richard,' said Jill Francis.

He glanced at the door, which was ajar. 'Yes.'

'I'm sorry to ring you at home – I tried the station first but they told me you weren't in.'

'What can I do for you?' He didn't know whether to address her as Jill or Miss Francis so in the end he said nothing.

'There's something I need to tell you.'

'All right.'

'I'd rather not do it on the phone. And it's confidential, so if you don't mind I'd rather not come to the station. I wonder if we could meet somewhere.'

Thornhill thought of Edith in the kitchen. 'Where?'

'It's not a bad morning. How about in the park?'

'Very well.' He appreciated that it was the best available choice. He wasn't sure how Edith would feel if Jill called at the house. On the other hand, he didn't particularly want to call at Jill's flat, especially not by himself.

He told Edith that he had to go out for a few minutes. She had been a policeman's wife for too long to ask questions, but he felt her curiosity like the glow from a fire. He wished that Jill hadn't phoned at that moment. He and Edith had been moving towards a truce. It was too delicate a situation for him to feel confident that there would be another opportunity.

For the first time in weeks there was a blue sky overhead. He walked up to the park. The thin winter sunshine brought an improbable foretaste of spring to Victoria Road. At the top of the hill he glanced up at the gleaming windows of Raglan Court on the corner of Albert Road and wondered where Leddon was.

In the park, he saw Jill standing near the bandstand, and as he drew nearer he realised that she was watching a party of sparrows fighting for crumbs that someone had scattered on the platform. She appeared not to notice his approach but at the last minute she turned towards him. He touched the brim of his hat with a forefinger.

She looked at him, raising her chin a fraction. 'Thank you for coming.'

He said nothing.

'I came across some information last night that I think you ought to have. It's confidential, actually, which is why I wanted to meet like this. I'm not meant to know, either.'

'What does it concern?'

'I'm not sure.' Unexpectedly she smiled. 'I'm not being very helpful, am I? It's possible it might have a bearing on the death of Dr Bayswater. But you're the best judge of that. Shall we walk? It's too cold to stand around.'

She set off down the path leading from the bandstand towards the Whistler's Lane entrance to the park. He fell into step beside her. He was aware of her looking at him. He knew that he was too aware of her, too alert to every movement she made, every nuance in her voice. It wasn't healthy.

'I had a drink with Dr Leddon last night,' she said.

Thornhill's shoulder muscles tensed.

'He didn't have a very high opinion of Dr Bayswater's medical skills,' she went on. 'He thought he was out of date, too inclined to trust his own judgement.'

'Sounds possible. Bayswater seemed competent enough when I saw him in action, but that's neither here nor there.'

'Dr Leddon mentioned that there was someone in Lydmouth who'd never walk again because of a mistaken diagnosis that Dr Bayswater had made.'

'He wouldn't have said who the person was, surely? That would be unethical.'

'No, he didn't.' Jill sounded defensive. 'He did let slip a little later that it was a woman. And . . . and in the end I asked him more or less straight out if it was Doreen Rodley. He didn't deny it. And his manner suggested I was right.'

'So you're next to certain?' Thornhill ran the probabilities through his mind: it was hard to believe that Leddon's practice had many other women patients who had recently become crippled.

'You see where this is going, of course?'

He nodded.

'I hope I'm not complicating things.'

'No,' he said. 'I don't think you're doing that.'

If Bayswater had been to some extent responsible for Doreen Rodley's condition, and if her husband knew this, then Joe Rodley had a substantial reason to bear a grudge against Bayswater. As far as one could judge these things, Rodley was a man who was quite capable of taking grudges seriously.

If he had gone to see Bayswater on the night of his death – to threaten him? to blackmail him? – and if there'd been a quarrel, then it was perfectly possible that Rodley had given way to the temptation to hit the old man with whatever came to hand.

But how did the yellow glove fit into this? What about Paul Frederick, last seen at Lydmouth station, boarding a train? And before that an hour or two earlier outside Viney Cottage – and the person who had seen him was Doreen Rodley.

Jill slowed and turned. 'I must go back.'

He walked with her. 'You must see a good deal of Dr Leddon. As you're neighbours, I mean.'

She glanced at him. 'A certain amount.' Her voice was suddenly chilly. 'Why?'

'I . . . I wondered if he'd mentioned – or whether you knew—'

'That he's married?'

He blinked. 'Yes.'

'As a matter of fact I do.'

'I don't want you to think I—'

'Then why did you say it?'

'Because—' He stopped walking, and so did she. They faced each other like two boxers squaring up for a fight. He said, 'What you do with your private life is no concern of mine, Jill. I wish . . . anyway, I didn't want you to get hurt, that's all. I owed you that if nothing else. If he's told you, that's fine.'

She smiled at him, and he felt sick with longing.

'Thank you,' she said. 'As a matter of fact, he only got around to telling me yesterday evening.' She hesitated. 'He'd had rather a lot to drink. In a roundabout way, he even asked if I'd say I'd seen him that Friday evening.'

'I don't understand. I thought you had.'

'Yes, I did. But that was early on. He meant later. He told me about someone seeing him in the street and about the whisky bottle at Grove House. He knew it was too late to pretend that he had an alibi. I suppose he thought it might come in handy, if the worst came to the worst, if a relatively respectable neighbour were to say that she'd seen him after he was meant to have committed the crime, and that he seemed quite normal, that he wasn't acting like someone who'd just banged an old-age pensioner over the head with a blunt instrument.'

They smiled at each other and walked on. He had a premonition that Edith or even Elizabeth would be waiting for him on the other side of the gates, that Edith would find out that his meeting this morning had been with Jill Francis. But no one was there. He and Jill parted outside Raglan Court.

At home, he told Edith that something had come up and drove at once to Police Headquarters. Drake's car was not outside. He went upstairs and found a grim-faced Kirby going through the contents of a large envelope in the CID room. Thornhill glanced over his shoulder, at the papers strewn across his desk.

'What's all that?'

'Two days' worth of Bayswater's post.'

'Anything interesting?'

'The mixture as before. Business and medical stuff. Nothing personal, nothing out of the way.'

'I'll look through it later. Leave it on my desk. Is Mr Drake due in today?'

'No, sir. They've got family over for the weekend. Some big party.'

Drake wouldn't thank him for disturbing him at home, Thornhill thought; not for this, not until they had some evidence to show him.

'Come on, Brian,' he said. 'Leave that. We've got work to do.'

Kirby tried to retain his surly expression but could not prevent himself from showing a glimmer of interest. 'What's up?'

'Something or nothing. I've heard a whisper that Doreen Rodley's in a wheelchair because Bayswater misdiagnosed her.'

Kirby whistled. 'It would fit. Rodley gets rough with a few drinks in him, too. Just the sort of damned silly murder he would commit.'

'There's the glove, Brian.'

There was no mistaking Kirby's enthusiasm now. 'Maybe that's nothing to do with it, sir. Bayswater could have picked it up in the street for all we know. There's nothing connecting it with the murderer.'

'It's a coincidence,' Thornhill said.

'That's what life is all about. One damned coincidence after another.' Kirby brightened. 'Howard Mork's dad sold Frederick those gloves. Howard Mork goes drinking with Joe Rodley. Maybe there's the connection.'

'We'll pay Rodley a visit. We'll just have a nice quiet chat with him. Not a bad time to go – he's more likely to be hung over than drunk at this time of day.' He paused. 'How's Joan, by the way?'

'Desperate to get it over with. The baby wants to get out. He's kicking her about something cruel.'

Thornhill drove them both to Whistler's Lane and parked outside Viney Cottage. He glanced up the road. The Fuggles' car was in the drive of the bungalow. As they waited at the front door of the cottage, he heard the faint but persistent yapping of the terrier.

'Macbeth hath murdered sleep,' he muttered.

'What's that, guv?'

'Nothing.'

The door opened, and there was Joe Rodley. He glared at Kirby.

'You remember me, Mr Rodley,' Kirby said. 'Detective

Sergeant Kirby. And this is Detective Chief Inspector Thornhill. May we come in?'

'Why?' Rodley was unshaven and tousle haired. He wore a frayed striped shirt, without its collar, open at the neck to reveal the grubby vest beneath. 'We're busy.'

'Not too busy to see us, I hope,' Kirby said genially. 'Of course, we could come back with a warrant, but I don't think that's going to help anyone, do you?'

'Joe,' called Doreen from the other room. 'Who is it?'

Kirby raised his voice: 'Just the police, Mrs Rodley. We wanted another little chat.'

'Bring them in here, Joe, and shut the door. I can feel the draught from here.'

Rodley's shoulders sagged. He held the door open and stood aside to let them pass. 'Don't you go upsetting her,' he murmured. 'Or I'll bloody murder you.'

In Mrs Rodley's bedroom, the heat and the half-drawn curtains made a mockery of the sunshine on the other side of the window. It was a prison, Thornhill thought, a hot, airless little cell where Doreen Rodley was serving out a life sentence with no remission for good conduct. She was out of bed and sitting between the stove and the table. She fussed over her visitors, offering them tea and making Joe bring chairs.

At a nod from Thornhill, Kirby produced one of his winning smiles, the sort that had charmed a long procession of female friends until he had settled down with Joan and grown fat. 'It's about your illness, love, in a way.'

'What's that got to do with anything?' Joe said.

'Well, Mr Rodley, that's just it: we don't know. More than likely nothing, but we have to check if we're going to find out who killed poor old Dr Bayswater.'

'You'd better ask Dr Leddon,' Doreen said. 'I'll tell him you

can, if you like. He can explain it properly. I find it hard to get
my tongue round all those words.'

'It's not the illness exactly, Mrs Rodley. It's more what Dr
Bayswater made of it. Are we right in thinking he diagnosed
you one way, and then after he retired and Dr Leddon took
over, he said something else?'

'Yes. I don't understand the ins and outs of it.'

'He got it wrong,' Joe muttered. 'The bastard got it wrong.'

Kirby swung round and looked at Rodley, who was leaning
against the closed door. 'Bayswater got it wrong?'

'That's what the young one said. Reckon he knows what
he's talking about, too.'

'What's done is done, love.' Doreen shivered, as though the
room were cold. 'Nothing will change it.'

'He made a mistake, look,' Joe said, still in the same low
voice. 'Our Doreen paid for it. That don't seem right to me.
What do you think?'

'The gentlemen don't want to hear about our problems,
love.'

'Then they bloody should. It's always the same, isn't it? One
law for the rich, one law for the poor.'

'Did you tell Dr Bayswater how you feel?' Kirby said
suddenly, as though the possibility had only just occurred
to him.

Joe pulled himself away from the door and stood straight.
'He knew what I thought about him.'

'The thing is, someone hit Bayswater over the head last
week. So naturally we have to ask around – find out who didn't
like him.'

Thornhill was watching Joe's hands and saw the fingers
curling upwards into fists. He said, 'This is routine, Mr Rodley.
It's the way we work – we have to rule out the innocent before we
can find the guilty.'

'He's right, Joe,' Doreen said, leaning forward in her chair. 'They're just doing their job. They know you didn't do it. I know you didn't do it. You just have to tell the gentlemen the truth.'

Rodley shrugged. 'I never found the truth was much good for people like me.'

'Oh, don't talk nonsense,' his wife chided. She looked at Thornhill. 'He lost his job last week, sir, and he's upset. You mustn't take any notice of him.'

'Nothing to worry about, love,' Kirby said.

'Nothing to worry about?' Joe hooked his thumbs in his belt. 'That's a laugh.'

'What we'd like to do, Mr Rodley,' Thornhill said, 'is have a look round the house, if you wouldn't mind. We're not prying, you understand, we're just checking there's nothing that could have any bearing on our investigation. We're certainly not trying to cause you trouble.'

'There, love,' Doreen said. 'They can't say fairer than that, can they?'

Joe shrugged. 'And if we say no?'

'Then, as Sergeant Kirby said, we'll come back in an hour or two with a warrant which will allow us to search your home. We may also have to take you down to the station for questioning.' He paused, allowing the implications to sink in. 'I'm not sure how long we'll have to keep you there. It's up to you, Mr Rodley.'

'So it's true.'

'What is?' Thornhill said.

'What you read in the papers, about the police round here.'

'Joe—' Doreen began.

'I don't think you meant to say that. I'll pretend I haven't heard it. It's the sort of comment that won't help anyone.'

'If you mess me around, I'll tell them, I'll tell the papers. I swear to God I will.'

'Will you?' Kirby said. 'Any newspaper in particular? Do you know someone who works for the papers? Someone who lives locally?'

Rodley snarled, 'You're putting words in my mouth.'

'Mrs Rodley, tell me what you think,' Thornhill said. 'Would you mind us having a quick look round?'

She glanced at Joe. 'Of course you can. Joe will show you everything, won't you, Joe? Come on, love, it's for the best.' The lines in her face had deepened. 'Please, love.'

Joe grunted. He took two quick steps towards them. Thornhill felt his muscles tensing. Kirby moved forward in his chair as if ready to spring up. Joe bent and took his wife's hand.

'Don't you worry.' He patted the hand as though it belonged to a child who had woken in the night from a bad dream. 'It's all right.'

She smiled up at him, and for an instant Thornhill and Kirby might have been in another room, another world, for all their presence mattered.

Joe straightened up and looked down at Thornhill. 'Okay, then. Let's get it over with.'

The cottage was small and sparsely furnished. The search did not take long. They began in Mrs Rodley's room, with her urging Joe to open drawers and lift the mattress so the officers could see they had nothing to conceal.

The other downstairs rooms consisted of a small, unloved parlour where dust gathered on dark furniture, cobwebs clung to the cornices, and the clock on the mantel had stopped ticking at a quarter-past four. A single-storey extension at the back housed a kitchen and a scullery, which also served as the bathroom. This was warmer than the parlour, because there was a boiler for the water. A tap dripped into a stone sink full of unwashed dishes. On the floor by the table lay the remains of a broken plate and half a slice of toast.

It was even colder upstairs. One of the two rooms was used as a boxroom. Thornhill and Kirby poked through an old trunk containing darned sheets and faded curtains, once considered too good to be thrown away. In a suitcase they found a wedding dress and a wilted carnation. Rodley stood watching them from the doorway but said nothing.

The other room had once been the marital bedroom. There was a big iron bedstead and more of the dark furniture. The sheets and blankets were in a grubby, fusty-smelling tangle at the foot of the bed. A soup bowl piled high with cigarette ends stood on the bedside table. When Kirby opened the wardrobe, a dead moth fell out. On the rail inside, Mrs Rodley's clothes hung like discarded selves, quietly decaying.

'I hope you're satisfied,' Joe said as they went downstairs.

In the garden, Thornhill lifted the lid of a bunker half full of anthracite. The only other building was a shed built of crumbling local stone with sagging pantiles on the roof and a ruined pig cot beside it. In the shed Kirby picked over garden tools, a rusting cage for trapping small animals, a pile of kindling and two bicycles. But it was in the pig cot, tucked into the angle between the top of the back wall and what was left of the sloping roof, that they found the string bag.

With Joe Rodley looking on, Kirby lifted it down. It contained a pair of pliers, a tarnished silver cigarette box, a cheque book and a brown leather wallet.

'What you got there?' Joe demanded, his breath hot on Thornhill's neck. 'I never seen that bag before.'

'I have,' Thornhill said.

The last time he had seen the string bag, it had held a bottle of Cutty Sark whisky.

Chapter Fifty-One

At Troy House, Philip Wemyss-Brown was fast asleep. Pale and shrunken, dwarfed by the mound of bedclothes, he lay on his side with his legs drawn up. The only sound in the room was the air moving noisily through his partly blocked nostrils, punctuated by a moment of silence after each in-breath and out-breath. On the bedside table were the amylnitrate ampoules and all the pills in their bottles, drawn up in ranks of chemical soldiers ready to march into action in the great battle against death.

'We'd better not wake him,' Charlotte whispered. 'The doctor said he needs all the sleep he can get.'

'We can save him some lunch,' Jill whispered back.

'He doesn't eat enough.'

'That's understandable. It's . . . it's not as if he needs a great deal of physical energy at present.'

Charlotte was staring fixedly at her husband, as if trying to record his features in her memory, pore by pore. 'It's horrible,' she whispered in an even lower voice. 'He's so tired all the time.'

'It's part of getting better.'

'But it's as if he's not really here at all,' Charlotte said. 'As if he's really somewhere else. Somewhere I can't go.'

'Come on.' Jill touched Charlotte's arm. 'We need some lunch.'

'Yes – one must be sensible.'

Jill wasn't sure how one set about being sensible. She looked at Philip. She could have sworn that his eyelids twitched but the rhythm of his breathing did not change.

The two women went downstairs to the kitchen. Charlotte heated cream of celery soup from a tin while Jill hacked at a loaf of bread. There was home-made chicken broth in the larder but that was sacred to Philip. By the time Jill had laid the table, the meal was ready.

Charlotte laid down her spoon after the first mouthful. She picked at her bread, tearing off fragments and rolling them into stumpy white worms.

'That man,' she said. 'Do you think it really was him?'

'Joe Rodley? We've nothing to connect him with Fuggle.'

'They're neighbours.'

'Yes, but that's not enough, is it? And it's hard to know who's done what.'

'Someone's got it in for the *Gazette*, that's plain enough.' Charlotte gave up the pretence of eating and burrowed in her handbag for cigarettes. 'All I know is that Fuggle must be behind it.'

'The two arson attacks, yes. And the attack on Mr Cubbitt. They're all in a group. But what about Dr Bayswater? Why was he killed? What happened to Mr Frederick?'

'And whoever was urinating through letter boxes must—'

'I don't think we need worry about that any more,' Jill interrupted.

Charlotte arched her eyebrows. 'Really? Who was it?'

'It's not important. It was completely separate from everything else and it won't happen again.'

Charlotte began to speak, then thought better of it. Jill finished her meal in silence. Afterwards, while the kettle was boiling, she used the previous day's *Gazette* to wrap up the carcass of a chicken from which Charlotte had made broth for Philip. When she returned to the kitchen, the rest of the newspaper was on the table. It jogged her memory and she leafed through the pages until she found the picture of Paul Frederick.

'What did you mean on Thursday evening?' she said to Charlotte, who was drying the cutlery.

Charlotte turned. 'About what?'

Jill tapped Paul Frederick's monochrome chest. 'You said something about the style, that it was unmistakable. Was it his uniform or his hair or something?'

Charlotte glanced at the photograph. 'Not Mr Frederick's style, dear. Pugin's.'

'Who?'

'Not who. What.' Charlotte pointed at the photograph. 'Though Pugin was a man, of course.'

'Yes, but—'

'The point is, when I saw that church, I thought it must be Pugin. You know – Augustus Pugin. The Younger, that is.'

'How can you tell? You can't even see the whole church, just one end.'

Charlotte put down the tea towel. For a moment her old self was there, firmly seated on a hobby horse. 'It has all the obvious hallmarks.' She used the spoon she had just dried as a pointer. 'Here we have a nineteenth-century parish church in the Decorated style, which suggests it's from Pugin's later period. And you can see that the tower is placed asymmetrically to the body of the church. That's another typical touch.' She poked the spoon at the doorway. 'And look at the moulding here, and that lovely little spire. It's really very nice. But as a matter of fact it's not Pugin.'

Jill looked blankly at her. 'What on earth do you mean? You've just said—'

Charlotte flapped her hand at her. 'I know, it must seem

confusing. I remembered I'd seen the church before, so after you'd left the other night, I looked it up. It turns out the architect wasn't Pugin himself but one of his followers. A man called Henry Woodyer. A very competent architect – he built one of our local churches, you must have noticed it: Highnam, just outside Gloucester.'

Jill nodded. 'So you've seen this church before?'

'Not in the flesh, as it were. Only a photograph in a book. I've got it in the study, if you're interested. And that's as much as one can see now, unfortunately.'

'Why's that?'

'It was badly bombed in the war. I very much doubt they'll rebuild it. Not in our present age of unbelief.'

Jill stared at the grainy print and cast her mind back a few days. All she remembered clearly was a wolf whistle and a pair of tramps playing cards in the shelter of a wall.

She said, 'Where exactly is it?'

'North London.' Charlotte squeezed her eyelids together as if extracting the memory by muscular pressure. 'St Benedict's, Yorkley Grove.'

Chapter Fifty-Two

When the first stage of Rodley's interrogation was over, Thornhill ordered sandwiches to be brought down from the canteen. He and Kirby wolfed them in his office. Shortly before two o'clock, they went downstairs. PC Porter was waiting outside the front entrance at the wheel of a marked police car.

'Are you sure this is wise, sir?' Kirby murmured. 'He's going to say we're harassing him.'

'That's rich, coming from you.'

Kirby had the grace to look embarrassed.

'He's going to say that anyway,' Thornhill went on. 'In any case, some people need a bit of harassing. But only in ways the Home Secretary approves of. Got that, Sergeant?'

He climbed into the back of the car. Porter already knew where they were going. No one spoke as they drove sedately down the High Street, round the corner by the *Gazette* offices and then sharp left beyond Grove House. The road levelled out. They passed Viney Cottage and Thornhill glanced at the windows, closing his mind to the misery inside it.

A few yards farther on, near the end of the metalled roadway, the Fuggles' gates were open. The Humber was parked in the barn at the far end of the drive.

'Block him in,' Thornhill ordered.

Porter reversed neatly between the gateposts and killed the engine.

'Stay here for now,' Thornhill told him. 'Brian, I'll do the talking at first.'

Smoke was coming from one of the chimneys. Macbeth was already barking. Thornhill rapped on the front door. They waited. He knocked again.

'Door!' Fuggle shouted somewhere inside the house.

The yapping increased in volume, as though Macbeth had been let into the hall. A shapeless shadow materialised in the frosted glass in the upper half of the door. A bolt rattled across and the door swung open. From somewhere in the house came the sound of a radio or television audience clapping.

'Yes,' Mrs Fuggle said in a faint voice, her eyes straying down the drive to the police car.

Macbeth barked even more loudly. He was attached to his lead, which was looped over the newel post at the foot of the stairs, as it had been before. He leapt against the restraint, careless of the collar tightening across his windpipe, careless of anything except his need to attack.

'Mrs Fuggle—' Thornhill began.

Frowning slightly, she stared at him as if he were an apparition from another world. She rubbed her forehead with two fingertips, the nails bitten to the quick.

'Mrs Fuggle, you remember me, I'm sure,' Thornhill went on, wondering whether she was ill. 'I'm Detective Chief Inspector Thornhill and this is Detective Sergeant Kirby. Is your husband here?'

Mrs Fuggle bent down and patted Macbeth, who quietened under her touch. The action seemed to bring her back to normal. She looked up at Thornhill.

'I'll see if he's in.'

'Of course I'm bloody in,' said Fuggle, appearing in the doorway of a room leading off to the left.

'May we have a word, sir?'

'I suppose so. If you must. You'd better come in here.'

His wife unlooped the lead and dragged Macbeth down the hall to the kitchen. Fuggle looked after her for a moment, his face purple and expressionless. He was wearing slippers, the backs broken down by his heels, old flannel trousers, a cardigan with a zip and a cravat with a pattern of horses' heads emerging from horseshoes. He shrugged and went back into the room, leaving Thornhill and Kirby to close the front door behind them and follow him in.

In the sitting-room, a log fire glowed red and sullen in a grate designed for coal. Fuggle turned off the radio and sat down in one of the armchairs, part of a three-piece suite covered with a cream material speckled with pink flowers. The pictures on the walls were mainly reproductions of paintings of ballet dancers and ladies on swings. China ornaments covered most horizontal surfaces. Apart from its owner, Thornhill thought, there was nothing noticeably masculine about the room.

'Well? What do you want?'

Thornhill sat down, motioning to Kirby to do the same.

'Some serious allegations have been made, sir.'

'Who by?' Fuggle snapped.

'That will emerge in due course, I expect. I'd like to discuss the content of the allegations rather than the source.'

'And I'd like you to leave my house.'

Thornhill stood up. 'Very well, sir.'

Fuggle squinted up at him. 'You can leave in a moment. I'll hear what you have to say first.'

'Thank you, sir.' Thornhill sat down again. 'You know Mr Cubbitt, I'm sure?'

Fuggle reached for his cigarettes. 'I knew him slightly. We met occasionally in the line of business. Never made much impression.'

'Shortly before he resigned from the *Gazette* he was beaten up. Then he moved to a job with the Champion Group, your own employers as it happens.'

'And you're still looking for the person who attacked him. Another of those cases where the local police force has failed to shine.'

'More recently, only last week in fact, you'll remember that someone set fire to the printing office of the *Gazette*. And more recently still, someone threw what seems to have been a Molotov cocktail through the drawing-room window of Troy House, which is—'

'I know perfectly well where Troy House is, Inspector, and who lives there. I've lived in this town a damned sight longer than you have.'

Thornhill nodded, as though acknowledging a hit, and continued in a bland voice: 'You'll understand, sir, that in cases like this we have to ask who benefits.'

Fuggle snorted. 'For God's sake!'

'We have someone in custody who claims you paid him to attack Mr Cubbitt and to start fires on two separate occasions. Also to break into a car belonging to Miss Francis and booby-trap it with rats.'

'Nonsense.'

'We have to take the allegations seriously. It's not very hard to see what your motive might be.'

Fuggle stared up at him. 'Enlighten me.'

'Because all these crimes affected the *Lydmouth Gazette* and you're the editor of the *Evening Post*. We understand that the *Post* and the *Gazette* are trying to increase circulation at the expense of each other. And the *Post* seems to be doing rather better. Especially since these crimes have occurred.'

'The *Post* is the better paper. No need to use other tactics.'

Thornhill sat back in his chair and crossed his legs. 'So you say.'

Fuggle said nothing. Thornhill felt a tingle of excitement, the thrill of the chase. Fuggle was not an easy man to browbeat and his face was only slightly more expressive than that of the Sphinx; but he wasn't fighting back with quite his usual energy.

Thornhill said, 'And then there's Mr Frederick. Last seen at the railway station, as far as we know, just over a week ago.' And it was odd, Thornhill thought, that no one had come forward and admitted to seeing him on the train. 'But before he went to the station he was seen at this end of Whistler's Lane.'

'We've been through that. It's nothing to do with us. I've never met the fellow, and I never want to.'

'Really? Just for the record, sir, where were you that morning?'

Fuggle shrugged. 'Here and there.'

'Oh – so you weren't in your office at Framington all the time?'

'As it happens, no. I went over there later in the morning. But I had one or two things I needed to do in Lydmouth early on.'

'Such as?'

'I had a haircut.' Fuggle patted his head. 'I went to the bank. Had a bit of a slow start, I suppose – I wasn't in a hurry to get out of the house.'

'I see, sir. Which bank was that, by the way, and which barber's?'

'The National Provincial. Falconer's.'

Fuggle glanced at Kirby, who was recording the interview in his notebook.

'You didn't go to Gloucester, by any chance, did you?' Thornhill asked.

'Of course I bloody didn't!'

'You might have done. It wouldn't have taken you very long in the car.'

'I didn't, and that's all there is to it.'

'Yes, sir.'

'I don't like your tone, Inspector.'

'It's Chief Inspector, actually.'

Fuggle shuffled his body forward in the chair and levered himself to his feet. He glowered at his visitors. 'These are bully-boy tactics. You can't get away with that in this country.'

'May I remind you that several very serious crimes have recently taken place in this town, as your newspaper has frequently pointed out? We have to investigate them to the best of our ability. You're not suggesting you should be above the law, I hope?'

For a moment Thornhill thought that Fuggle might have a fit, or keel over, or even physically attack him. In the end, the old journalist – one thought of him as old, although he was under sixty – did none of these things. He simply stood there, swaying slightly like a top-heavy tree in a strong wind.

Thornhill waited a moment and then got to his feet. Kirby glanced at him, snapped shut his notebook and followed suit.

'Thank you for your co-operation, sir,' Thornhill said.

'You haven't heard the last of this.'

'I expect you're right. I doubt if you have either.'

At the door, Thornhill paused and looked back. 'One more thing, sir. You don't mind if we check your car, do you?'

'Yes I bloody well do.'

'Why is that, sir?'

'Because I was hoping for a bit of peace and quiet this afternoon. Why do you want to look at it?'

'We want to check the truth of a further allegation our informant made in connection with the other ones.'

'What allegation?'

Thornhill ignored the question. He said, 'Of course, if the allegation proves incorrect, then it rather undermines the rest of what the informant said.'

Fuggle hawked and worked his cheek muscles as if about to spit. 'Suit yourself. I've nothing to hide.'

He took his time finding shoes and jacket; and this was not simple bloody-mindedness. Fuggle had aged, Thornhill thought; seeing him here at home after a heavy lunch made it painfully obvious.

In the hall, the sound of Macbeth barking on the other side of the kitchen door was much louder. Without a word, Fuggle collected a stick from the hall and took them outside. Moving slowly, and supporting himself on the stick, he led them up the drive to the barn at the end of the garden, beside the vegetable patch. Thornhill glanced back at the house. Mrs Fuggle was watching them from the kitchen window. She saw him and ducked back into the dark depths of the room.

Porter got out of the car and came after them, moving at a ponderous trot. 'Message for you, sir.' He screwed up his face in the effort of memory and lowered his voice to a confidential whisper. 'DC Kear radioed it through. He said to say that Rodley thought it had the word *paraffin* on its side.'

'That's original.'

Porter stared. 'Sir?'

'It doesn't matter.'

'In blue paint, sir,' Porter added.

Thornhill nodded and walked on. The Humber's boot poked out of the barn's doorway. Kirby had already opened it and was examining the contents. He straightened up and glanced at Thornhill; his shoulders twitched in an almost imperceptible shrug.

Thornhill went into the barn itself. The air smelled of fresh paint and old vegetables. Fuggle was standing just inside the doorway with his lips pursed in a silent whistle. In his hand was an unlit cigarette. Thornhill ignored him and walked along the nearside of the car. A trailer-load of logs had been piled against the back wall of the barn, encroaching on the space usually devoted to the car. An axe was propped against a scarred saw-horse. Some of the logs had already been chopped and stacked, but more remained in a low, untidy heap. Near by was an old kitchen table, partly repainted a deep rich purple.

Kirby opened the driver's door and looked inside the car.

Porter wandered into the barn, jarring his leg against the handle of a small motor mower. As so often, he seemed in a dream, or at least to be inhabiting a slightly different reality from everyone else's. He sniffed.

Fuggle said, 'If you tell me what you're looking for, gentlemen, perhaps I could help.'

'What's that?' Kirby said, pointing at the workbench in the corner beside the saw-horse.

Porter picked up a red can and handed it to Kirby, who unscrewed the top and sniffed. 'Petrol,' he said.

'Turn it round,' Thornhill ordered. 'There's something on the side.'

Kirby rotated the can in his hands. On one side the word *paraffin* had been stencilled in pale blue paint.

'That's it,' Thornhill said.

'That's what?' Fuggle said, and lit the cigarette.

'That's what we were told we would find in your car.'

'You found it in my garage instead.'

'Yes, sir.'

Fuggle tossed his match outside. 'I use it for petrol.'

Porter frowned. 'Why does it say paraffin on the side?'

'My mother used it for paraffin. I use it for petrol. Is that clear?'

Kirby shook it. 'It's empty.'

'I'm not surprised. The tank was low the other morning, so I filled it up from the tin.'

'You usually keep the can in the boot of your car, sir?' Thornhill asked.

'Yes, I do. It's no secret. I'm sure plenty of people will have noticed it.'

Porter coughed. 'Excuse me, sir.'

'What?'

The back door opened. Mrs Fuggle came out on the step.

Porter was craning his neck and looking at something on his leg. 'Sir, there's something here that—'

'Chief Inspector,' Mrs Fuggle called. 'It's the phone for you.'

Thornhill went out of the barn. She waited on the back-door step. When he reached the house, he glanced over his shoulder. The others were trailing after him, first Fuggle, then Kirby, still carrying the can, and finally Porter, looking perplexed.

Mrs Fuggle led him across the neat little kitchen, furnished to the height of modernity in about 1938, and into the hall. Macbeth was now shut in the sitting-room, still barking. She nodded unsmilingly at the telephone on the small table beside the hatstand and stood aside to let him pass.

Thornhill picked up the receiver. 'Hello?'

All he heard was the dialling tone.

He turned swiftly. Mrs Fuggle was watching him from the kitchen doorway.

Chapter Fifty-Three

Roger Leddon looked perfectly normal but he smelled as if he had had lunch in the pub. He had a box of Mackintosh's Week-end Assortment in his hand. Jill was wary of presents. Too often they were also bribes or something worse.

He held out the chocolates. 'For you.'

She did not take them from him. 'What are they for?'

His face broke into a smile. He was good at giving the impression of understanding exactly what was on your mind, of complicity with your most secret thoughts, as though you and he were willing conspirators in a dangerous but thoroughly enjoyable game. 'I wanted to apologise. I had too much wine last night and I'm afraid I said more than I should.'

'It's all right.'

'I thought we could start again, over a cup of coffee perhaps. Your place or mine: whichever you prefer.'

'No, thank you,' Jill said, and then heard herself adding, 'I've already had some coffee.'

'Jill, please. Listen, I know I behaved like an apeman last night, and I regret it. It's been such a worrying time – anyway, it won't happen again, I promise.'

'I'm glad. But – sorry – I really must get back to work.'

For an instant his mask slipped. If you took away the charm and the excitement then what was left? Just a face equipped with the usual features; not even a very pleasant face. Bright eyes and thick lashes weren't enough.

He tried the smile again and came a step nearer.

'No,' Jill said. 'I mean it. Goodbye, Roger.'

She closed the door and went back into the living-room. Usually, at this stage, when she had met a man she liked and then found he was not so likeable or suitable after all, she felt unhappy. Not this time. All she felt was relief.

Leddon banged on the door.

She stood by the window, looking down at the gates of the park. She glimpsed Mrs Fuggle and Macbeth zigzagging aimlessly across the sodden grass.

'Jill!' Leddon shouted. 'You surely don't believe all this rubbish they're saying?'

Was it rubbish? she wondered. Perhaps he had killed Bayswater. But that wasn't the point, not at present. What mattered were the glimpses she had had of a slippery and selfish person underneath Roger Leddon's appealing exterior.

He rang the door bell. He rang it again. Then, at last, he went away. Jill examined her face in the mirror. She looked quite normal, she thought, though surely the eyes were a little puffy today and the lines a little deeper.

Mrs Fuggle and Macbeth were now out of sight. Jill went to the telephone and dialled Directory Enquiries. She asked for the Wintour Arms, Yorkley Grove, London. In less than a minute, she was talking to an unidentified man at the other end.

'Maisie Lawrence?' he said. 'Hang on.'

Jill heard him bellowing Maisie's name. Her ears filled with the sounds of a busy pub on a Saturday afternoon. Then, after what seemed like half an hour, she heard Maisie's voice at the other end of the line.

'It's Jill Francis. Do you remember? I came to see you on Thursday.'

There was a cackle on the other end of the line. 'Of course I remember. I may be old but I haven't lost my marbles or my memory. So you ain't found Jenny Ellwood yet. Otherwise you wouldn't be ringing me, would you?'

'That's it,' Jill said. 'You mentioned that Genevieve had a fiancé.'

'Tony,' Maisie screeched. 'Lovely man. Worshipped the ground she trod on.'

'You mentioned he came back looking for her after he'd been demobbed.'

'So someone said. I didn't see him, though.'

'Which branch of the services was he in?'

'He was in the RAF, dearie. Flight sergeant. I tell you this: he was one of those men who looks nice in a uniform.'

'I don't suppose you can remember his full name?'

'He had a foreign surname – well, I suppose he would, being foreign. He was Dutch, come over to join the RAF and fight Jerry. But his name sounded English. Frederiks, I-K-S.'

Jill sighed.

'What was that?' Maisie asked.

'Nothing. You've been very helpful. Thank you very much.'

'Let me know if you find him,' Maisie said. 'Or Jenny, of course.'

'All right, I will.'

'You come down the Wintour and tell me all about it.' There was a cackle on the other end of the line. 'Be a good girl and I might buy you a drink.'

Jill said goodbye and rang off. She lit a cigarette and went back to stand by the window. At last there was a pattern, a connection. Flight Sergeant Tony Frederiks had courted Genevieve Ellwood in Yorkley Grove in the war. Flight Sergeant Paul Frederick had his photograph taken in Yorkley Grove, also in the war. The chance that they were not the same man was so small as to be negligible. Richard Thornhill could probably confirm the identification in a moment.

The sound of a revving engine diverted her attention. Leddon's Ford Consul emerged out of the Raglan Court driveway. Without stopping, he swung on to the road and drove rapidly away.

But how did Bayswater come into it? Had Frederick come back to kill him? Why?

Something niggled: something so indistinct she had no idea what it was. She had forgotten something. Something did not quite fit.

The flat seemed suddenly airless, a place that smothered thought. She put on her coat, hat and gloves and picked up her handbag. She would walk in the park. If Mrs Fuggle were still there, she might even talk to her.

Jill left the flat. While she was walking down the communal hallway to the stairs she heard the muffled ringing of a telephone, which might have come from any one of half a dozen flats, hers included.

She went down the stairs. The ringing grew fainter and at some point was completely overlaid by the sound of another, more urgent bell, farther away. The bell of an ambulance.

Chapter Fifty-Four

A s Thornhill was walking towards the door from the car park at Police Headquarters he heard the clanging of an ambulance bell in the High Street but paid it no attention.

Buoyed with excitement, he took the stairs up to the first floor two at a time, Kirby and Porter pursuing him. He led the way into his office, where the pile in his in-tray was even higher than it had been that morning, and sat down behind the desk. The others lingered by the doorway.

'Now we're getting somewhere,' Thornhill said. 'Well done, Peter.'

Porter stared at his gleaming boots and executed a shuffling dance of embarrassment.

'Brian, ring Sergeant Carney. I want him here this afternoon. We know the pliers were probably the weapon but I'd like some prints from them, if there are any, and from the cigarette box, the cheque book and the wallet as well. And check to see if he's got anything from the fragments of glass from the Kia-Ora bottle at Troy House. We can't have Rodley bang to rights for the arson but I'd like the next best thing. Otherwise it all rests on his confession, so there's a risk his brief will find a way for him to wriggle out of it.'

'The lab will need the pliers too,' Kirby pointed out.

'That's why I want any prints first. But get hold of Murray while you're waiting for Carney to do his stuff. We need him to establish whether there's a fit between the pliers and

Bayswater's injuries. And the lab will need to compare the sample Porter found with the one we got from Gloucester.'

'It would be the bloody weekend, wouldn't it?'

'Twist the duty officer's arm. We should be able to bike the sample and the pliers down to Cardiff this evening.'

'But, sir, if—'

Thornhill raised his hand. 'I want chapter and verse, and I want it as soon as possible.'

'When are we going to charge him, sir?' Kirby asked.

'We'll see. I need to talk to Mr Drake first.' Thornhill turned to Porter. 'In the meantime, I don't want anyone talking to Rodley until I say. Make sure they understand that downstairs. Put him in a cell by himself, give him a cup of tea and let him stew. Off you go.'

When he was alone, Thornhill picked up the phone and asked for the Deputy Chief Constable's home number. Mrs Drake answered. When Thornhill said his name, a surprised note came into her voice.

'It's not the best of times, Richard. Are you sure it can't wait?'

'I'm afraid it can't.'

'All right,' she said reluctantly. 'I'll fetch him.'

'I'm sorry, Mrs Drake, but I have to see him in person.' Thornhill had no intention of discussing this particular subject over the phone. 'I'd like to come over for a few minutes.'

'If you must.' Mrs Drake knew how to recognise the inevitable but her husband's seniority meant that she did not have to accept it with good grace. She said she would tell Mr Drake that Thornhill was on his way and rang off.

Thornhill picked up his hat and left the office. It was a relief to be physically active again. The adrenalin was pumping through him, as it always did when the final stage of an investigation was about to take shape.

The High Street was crowded with Saturday shoppers. Although it wasn't raining the weather was so gloomy that already the afternoon had slipped into a premature twilight. The Chamber of Commerce had put up the Christmas lights and coloured bulbs twinkled across the road and above the shopfronts.

Less than three weeks until Christmas, Thornhill realised, and he hadn't even thought about what to buy Edith. He remembered she was going up to London for the sales after Christmas – perhaps she would find something there. The prospect of her going to London for a night or two by herself gave him a twinge of anxiety, like a small insect passing over his skin.

He turned into the Chepstow Road. The Drakes lived in a cul-de-sac just south of the town. Their house was detached, double fronted and surprisingly large. But they needed the space, Drake had once confided to Thornhill, for when the family came to stay.

It was clear that the family had turned out in force today. The drive was full of cars. Thornhill parked on the road. As he walked towards the door he heard the sound of a piano and voices raised in song. He recognised the tune of 'Ten Green Bottles'. When Mrs Drake opened the door, the music surged in volume and swept out to meet him, bringing with it memories of children's birthday parties, including his own.

Mrs Drake was a slim, stringy woman with a face almost as red as her husband's and tightly cropped hair the colour of pepper and salt mixed up on a plate. She looked as though her years in India had burned or sweated off all the excess flesh, all the excess moisture, leaving only the essence behind, as leathery as dried meat. Edith liked her, and respected the way she had coped with moving back to the cramped, grey austerities of post-war England, leaving behind the big house, the staff of servants and the holidays in Srinagar and Ootacamund without a visible pang.

'I hope you know what you're doing,' she said to Thornhill. 'He's not best pleased, I'll tell you that.'

The hall was inhabited by a small army of hats and coats. A brand-new Raleigh bicycle, child size, was propped against the wall.

'I'm sorry,' Thornhill said. 'I would have avoided it if I could.'

She gave him a quick nod and opened the door of her husband's study. 'You can wait in here. Do sit down. He won't be a moment.'

She switched on the electric fire and left him to wait. The study was already too warm from the central heating. The Malay heads stared at him from the bookcase to the left of the mantelpiece. He did not sit but prowled round the room, driven by the restless energy the investigation had generated.

The door opened, the music swelled again in volume and the DCC swept into the room, propelled by the tide of sound. He wore a tennis shirt, open at the neck, an old cricket jersey with what looked like a smear of jam on one sleeve and baggy brown corduroy trousers. Thornhill had never seen him so informally dressed. His sparse hair was awry as though somebody had been running their fingers through it.

'Come and sit down, man.' Drake took the sofa and stretched his legs over the hearthrug; even his posture had lost its usual stiffness. 'Put that overcoat on the chair. Why are you here?'

'We've had some major developments, sir.'

Drake grunted, though his face gave no indication whether this was from mirth or irritation or something quite different altogether. 'I didn't think you'd disturb me for something minor, Thornhill.'

'We paid a visit to Joe Rodley at Viney Cottage this morning. We conducted a routine search. In one of the outhouses, we found a string bag containing several items, including Dr Bayswater's cigarette box, wallet and cheque book. And a pair of pliers.'

'The murder weapon?'

'Very possibly. We'll soon know.'

'And Rodley? What does he say?'

'He denies all knowledge of the bag and the murder, sir. On the other hand, he has admitted to several other offences. As you know, he has been spending rather more freely than one would expect for a man in his circumstances. At first he wouldn't say why, but after we'd arrested him and taken him down to the station, he claimed that the money had come from Ivor Fuggle.'

'Which offences, exactly?'

'He says that Fuggle bribed him to waylay Mr Cubbitt and beat him up, and also to fire-bomb the *Gazette* and Troy House. He says that Fuggle assured him that no one would be hurt, otherwise he wouldn't have done it.'

'The Gwyn-Thomas woman was hurt.'

'Yes, sir. And she was also hurt when she discovered the rats in Miss Francis's car. Which was also Rodley's doing.'

Drake scowled. 'Not easy, I wouldn't have thought, managing that little stunt.'

'No, sir – he tried to put them in the car as early as the Thursday evening, but Miss Francis almost caught him at it. Then the car was at Gray's Garage. But actually catching the rats was less of a problem for Rodley than for most people: according to Porter, his uncle was a rat-catcher. He set a trap in the Grove House garden. That was before the murder – on Wednesday night: so there was nothing to stop him nipping through the gate after dark. We found the cage he used in the shed.'

'He's admitted nothing else, I suppose?' Drake said, with heavy irony. 'Such as Mr Prout's little problem and Mrs Fuggle's grave?'

'He denies both. On the face of it, there's no reason to doubt him.'

'I don't like this,' Drake said.

'Sir?'

'Use your head, man. Half the county knows that Ivor Fuggle has been conducting a feud against the police because they read about it on a daily basis. The danger is that if we try to pin something on him, he's going to cry foul. And he's going to use his damned newspaper to say so loud and clear. We're not going to get very far if the entire case relies on the word of someone like Joe Rodley. I know Fuggle's got the motive but that means next to nothing, as you well know.'

Thornhill studied a brass ashtray on the table beside his chair. 'I paid a visit to Mr Fuggle, sir.'

'You did what? You should have checked with me before-hand.'

'I'm sorry, sir. But it occurred to me that there was a danger that Mr Fuggle might have noticed us at Viney Cottage, even seen us arresting Joe Rodley. After all, they're the next best thing to neighbours. So I thought it important we should move quickly.' He hesitated. 'As you're off duty today, sir, I wasn't able to contact you easily.'

'You could have picked up the phone.'

'Yes, sir.' Thornhill let his reply hang for a moment, aware that his unwillingness to contact Drake beforehand had come at least partly from his suspicion that Drake would be reluc-tant to disturb the Saturday afternoon tranquillity of Ivor Fuggle.

'Well?' the DCC demanded. 'What happened?'

'Mr Fuggle denied any involvement in the attacks on the

Gazette. But when we questioned Rodley, he told us that Fuggle gave him some petrol before the attack on Troy House, and that he poured it into the Kia-Ora bottle from a red can which he kept in the boot of his car. He said the tin was labelled *paraffin*. Sure enough, we found a tin like that in Mr Fuggle's garage. Judging by the smell, it recently contained petrol.'

Drake nodded. 'It's a point, but not a conclusive one. It's easy to imagine other circumstances when Rodley might have seen the can.'

'Yes, sir. In effect that's what Mr Fuggle said. On the other hand, when we asked if we could search his house and out-buildings, he refused.'

'He was perfectly within his rights.'

'Yes, sir, but in the circumstances you must grant it seems suspicious.'

Drake shrugged. 'Depends on the man involved, surely? With Ivor Fuggle, it seems entirely true to character. He's hardly going to go out of his way to co-operate with the police.' His face grew redder and harsher. 'I'm not satisfied with this, Thornhill.'

'There's more, sir.'

'I hope it's good news. For everyone's sake.'

'To go back to Rodley: if the pliers really are the murder weapon, then we have a good case against him for the murder even if we don't find his prints on them.'

'But why would Rodley want to kill Bayswater? There's no sense to it. It's not as if much was stolen.'

'If he killed him, it wasn't for money.'

Drake drew back his upper lip, giving his face an appearance that was as foxy as his colouring. 'Then for what?'

'I think Mrs Rodley's medical history holds the answer to that.' Thornhill shifted in his chair, trying to edge away from the fire. 'I heard a hint that Bayswater misdiagnosed her, and was indirectly responsible for the state she's in today.'

'A hint? What do you mean? You're talking in riddles.'

'Sorry, sir. You know what it's like in Lydmouth: one hears things.'

Drake stared at him with eyes like blue marbles. 'What we used to call bazaar gossip, eh? You'll need a damn sight more than that.'

'I think there is every chance we'll get it.' Here Thornhill felt himself on safer ground. 'I put it to Mr and Mrs Rodley and they admitted that Dr Leddon had let something slip to them, something about Bayswater's original diagnosis.'

'Not what I would have thought was professional behaviour for a doctor.'

Thornhill felt a rush of anger. 'With respect, sir, the point is that it's more than rumour.'

Unexpectedly, Drake grinned. 'Odd, that.'

'What?'

'How people always say "with respect" when they mean the opposite.'

Thornhill transferred his attention to a small mahogany elephant with ivory tusks that stood guard beside the fireplace. 'Yes, sir.'

Drake flapped his hands, as though shooing away the moment of levity. 'All right. It's a motive of sorts, I grant you. But if Rodley killed him, the choice of weapon suggests it was unpremeditated.'

'Perhaps Rodley went there to extort money, or simply to tell Bayswater what he thought of him. And it got out of hand. It happens.'

Drake tapped his fingers on the arm of the sofa. It was growing darker, and the only light came from a table lamp beside Thornhill's chair and the glowing bars of the electric fire. Elsewhere in the house, the musicians had shifted their attention to 'Row, Row, Row Your Boat'. The tempo was gradually accelerating. There was also a good deal of thumping, which suggested that an element of dance had entered the performance.

'What about Leddon?' Drake suggested. 'I thought you had your doubts about him. He has a motive of sorts, and we've got him on the scene.'

Struggling to be fair, Thornhill said, 'Leddon can't have known what Bayswater's heir would do with Grove House. It's unlikely he even knew who Bayswater's heir would be.'

'Chap lost his temper when Bayswater said he wouldn't sell yet again. Lashed out.'

'I'm not convinced he's the right type, sir. He's too controlled. Too calculating.' Thornhill hesitated. 'I can't help feeling that we're looking at this from the wrong angle. We're leaving out Frederick altogether. As far as we know, neither Leddon nor Rodley has any connection with him. But he travelled to Gloucester on the same train as Bayswater and his glove was under Bayswater's body.'

'It's tricky. Two cases, a murder and a disappearance. And that damned glove links them.'

'But we don't know how. Which brings me back to Ivor Fuggle.'

'Oh, for God's sake, haven't I made that sufficiently clear?' Drake sat bolt upright. 'We can't afford to stick our necks out, not where Fuggle's concerned.' He paused and then leaned forward, lowering his voice: 'This is in confidence, Richard: Mr Hendry is very concerned about this and so is the Standing Joint Committee. Ivor Fuggle is off limits unless declared otherwise. That's an order, and I'm passing it down to you.'

'There's something I haven't told you yet, sir.'

'Eh?'

'When we were looking at the petrol can this afternoon we were in Fuggle's garage. It's more like a little stone barn – not purpose built. He also uses it as a wood store and somewhere to keep garden tools. Porter was with us and he noticed—'

'Porter?'

'Yes, sir. His coat brushed against a mower in the garage. When we came outside, he noticed it had left a smear of oil and sawdust on the hem.'

'Well?'

'We found a similar mark on Frederick's overcoat.'

'For God's sake! A bit of oil and sawdust – you could pick that up anywhere.'

'Yes, sir. But I've arranged to have samples biked down to Cardiff. Just in case.' Thornhill glanced at Drake and hurried on. 'There's no harm in that, is there, sir? It doesn't involve Mr Fuggle at all. But if it turns out that the mark on Porter's coat may have come from the same source as the mark on Frederick's, then it's one more indication that—'

'Find Frederick,' Drake said, standing up abruptly and switching off the electric fire. 'But leave Fuggle alone unless I tell you otherwise. Is that clear?'

The two men stared at each other. Behind Fuggle was the Champion Group, Thornhill knew, with its army of provincial newspapers. There were several aspects of his job that Thornhill loathed, and this was one of them: when external influences affected the operational direction of an investigation.

Somewhere on the other side of the door 'Row, Row, Row Your Boat' came to an unscheduled end as the piano went one way, the singers went another and there was a crash that shook the house, as though a heavy piece of furniture had toppled over.

In the silence a child laughed.

Chapter Fifty-Five

Someone tapped on the nearside window of the car.

'Yoo-hoo, Miss Francis!'

Jill glanced to her left. Amy Gwyn-Thomas was on the pavement, stooping and peering into the car. She was smiling so widely that for an instant Jill failed to recognise her. Her left hand was hooked round the arm of Mr Prout.

'I've got something to tell you!'

A car horn hooted. The Morris Minor was standing in a short queue of traffic waiting at the zebra crossing in the High Street, and now the head of the queue had begun to move. Jill pulled over to the kerb and rolled down the window.

'Look!' Amy cried, the end of her long, thin nose glowing pink with cold and excitement. She released Mr Prout, removed the glove from her left hand and went on in a hushed, breathless voice: 'The next time you see that hand, Miss Francis, there'll be something different about it.'

Jill blinked at the bony fingers with their prominent knuckles, which were now resting on the sill of the nearside window.

Amy simpered. 'Can you guess?'

Her face was blazing with joy. Mr Prout, debonair as ever, smiled at her. He looked dazed, Jill thought, perhaps a little embarrassed.

She said, 'You're not—?'

'We are!' Amy shivered with pleasure. 'We are!'

'I'm so glad. I'm sure you'll both be very happy. Congratulations, Mr Prout.'

There was nothing for it. Jill got out of the car and embraced Amy, who clung to her, squeezing, poking the corner of her glasses into Jill's cheek. Then Jill shook hands with Mr Prout.

'We're off to look at rings in Masterman's,' Amy confided. 'Ronald insisted.' She gazed at her fiancé. 'I told him I could wear an old ring of my mother's but he wouldn't hear of it.'

Jill smiled at them both until her face felt stiff. A joy shared is a joy increased. All the while the shocking implications of what she had so recently discovered careered through her mind.

Amy tapped Mr Prout proprietorially on the arm. 'Mind you, I'm staying at the *Gazette*, Ronald, aren't I? A modern girl needs her independence, doesn't she, Miss Francis?'

'Oh yes. Though of course it's your decision – but we'd hate to lose you, so I hope you'll stay.'

Jill had spoken automatically, but hardly were the words out than she realised that she meant them. At one time she had disliked Amy intensely. But now she valued her, even liked her. It struck her out of the blue how often it was that one's feelings for people changed. No one warned you about that. It rarely happened in novels, or only for very obvious and usually very dramatic reasons. In practice, as opposed to in fiction, feelings grew and changed slowly, like plants, often in ways difficult to predict. And like plants, perhaps, within their growth was the secret of their death.

'I mustn't hold you up any longer,' Jill said.

Amy kissed her again and she and Mr Prout shook hands once more. Jill returned to the car. For a moment, thankful for the distraction, she watched them walking arm in arm up the High Street.

How long would it last, this joy of ownership? How long would Amy be glad that she was no longer solitary? At one time Jill might have envied her – not Mr Prout, perhaps, but Amy's engaged state considered in the abstract. Now she was not so sure. She tried and failed to imagine Mr Prout overcome with passion. The very thought of it was mildly indecent. Still, one had only to look at one's acquaintances to realise that there was no earthly reason why sex should play an important part in marriage, or even any part at all.

Jill put the car into gear and slid into the stream of traffic. Police Headquarters loomed up on the left-hand side. All the parking places at the front were taken so she drove round to the half-empty private car park behind the building and left the Morris Minor in the slot reserved for the Chief Constable. She switched off the engine. Flecks of rain spotted the windscreen. *Bloody rain, bloody everything.*

She walked round to the front of the building, up the steps and into the reception area. She had not seen the sergeant behind the desk before. She asked for Chief Inspector Thornhill.

'I can take a message, if you want, or maybe I can help.' The sergeant leaned over the counter towards her, bringing with him his personal atmosphere composed of halitosis, vinegar and tobacco. 'What's it about?'

She backed away. 'I need Mr Thornhill himself. Is he in the building?'

'He's just come in but—'

'Then would you kindly let him know that Jill Francis of the *Gazette* is here?'

The sergeant reached reluctantly for the phone. A moment later, Thornhill came downstairs. He was still in his overcoat.

'Good afternoon,' Jill said. 'I came across a piece of information I think you ought to have.'

He nodded, as though this was the most usual thing in the world, and said, 'You'd better come up to my office.'

He raised the flap of the counter and ushered her through. Jill was conscious of the desk sergeant's curious eyes following her. She and Thornhill went up the stairs side by side. Neither spoke. She glanced sideways at him as the stairs turned back on themselves. His had never been an expressive face. But she thought there was something too controlled about it today. Something had angered or upset him. How odd that the ability to second-guess a person's emotions could survive a three-year absence and an emotional volte-face.

Assuming, that is, that an emotional volte-face had really taken place.

On the first floor, he showed her into his room. Thornhill had a different office from the one she remembered – larger, and with two windows instead of one, both of which looked down on the High Street. He murmured an apology and, half closing the door, spoke for a few seconds to someone in the corridor: ordering a prisoner to be taken to an interview room. He returned almost at once, took her coat and lit the gas fire.

A knot of tension had developed in her stomach. She sat down and opened her handbag, intending to look for a cigarette. Then she changed her mind. The only ashtray in sight was on the desk, and it was full of paper clips. Apart from the ashtray and a blank, lined pad of foolscap paper, all it contained were two wire baskets, an in-tray and an out-tray. The out-tray was empty. In the in-tray was an untidy pile of papers that told their own story, that Thornhill was too busy to look at them, or even to straighten the pile.

He sat down behind the desk. He smoothed the hair back on either side of his head. It was an unconscious gesture which she remembered from the past: he often did it when tired or worried.

She said, 'I'm sorry to barge in like this. I realise you're very busy.'

'You've got something to tell me?' He hesitated. 'Something about the Bayswater case?'

As opposed to something about us?

'Not directly.' Jill watched a shadow cross his face. 'There may be a connection, though. It's about the man who's gone missing.'

'Paul Frederick?'

'I wondered if you had his wartime service record. Where he was stationed, what name he enlisted under, that sort of thing.'

'I thought you had something to tell me rather than the other way round.'

She laughed, responding not to his words but to the glint in his eye. 'All right. I'm going about this the wrong way, aren't I? This really starts with Ivor Fuggle.'

He leaned across the desk, all attention now, but wary. 'Go on.'

'He has to be the person orchestrating the attacks on the *Gazette*. He's very difficult to touch so I wondered . . . I wondered if he had any weak points.' Suddenly it sounded shabby, as though she were sinking to Fuggle's level. 'In particular, I wondered about Mrs Fuggle. I managed to get hold of a letter that she'd written from her old address in Bournemouth, where she was living when she met Mr Fuggle. She was using up old letterhead, so there was another address on the letter, an even older one, which she'd crossed out. In London – Yorkley Grove.'

'Where's that?'

'North London. I was in town the other day with an hour to spare so I thought I'd have a look. I talked to a lady who'd lived there during the war. She remembered the Ellwoods quite well.'

'The Ellwoods?'

'Sorry – of course, you don't know: Mrs Fuggle's maiden

name was Ellwood. There were three of them – Genevieve, her brother and their mother. They used to live in Tufnell Park but in the war they rented a flat in Yorkley Grove. Genevieve was a waitress. The brother was called Mike, some sort of civil servant. Then the mother died of pneumonia and that left the brother and sister. The house took a direct hit in one of the first V-2 raids. Mike was killed and Genevieve moved away.'

Thornhill was sitting very still, watching her. Gradually she felt herself relaxing. The knot in her stomach began to un-clench.

'Genevieve had a fiancé. He was a Dutch airman in the RAF and his name was Tony Frederiks.' She spelled out the surname. Afterwards her hand flew to her forehead. 'I forgot – I don't know why, I can't think straight at present. The church.'

'What church?' he said gently.

'The one in the photograph you sent us. Paul Frederick in his RAF uniform, with a church in the background. Remem-ber? Well, that church is in Yorkley Grove. Except it's not in that state any more. It's a ruin.'

'Wait a moment.'

Thornhill opened one of the bottom drawers of his desk and took out a file. He skimmed through it and looked up.

'When he joined the RAF he gave his name as Anton Paul Frederiks. When he became a naturalised British citizen, he anglicised the name to Frederick.'

'So there's no doubt he was Genevieve Ellwood's Tony.'

'It looks like it.'

'According to Maisie, he—'

'Who?'

'Maisie Lawrence,' Jill said. 'My informant in Yorkley Grove. She said that Tony came back looking for Genevieve after the bomb. But Genevieve had moved away. She never came back.'

'Understandable enough, I suppose.'

'Is it?'

'She'd lost everything. What had she got to stay there for? She probably found a room nearer where she worked.'

'But she didn't leave a forwarding address. It's as if she didn't want to see Tony. And that's odd, if you come to think about it. She'd just lost her home and her brother. You'd have thought he was all she had left.'

'She was in shock. People do strange things when they are in shock.' But he spoke idly, as though his mind were elsewhere. Suddenly his voice sharpened. 'You're sure about all this?'

'Of course I'm sure,' Jill said. 'You realise what this means? There was someone Frederick knew in Lydmouth, his former fiancée. He could have gone to see Mrs Fuggle in those missing hours on Friday morning.'

'It's more than that.' He smiled at her. A pulse was beating in the hollow above his left cheekbone. 'It's much more. You've given me exactly what I needed to hear. It's not generally known – and it mustn't be for a while – but there was a sighting of Paul Frederick on Friday morning – before you saw him running for the train at Lydmouth station. Someone saw him at the upper end of Whistler's Lane. He was seen twice, in fact. Once going up there, and then again returning.'

'But how did he know she lived here?'

'There was a photo of the Fuggles in Wednesday's *Post*. He probably saw that.'

'Of course – Amy showed me.' Jill retrieved the memory. *The* Post's *editor Mr Ivor Fuggle and his wife Genevieve share a joke with Lady Ruispidge*. 'And Genevieve would have caught his eye – it's an unusual name.'

He stood up. 'Would you excuse me? I need to get things moving, and then I'd better take down some names and addresses from you.' He picked up the ashtray and turned it upside down, so that a gleaming silver mound of paper clips appeared on the immaculate surface of the desk. 'Do smoke.'

The door closed behind him. Jill took her cigarettes and lighter from her handbag. She stretched across the desk for the ashtray. The cuff of her coat caught the edge of the in-tray. The wire basket slid a few inches across the desk. One corner overhung the edge. For an instant as long as a lifetime it stayed there. The pile of papers wobbled. Jill dropped cigarettes and lighter and lunged inelegantly towards it.

She was too late. The basket tilted. It dived to the floor, disgorging its contents over the carpet.

'Oh, bugger it,' she muttered.

She picked up the basket, then squatted beside the heap of papers – single sheets, files, envelopes – and did her best to shuffle them back together in their original order. She felt flustered, as though she were doing something surreptitious, even underhand. That was not at all what she was doing, but if Richard came back, if somebody else came in, that might be the construction placed on her actions.

She put the pile back in the in-tray. It did not look the same. On the other hand, she could not remember what it had looked like. It would have to do.

She sat down again and at last reached for her cigarettes. She had just taken one from the packet when she caught a flash of something pale between the side of the desk and the metal wastepaper basket.

It was a sheet of paper, something she must have missed when she was gathering up the others. She picked it up and automatically glanced at it. Bayswater's name caught her eye. She sat back in her chair. Even as she was returning the sheet of paper to the pile, her eyes were scanning it with the rapid and unthinking promiscuity of the habitual reader. It was a letter from another doctor, a man named Lindsay Pirk who worked at the Eastville Clinic in Newport. Her eye floated down the page.

> You raise an interesting point in your letter of the 2nd. There is no doubt that Eonism is idiopathic. But there is still some uncertainty about the precise mechanisms involved. Havelock Ellis refers to it as 'sexo-aesthetic inversion', which to my mind is a more accurate term than Hirschfeld's . . .

Jill abandoned the pretence that she was not prying. She glanced at the date at the top and read the letter carefully once, and then again. Bayswater's mail must now be automatically redirected to the CID office.

At that moment a bell began to ring, shatteringly loud, the sound harsh and penetrating.

Jill shot to her feet. For an instant she thought the bell was ringing because of her, because of what she was doing. Fire alarm, she thought, and thrust the letter at random into the pile towering in the in-tray. She put on her hat and coat and picked up her handbag.

She was reaching for the handle on the door when it opened from the other side. Richard barged into her. All the while the bell rang on, as relentless as a pneumatic drill. She heard running footsteps in the corridor.

'I must ask you to leave, Miss Francis,' Thornhill said, formal once again. 'I'm afraid we have a suspect on the loose.'

'Here? In the building?'

'You're quite safe. Porter will see you to your car.'

'This way, miss.' Grim faced, Porter beckoned her. 'You got your things?'

She began to speak: 'There's something else—'

Thornhill interrupted. 'I'll be in touch as soon as possible.'

She nodded but said nothing. Porter marched her along the corridor and down the stairs. In a situation like this, Porter's dark blue bulk stopped being faintly comic and became reassuring. He seemed as invulnerable as a cartoon character. Hit him over the head with a sledgehammer and the sledgehammer would bounce.

In the car park, two uniformed officers were checking the sprinkling of Nissen huts, sheds and garages, the temporary structures that seemed to breed among themselves as the years passed. Porter opened the driver's door of the Morris Minor for Jill.

'Lock the door from the inside, miss,' he advised. 'Safe journey.'

'Can you tell me who's escaped?'

'No, miss.' It was too dark to see Porter's face but he sounded shocked. 'It wouldn't be right.'

Jill felt that somehow she had disappointed him. 'Of course not – I understand. Thank you.'

He closed the door. She locked it and started the engine. It was now raining steadily but not heavily. She felt as though she had been passed through a hand wringer and most of the vitality had been squeezed out of her. She drove slowly back to the flat, which she still could not think of as home.

A cup of tea, she thought, with lots of sugar – and at last I'll be able to have that cigarette.

She pulled into the little car park behind Raglan Court. None of the lights at the back of the building was on, and the overhanging trees increased the gloom. She turned off the engine and reached for her handbag. It was at that moment that she heard the sound in the back of the car.

Oh God, she thought, no more rats. *Please.*

Chapter Fifty-Six

It was slack, it was unforgivable, it was embarrassing.

Someone, Thornhill told himself, was going to spend the rest of his days regretting it. But the time for apportioning blame would come later. He already knew the essentials: that Brian Kirby had detailed a couple of constables, one experienced and one a rookie, to escort Joe Rodley from the holding cell to one of the interview rooms. The older of the two officers had only just come into the building and had no idea what was going on or who Rodley was. He had a desperate need for a pee, so he had told the rookie to carry on escorting the prisoner to the interview room.

Rodley himself, no fool, had acted meek and mild and subdued – until he was on the stairs, at which point he threw a roundhouse punch at the rookie which brought the side of the lad's head into violent collision with the iron handrail.

No one saw it happen. No one saw where Rodley went. The senior constable came back from the lavatory and found the rookie sitting on the bottom step with his head in his hands and moaning. He raised the alarm immediately. The trouble was, immediately wasn't fast enough.

Thornhill had set guards on the exits and organised two search parties that combed the building, floor by floor. A third group of officers examined the yard at the back and a fourth went into the High Street and questioned passers-by. The control room radioed an alert to all patrols.

Thornhill felt sour and furious. This was a mistake that should not have been allowed to happen. The search for Rodley was wasting resources just at the time when those resources were needed elsewhere. There was also the point that Rodley's escape made the police look inept – it was a gift for Fuggle, and Thornhill had no doubt that he would use it to the best of his ability. As the senior officer on duty, Thornhill knew that the responsibility for the debacle would eventually fall on him.

The search of the building was completed within ten minutes. In the meantime, Thornhill had a car brought round. As he was leaving, the phone rang. Thornhill motioned to Kirby to answer it.

Even with the phone clamped to Kirby's ear, Thornhill heard the raised voice on the other end of the line.

'Yes, sir,' Kirby said. 'Mr Thornhill? No, sir, I'm afraid he's not in the building.' He mouthed the word *Fuggle* and raised his eyebrows at Thornhill, who shook his head. 'I'm afraid he's just left, sir.' He held the phone away from his head and the angry voice snarled and snapped at the other end of the wire. 'No, sir . . . Yes, sir. I'll tell him.' There was a final crackle of invective on the other end of the line. Kirby replaced the receiver. 'That was Mr Fuggle,' he said demurely. 'Seemed to want a word with either you or Mr Drake.'

'Why?'

'Said something about wanting a statement from the police justifying their behaviour this afternoon. He's going round to Mr Drake's now.'

'To his house?' Thornhill shrugged and moved towards the door. 'What did Fuggle say at the end?'

Kirby looked faintly embarrassed. 'He said: why talk to the monkey when you can talk to the organ grinder?'

'Sometimes I'd rather be the monkey. You'd better ring

Mr Drake, tell him what's happened, tell him Fuggle's on his way.'

Thornhill ran downstairs. The car was waiting at the back, its engine running, wipers slapping across the windscreen and Porter behind the wheel. They drove in silence through streets that were much quieter than they had been. By now it was a little after five o'clock and most of the shops were closed or closing. The town was entering the dead time of the evening before the pubs opened.

They drove up Whistler's Lane. The lights were on in both the Fuggles' bungalow and Viney Cottage. When they had parked, Thornhill told Porter to check whether Fuggle's car was still in the garage. It had gone.

A constable emerged from the shadows surrounding the gate to the park. Thornhill waved him over. Whistler's Lane was on the man's beat and he had been detailed to keep an eye on Viney Cottage until Thornhill's arrival.

'No sign of life, sir. No one's gone in or left.'

'She must have someone with her, surely?'

'If she has they got here before I did, sir. Do you want me to stay here?'

'Yes, for the time being.'

Thornhill crossed the road, back to Porter at the gate of Viney Cottage. He felt sorry for the constable behind him, shivering in his dark blue cape on a wet winter afternoon, waiting for something that might or might not happen.

A moment later he knocked on the cottage door. There were footsteps in the hall. He found himself looking at the huge, murky eyes and black-rimmed glasses of Mr Prout.

'What are you doing here?' Thornhill asked, surprise making him speak more bluntly than usual.

Mr Prout sniffed. One hand played with his cravat. 'Mrs Rodley phoned Miss Gwyn-Thomas. I . . . I happened to be having tea with her so I thought I'd escort her up here. A sorry business, I must say.' He lowered his voice. 'What exactly has Rodley done?'

'I'm afraid I can't discuss that at present, sir.'

Mr Prout stared up at him, his mouth twitching. Then he turned and led the way into the bedroom on the right. The small room was stiflingly hot and already crowded. Doreen Rodley was in bed. Amy Gwyn-Thomas was measuring a spoonful of medicine from a bottle. Genevieve Fuggle sat smoking at the table in the window, so Mrs Rodley or Amy must have phoned her as well.

'Shut the door,' Amy said without turning round. 'There's a draught.'

Thornhill cleared his throat. 'I'm sorry to disturb you again, Mrs Rodley.'

She opened her eyes and looked at him. 'Where's Joe? What have you done to him?'

'Perhaps I should have a word with you alone.'

Mrs Rodley shook her head with surprising violence. 'If you've got something to say, you can say it in front of my friends. What's going to happen to Joe? That's what I want to know. I can't cope without him, I can't manage, I—'

'There, there.' Amy patted her hand firmly. 'I'm sure everything's going to be all right.'

'I'm not sure.' Doreen's eyes were wild. 'I'm not sure of anything any more.'

'We were questioning Mr Rodley at the station,' Thornhill said. 'Unfortunately he ran away.' He hesitated. 'And in doing so, he assaulted one of my officers.'

Doreen Rodley's white, papery face crumpled as if squeezed in a giant hand. He watched silent tears trickle down her cheeks. An invisible reservoir of grief was gently overflowing.

'You've not seen him?' Thornhill glanced at each of the three women in turn. 'Has he phoned?'

'No,' Genevieve Fuggle said huskily. 'I've been here for nearly half an hour, and no one's phoned, no one's come.'

Amy nodded in confirmation.

'He'll go to prison now, won't he?' Mrs Rodley said. 'It's the end, you know. The end of everything.'

Thornhill thought of the anodyne things he might say in reply. Instead he told her: 'One of my officers is on guard outside, Mrs Rodley. I'm going to send a woman police officer up to be with you. It may be best if you go into hospital for a few days. Or stay with a friend, if you prefer. But in either case we shall need to know how to find you.'

Mr Prout ran his finger between his cravat and his neck.

Thornhill turned to go. Mrs Fuggle came into the hall with him to let him out.

'He's a murderer, Joe Rodley, isn't he?' she hissed.

Thornhill said nothing. She was very close to him. Her face was shiny with perspiration, which wasn't surprising, given the heat of the room.

'That's what you think,' she told him. 'He killed that old doctor.'

Chapter Fifty-Seven

The telephone was ringing as Jill Francis unlocked the door. With his free hand, Joe Rodley twisted the handle and nudged her into the flat with his shoulder. He glanced up and down the corridor and followed her, closing the door. Jill looked at him, a mute question.

'Leave it,' he said.

The phone rang on.

Joe let go of her arm. That was something. But she was aware of his physical presence. He wasn't tall but he was broad. He smelled sour. It occurred to her that he no longer had anything to lose.

The phone stopped ringing. She heard the click as Joe put down the snib on the Yale lock. For a moment he stared at her with bloodshot eyes. He needed a shave.

Jill said, 'Can I get you a drink? A cup of tea?'

She spoke without forethought. Anything to inject a touch of normality into the proceedings. You don't offer hospitality to someone who might kill you. You don't kill someone who has offered you hospitality.

Joe shook his head. 'Money,' he said. 'Cheque book. Jewellery.' He held out his hand. 'I'll take the car keys now.'

She felt a shameful rush of relief. He was going to steal what he could and then drive off in her car. She had no objection to that at all. On the contrary, she would do everything in her power to make his departure as smooth and pleasant as possible.

Four internal doors gave on to the hall. He opened each of them, one by one, checking the rooms beyond, his eyes darting back to Jill every few seconds. Finally he jerked his head, motioning her into the living-room.

'Sit down,' he ordered.

'Shall I turn on the fire?'

He shook his head. He prowled round the room, opening drawers and riffling through their contents. He found her passport and cheque book, both of which he dropped on to the table beside her typewriter.

'Listen,' Jill said. 'Are you sure this is a good idea?'

He glanced at her but said nothing. She still did not know what he had done but it seemed more and more likely that he had killed Dr Bayswater.

He picked up her handbag, opened it and emptied the contents. The muddle of her private life tumbled on to the table. A bottle of perfume bounced and fell to the floor, where it shattered. Gradually the room filled with the scent of Chanel, transforming an expensive pleasure into a problem. Rodley snatched the purse.

Even in her fear, Jill found herself staring at her belongings, half surprised and half ashamed. Why were there so many London bus tickets? Did she really need at least three handkerchiefs, none of them clean?

Rodley went through the purse and put it with the cheque book. All the time, his eyes were moving, flicking towards her and then back to what he was doing. He licked his lips repeatedly with the tip of a pink, gleaming tongue. She felt queasy with fear. Some men, she knew, were sexually stimulated by danger. She wondered whether Joe Rodley was one of them.

He abandoned her handbag and went into the kitchen. The door was open and so was the serving-hatch. She was never out of his sight. She stared at her discarded possessions on the table, at a dog-eared library ticket, a pencil stub, a key she did not recognise and two lipsticks, one without a top.

She heard Rodley opening cupboards and drawers and the rattle of cutlery. When he came out, he was carrying a loaf of bread, a packet of ginger biscuits and a carving-knife. He put the bread and the biscuits down on the table. Then he showed her the carving-knife and ran his finger down the blade, as though testing its sharpness. Jill tried to smile. She desperately sought words that might ease the situation.

The telephone began to ring again. They both jumped. Rodley swore. Jill instinctively reached out a hand towards the phone. He leapt in front of her, lunging towards her with the knife. The tip snagged in the tweed of her coat. She flung herself backward with a little cry, a whimper. She was ashamed of herself. She was acting like a weak and feeble woman. But at present there seemed to be no other way to act.

He glanced at the telephone, still ringing. He approached it warily, as though it were a wild and possibly dangerous animal. Frowning, he scooped up the wire that ran down to the connection point on the skirting board. He made a loop, inserted the blade and sliced the wire in two.

The bell stopped in mid-ring. He looked at her and smiled, revealing jagged, yellow teeth.

'Bedroom,' he said, and pointed the knife in the direction he wanted her to go.

He walked just behind her, into the hall and the bedroom beyond. The bed was unmade and there were unfolded clothes on the chair. Jill wondered what she would do if he tried to rape her. She must find a weapon. All she could think of were the china candlesticks on the dressing-table; but even if she could reach them, they would break so easily they would quite possibly damage her more than they damaged him.

Go for the eyes and testicles, she told herself, hearing in some remote part of her memory a friend using the same words, a friend who worked as a nightclub hostess and who knew all about the beastliness of men.

Joe Rodley stood in the doorway. 'Jewellery,' he said. 'Where is it?'

She nodded at the dressing-table. 'The top left-hand drawer.'

He strode across the room to it, forcing her to back away. He pulled out the drawer and upended it over the bed. Half buried among the underclothes were two jewellery boxes and a jewellery roll. He tore open the roll and the boxes and crammed their contents into the pockets of his jacket with an unthinking greed that reminded Jill of a schoolboy hoarding sweets.

She stood watching him with her arms crossed tightly over her chest and her heart pounding. She would have liked to use the lavatory but did not dare ask.

He opened the sliding doors of the wardrobe and looked at her clothes. Gesturing with the knife, he took her into the hall and opened the door of the cupboard there.

'Haven't you any men's clothes?'

Jill shook her head.

'Car.'

'What?'

He said, using the same low, rather monotonous voice: 'Are you fucking stupid? The car. Your car, the one we came in. We're going for a drive.'

'But why? Why do you need me?'

'Because maybe you'll drive some of the way. Because they'll be looking for one man, not a couple. And because I may need something to bargain with.'

It took Jill a moment to realise that 'something' meant herself. 'What about Doreen?'

A shadow passed over his face. 'I'm no good to her if I stay here, am I? They're going to hang me. You won't believe me but I didn't kill Bayswater. He deserved it, mind.'

'If you didn't do it, then you must give yourself up. They won't want to get the wrong man.'

'That's not the way it works. It may be for your sort, but it's not for me. They want to find a killer and they don't really care who it is, though if it's someone like me it would suit them fine. They arrest me, I get hanged and everyone goes home happy.'

'It's not like that,' Jill said. 'I promise, if you let me—'

'I don't want promises. I want something like a clothes line.'

'In the cupboard underneath the sink in the kitchen,' Jill said automatically.

He touched her with the tip of the blade, forcing her into the kitchen. With the knife resting on the nape of her neck, she found him a ball of heavy twine she used for parcels.

'That'll do,' Rodley said, and prodded her, this time with his finger, pushing her into the living-room. His eyes fell on the briefcase on the floor by the sideboard. 'Empty that out.'

She obeyed him. There was nothing of value in it, not to him, only notes for stories, a newspaper and a couple of magazines. He instructed her to put the twine, the food and, as an afterthought, the gin and the whisky from the drinks tray into the briefcase.

'Right, then,' he said. 'Off we go. If we meet anyone on the way to the car, try not to talk to them. If you have to, don't bring me into it. If you can't help it, I'm the new mechanic from Gray's, and I've come to look at your car. You think you might have a rattle in your engine. If—'

There was a ring on the bell. Rodley drew in his breath sharply. His eyes locked with Jill's.

There was another ring.

Joe gripped her shoulder with one hand. She felt the knife

pressing against her coat, less than an inch from the soft flesh between rib cage and hip bone.

'Jill!' Leddon called. 'Jill, it's me, Roger.'

The grip on her shoulder tightened still further.

Leddon knocked this time. 'Let me in. I know you're there – I saw the lights.'

There came another burst of knocking, oddly frenzied. Jill and Rodley stood motionless, as though posing for a life class.

'Are you all right? Is something wrong?'

A few seconds of silence crawled by. Jill listened to her breathing and the heavier sound of Joe Rodley's just behind her.

'Jill, I'm worried. Are you ill? You must be able to hear me.'

She opened her mouth. Simultaneously the pressure on her right side eased. She saw the knife blade glinting in the light. The tip burrowed into her clothing until it pierced the skin just below her left breast. She gasped.

'Jill?'

Even now part of her remained cynical and detached. Was Roger Leddon really concerned about her well-being or was he merely trying to woo her back into the morally elastic universe he inhabited?

The handle turned. The door rattled in its frame.

'Jill, I'm going to get Merton. He's got a pass key.'

Mr and Mrs Merton had a flat on the ground floor overlooking the car park. Jill felt Joe Rodley's lips brushing her right ear and the knife pricked a little harder.

'Put the door on the chain,' he murmured. 'Then open it and say you're okay but you've got a headache, you've been dozing, and all you want to do is go to sleep. Anything other than that, and it's the last thing you say. They can't hang you twice, can they?'

Leddon knocked again. Jill and Rodley moved into the hall.

He let go of Jill's shoulder and put the chain on the door. His left hand returned to Jill's shoulder.

'Open it,' he breathed.

Jill lifted the snib on the Yale. She drew the door back as far as the chain would allow, no more than two or three inches. Most of her body and all of Rodley's was still shielded from anyone outside. She craned to her left, so her face would be visible to Leddon through the gap.

'Jill! What is it?'

'Nothing.' The blade dug a little deeper. 'I . . . I've got a headache. I was dozing.'

His face sharpened. 'Well, let me come and look at you. Hang on a second, I'll get my bag.'

'No, Roger – it's all right. I get these headaches sometimes. Some sort of . . . some sort of migraine. The best treatment is just lying in a darkened room.'

'You haven't been answering your phone, either.'

'There's something wrong with the line, I think.'

'Have you reported it?'

'Yes,' Jill said wildly.

'I know Charlotte's been trying to get hold of you too.'

'Charlotte – why?'

'Bad news, I'm afraid.' He screwed up his face and for an instant she felt the meretricious warmth of his sympathy oozing through the gap like warm gas. 'If you've got a headache, this isn't the moment. The trouble is it's never the moment.'

'Philip?' she said.

He nodded. 'I'm so sorry.'

She clung to the edge of the door. For a moment she feared she might faint. She remembered the ambulance bell and the repeated ringing of the telephone. Feeling drained away, leaving her numb and somehow unreal.

'Is he . . . is he dead?'

'I'm so sorry,' Leddon repeated. 'Another heart attack. He . . . he can't have felt anything. I've been over there – I've just come back.'

The only thing that kept her from giving way was the knife digging into her chest just below the line of her brassiere. The pain, sharp and physical, was something to cling to, something indisputably real. If her knees gave way and she fell, Jill thought, the blade would dig deeper and deeper and deeper.

She said, 'Charlotte – how is she?'

'Not too good, I'm afraid. I've given her something to calm her down. She's probably asleep by now. The vicar's wife is with her – luckily she and her husband were at Troy House when it happened.'

'I'll go myself as soon as I can,' Jill said, conscious not just of the pressure of the hand and the knife but also of the feral smell of Joe Rodley, of a terrified man.

'Jill, as a doctor, I really think you should—'

'I'm perfectly all right,' she said. 'All I need is rest. If you really want to help, though, you could let Charlotte know – or Mary Sutton if Charlotte's asleep – that I'll come as soon as I can.'

Rodley's shoulder leaned against the door. It closed gently in Leddon's face.

Jill was trembling. Rodley moved the knife and, holding it where she could see it, took her arm and guided her back to the living-room. He pushed her into an armchair. She sat there, staring at him and wondering what she thought, what she felt.

He picked up the sherry bottle and extracted the cork with his teeth. He poured two inches of amontillado into a whisky glass and handed it to her. Automatically she drank. The fortified wine ran down her throat like liquid fire and settled in a warm medicinal lake at the bottom of her stomach. Without moving his eyes from her, Rodley poured himself a rather larger glass and drank it in a couple of mouthfuls.

'Friend of yours?' he said.

Jill nodded.

He shrugged. 'Oh well.'

She frowned, trying to work out what his behaviour meant: whether he was being sympathetic or simply couldn't care less. Or did his feelings occupy an ill-defined area somewhere between those two extremes? She sipped the sherry.

'Come on,' he said. 'Sup up. We got to get going. Which is Leddon's flat?'

Jill said, 'Downstairs – first floor at the front.'

'Can he see the car park?'

She shook her head.

Rodley seemed to fill with feverish energy. They were going, and they were going now. Leaving the lights burning, he hustled Jill out of the flat. He made her carry the briefcase. He kept one hand wrapped round Jill's upper arm, holding the knife concealed under the cuff of his jacket in the right hand. He led her almost at a trot down the stairs, along the hallway and out of the back door into the car park.

The Mertons' windows were dark. No one had turned on the outside light. Rodley told her to get into the back of the car. Then, while he whistled very quietly under his breath the tune from *Oklahoma* about a surrey with a fringe on top, he cut off a length of the twine and bound her thumbs tightly together behind her back.

'You can't make me sit like this. It's going to be excruciating.'

'You'll cope,' he told her. 'Open wide.'

He produced what looked like one of her tea towels from his pocket.

'What are you going to do?'

'Gag you.' Still filled with that manic excitement, he grinned, and for an instant she glimpsed another side of Joe Rodley: the side that liked a drink and a laugh; the side that had probably wooed and won Doreen.

'No – please. I promise I won't call out. And the windows are shut, anyway.'

He looked at her, his face expressionless.

'I'll choke,' Jill said desperately. 'I'll be sick.'

He cleared his throat. 'Our Doreen is sick sometimes, if her mouth's covered. Happened at the dentist's once.'

'There you are. I could suffocate. I wouldn't be much use to you then.'

Turning, he touched her cheek with the cool blade and said: 'All right. Just for Doreen. But you be a good girl, eh? Otherwise I'm going to put this knife in you. No skin off my nose, not now. All right, sweetie?'

Rodley let out the clutch and drove out of the car park. As the Morris Minor rolled sedately down Albert Road, she stared at the outside world, hardly able to believe that it was carrying on just as normal while inside the car she and Joe Rodley were locked in this strange and painful aberrant reality. She saw two schoolboys fighting under a street lamp and a woman half running through the slanting rain with a pint of milk clutched in her hand. Joe was whistling louder now, still about that bloody surrey with the fringe on top.

At the bottom of the hill they turned right, and then left up the High Street. The rain-washed tarmac reflected a black metallic gleam. Surely someone would notice them? But it was never easy to see into a darkened car at night. Few people were about. But there was someone ahead on the zebra crossing. She waited for Rodley to brake. Instead he dropped a gear and pushed the accelerator down hard.

The car leapt forward and there was a jolt as it collided with a man on the crossing. For an instant Jill saw the face of the Morris Minor's victim – grey hair, staring eyes, a gaping mouth, flapping coat-tails. The man fell forward on to the bonnet with a bang before rolling off to the nearside. His umbrella caught a puff of wind and skittered across the road, turning and twisting like a dancer.

'Bastard,' Joe Rodley said, and laughed. 'That'll teach you to be a skinflint.'

Jill craned her head. A dark shape lay half on the crossing and half on the pavement. She tried to speak but the words stuck in her mouth and made her feel sick.

'Yeah,' Rodley went on. 'That was him, all right. Lying bugger. That'll teach him to—'

A few yards farther on, a large figure stepped from the kerb and held up an arm. The car's headlights caught his face, blank with incomprehension beneath the familiar shape of a policeman's helmet. It was Peter Porter.

Rodley swore and dragged the wheel hard to the right so that the Morris swerved, narrowly avoiding a collision with an oncoming bus. Horns blared in a discordant chorus. Jill twisted in her seat. PC Porter was pounding along the pavement after them, one arm raised as if trying to grab the car while the other held a whistle to his lips.

'Bloody loony,' Rodley said. 'I can't stand fucking heroes.'

Jill bounced up and down on the seat, hoping that Porter would see her.

Without slowing, Rodley turned right. At the bottom of the hill, where the road crossed the railway tracks, the great gates of the level-crossing were beginning slowly to close. The Morris Minor surged forward, faster and faster, towards the diminishing gap between the gates.

Jill thought: if I ever get out of this, I'm going to sell this car. She closed her eyes.

Chapter Fifty-Eight

Rain was falling – not heavy but steady and penetrating, whipped away from the vertical by a strong south-westerly wind. Richard Thornhill sat beside his phone. The building was overheated but he was cold. The crisis was unfolding around him. There was nothing he could do apart from wait and listen and give orders and then wait again.

Vincent Drake phoned, coldly furious not just because of the blunder but because Ivor Fuggle had burst into his family party like a wicked fairy at a christening. Drake rarely lost his temper but when he did he was formidable. Fuggle had been forced to retreat, mouthing threats; some of which he was undoubtedly capable of carrying out. Unfortunately his car had failed to start, which had improved neither Fuggle's temper nor Drake's.

'Bloody man left his rust heap across the mouth of my drive. Goddam it, I've got a house full of people trapped here and Millie tells me she's got nothing to feed them with. Have a word with Transport – as soon as someone's free I want them up here with the Land Rover. In the meantime, keep me posted, Richard. You're in charge, but if you need me you know where I am.'

That was the good side of Drake and the bad side too. He knew how to delegate and he knew Thornhill could take the responsibility. He also knew that a full-blown catastrophe was looming at Police Headquarters, but he wasn't going to interfere unless he had to; and if it all went wrong he would not be first in line for the blame. Thornhill wasn't clear whether Drake's motive was altruistic or selfish or just the usual mixture of the two.

He stared at the rain gliding down the window pane, seeing Jill's face darkly in the glass. Under the shifting patterns of the water, the face formed, disintegrated and re-formed. He forced his mind back to the problem of Rodley, to the embarrassment of losing a prisoner and to the possibility that they might never get him back.

Kirby barged into the office without knocking. 'We've got a sighting, sir.'

'Where?'

'Raglan Court. Leddon thinks he saw Rodley getting into Miss Francis's car and driving off.'

Thornhill pushed back his chair so quickly it fell over behind him. 'Miss Francis? Where is she?'

'Leddon doesn't know. He knocked on her door a few minutes earlier and for a while she didn't answer. When she did, she kept the door on the chain and said she had a headache and was going to lie down.'

'Has anyone phoned?'

'No luck. The line's dead.'

'Quite sure?'

'Yes, sir. That's what Leddon said, and Dyke tried again just now. It's not ringing at the other end. We're checking with the exchange.'

Thornhill said quietly, 'So Rodley stowed away in her car – is that how he got away from here?'

'Probably. It was parked near the back door, in the Chief Constable's space. Ten to one she didn't bother to lock it. The question is—'

'The question is, whether Miss Francis is with Rodley now.'

'Leddon says she was acting very strangely. You know Philip Wemyss-Brown has just died?'

Thornhill stared blankly at him. 'What?'

'Heart attack. Leddon mentioned it. He'd been up at Troy House before he called on Miss Francis. He said she didn't really seem to register it.'

'When did he see them leaving Raglan Court? How long ago was it?'

'Hard to say with any accuracy. Leddon was going out to his own car – that's when he saw the Morris Minor with Rodley driving off. He went back inside and banged on Miss Francis's door again. No answer, so he went back to his own flat and tried phoning her again. He wasted another few minutes trying to find the caretaker who's got a pass key, but he was out. Then he phoned 999. The emergency services routed him on to us but it took another minute or two to reach CID. Somewhere between fifteen and twenty minutes is my guess.'

'So they're probably out of town by now?'

'We can't be sure.'

'You'd better go up to Raglan Court, and if there isn't an answer, force an entry. We'll set up roadblocks and alert all patrols.' Thornhill had been speaking in a flat, soft voice but suddenly, without warning, he lost control of it and the volume rose and the tone sharpened. 'Hurry, man.'

Kirby almost bolted from the office. Thornhill followed, on his way to the Communications Room. He was passing through reception just as Peter Porter burst through the main doors from the High Street.

Porter had lost his helmet and there was a long smear of mud down one side of his cape. When he saw Thornhill he opened his mouth but all that came out was a gargle.

'What is it?' Thornhill snapped.

'Joe Rodley, sir.'

For the second time that evening, the clamour of an ambulance bell cut through all other sounds.

'Where?'

'He's got Miss Francis's car, sir. And she's in the back – I saw them in the High Street. And Mr Fuggle's—'

'He's in the car too?'

'No, sir. He was on the zebra crossing.' Porter swallowed. 'Rodley knocked him down, just drove straight at him. I saw it happen.'

'Where did they go?'

'Towards the station.'

'And Fuggle? Is he badly hurt?'

'I don't know. He's knocked out.'

The thought of Jill alone in a car with a murderer filled the forefront of Thornhill's mind, obscuring everything else. On some level he was aware that he was moving to and fro, snapping out orders. He phoned the railway police and sent a couple of men down to the station. If, as was more likely, Rodley had driven over New Bridge instead, he had three choices: going up the hill into the forest, turning right along the line of the estuary towards Eastbury, or turning left into a lane that after a mile or two dwindled into a farm track. Thornhill sent cars out in all three directions and alerted the sub-stations at Eastbury and Ashbridge.

At some point during this confusion, Brian Kirby returned with the news that Jill's flat was empty, and that there were signs that her belongings had been ransacked.

'Where is he heading?' Thornhill said. 'Maybe his wife will know.'

Porter coughed. 'Might be Ipswich, sir.'

Kirby and Thornhill turned to him simultaneously.

Porter slouched and stared at the ground, as though trying to shrink his bulk into insignificance. 'I thought you'd know.'

'Know what?' Thornhill demanded, unable to keep the irritation out of his voice.

'Joe's dad's local, sir, but his mum was a foreigner. He was a groom, look, before the war – the first war, that is, and he was working at this big house in Suffolk. She was in service there, and he courted her and when they were wed, they came back to Lydmouth.'

'So he's got family in Ipswich?' Thornhill said, too used to the strange depths of Porter's local knowledge to feel surprised by it.

'His auntie lives there, family works on the ferries out of Harwich. Couple of cousins were done for smuggling cigarettes last year.'

'So maybe he's hoping to leave the country,' Kirby said. 'But what about his wife?'

'What about her?' Thornhill thought of the desperation and the anger that must have fuelled the hit-and-run attack on Fuggle. 'He's afraid of being hanged. He can't afford to worry about her. On the other hand, you can't be hanged twice.'

There was a tap on the door and one of the sergeants from Uniformed sidled into the CID office.

'We've got a sighting, sir. Jack Sneddon was on patrol on the Eastbury Road. Saw a Morris Minor take the turn up to the forest. They were driving so fast he tried to take their number.'

'Then we've got him.' Thornhill crossed the room to where the map hung on the wall. 'If we get Ashbridge to seal off the road there' – he stabbed at a point on the Lydmouth side of the village – 'and we send a couple of cars up behind, there's nowhere for him to turn.'

There was another cough from Porter. 'Excuse me, sir, he might take the back road – he knows all the byways, look, because his dad worked for the Forestry after he came out of

the army and he lost his place because the estate was sold, and
the stables—'

Thornhill cut into the flood of words: 'Which road?'

Porter gaped at him. 'The . . . the gated road over the top,
sir.' He frowned at the map for a moment. Then he traced with
a chewed fingernail a dotted line that led north through the
forest off the Ashbridge road. 'See?'

Kirby peered round Porter's massive shoulder. 'You
wouldn't get a vehicle up there. Not in a million years. Me
and Joan went there for a picnic once. Meant for deer and
horses, not cars.'

'It's wider than it looks, Sarge. See the dog-leg? Once you're
past that it broadens out, and it's a good surface, a lot of hard
core, because the army used it in the war. I'm not saying you
could get a car up there, but you might.'

Thornhill was staring at the map. On the Lydmouth side of
the road the land climbed. The path that Porter had indicated
followed the line of a watercourse. Near the top of the ridge it
ran into a metalled road running roughly parallel with the road
below. Once you were past that, you had a choice of several
routes, to both Birmingham and Bristol. If Joe Rodley got that
far, they might lose him if he was clever. And he was a driver
by trade, Thornhill remembered, he knew the roads and the
back roads.

'We could send another car after him,' Kirby said. 'Assuming that's where he went.'

'Not so easy if you don't know your way, and in the dark.'
Porter spoke with the unfeigned assurance of a man who
knows his subject. 'And he's got a good start. But you could
cut him off.'

'How?' Thornhill said.

Once again, Porter's massive forefinger prodded the map.
'See that line there, sir?' This was another path running up

from the Ashbridge road, at a lower point from the first. 'You wouldn't get a car up there in a month of Sundays, or even a Land Rover. But maybe a motorbike. You could if it was dry.'

Thornhill followed the line of the track with his eyes. It met the top road, little more than a lane, perhaps half a mile west of the first track. Because of the lie of the land, it was a much shorter distance, though judging by the contours the track was much steeper as well as narrower. He calculated the man-power at his disposal.

He said to Porter, 'Find yourself a motorbike. And Dyke as well. Stay together. Up to that top road, then cut along and block him off. It's probably a wild-goose chase but we can't afford to take the chance.'

He watched Porter blundering from the room, jarring his side against the corner of a desk and knocking over a waste-paper basket. He saw the expression on Kirby's face and wondered whether he had made yet another mistake.

Chapter Fifty-Nine

There was a uniformed constable at the gate of Viney Cottage in case Joe Rodley unexpectedly came home but Amy suspected that no one really thought this was likely. At last, a little after six o'clock, a woman police officer and a nurse appeared on the doorstep. Amy was so pleased she could have hugged them.

The newcomers might have been twins. It was not that they looked particularly similar – they were respectively thin and plump, tall and short – but they both exuded the same professional confidence in their own fields of expertise.

'Right, dear.' The nurse pulled Doreen up. She plumped the pillows and let Doreen fall back against them. 'There! That's better, isn't it?'

Doreen Rodley seemed not to notice what had happened. She continued staring at her left hand, the one with the wedding band. She had not spoken for over an hour.

'Gosh, it's hot.' The woman police officer loosened her collar and fanned herself with a magazine. 'Shall I open the window?'

'She feels the cold,' Genevieve Fuggle said.

The police officer gave a jolly laugh. 'I feel the warmth!'

'Stuffy rooms aren't healthy,' said the nurse, throwing open the window. 'Breeding grounds for germs.'

Amy went into the kitchen to make tea for the newcomers. While she was waiting for the kettle to boil, she opened the back door and stood on the step for a moment. In the distance, faintly, she heard the sound of an ambulance bell. Life, she thought, was going on elsewhere. She made the tea and carried the tray into Doreen's room.

'Now you mustn't let us keep you two any longer,' the policewoman said. 'We'll soon find our way around – and I'm sure you're longing to get home.'

She smiled and the nurse smiled too, the pair joined in their despotism like Siamese twins. Without a word Genevieve picked up her handbag. Amy reluctantly followed suit – she had wanted to leave Viney Cottage but now she was more or less being expelled from it, she felt cheated. They said goodbye to Doreen, who gave no sign of having heard. Amy and Genevieve looked at each other and their lips pursed with shared disapproval.

When they left Viney Cottage, the constable opened the gate for them and wished them goodnight. The two women hesitated on the pavement.

'Well!' Amy said.

'Quite!'

'Like a pair of prison wardresses, I thought.'

'Yes – it was horrible.' Genevieve's voice sounded tremulous. She glanced up the road at her bungalow, whose windows were in darkness. 'I don't suppose you'd like . . . a cup of something? Or even a glass of sherry?'

'That's very kind.' Amy's curiosity was piqued. The Fuggles rarely entertained. In a split second, she imagined herself at some point in the future telling Philip Wemyss-Brown what she had seen there and making him laugh.

'Ivor's out still,' Genevieve continued hastily, sounding appalled by her own daring. 'I think he was going to see the police. He . . . he's very cross with them, you know.'

Amy nodded but said nothing. The two women walked in

silence up to the Fuggles' front door. As soon as Genevieve put a key in the lock, Macbeth gave tongue within. When the door was open, Genevieve flicked on the light and swept the little dog into her arms. She held Macbeth as though he were a baby. The terrier paid no attention to his mistress. He craned his neck to what looked like an impossible position and barked furiously at Amy.

'You're a good doggie,' Genevieve said. 'Aren't you, darling? Now you be nice to our visitor.'

Macbeth continued to bark. In the end Mrs Fuggle was forced to shut him up in the kitchen.

'He's so highly strung,' she confided. 'The slightest thing sets him off.'

Amy wasn't sure she liked being referred to as 'the slightest thing'. She allowed Genevieve to take her hat and coat. They went into the sitting-room, which smelled of Ivor Fuggle's cigarettes and indeed of Ivor Fuggle himself. Amy shivered. In a manner of speaking she was in the bear's lair.

A fire smouldered dully in the grate. Genevieve riddled it with a poker and put on another log and a shovelful of coal. The glasses were dusty and the sherry came from Cyprus. Amy settled in her armchair, feeling comfortably superior. She watched Genevieve moving awkwardly around the room, like a moth dazed by the light.

At last Genevieve sat down. She leaned forward in the chair and wrapped both hands around her tiny glass as if afraid she might drop it.

'Poor Doreen,' Amy said, because poor Doreen was all they really had in common. 'I wonder what will become of her now.'

'You think her husband won't come back?'

Amy looked pityingly at Genevieve, wondering at her naivety. 'I think it's very unlikely.'

'Where's he gone?'

'Heaven knows. Wherever it is, I'm sure the police will soon track him down.'

Genevieve swallowed her sherry in a single mouthful and looked at the empty glass. 'Do you think he did it?'

'Killed poor Dr Bayswater? Well, it does look like it. I mean, you don't run away unless you've done something very serious, do you? No, I'm afraid there's not much doubt about it.'

'What do you think they'll do to him when they catch him?'

'Hang him, I suppose.' Amy sipped her sherry, extending her little finger as she raised the glass. 'If he really killed Dr Bayswater, of course. And I wouldn't be surprised if he did, I'm afraid. I mean, he's a frightfully violent man, everyone knows that.' She hesitated, aware that she might be treading on dangerous ground if Mr Fuggle had hired some of Joe Rodley's violence for his own purposes. But the subject was too interesting to let drop. 'And for a man like that to beat a helpless pensioner to death in his own home – I think a judge is going to take a very dim view of that.'

'Yes, and so he should.'

'I know it will make it much harder for Doreen in the short term,' Amy went on. 'But we must think beyond that, mustn't we? If he's . . . if he's no longer there, it would be much easier for her to make a fresh start. It must be so awful if you know your loved one is in prison for murder. You'd be in a sort of limbo, wouldn't you?'

Genevieve Fuggle nodded. 'But it just seems so final – hanging someone, I mean.'

'That's what it's meant to be, dear,' Amy said.

Genevieve Fuggle nodded again – and then again and again, to and fro, to and fro, until her dumpy figure and repetitive movements reminded Amy of the wobbly-men in Prout's Toys and Novelties. 'I'm sure you're right,' Mrs Fuggle said. 'I think I might have another glass of sherry – shall I top up your glass too?'

Chapter Sixty

The canteen had labelled it the Curse of Kirby. The symptoms were griping pains, leading to a pressing and recurring need to evacuate the bowels in an increasingly liquid manner. Secondary symptoms included the sense that the world was shortly about to come to an end, and the sufferer couldn't care less if it did.

Kirby himself was more or less back to normal. But four or five of his colleagues at Police Headquarters were now afflicted. It was unfortunate that PC Dyke was next in line, and that the Curse of Kirby should have struck at the precise time it did. Dyke and Porter had gone down to the transport pool where Sergeant Tanhouse reluctantly allowed them to sign for a couple of motorbikes. They were about to set out when Dyke turned a pale face to Porter and said, 'Won't be a minute. I got to see a man about a dog.'

One minute stretched into two, and the sounds – and indeed the smells – made it quite clear that it would be some time before Dyke went anywhere.

Porter glanced at the clock on the wall. With every minute he lingered, Rodley's chance of escape improved. He told Tanhouse he was going alone, and that Dyke could follow. Tanhouse nodded sourly at him and told him not to get the bike dirty or he'd have his bloody guts for garters. Porter strapped the helmet on and kicked the bike into life.

Peter Porter became another man when he was behind the

wheel of a car or riding a motorbike. When he was in charge of an internal combustion engine, his habitual clumsiness vanished. He knew instinctively what the engine wanted, what the engine could do for him if he treated it in the right way.

There was little traffic. He rode through the rain down to the station and over New Bridge. There was a roadblock at the junction beyond but they waved him through. Soon he was climbing upward in a tunnel between trees. The lights of the town dropped away. The beam of his headlamp drew him onward.

The track on the right-hand side was so well concealed that he nearly missed it. He rode slowly into the mouth of the path and dismounted. At this point, the journey plunged into nightmare, for the path was muddy as well as steeper than he recalled. Pushing the bike uphill, slithering and slipping, he covered less than a hundred yards in ten minutes. Twice he fell. Part of him wondered how he was ever going to get the mud off his uniform. The rain pattered on the branches and dead leaves. Despite the cold, Porter was basted in his clothes.

It wasn't going to work. If he tried to haul the bike up to the top road, he would still be here at daybreak tomorrow morning. Closing his mind to the thought of Sergeant Tanhouse, he dumped the machine in a sea of brambles. He fumbled in the bike's panniers until he found the torch that was part of the standard equipment. Following its dancing beam, he ran uphill.

His breath was now coming in great ragged bursts from his chest. He tore at his uniform, trying to get the cool night air to his body. Branches and suckers slashed his face and body. Twice more he fell, once measuring most of his length in a puddle full of icy water. The path forked. He chose the left-hand branch but was forced to retrace his squelching steps when the path petered out among a thicket of saplings.

He staggered on. The path twisted round corners, swooped and climbed in ways that seemed to bear no relationship to the dotted line on the map. Perhaps he should have persevered with the left fork. But at last, and with surprising suddenness, just as he had given up all hope, the trees fell away on either side and he stumbled out on to a hard surface. He had reached the lane.

Apart from the torchlight, it was absolutely dark. The rain appeared to fall from a black nothing. Porter ran slowly along the lane, fighting the stitch that now developed. He held the torch angled to the left, so its beam chased along the verge. His wet clothes felt as heavy as a suit of armour. While he ran, he listened, terrified that he would hear the sound of an engine.

The night was full of abnormally loud sounds – the flapping of waterlogged clothes, the pounding of his boots on the tarmac, and the ragged gasps of his breathing. Time passed but lost its usual dimensions – was it ten minutes? twenty? an hour? He checked his watch and discovered that it had stopped at a quarter-past six.

A gatepost skipped into the torchlight and danced away into the darkness. A few seconds later, Porter's mind interpreted what he had seen. He stopped and retraced his steps. Attached to the post was a five-bar gate that sagged across the mouth of a broad ride. He opened it far enough to squeeze through the gap.

On the other side he crouched and shone the torch on the ground. It was much wider than the track he had used and the surface was at least partly composed of hard core. However, there was enough mud in the area immediately behind the gate to show that neither people nor vehicles had recently passed this way, only deer. He was in time.

But was this the track that Joe Rodley might use or was it farther along the lane? And then there was the other problem:

Porter could not be sure whether there was any point in his being here in the first place. At the police station, he had spoken without thinking, from the depths of his own knowledge. Now, shivering in the rain, he felt much less sure that Joe Rodley would use this route. He knew from the experience of a lifetime that in matters of the intellect he usually contrived to come up with the wrong answer. He did not know why, only that this was the way things usually happened. Why should it be any different now?

He went back to the lane. His breathing had returned almost to normal. He switched off the torch to save the battery. He was growing colder by the minute, and increasingly aware of how wet he was. There was no way that headquarters could get in touch with him, assuming that headquarters remembered his existence. If Joe Rodley had used another route, they might not remember to let Porter know. He might be stuck up here for hours.

He paced up and down the lane, fifteen yards one way, fifteen yards the other, waving his arms in a vain attempt to warm himself. After a while, despair lapped over him and he stood quite still, growing colder and wetter and gloomier. The night was full of rustles, the sounds of small animals going about their business. Once there were louder footfalls, which brought him back to full attention before he realised that it was a deer.

Then, at last, he heard a sound rising and falling among the other noises of the night, gradually becoming louder: the sound of a labouring engine.

He knew, without quite knowing how he knew, that the engine was labouring because it was climbing an incline in too high a gear. In the same mysterious way, he also knew that the engine note probably came from a Morris Minor's 800cc overhead valve A Series engine.

Torch in left hand, truncheon in right, he walked as quietly as he could along the grass of the verge to the gate. He drew back among the bushes on the verge and peered down the track. The car was drawing closer. Light flickered among the trees.

The light became much brighter, became a pair of dipped headlights. Without warning, terror seized Porter. Unwanted memories flooded into his mind. Joe Rodley beating up a pair of Welsh rugby players in the yard of the King's Head a couple of years ago. The battered face of that journalist from the *Gazette* after he had met Joe Rodley on a dark Saturday night. There was another lesson Porter had learned from experience, that in any fight he tended to come out worse, regardless of the gender, size or age of his opponent.

His stomach writhed with griping pains. *Oh God, not the Curse of Kirby, please.* Or was it simply terror? He shrank back into the trees, pressing his belly in the hope he could stop it exploding.

The Morris Minor came closer and closer, bouncing and slithering over the ruts and potholes, until it came to a halt five yards from the gate. The wipers slapped to and fro across the windscreen. Porter's eyes were dazzled. He saw the lights, not the car.

The driver's door opened. Joe Rodley climbed out.

'Stop!' Porter quavered. 'This is the police.'

For an instant, nothing happened. Rodley did not speak. Then the car shifted slightly as he climbed back in.

Porter stepped out of the trees, switched on the torch and turned the beam on the car, which was streaked with mud. He rapped on the driver's window with the truncheon. Rodley wound down the glass a few inches.

'I arrest—' Porter began.

'Shut up. Open the bloody gate.'

'I'm not—'

'You are. I've got that *Gazette* woman, the new one, in the back. If you don't do what I say, she'll wish she'd never been born.'

'I . . . I don't believe you.' Porter shone the torch into the back of the car. He saw Jill Francis huddled on the back seat.

'I'll make her scream if you like,' Rodley said casually. 'Is that what you want?'

Porter stood there in the rain and wished someone would tell him what to do.

'Just open the goddam gate, will you?'

He heard the click as Rodley locked the driver's door from the inside. The torch was still shining into the car, where Miss Francis sat awkwardly on the back seat, with her arms behind her back. Her face was haggard, her mouth distorted as if she had eaten something bitter. Porter had always thought of her as beautiful but she was not beautiful now. Joe Rodley stretched between the front seats and grabbed her round the neck. He hauled her towards him and kissed her.

'See?' he said. 'I can do what the fuck I want with her. And I'm going to unless you open that gate.' With his free hand he reached for something on the front passenger seat beside him. 'I've got a knife. See? I can cut her a little bit, or I can cut her a lot. Or I don't have to cut her at all. It's up to you.'

Porter knew that if he were a better policeman, someone like Dyke perhaps or Kirby or better still Thornhill, he would be able to reason with Joe Rodley or outwit him or find some other way of rescuing Miss Francis.

A high, shocking scream burst out of the car.

The scream continued, jagged as a saw blade. Porter himself cried out, a high and wordless sound. The scream paralysed him. Inside the car, Joe Rodley and Miss Francis were clamped together. Joe was hitting Miss Francis over the head with his right hand balled into a fist: bang, bang, bang, as though he were hammering a nail in a desperate hurry.

But it was Joe who was screaming.

Porter slammed the truncheon into the window. The glass held. He hit it again with the end of the truncheon, much harder, with all his formidable strength. The window shattered. He thrust an arm through the gap, careless of the jagged edges of the glass, and fumbled for the handle that released the lock. The door swung outward. He groped inside the car, into the heart of that terrible scream.

Rodley had stopped hitting Miss Francis's head. Instead, he was frantically patting the seat beside him. Porter understood what Rodley was doing when he saw the glint of steel in the man's hand. He had dropped the knife. But now he had it again. The blade was sliding through the air – aimed not at Porter but at Miss Francis in the back seat.

Without thinking, Porter pushed out his arm to protect her and caught the force of the blow. Pain seared through his arm. With a surge of rage, he wrenched Rodley towards him and slammed the truncheon into the side of his head. The man grunted, slumped across the passenger seat.

Porter wondered where his handcuffs were. He wished he hadn't hit Rodley quite so hard. He had never hit anyone like that. In a daze, he picked up the torch, which he had dropped as the blow connected.

The beam danced about the car's interior. A black smudge glistened on Rodley's left hand. The beam ducked and wove over the seats and landed on Miss Francis's face. She was sitting forward in the seat and staring straight at Porter. There was something black around her mouth, too.

'Thank you, Porter,' she said.

Her face crumpled. She turned her head and spat. She

looked at him again, squinting in the torchlight, and tried to smile. She keeled sideways.

Porter straightened up. Cramp squeezed his stomach. The truncheon in his right hand was slippery and sticky. He listened. All he heard was his own laboured breathing and the sound of a small creature moving in the undergrowth.

Chapter Sixty-One

For a moment Thornhill waited outside Drake's office. He was afraid to go in. He didn't know what he would find or how he would feel. He smoothed back his hair, knocked and opened the door.

The first thing Thornhill noticed was the smell of cigarettes. Drake's room was one of the few places at Police Headquarters where smoking was banned by anyone under the rank of Chief Constable. The office was much larger than Thornhill's. The DCC was fussy about his surroundings, as about much else; and it was the tidiest room in the building and also, less predictably, the most homely. Drake had removed most of the standard-issue furniture and replaced it with his own – the two leather armchairs in front of the gas fire, the circular walnut table between them, the mahogany desk with its infinity of small drawers. On the walls was a series of eighteenth-century engravings showing the cathedrals of England.

Jill was alone. She looked up at him from a nest of blankets in one of the armchairs. Her eyes were wide and startled, larger and bluer than ever in the pale, drawn face. She tried to struggle out of the armchair.

'Don't stand up, Jill,' he said, and again the Christian name slipped out of him before he was aware of it.

She sank back in the chair and pulled the blankets more tightly around her. 'It's so odd. I . . . I can't stop shaking.'

'It's perfectly natural. Shock, that's all.' He drew nearer and touched her shoulder lightly. 'I thought one of the WPCs was meant to be with you.'

'I sent her away.' She sucked hard on her cigarette. 'She brought me some tea and the blankets, though.'

Thornhill glanced at the cup beside the ashtray on the table. It was empty. 'But she shouldn't have left you.'

'It's not her fault. I told her to go. I . . . I didn't want to talk to her. I said I wanted a toothbrush and toothpaste. I . . . I bit his finger down to the bone, you know. I thought I might bite it off.'

'It's over now.'

'It's not. I can still taste the blood, you see, and the nicotine on him. That's why I want to do my teeth. He went mad, thrashing about. Like a landed fish.'

She stubbed out the cigarette and closed her eyes. Neither of them spoke. After a minute he wondered whether she had fallen asleep.

'Jill?' he said softly. 'Would you like me to go?'

'No.' She yawned. 'That's to say . . . I'm sure you've got more important things you need to do.'

Thornhill sat down in the other armchair. 'In a moment. The doctor will be here soon.'

'Which one?'

'Leddon.'

She glanced at him. 'I don't need a doctor.'

The realisation that she had no desire to see Roger Leddon gave him a surge of illicit pleasure. 'I think you should. We need to make sure you're okay. If you prefer, I can order a car and someone will take you to hospital. But I thought that having someone come here would be less trouble for you.'

'It doesn't matter.' Her fingers picked listlessly at a blanket. 'He can come here.'

'We'll need to take a statement, of course, but not now.'

'It was horrible. I thought . . .'

'What?'

'I thought Rodley was going to kill me.'

'You're all right now. It's over.'

'But it's not over, is it?' she wailed. 'This is only the beginning. And I can't get the taste of his blood out of my mouth.'

'You will,' he said urgently. 'I promise.'

'I should never have come back to Lydmouth. And now . . . I need to go to Charlotte.' Her face seemed to grow younger, grief expunging the evidences of maturity and leaving only the child. 'Charlotte. And poor Philip.'

She began to cry, the tears spilling out of her eyes as if wrenched from some internal reservoir by the silent sobs that shook her body. Thornhill watched. She wasn't beautiful now. She was as raw and vulnerable as Susie after a bad dream or a painful fall. He knew from long experience that you could not hope to erase a child's grief, only contain it, and often containing it was better than pretending that it could be cured or that it did not exist in the first place.

He was thinking of Susie as he got out of his chair and knelt beside Jill's. He put his arms around her shoulders and drew her gently towards him.

She buried her face in the angle between his neck and his right shoulder. Her arms were crossed tightly across her chest, her hands gripping the blankets. He rested his cheek gently against her hair. He smelled cigarettes and the familiar perfume.

After a while the sobs subsided and her breathing steadied. When she shifted in the armchair, he sensed that she wanted to pull away. He released her and she sat back. Like a child, she rubbed her eyes with her hands. He took out his handkerchief and gave it to her. He stood up and moved away from the heat of the fire, which had been scorching his left leg.

'There's one thing I need to know now,' he said.

Jill blew her nose. 'What?'

'Whether Rodley admitted killing Bayswater.'

She looked away from him. 'He said he hadn't, but it didn't matter because the police had decided he'd done it and were going to frame him in any case.'

'Of course we wouldn't.'

She blew her nose. 'I know you wouldn't.' She put an uncomfortable stress on the word *you* which brought the silent and invisible presence of Kirby into the conversation.

'Did he say why he tried to run Fuggle down?'

'Something about teaching him a lesson because he was a skinflint.'

There was a knock on the door.

'Come in,' Thornhill called, moving even farther away from the fire and the armchairs. 'We'll talk tomorrow,' he added in a lower voice.

Kirby came into the room, followed by the WPC and Dr Leddon. The WPC was carrying a toothbrush and a tube of toothpaste.

'Okay if the doc sees Miss Francis now, guv?'

'All right.'

Leddon hurried across the room. 'Jill – how are you?'

She ignored him. 'I'd like to go to Troy House.' She was looking at Thornhill. 'If that's all right.'

Leddon said, 'We'll see. Let's—'

Jill pulled the blankets more tightly around herself. 'I want to go now.'

Thornhill paused at the door. 'There'll be a car for you when you need it, Miss Francis. When you're ready.'

'Thank you.'

He glanced across the room and glimpsed the old woman she would become, just as he had glimpsed the child she had been. She's mortal, he thought, she's just like me.

Brian Kirby followed him out of the room. 'She's been in the wars, hasn't she?'

Thornhill did not reply. But on the stairs he said over his shoulder, 'Rodley told her he didn't kill Bayswater.'

'At least he's consistent.'

'He thinks we're going to frame him.'

Kirby shrugged. They reached the ground floor. The duty sergeant raised the flap of the counter for them.

'The hospital rang while you were upstairs, sir,' Kirby said. 'They're operating on Fuggle.'

'What's the damage?' Thornhill asked.

'Ruptured spleen and a fractured pelvis. It's the spleen that's urgent.'

'They think he'll live?'

Kirby laughed. 'It'll take more than a Morris Minor to kill Ivor Fuggle. It's not going to help Joe Rodley, though.'

The car was waiting for them with its engine running and two uniformed officers sitting in the front. Thornhill paused on the pavement, his hand on the door handle.

'What about Rodley himself?'

Kirby grinned. 'Leddon says his finger will never be the same again. The lady's bite is worse than her bark.'

'You can keep your jokes to yourself, Brian, all right?' Thornhill climbed into the car. 'Whistler's Lane.'

They drove up the High Street. Thornhill glanced at his watch, angling it so the dial caught the light from the street lamp. So much had happened that it felt later than it was, long after midnight. But it wasn't even ten o'clock. It seemed bizarre that life should continue, safe and uncaring, as bizarre as what had been happening on its dark margins.

He watched a sleek middle-aged couple in evening dress climbing into a car outside the Bull Hotel. On the other side of the road, a crowd flooded out of the Rex Cinema. Even through the closed windows of the car, he heard faint sounds of dance music. Two beat officers in glistening capes walked briskly along the pavement, patrolling from pub to pub, where checking the clientele at least gave them an opportunity to stand for a few moments in the warmth. Ordinary people, Thornhill thought with a twinge of envy, on an ordinary Saturday night.

He patted the inside pocket of his overcoat and felt the reassuring outlines of the envelope it contained. Drake had given way in the end and permitted Thornhill to apply for a search warrant.

The car rounded the corner into Broad Street and turned left into the dark, narrow mouth of Whistler's Lane. Grove House reared up on the corner, its windows blank, looking more forlorn than it had even a week ago: a Gothic fantasy slipping rapidly into a decay that mirrored its late owner's.

No one spoke as the car nosed up the lane. There were lights in the downstairs windows of Viney Cottage, where the nurse and the WPC were on duty with Doreen Rodley while outside the constable waited for someone to send him home. As they passed, Thornhill glimpsed the silhouette of the outbuilding where they had found the string bag.

It would have been easy enough to plant the evidence that linked Rodley with Bayswater's murder. On the other hand, it was possible, even likely, that Rodley had hidden the bag and its contents there himself. A broad vein of stupidity ran through most of the criminals Thornhill had known. Perhaps you had to be stupid to think you could beat the odds.

He placed no reliance on Rodley's denial. Of course he wouldn't admit to killing Bayswater. It was one thing to admit to the other offences, especially when the evidence against him was so strong – and what did it mean, a few years in prison at most, a relatively insignificant price to pay. But murder was quite different. If the circumstances were right – or wrong – a conviction for murder could lead Joe Rodley to his own death in a hangman's noose. All it needed was a strong enough prosecution case and one of the many judges who still believed that there was only one way to deal with a murderer.

'Park on the road,' Thornhill said to the driver. 'Across the driveway.'

The drive was empty – Fuggle's car was still outside Drake's house, though no longer blocking his gates. In the bungalow, the curtains were drawn but lights showed in several windows, including the hall and the sitting-room.

The driver climbed out and opened Thornhill's door. As he left the car, a flurry of rain caught him under the brim of his hat. Water trickled down his neck. He felt suddenly weary. There was no satisfaction in this sort of case, he thought, and no sense of intellectual achievement either: all they were doing was trying to limit the damage when messy, unhappy people made even more of a mess of their lives than usual.

The four police officers marched up the drive. Macbeth started to bark, rapidly working himself up to a frenzy. Kirby rapped on the front door. No one came. He tried the handle. The door was locked.

Thornhill left one constable at the front of the bungalow and walked along the side. The lights were on in the kitchen too, though the window was covered by a blind. He tapped on the back door, waited a couple of seconds and twisted the handle. The door opened.

Yapping and snapping. Macbeth shot between Thornhill's

legs, nipped his left ankle, made a sharp, right-angled turn and bolted down the garden towards the stone barn.

'See what that bloody dog's up to,' Thornhill said to Kirby.

He stepped inside the kitchen. It was immaculately tidy, the surfaces clear and clean, the table and chairs precisely aligned. The air smelled strongly of bleach. No one was there, and the room looked as if nobody had ever been there. It was forlornly perfect, like an advertisement in a pre-war housewife's magazine, and the addition of a living creature would have made it untidy.

'Guv,' Kirby shouted from outside. 'Guv, you'd better take a look.'

For a moment, Thornhill hesitated. A brown envelope had been propped against the white enamel bread bin. The envelope was the only item that had not been put away in its proper place.

He told the remaining constable to wait in the kitchen and not touch anything, then walked quickly through the rain to the open doors of the barn. Macbeth was snarling within, a deeper and if possible even more malevolent sound than the dog usually produced.

Kirby was standing in the doorway, the beam of his torch playing over the interior. Thornhill glimpsed a dark rectangle on the floor and, beside it, the whites of Macbeth's eyes and teeth and the pink of his mouth. The saw-horse that Thornhill remembered from his last visit was lying on its side. Not easy to knock over a saw-horse, he thought, not by accident.

The torch beam floated higher. Thornhill saw black, lace-up shoes above which were thick calves in grey stockings. He saw all this in the instant before his arrival goaded Macbeth into further paroxysms of fury. The little dog darted forward and snapped at Kirby's ankles. Kirby swore obscenely and kicked the dog as if it were a rugby ball. Macbeth flew through the air, in and out of the beam of light, and thudded into the back wall of the barn.

'Cut her down,' Thornhill said as he moved forward. 'I'll take the weight. For God's sake, cut her down.'

Sunday, 11 December

Chapter Sixty-Two

The bells were ringing from the churches and chapels of Lydmouth. Jill Francis stared out of the window at a grey sky smudged with the smoke from a hundred chimneys. She thought about women peeling Brussels sprouts in a hundred kitchens, while their husbands, stiff and useless in their Sunday finery, read newspapers and sipped cups of tea.

That was the oddest thing – that when you felt the end of the world had come, for most people life went on just the same. Jill wanted an objective correlative to grief – a flood of lava pouring towards Lydmouth down the slopes of the forest hills, perhaps, or a tidal wave roaring up the estuary. Not this grey normality, not the sound of bells over Lydmouth on a Sunday morning.

She sat at the dressing-table, delaying the moment when she must leave the sanctuary of her room. She frowned at her reflection in the mirror: nothing but a bit of borrowed powder on her face and the clothes she had worn yesterday. She looked and felt a mess, and that was as good as could be expected in the circumstances.

She considered the circumstances and thought: now what?

No point in delaying any longer. She went on to the landing. Charlotte's door was closed. Jill listened for a moment outside. Leddon had given Charlotte something to make her sleep so she might not wake for hours.

She glanced at the door of the neighbouring room, the

bedroom that Charlotte and Philip had once shared, where now Philip lay alone, waiting for the undertaker. Jill imagined herself opening the door and Philip tugging the sheet away from his face and grinning at her.

'Fooled you.'

She went quietly down the stairs. The kitchen was warm and smelled of fresh cigarette smoke. Puffs of steam were emerging from the spout of the kettle. Charlotte's handbag was on the table.

It at once seemed quite obvious what had happened. Unable to bear the prospect of widowhood, Charlotte had got up early, put the kettle on, smoked a cigarette and gone off to find a nice quiet place to kill herself.

Jill's heart thudded as she walked from room to room. Less than forty seconds later, she found Charlotte in the little room beyond the dining-room, which Philip had used as a study. She was sitting at the desk with a grey box file open before her. She had a pen in one hand and a cigarette in the other. She was frowning, though the frown faded as she looked up and saw Jill.

'Hello, dear,' she said. 'Did you sleep well?'

'Yes – well, no, actually, not particularly. But what about you? Roger Leddon said you probably wouldn't surface until lunchtime.'

'I flushed the tablets down the lavatory,' Charlotte said. 'I don't want to walk round like a zombie.'

Jill thought that Charlotte looked rather like a zombie even if she wasn't walking around like one. Her hair was awry, her face pale and lined, with none of its usual powder. She too was wearing the same clothes as last night and in her case they looked as if she had slept in them.

Charlotte frowned at the cigarette in her hands as if wondering how it had got there. She stubbed it out. 'Anyway, there's too much to do. So many arrangements need to be made.' She looked down at the file in front of her and her voice faltered for the first time. 'I was looking through one or two papers.'

'Can't it wait?'

'No.' An expression of low cunning passed over Charlotte's usually guileless face. 'I'd love a cup of tea, though.'

'I'll be back in a moment,' Jill promised. 'The kettle's coming up to the boil.'

When she returned with a tray, Charlotte had emptied the box file and sorted its contents into three piles. She looked at Jill and her eyes were brighter than they had been. 'Do you know, he kept all my letters? I never realised. How very odd. Of course, I kept his, but I never thought he'd keep mine. Why did he never say?'

'That's men all over,' Jill said, wondering whether in fact it was: whether for example Richard Thornhill had kept Edith's letters to him, and not told his wife that he had done so. She poured the tea. 'I brought some biscuits.'

'I'm not hungry.'

'Nor am I,' Jill said. 'But I think we ought to eat a biscuit. Otherwise we really will turn into zombies.'

Charlotte shook her head. She lit another cigarette but then left it smouldering in the ashtray. She was looking at the sheet of paper on the desk. As she read, she picked up a biscuit and began to eat, mechanically brushing away the crumbs that fell on the sheet of paper. Jill sat in the only armchair, drank tea and looked about her.

Neither Charlotte nor the cleaning lady had ever brought a duster into this room. It had been a bachelor island surrounded on all sides by a marital sea. The horizontal surfaces were coated with grey dust, speckled with fragments of pipe and cigarette tobacco. Nevertheless, it was very tidy. One wall was lined with bookshelves from floor to ceiling. Jill remembered the battered roll-top desk from the flat where Philip had lived when she first knew him, long before he met Charlotte. There were no pictures on the walls, only a photograph of a smiling Charlotte in a leather frame on the desk.

'It's very odd,' Charlotte said after a while, absently taking another biscuit. 'Read this.' She pushed the sheet of paper across the desk.

Jill picked it up, looked at the heading and skimmed the first few lines. It was a policy from the Scottish Provident.

'I never knew he'd taken out life insurance,' Charlotte said indistinctly, speaking through a mouthful of biscuit. 'He might have told me.'

Jill said nothing. She read on until she saw the sum assured. 'Good Lord.'

'Yes,' Charlotte said. 'Eighty-five thousand pounds. It's ridiculous. The premiums must have been crippling. I've no idea how he managed to find the money. And there he was, the foolish boy, he needed a new suit last spring, and nothing I could say would make him have one. He said we couldn't afford it, that we had to draw our horns in. Well, really!'

'Yes,' Jill said. 'You see what this means?'

'It means rather a lot of money. I would have thought that was obvious.' She tapped the policy. 'It should be quite straightforward, don't you think? Roger Leddon had been treating him, and he saw Philip within twenty-four hours of his death.'

It wasn't so much Charlotte's words which alerted Jill as the tone of her voice. Jill thought of Philip lying upstairs, feeling himself useless, seeing a future in which he was a drag on his wife; seeing a future in which the *Gazette* passed out of the family's control and Charlotte was left in relative poverty.

Jill said, 'You never told me what exactly happened.'

'When Philip died?' Charlotte spoke quite naturally, as though 'died' were a word like any other. 'He was alone in the room. It was some time after lunch. He said he wanted a snooze, and I was sleepy too so I went and lay down. When I woke up, I went straight back to see him.' Charlotte blinked rapidly. 'He was lying on the floor. He had got himself out of bed, the silly boy. But the bell was beside his bed as usual – all he had to do was ring and I'd have been there in a jiffy.'

'What did he want?'

Charlotte said, 'Just between ourselves: there was a bottle of whisky in the wardrobe. He . . . he'd drunk rather a lot of it.'

She looked at the half-eaten biscuit in her hand and put it in the ashtray. For a while there was nothing more to say, or rather nothing more that it would be wise to say. But thoughts were another matter. Philip had known as well as anyone the effects that a substantial quantity of alcohol and sudden exercise might have on him.

Jill thought that he had taken the gambler's way out, knowing that whichever side the coin fell, he would win. If it fell one way, he would have a satisfying slug of whisky and perhaps the gratifying knowledge that he had fooled his friends and relations. If it fell the other, he would have his whisky – and then the consequence of that brief pleasure would ensure that Charlotte would be well provided for and that he would no longer have to endure the dreary twilight existence of an invalid. If you found yourself in a situation where you had to gamble with fate, Jill supposed, there were worse games that you could play than this.

Charlotte whispered, 'He did everything for me, you know.'

The words were ambiguous. The tears that spilled out of Charlotte's eyes were not. Jill stood up and put her arms around her friend. They clung together. We need to do this, Jill thought, as Charlotte heaved and spluttered, it's part of the ritual. She herself was heaving and spluttering as well. Grief was not an elegant emotion.

In the hall, the telephone began to ring. Charlotte pulled away from Jill.

'I don't want to see anyone,' she said fiercely. 'Or talk to them. Especially Amy. I'm not sure I could bear it.'

Jill stood up. 'I'll answer it. What will you do?'

Charlotte patted the desk as though it were a large dusty dog. 'I'll stay here.'

Jill went into the hall, wiping her eyes with the back of her hand. As she picked up the receiver she glimpsed her face in the mirror above the hatstand and noticed with numb surprise what a ruin it had become. Men had sometimes told her she was beautiful, and she had come to take good looks almost for granted. Men wouldn't think she was beautiful now.

Amy Gwyn-Thomas's voice squawked on the other end of the line. For at least a minute the torrent of words was unstoppable, sweeping wildly from the depths of grief about Philip's death to the heights of joy about her impending marriage to Ronald Prout. Jill told her that Dr Leddon had given Charlotte some sleeping tablets and that it would be better not to disturb her – no more than the truth but, as so often with the truth, selectively presented so that its implications amounted to a lie.

She had hardly put down the receiver when the phone began to ring again.

'Jill?' said the voice on the other end. 'Jill, it's Richard.'

She sat down on the chair beside the telephone table. 'Hello.'

'I hope I haven't woken you. I wasn't sure if—'

'No, no.' With mild curiosity she watched herself waving her free hand palm downwards in the air, as though trying to calm a restless child. 'I've been up for a while.'

'How's Mrs Wemyss-Brown?'

Going mad like the rest of us. 'As well as can be expected. It's been a dreadful shock, obviously.'

'I wondered if we could have a word at some point. You and I, that is.'

'Of course.'

'I hate to disturb you at a time like this but there are one or two loose ends that need to be cleared up.'

'All right. When?'

'I don't suppose you'd have a few minutes now?'

Jill's hand flew to her hair. 'I . . . yes. When exactly?'

'I could be with you in five minutes. But perhaps Mrs Wemyss-Brown would prefer not to have too many callers at present. We could meet outside if you'd prefer.'

'I think I'd better stay here,' Jill said. 'Charlotte needs someone to answer the phone and the door bell. I'll check with her and see what she thinks. I'll phone back if there's a problem. But in any case I don't think she'll want to talk to you, not at present.'

'I don't want to talk to her. I want to talk to you.'

'Yes,' Jill said, trying not to read more into that remark than it warranted.

They rang off. She went back to Charlotte, who was still seated at Philip's desk. She was turning the pages of an album of photographs. Jill told her what had happened.

'Of course he can come,' Charlotte said.

'I can tell him to go away if you want.'

'You've done that too often already,' Charlotte said, turning another page of the album. 'Life's too short.'

Chapter Sixty-Three

Not for the first time, Jill wondered what Charlotte knew or suspected about her feelings for Richard Thornhill, past and present. She went upstairs, hoping she had time to make emergency repairs to her ravaged appearance. But she was too late.

While she was still mounting the stairs, there came a short, discreet ring on the door bell. She turned and went back to the hall. Thornhill was on the doorstep, hat in one hand, briefcase in the other. The shoulders of his overcoat were flecked with silver drops of rain. There were dark smudges under his eyes.

'You walked?'

'Only from the bottom of the hill. I thought it might be better not to leave the car outside Troy House.'

She took him into the kitchen, where it was warmest. He draped his coat over a chair and put the briefcase on the table. Automatically she offered tea or coffee, which he declined. They sat opposite each other.

'How is she?' he asked in a low voice.

'I don't think it's really sunk in yet.'

'I liked him,' Richard said. 'I liked him very much.'

Jill said brightly, in an attempt to head off her own tears. 'And how's Mr Porter?'

'He's fine. As strong as an ox, that one. In fact his landlady phoned this morning to say he was ill, but that's nothing to do with this, just an upset stomach.'

'He saved my life. He was very brave, you know.'

'I know. He wasn't just brave, either. He was the one who worked out that Rodley might take that route through the forest.'

The church bells had stopped ringing and the sky was slowly becoming lighter. The kettle on the Aga was still emitting little puffs of steam.

Jill said, 'Can you tell me about Rodley?'

'No reason why not – it'll be all over town by the end of the day. Fuggle bribed him to undermine the *Gazette*. He attacked Mr Cubbitt, and he put the rats in your car. He was responsible for both the fires. But then he tried to get more money out of Fuggle, and Fuggle refused. After that, he was convinced that Fuggle had set him up for the murder of Bayswater, which was why he had no compunction about running him down last night.'

'What happened to him – Fuggle, I mean?'

'He'll live, all being well – luckily for Rodley. As long as there aren't complications after the operation. And Rodley's okay too, though he's badly concussed.'

Jill looked away. Her mind filled with that last, dreadful scene in the car, with that thing in her mouth, the thing that tasted of nicotine and blood, her teeth grinding down on something with the texture and toughness of living wood until at last they jarred on bone; and all the time the blows raining on her head, the sour tang of sweat and fear and the scream that she had heard even in the broken dreams of the night. She felt Thornhill's hand cover hers.

'You did what had to be done,' he said. 'Rodley was in a corner, he could have killed you.'

Jill swallowed. 'I know. I . . . I don't want to think about it. Go on with what you were saying.'

He released her hand. 'Are you sure? I can come back another time.'

'Of course I'm sure. It's the best thing. The more you know, the less you can imagine.'

He nodded. 'The problem with this business, all along, is that there were two cases, not just one. We knew they intersected, but not how or why.'

'Paul Frederick.'

He nodded. 'Exactly. That confused the whole issue. The yellow glove.'

'He went to see Mrs Fuggle, didn't he? Because they had known each other in London during the war.'

'I'm going to show you something.' Thornhill opened his briefcase and took out a file, from which he removed a sheet of paper. 'It's all right,' he said as he handed it to her. 'It's a transcript. Last night we went to the Fuggles' house and we found Mrs Fuggle hanging herself in the barn at the bottom of the garden.'

'Is she dead?'

'We got her down in time. But I wouldn't be surprised if she wishes that she were dead Under the barn there's an old rainwater cistern. The hatch was concealed by the log pile. We were within a few feet of it when we went up there yesterday morning. She must have been terrified – she faked a phone call to distract me.'

'Frederick was down there? In the cistern?'

'Yes. There was only a few inches of water in the bottom – you could see the body as soon as you shone a torch down there. She was beginning to fill it with earth, hoping she could bury him. There was also a half-empty tin of white paint, a brush and a paint-stained coat. It looks like she desecrated her mother-in-law's grave. She never knew Fuggle's mother but she must have hated her all the same.'

'I wonder whether she was jealous of her,' Jill said harshly, because she knew something about jealousy and its corrosive effects. 'Fuggle didn't know any of this?'

'I doubt he had the slightest idea. Still doesn't.'

'I don't understand. I can see why she might have killed Frederick, but Bayswater—'

Thornhill interrupted her, sliding the sheet of paper across the table. 'Read this. She'd left a sort of diary behind in the kitchen, random notes she'd made over the last week or so. I think she felt it was a suicide note. That's the last entry. But it's not always easy to follow. She's got flu.'

Temperature 103.2° this morning. My head hurts.

They're going to hang me anyway. Can't do it twice. I dreamed last night that Jenny and Tony and the old doctor were laughing at me. Come on, they say, you're better off dead.

Simpler to do it myself, save everyone a lot of trouble. It was all Tony's fault. Nasty man. He shouldn't have come back. He knew, he said, he knew all along – she told him about what I used to do. Think of them laughing at me.

BITCH.

He said she could still be alive if I hadn't gone out. Because Jenny couldn't leave the house without her things. LIAR. He said he'd tell Ivor exactly what sort of woman he'd married.

His clothes felt so strange, so COARSE, after all these years, so SMELLY!!

The yellow glove. The doctor found it on the toilet floor in the train. The bloody nerve of the man, phoning me at home. The Case of the Yellow Glove, he said he'd call it, like some silly story, and write about it and people would never know it was me but they would, they would. And if the glove came into it, people would know everything.

Didn't mean to hit him, though. But he just wouldn't change his mind. Then I saw the rat and had to run, and I never found the glove. In the park the policeman was shining his light so I threw away the bag.

Later I found the bag and put it in Rodley's shed. Safer there. Not a nice man but I don't want him hanged for killing Bayswater.

Better this way. Someone will find out sooner or later. Head hurts so badly. Darling Macbeth, look after him. Hanging is so

Jill looked up. 'There's nothing else?'

'The earlier entries tell us a little more. We think she hit Frederick with the blade of a spade. He probably found her in the garden or the barn. But afterwards she kept her head – tried to make it seem as if he left Lydmouth. She put on his clothes and used his return ticket to take the train.'

'So she was the one I saw at the station?'

Thornhill nodded. 'She got off at Gloucester, where she dumped Frederick's clothes and posted a card he'd already written to his kids. Then she came back to Lydmouth. It would have worked if it hadn't been for Bayswater.'

'You think Bayswater saw her go into the lavatory on the train as a man and come out as a woman?'

'Probably. Then he went into the lavatory himself and found the glove. And it was the glove that linked her to Frederick. And it was when Bayswater wouldn't give her the glove back, wouldn't change his mind about writing up her case, that—'

'That was when she killed him,' Jill said in a flat voice. 'Because she couldn't see another way out.' She glanced at the sheet of paper. 'But then she saw the rat and ran away before she could search for the glove.'

Thornhill rubbed his eyes, which were heavy-lidded with tiredness. 'It seems odd to be more scared of a rat than a possible murder charge.'

'Not at all,' Jill said. 'I'd have screamed and run like blazes.'

'I think she ran home across the park. But she must have panicked again.'

'The policeman?'

'Yes. Our patrols check the park at night. She probably saw the beat constable shining his torch on the public lavatories. So she threw away the string bag with the pliers. A few days later she went back and found it.'

'Will she hang, do you think?'

'Who knows?'

'Surely there are mitigating circumstances?'

'If the jury come in with a guilty verdict, it's up to the judge. You know that as well as I do.'

'It's not justice,' Jill burst out. 'It's judicial revenge. And what if you get the wrong person?'

Thornhill said. 'I don't think there's much doubt that she was responsible for two murders. What happens next is out of my hands.'

'You can't refuse to take responsibility.'

'I have a job to do. That's my responsibility.'

'But what do *you* think?'

He sighed. 'I think there's been enough killing.'

They sat in silence for a moment. Jill yearned for a cigarette but did not want to move.

'There is one thing that you don't know,' Thornhill said at last. 'The reason for all this.'

She smiled at him. 'Don't I? Have you only just found out?'

'If we're talking about the same thing, there's no way anyone could have found out until last night.'

'At the hospital? I bet it caused quite a stir.'

His eyes narrowed. 'I didn't know myself until the hospital rang up.'

'I was alone in your office for a few minutes yesterday evening,' Jill said, feeling the colour rising in her cheeks. 'Do you remember – it was just before the alarm went off. It was a complete accident but I knocked the in-tray off your desk. As I was picking it up, I couldn't help reading something, a letter to Dr Bayswater from another doctor.'

'What did you see?'

'A reference to Eonism.'

'What's that?'

'A psychological aberration. It's named after the Chevalier d'Eon, who lived in the eighteenth century. He sometimes dressed as a woman, sometimes as a man. So Eonism is wanting to adopt the manners and clothes of the opposite sex – transvestism. Once I saw that word, everything fell into place. And it fitted with what I'd heard from the old lady in Yorkley Grove. She said Genevieve always had a smile on her lips and a song in her heart, which didn't sound much like Mrs Fuggle. But apparently the brother, Michael, was much gloomier.'

'But why did you think the letter referred to her – him, I mean?'

'The date. The letter was dated last Wednesday, but it referred to Bayswater's letter of the second – of December, presumably.'

'Good God. I think I saw Bayswater posting it late on the Friday afternoon.' Thornhill put his head in his hands. A moment later, he looked up. 'What about Fuggle? He must know, surely?'

'Not necessarily. There's not much sex in some marriages.' She was watching him as she spoke but he turned his head so she could see less of his face. She went on, 'And there's nothing wrong with that, of course. They got married when they were both middle aged. His mother had just died. He was in the middle of a nervous breakdown, and he was probably lonely. He must have needed a housekeeper, too. I bet he's hopeless in the kitchen. And poor Genevieve – Michael, or whatever you want to call him – well, I imagine he was lonely too. They probably made it quite clear to one another that sex wasn't part of the bargain.'

Thornhill said slowly, 'They slept in separate rooms. Single beds.'

'I wouldn't be at all surprised if Ivor Fuggle's a virgin. That's why he's so rude to women. We scare him. Anyway, not everyone's obsessed by sex – it's as simple as that.'

She found him looking at her. It was her turn to look away.

Thornhill cleared his throat. 'To go back to the diary: some of the sheets of paper were dated, some weren't. But I think the first entry probably refers to Wednesday, 30 November.'

'The day I came back to Lydmouth.'

'And the day Mrs Fuggle saw Paul Frederick coming out of Butter's. He'd been buying the gloves.'

'And the day the *Post* had a photo of Mr Fuggle and his wife Genevieve. Frederick must have seen it.' Jill remembered the diary entry: *He knew, he said, he knew all along – she told him about what I used to do.* About Michael's habit of dressing up in his sister's clothes? She said, 'So she must have been half expecting Frederick to turn up on the doorstep.'

'Yes.' He reached into the briefcase and drew out another typed page. 'There's also this: it's out of sequence, probably written much earlier. In the war, even.'

She was dead. Everyone was dead. I didn't even make any choices. I came back and found the house wasn't there, most of the street wasn't there. I was wearing her clothes, I had her handbag, I had her ration book and everything. I WAS her.

In the blackout everyone thought I was a woman. It was lovely. Once a sailor kissed me. And when I got back to Yorkley Grove that night, the policeman was so nice, he said, 'You go and sit over there, love, have a nice cup of tea.' And the woman who gave me the tea called me 'miss'. It just went on from there. I didn't mean to do it. It sort of happened to me.

That's the way it's always been in my life. Things happen to me.

Jill pushed the sheet of paper back to him. 'Michael coming home after the bomb?'

'Dressed as Genevieve, as Jenny. And finding the house gone, and probably his sister with it. And the road full of strangers who assumed he was a woman.'

He slid the page into his briefcase. Jill examined her nails, which were in a shocking state. She knew he was looking at her.

'Now what?' he said.

'For Mrs Fuggle?'

He shook his head. 'You and me.'

The change of subject was so abrupt that her stomach lurched. She thought of Philip lying dead upstairs. She wondered whether the cigarettes and the whisky had killed him or whether it would have happened anyway. Must drink less, she told herself, must smoke less.

'Why didn't you come and see me in London?' she said. 'I hoped you would.'

'I was trying to do what seemed best for all of us. If it's any consolation, I've thought of you every day. Literally. Every day.'

Jill bowed her head.

'Will you stay in Lydmouth?' he asked.

'It depends on Charlotte. If she still wants me to run the *Gazette*, I shall.'

He said, 'If you stay here, I don't know what will happen.'

'That's our choice, isn't it? We can't be like Mrs Fuggle and blame the way things just happen to us.'

He smiled at her. Jill told herself that she was too old to fall in love again, especially with a man she had already been in love with once before. But Philip was dead and even Charlotte had said that life was too short: too short to waste.

Thornhill stood up and she repressed an urge to seize his hand and ask him to stay.

'Brian Kirby's a father.' He sounded breathless. 'I had a phone call at eight o'clock this morning.'

'Are Joan and the baby okay?'

'Doing fine, I understand. It's a boy. They're going to call him Charles Louis.' There was the hint of another smile. 'Mrs Kirby is a great admirer of the royal family.'

They went out into the hall together. At the front door they both paused. Neither of them tried to open it.

He touched her arm. 'I must go – there's an awful lot to do. Thank you – thank you for your help.'

Jill looked at the place he had touched. 'Not at all.'

He opened the door. On the step outside he turned back to her and said in a much lower voice, 'I hope we see each other soon.'

'Yes.' Jill smiled like an idiot. 'That would be nice.'

'At least it's over. Though we haven't found the Pisser yet.'

'He won't be troubling you again, I can promise you that,' Jill said. 'Mr Prout's fish slice solved that one.'

Richard Thornhill stared at her. 'You don't want to tell me more?'

Jill shook her head. 'A woman likes to have her secrets.'

She watched his face lighting up with amusement. Too old to fall in love again? Too late to worry about that now.